FALLING FOR THE COLONEL

A REGENCY ROMANCE

VICTORIA HART

ISBN: 978-1985783843

Printed in the United States

MAPLEWOOD
— PUBLISHING —

CHAPTER ONE

Summer, 1815
Falmouth, Cornwall

"I DO WISH you would hurry; the weather is so unbearably warm today," Lydia Wells complained to her sister, Charlotte, as she paced the floor of their shared room.

"Don't rush me. You know I don't approve of bathing machines," the frail young woman lamented as she tied a perfectly symmetrical bow in the ribbons of her bonnet.

"It's completely safe. I'm your older sister; would I ever let anything happen to you?" Lydia replied, gazing out the window.

The view from the third-floor garret of Mrs. Peyton's School for Girls in Falmouth was extraordinary and never failed to impress Lydia. From the small window tucked under the eaves, she could see below to the busy port, bustling with activity. Tall ships of the line and speedy frigates from His Majesty's Navy lined the quay crowded with merchant ships. Past the quay, along the sliver of white sand beach, the fishermen brought in their catch, to be sold by their wives along the harbor. The small, shack-like bathing machines pulled by docile steeds dotted the waterfront as intrepid tourists took their turns taking a dip in the cool waters as the bright summer sun shone down on the beach.

The view was one of the only reasons that Falmouth had any appeal to Lydia. The port was bustling with ships coming and going, a welcome sight that thrilled her, but the town itself was quiet and unassuming. The public houses that lined the harbor were forbidden to respectable young ladies, which confined her adventures to shopping trips for small tidbits that she could afford and strolling along the trails leading to the hills above the town.

Occasionally, if she was feeling daring, she would walk alongside the harbor; the enormous ships that smelled of salt water, oak, and gunpowder thrilled her. The naval ships, she knew, had been to places she could only imagine, and the merchant ships had explored all parts of the world and came back laden with silks and spices. The harbor, which she could see clearly from the window, was a place that reminded her that somewhere, out in the world, men had adventures while women stayed home and waited for them to return.

Mrs. Peyton, the kind widow who ran the school, would have been mortified if she knew just how much time Lydia spent at the harbor, but Lydia did have an excuse. Her father was a captain in the Royal Navy and could return at any time, a likely reason for Lydia to visit the harbor, or so she told herself.

Turning to face her sister, she resumed her impatient ordering. "Charlotte, come on, the weather won't hold for long; you know how changeable the skies are this time of year. I long to go for a bathe before it rains. They won't accept bathers if it's raining."

"Rains? Do you think it's wise that we go to the shore on a day when you expect rain? We could catch our deaths of cold."

"If we go bathing, we will be wet all over from the sea water, so what harm will a little rain do?" Lydia asked as she completed a cursory check of the contents of the basket suspended from her arm.

She had her bathing clothes and her sister's, and an old torn bed linen from the laundry that she hoped Mrs. Peyton would not mind being used at the beach.

"I hadn't thought of that," Charlotte confessed as she tucked an errant blonde curl under her bonnet.

"Hurry, Mrs. Peyton has promised to have Cook fill a hamper for our luncheon. We shall go bathing and have a nice lunch on the beach; won't that be delightful?"

"If you say so, but I do hope I won't catch a chill."

"You won't catch a chill on a day like today. It's terribly hot – we'll waste away in the heat before we catch our deaths of cold. Come on, I cannot wait a moment longer."

The younger girl reached for her parasol as her older sister, who was taller and stronger, grabbed her hand and dragged her down the narrow stairs leading to the second floor. One more flight down and they arrived in the foyer where the maid, Moira, curtseyed at the sight of them.

"You're off to the sea, then? I should insist that you have a proper chaperone but at your ages, I will rely on you both to conduct yourselves with decorum. Girls, please behave as proper young ladies. Lydia, I am counting on you to set the example," an older woman said as she emerged from the modest but comfortable drawing room.

"We will, Mrs. Peyton, you have our word," Lydia said with a smile.

"Moira, fetch the hamper from the kitchen; Cook knows the one I mean," the older woman said to the buxom maid.

The maid left the foyer, bustling down a flight of stairs to the kitchen.

"Promise me," Mrs. Peyton said a she addressed Lydia, "That you won't let your sister take in too much sun. You know how delicate her constitution can be."

Charlotte looked down at the floor, demure and modest. Lydia replied, "I have always taken care of her. I will ensure that she doesn't get any more sun than is good for her. With her frailty, salt air may be restorative."

"Very well. Do be careful, I think those bathing machines are dangerous. You could be dragged out to sea or drown within sight of the shore."

Lydia adored Mrs. Peyton, but she could be as impossibly anxious as Charlotte. Still, Lydia knew it wasn't the fault of either lady; women were taught to be submissive and dainty, to fuss over illnesses and worry over everyone's health. She knew that she herself was unusual; her love for adventure and disdain for consequences were greatly discouraged. Yet she could not be unhappy; Mrs. Peyton didn't agree with bathing machines but she allowed the older girls at her school to partake in the unique pleasure infrequently, even providing a luncheon for the occasion.

Moira climbed the stairs, a hamper in her hand. As she thanked Mrs. Peyton, she considered herself fortunate to have someone in her life who cared about her and Charlotte. She knew all too well that as daughters of a sea captain, they were both lucky indeed to have Mrs. Peyton. Like a kindly old aunt, she fussed over them and worried they would fall ill. She was the only family they had ever known, and Falmouth was their only home.

Lydia handed the smaller of the two baskets she was carrying to Charlotte, wondering to herself if they should not have engaged a carriage. Leading her sister down the hill towards the beach she thought about her future, wishing she could see other places besides this sea port.

"Charlotte, have you wished you could go to sea, like Father?" she mused as they walked past two young officers on High Street.

"Of course not. Why would I wish for anything so ridiculous? It's dangerous on the ocean, there are storms, sea monsters, and terrible waves."

"You, my dear, worry far too much for your own good. If not the ocean, what about being a soldier? Have you ever wanted to be garrisoned in a town far away, or travel to another country and fight?"

"How dreadful! Lydia, where do you get these ideas? A proper young lady does not long to be in the world of men. Do you have no interest in a home and a family?"

"One day, perhaps, but are you not curious what lies outside of Cornwall? Our father has been all over the world, and we sit here in this little town with nothing to do but attend to our studies, take afternoon strolls, and wait for something to happen in our lives."

"I like to play music; there is that, you know. We are fortunate that Mrs. Peyton has a piano."

Lydia stopped in her tracks. "A piano? *That* is the extent of your imagination? Playing music and having a house of your own? Look around you! Every day these ships come and go from here. The men see exotic lands and have adventures while you are left to our needlework and I to my teaching."

The younger of the two women looked down at her feet as she answered, "I am not like you, Lydia, no one I know is. How can you be obsessed with ships and a life that is fraught with danger upon the sea? Can you not be content that you have a position at Mrs. Peyton's, a place to live, and a comfortable life?"

"I am grateful for those things, but I cannot be content that this is all I will ever be. I don't want to be an old maid one day, still living in Falmouth, never having seen the world."

"The world? I think it's a scary place."

Lydia looked at the sky overhead, the sun shining down through white clouds, but those clouds could darken suddenly in the summer heat. Returning to her speedy pace, she urged her sister onwards to the beach. She did not want to miss the opportunity to dunk herself in the ocean, an exhilarating feeling that she rarely had the opportunity to enjoy. As she reached the edge of the water she dropped the hamper on the sand, and turned to check that her sister had kept pace behind her.

"Come on, last one in has to pay five pence."

"That seems like an exorbitant amount of money," Charlotte

replied, as she eyed the water warily and placed her basket on the beach.

"Then you'd better hope I'm not the first one to the bathing machines!" Lydia teased.

Charlotte retrieved the dark wool bathing suits, a gift from their father on his last trip home. "How much should I pay if I want to stay firmly in the sand, while you drown yourself fin the ocean?"

"A new bonnet."

"Then you shall have it. I intend to stay right here, eating your lunch while you catch your `death in the briny water."

"Poor Charlotte, if you insist. I shall want a straw bonnet with a red ribbon; it will go well with my hair, don't you agree?"

"If you insist, but it's terrible of you to extort money from me when you are the only one who has a position."

"Well then," Lydia said, as she untied her worn old bonnet, unveiling a head full of dark curls tucked into a messy bun, "You'd better move fast, because I have the advantage."

Charlotte methodically untied her bonnet, carefully placing it in the basket. "I suppose if I take a dip in the ocean and catch my death or am eaten by a sea monster, you can explain to our father that it was your fault."

"Gladly. Come on – if you must die, I cannot think of a more delightful way than bathing in the sea."

"I can," grumbled Charlotte.

Lydia and Charlotte made their way to the water's edge. Lydia smiled and Charlotte frowned, convinced that she would meet her fate in water that barely came up to her knees.

———

SITTING on the bed linen spread across the soft sand of the beach, Lydia leaned back, letting her hair dry in the summer sun. It fell in dark curls that matched her long lashes, an attribute she was rather vain about, though she kept that to herself. Charlotte sat under her parasol, a beef pasty held daintily in her gloved fingers, her wet hair tucked under her bonnet. They were as opposite as two sisters could be. One raven-haired and wild, and the other pale and proper.

"Do you ever think where Father can be?" Charlotte asked, her gaze fixed on the waves gently rolling to the shore.

Lydia looked down at her long legs spread out in front of her. The light cotton material of her dress, a faded ivory color, was a boon of his life upon the sea. The material to make the dress came from the Mediterranean. It was lighter than English material, and better suited for the summer heat.

Her own attention captured by the sight of the tall masts visible like a forest of trees in the harbor, she answered, "He captains a ship of the line, so he could be in the Mediterranean, the Indies, or just beyond the horizon," Lydia answered wistfully.

"Do you ever worry for him, that he is safe?"

Lydia remembered the enormous ship her father commanded, the HMS *Thames*, with her hundred guns and crew of seasoned sailors. The ship, like the man who commanded her, was battle-hardened and strong, and she thought both man and ship could weather any storm. She was certain that wherever he was, he was safe – or so she hoped.

Reassuring her younger sister, she answered, "He is a grizzled old captain and his ship is a solid vessel; there is no need to worry."

"Captain Wells, grizzled? Are you certain you're talking about Father and not another Captain Wells?" Charlotte laughed.

She'd been kidding. Her father was not grizzled but always smooth-shaven, his uniform – like the man himself – never ruffled. He was impeccable in his speech, his manners, and his presentation.

"Aye, matey, he is a grizzled cap'n, that one, he is," Lydia affected her finest impression of an old sailor, squinting and twisting her face into a scowl.

Charlotte laughed at the sight of her beautiful sister impersonating any one of a hundred men they saw along the quay. A cool breeze drifted from the sea, giving Lydia the slightest case of delicious chills after the heat of the early afternoon. Reaching for the last bite of her pasty, she looked at the hamper and wondered what other delights awaited in inside it.

"The sea air always gives me an appetite; do we have anything else delectable in that hamper? Surely cook must have packed something sweet? Cake, or pies perhaps?"

Charlotte gently set the parasol on the sand, opened the hamper, and reached in to its depths. She removed some apple tarts carefully wrapped in a linen napkin, just as a gust of wind blew in from the ocean, catching her parasol.

"Oh, Lydia, my parasol!" Charlotte cried, forgetting about the tarts. She rushed to chase the errant accessory.

Lydia jumped up to help her sister give chase. The parasol was as buoyant in the air as any small boat on the sea, being tossed and carried by the current. The parasol showed no signs of slowing down – it floated up to the stone quay and out of Charlotte's reach.

Lydia was just about to comment that the parasol may be beyond saving as it floated away. She was astonished by the sudden appearance of a young man on the quay. He had hair in a darker blond hue than her sister's, he was taller than she was, and he had a brilliant smile, a detail she noticed as he quickly retrieved the parasol before it headed across the harbor.

"Miss, is this yours?" he asked with a bow, standing on the stone quay well above the beach.

From the blush of Charlotte's cheeks, Lydia knew she was not the only Wells sister to think the young man was as handsome as he was helpful.

"Yes, thank you," Charlotte demurely replied.

"Hugh Burton, at your service, ma'am," he answered, as he bowed once again with a flourish of his hand.

Charlotte was visibly confused as Lydia caught up with her. They had not been properly introduced to this man and she was certain Charlotte was unsure what to do. The young man was pleasant, but he displayed a cavalier attitude and was not following the rules of polite society.

"Mr. Burton, thank you for saving my sister's parasol," Lydia said, as she looked up at him.

"It was no trouble. For the lady," he replied as he passed the parasol down to Charlotte.

He shouldn't be speaking to them without a proper introduction, but his Cornish accent was charming. His hands were large, dwarfing the parasol in his grip, and his face was handsome but tanned from the sun. His features were not unfavorable but were common among the local population of fishermen and tradesman. Lydia was struck by his twinkling green eyes, which sparkled like sun on the waters, a feature she suspected was also mesmerizing to her younger sister.

"We have yet to been formally introduced. Since you courageously came to our aid, I am sure we are past such formalities," Lydia said as she looked at her sister.

Charlotte was looking at Hugh Burton as though he was the most captivating view in Falmouth.

"I give you my solemn oath that I would not think any less of either of you two ladies if I were to know your names."

"I am Miss Lydia Wells, and this is my sister, Miss Charlotte Wells. It is a pleasure to make your acquaintance."

"Miss Wells, ma'am," he said as he nodded to Lydia. He directed a wide smile in Charlotte's direction and said, "Miss Charlotte, I wish you a good day."

"Goodbye," Charlotte managed weakly as she watched him turn to walk down the quay.

"Goodbye, indeed." Lydia laughed to herself as she watched her sister.

Charlotte was touching the parasol as though it was a holy relic, softly running her fingers over the place where the handsome young man had touched it.

"Hugh Burton," Charlotte murmured quietly as she stood on her toes and tried to get a better look at the quay overhead.

"Are you unwell?" Lydia asked, as her gaze followed Hugh Burton's form until it was out of sight.

"Unwell? I feel lightheaded, as though I may faint. Perhaps I need to sit down for a while."

"Rest here in the shade of the stone wall; I will gather our hamper and bonnets."

"Don't do that, not yet."

"Sister, dear, we must return if you are feeling unwell. If I return you to Mrs. Peyton in any state other than perfect health, I fear to think of the consequences. It has been many years since she had to punish me, but I doubt she would hesitate. You know you were always her favorite student."

"I am not unwell. I cannot describe what I am feeling, my heart is fluttering, I can barely breathe, and I may not be able to walk back up the hill to the school."

"Charlotte Wells, we must get you home immediately. Wait here; I will gather our things and hail a carriage to hire."

"Don't you dare. Give me a moment to collect myself; I have no desire to go home just yet. There are hours left in the day and I don't want to be anywhere else but here."

Lydia narrowed her eyes at her sister, and smiled as the realization struck her – Charlotte was smitten. Mr. Hugh Burton had breezed into Charlotte's life as lightly as the sea breeze that carried away her parasol.

"If you insist that you are quite well, we may continue our luncheon on the beach...unless you have other pastimes you wish to pursue this afternoon?"

"As a matter of fact," Charlotte sad as she looked up at the quay, "I was wondering if we could take a stroll before finishing our luncheon? The quay looks like a fine place for walk."

Lydia concealed her overwhelming desire to giggle. "You, my sister who despises long strolls or being outside for very long, would like to stroll along the quay?"

"I have never seen the quay look so inviting as it does today.

Perhaps you're right; there is more to life than what I presumed. Perhaps I should begin by taking a nice long walk with you along the harbor. The walk would do me good; the exercise would be beneficial."

"When did you become interested in walking along the harbor?"

"Lydia, please just gather our things while I regain my composure. I know it may seem like a strange request to walk among the ships but I feel different this afternoon. I am quite sure you can guess the reason why."

"Indeed, I can. I was teasing and having a bit of fun, you must forgive me. Mr. Burton was a handsome fellow and he seemed pleasant – I fully understand why you feel a sudden compulsion to take a walk along the harbor. Stay where you are and I will gather our hamper."

"Do you think he was a sailor?"

"Mr. Hugh Burton, savior of parasols? He had a weathered look about him, but no uniform. No, I don't think he was a sailor – but he may be here along the harbor enlisting in the fleet, so perhaps he is not a sailor *yet*."

"If not a sailor, then who could he be?"

"A charming young man who happened to come to your aid."

Charlotte's gaze fell to the parasol then once more went to the quay overhead. "Oh, do hurry. We mustn't lose any time; he could be upon a ship already and I will never see him again."

Lydia wanted to tell her younger sister that the chances of seeing the young man were not very good. Falmouth was a small town but one of the busiest ports in England; a great many ships sailed in and out. On these ships men of all ages earned their livelihoods. Mr. Burton could be just such a man, and as many young men from Cornwall did, he could be joining a crew this very afternoon. She could only hope that her sister would be able to forget her chance meeting with him and return to her studies and her music. If Hugh Burton was a sailor he would never be home, a dilemma they knew far too well already.

CHAPTER TWO

The garret was pleasant, if slightly chilly during the nights of early autumn. Lydia liked to sleep with the window open, despite repeated warnings of the dangers of the night air. The cool breeze from the ocean was a welcome respite after the stifling temperatures of summer. It was one night in late September that she and her sister were lying in their narrow single beds, neither one able to sleep.

At the age of eighteen, Charlotte was finishing her instruction in music and drawing at the school before she, like her older sister, would be prepared to find her way in the world. These last few months of musical instruction were vital to Charlotte's prospects; she could not afford to ignore her practice as the weather turned cooler. And it was these last few months of instruction that concerned Lydia the most, because there was a change in Charlotte.

The difference was obvious to Lydia, but less so to those around her at school. The frail young woman who was normally devoted to her studies and the practice of piano was no longer so interested in them. Her playing seemed to be without spirit, and her drawings were rarely finished.

Lydia wasn't worried that anyone else would be alarmed by

Charlotte's behavior, as her behavior could be easily explained. Mrs. Peyton and the other teachers may have decided that her lackluster performance was only a signal that she was of the age when her studies were not the only thing she was thinking about. It was common, as Lydia had seen in the older girls, for their interests to turn to eligible young men and the planning of their future lives. This often happened at the age of fifteen, but her sister had only begun to express the same restlessness late that summer.

"Charlotte, are you asleep?" Lydia asked, knowing that her sister lay awake in her bed.

"No, I can't sleep."

"Neither can I," Lydia said in the darkness.

"Why are you awake?" Charlotte asked in a whisper, her soft voice barely audible in the stillness.

"If you must know the truth, I am worried about you."

"About me? Lydia, there is no reason to be worried about me."

"Isn't there? You haven't been practicing as you should be, and your drawings litter our room, none of them satisfactorily finished. I'm not trying to treat you unfairly, but you know our situation here at the school is not permanent."

Lydia's statement was met with silence. In the distance, down below in the street, she could hear the faint laughter of the sailors leaving the public houses. It was a sound that always seemed pleasant to her, although she knew they had been drinking. Charlotte hadn't answered, and Lydia wondered if she should not have taken the liberty to speak so candidly. Being candid was one of her faults.

"You're right," came the reply.

"Yes, but why? Charlotte, you have always been so dependable. I may be the older of us, but I've often felt like you were the one I should be modeling my life after."

"You don't mean that."

"Yes, I most certainly do. I am taller than you, and stronger, but you are far more settled than me. You have dreams of a house and family when all I can think about is reading novels and going on adventures."

"Your dreams of adventure may come closer than anything I have devised."

"You are only eighteen. Why give up on the dreams you hold dear, when they seem so practical?"

"Practical? I doubt you would think so if you only knew the truth," Charlotte said as she threw her covers off and sat up. Lighting a candle, she sat on the edge of the bed, her face illuminated in the glow of the flame.

Lydia tried to read her sister's expression in the dim light. Charlotte was a serious young woman, reserved and quiet, and her smiles did not come as often as Lydia wished they would. Tonight, however, her ordinarily unreadable expression seemed even more enigmatic.

Mrs. Peyton was responsible for the education and proper upbringing of the girls left in her care. Many of them were girls like Lydia and Charlotte, daughters of officers and sea captains without any family but their fathers, who were away at sea for months at a time. Her position teaching the older girls literature and history was an enormous responsibility and one she gave her every effort. It took a lot of her time.

After classes and meals, there may be the occasional stroll through the town and up the hills, but there was often no time for much else. During this past summer, her sister had changed and Lydia was despondent, believing that she had failed in her responsibly, since she could not account for the difference.

"Charlotte, I have no right to interfere in your private affairs but I've never been in this circumstance before. I used to understand you, and now I fear that I don't. Are you unwell? If I haven't been as attentive to you, it is only because I have never felt it necessary to treat you as anything other than a responsible young woman."

"There is no need to worry. If I have caused you concern, I do humbly apologize. Forgive me; it was never my intention to cause you distress."

"Distress? No that is too strong a word, but I have worried that the change in you was result of a failing on my part."

"No, my dear sister, you are incapable of failing me. As I have said, I owe my present happy circumstances to you. If it was not for your bravery and insistence that women could be adventurous, I should never have found the courage to conduct my own adventure. I doubt you will be impressed by my own modest attempts to fashion my life after a heroine in a novel, but it was not my intention to be a heroine, only to try to secure my own peace of mind and happiness."

Lydia's mind was reeling from the dramatic change in her sister's otherwise quiet demeanor. Charlotte was shy and retiring, all that a proper young lady should be, but in this circumstance in the tiny bedroom tucked into the attic, she was as bold and courageous as any woman in Lydia's books.

"Whatever do you mean?"

Her sister smiled as she jumped up and went to the diminutive writing desk they shared. Opening a drawer, she retrieved a bundle of letters. Aside from the odd letter from their father that made its way to them through the hands of sailors who came to port, or a letter from former students of the school, Lydia could not imagine what correspondent could have written such a great many letters.

"I am embarrassed to say that I have been keeping a secret form you, not because I didn't trust you, but because I didn't want you to discourage me or find me silly," Charlotte explained as she handed the letters to her sister. "I am in your debt for every one of these missives. They have brought so much joy to my heart."

"In my debt? Charlotte you have me at a considerable disadvantage; how am I responsible for these letters? I did not write them."

"You may not have written them, but the day you ignored formality and introduced us to a certain young man at the quay? Do you remember? It was that day you made each one of these letters happen – as though you wrote each one in your own hand."

Lydia gasped as she leaned close to the candle; the letters were all addressed to Charlotte in the same script. "Am I to understand that these all came for the same source?"

"Yes," beamed Charlotte. "They are from Hugh Burton."

———————

"HUGH BURTON? The young man who collected your parasol?" Lydia asked as she tried to make sense of what her sister was telling her.

Charlotte nodded. "Yes, the very one."

"I don't know what to say. I'm astounded."

A dark cloud passed over Charlotte's pale features. "You are not shocked by my behavior, are you?"

"Shocked? How can I be, when I don't know what your behavior may have been? I cannot act as judge unless I have some evidence and these letters are all the evidence you have provided."

"Forgive me, my mind has been in a state these last few weeks. Sometimes it seems I'm uncertain of what is real – my attention has been devoted to Hugh and little else."

"As evidenced by your lack of attention to your music and art studies," Lydia reminded her sister in a serious tone.

"I know, but if you only knew why I have been neglecting them, you could hardly find fault in it. I have been most happily distracted, I can assure you."

The night air was growing colder; Lydia rose and walked towards the window. The moon was full, and the view of the harbor was breathtaking. Torchlights glittered from the public houses down the hill and lights were visible from the many ships at harbor. The moonlight shimmered on the water. Shivering, she breathed in the scent of salt and cold, and closed the window with some regret.

She knew she should play the role of the responsible older sister and admonish Charlotte for conducting a relationship in secret, leaving herself open to speculation and gossip – but she found she could not. Charlotte was glowing in a way that Lydia had never seen.

Her first instinct was to protect her frail sister from any improper behavior the handsome Hugh Burton may have imposed upon her, yet she was very curious to hear the details of their relationship.

Carefully setting the letters beside the candle on the shared bedside table, Lydia pulled her covers around her and sat on the edge of her narrow bed. "I did not mean to criticize you; I have no doubt that you will find the necessary inclination to complete your studies before Christmas. I am curious about Hugh Burton, though. If I remember correctly, when we went walking along the quay after he retrieved your parasol, we didn't find him."

The change in tone seemed to return her sister to her previous state of youthful exuberance and joy.

"You remember correctly. If I may speak candidly?" asked Charlotte.

"I have often considered myself to be an expert in candor, but I am not accustomed to hearing you speak in such a way. Please do."

Lydia could see her sister was still anxious, and holding something back as Charlotte spoke. "You promise not to criticize me, or forbid me from continuing to write to Hugh?"

Knowing there was no genuine way to answer that question without hearing the details of the relationship, Lydia agreed, vowing to hold her tongue no matter what events her sister would share.

"Yes Charlotte, I give you my word not to treat you with condemnation."

Her sister's shoulders relaxed, as though an enormous burden was falling from her narrow frame. "I don't know quite where to begin, but I suppose I should start with the afternoon we walked along the quay."

Lydia made every effort to be patient as her sister slowly told the story. She pulled her blanket tighter around her shoulders and she slipped her feet under the blanket, sitting in an unladylike manner under her covers.

"He was a handsome, charming man, as I recall," Lydia replied.

Charlotte's voice matched the soft look in her eyes as she drifted away into the memory. "I can't tell you how profoundly disappointed I was that we didn't find him that day. If you must know, I felt terribly slighted by fate that I was permitted to make his acquaintance under chance circumstances, but then denied any further conversation with him. I wanted to speak to him, but I was far too terrified, so I tried to see him once more, to feel the happiness I experienced when he smiled at me."

Lydia was a reader of novels and prone to giving herself over to adventures and romantic notions – but she wasn't sure what to think of her sister's experience. Was love an emotion that was not slowly created over a long acquaintance with a gentleman, but could happen as suddenly as a lightning bolt in a summer storm?

Lydia encouraged her sister. "Please, you must continue, I cannot rest until I learn how you met him once more."

"Yes, about that. You know we did not see him again on that day, and I was very disappointed. As we made our way home that evening, I found myself despairing that I should ever see him again. If he was a sailor, he could easily set off for a port in a distant land and forget about me. As I went to sleep that night, I was determined that I would do everything in my power not to let that happen."

"But Charlotte, none of it was in your power to control."

"I didn't let that stop me. I decided that if I never saw him again, it would not because I allowed that to happen; on the contrary, if I never saw him again it was because it was not meant to be. But in the meantime, I was determined that I would do all that I could do to hasten any meeting, although I knew my actions would most likely be futile."

"I never would have imagined that you could be so determined," Lydia commented.

"Up until I met Hugh, I didn't know it myself. Determination is not a quality that comes naturally to me but in this circumstance, I found the strength to be very determined indeed. The following day was Sunday. As we came home from church, I made up my mind that

I would defy Mrs. Peyton's warnings about walking alone and return to the quay. I hoped to meet him again there."

"You must have been successful, although I can scarcely imagine you, my gentle sister, down on the quay in the company of sailors and fishermen."

"I was scared out of my wits. I feel quite secure in your company and the company of our father, but I don't know where I found the courage to go alone. Only my interest in seeing Hugh once more drove me to do it. I would have never considered going out alone before."

"You must have found him?"

"Yes, I did. I made several journeys to the quay, always quickly and without telling anyone where I was going. I felt terrible that I was lying, but I used every excuse to return. If cook needed an item from the market, or Mrs. Peyton needed a letter sent or a spool of thread, I was the first one to volunteer. Each time I went out, I made a trip to the quay. I did this for a month, and my optimism at finding Hugh began to wane. I can't understand how no one suspected me; my behavior must have seemed rather odd, volunteering for errands and always arriving back home out of breath from the exertion of running back up the hill."

"I confess I'm astonished. I never suspected you of any impropriety."

"No one else suspected me, either. It was nearing the end of a month that I was out on the quay, on a day that was not good weather. A cold mist blew in from the sea and I was sure I would become ill. The harbor and the beach were not as crowded as they often are in fine weather. As I was making my way around the ships, trying to avoid being struck by the men unloading the cargo, I was surprised to see Hugh and an older gentleman at the end of the dock."

Lydia could feel her pulse race as her sister recounted their meeting. "Charlotte, how exciting! Did he remember you?"

"He did remember me, although I could see that he was working.

He smiled at me, acknowledged that I was there. I remember smiling back at him and standing on the dock, watching him unload the fish from a boat. I think that I may have stood there for several minutes before I came to an embarrassing awareness of what I was doing. I must have looked foolish. I can still remember the instant that I turned to leave. I decided to walk away and let him finish working, that I could return later, when I heard someone running up behind me. It was Hugh."

"What did he say? What did you say?"

"He expressed his surprise to see me and asked me to wait there on the dock for him. He was nearly finished unloading the catch from the boat. I said yes, and stood there, although I was in a rush to return to the school. After all, I was not supposed to be at the docks, I was supposed to be purchasing ink for the school. He soon joined me and told me the most astonishing thing I have ever heard."

"What was that?"

"That he had been trying to find me! He knew my name but nothing else about me except that I had a sister and a parasol. He regretted not saying more to me that day we met, but he was sure that I was a lady just here for a holiday, to take in the sea breezes. He doubted that a lady such a myself would want to be seen talking to the son of fisherman. He admitted that his manners that day were crude, but his intentions were honorable."

"A fisherman, so that is what he was doing at the quay."

"Yes, he and his father fish from their boat. They don't live in Falmouth, but a village not far from here. He told me that he and his father come to port a few times each month to sell their catch down at the harbor. Lydia, he believed me to be a lady! Me, the daughter of a sea captain."

"Your deportment does you credit, my dear," Lydia answered.

"I suppose it must. He expressed shock that I had found him when he had looked for me at every trip to Falmouth. Isn't that something, we were both searching for each other? I immediately dispelled the notion that I was a high-born lady, and confessed that our father was a captain in the navy. We spent a few minutes that afternoon conversing as we walked along the harbor, and we promised to write to one another, and plan our next meeting in our correspondence."

"And so you have. Tell me, how many times have you met with him since that happy encounter?"

"Just a few times. When he is in Falmouth he is here to work. His father is very strict and they have a limited time to unload their catch, sell it, and return to their village before the sun sets. When I can steal away, I only have an hour or so to spare before I am missed."

"What do you do, if I may ask, when you are together?" Lydia tried not to let her face show her concerns.

"We have had tea at a public house near the harbor, but usually we strolled along the beach and harbor. Once we took a walk into the hills. And we write letters. When he comes to town, it's a rare occasion that we can be together."

"And his father, you said the man is strict?"

"He is. He never smiles, not for any reason. He isn't a mean person, he's just not cheerful, not like his son. Hugh is always smiling; he makes me laugh with his funny stories." Lydia sighed, and adjusted her own blanket around her shoulders. "He is a wonderful storyteller, and he is handsome and witty. You would approve of him; I just know you would. His family doesn't have a lot of money but he enjoys reading when he can. His father doesn't waste his money on the purchase of books, but the vicar of their parish lends Hugh books from time to time. In that way, he reminds me of you."

"Mr. Hugh Burton is not only a writer of letters, but a well-read fisherman? Charlotte, I am amazed. I have never been so surprised by anything you have told me. These letters are all written in his hand?"

"Yes, every one of them. Paper and ink are an expense that his father thinks of as foolish – he confided in me that his father cannot read a word – so he is forced to hide his writing supplies in the rafters of the barn."

Lydia smiled despite herself. She could see that Charlotte was in love, and judging from the stack of letters addressed to her, her young man shared the same feelings. Love was an emotion that heroines in novels experienced – or poets in literature. She had never seen anyone filled with the emotion until her sister met Hugh.

Hugh was a fisherman, which meant his status was below Charlotte's, but Lydia could not see any reason not to encourage the continued relationship. They were, after all, daughters of a naval officer, not high-born ladies. With their modest dowries, they could strive to better than themselves, but she could not discourage a match with a man who had a trade.

In the absence of her father, she gave her approval for the relationship to continue. Promising to do all that she could to assist Charlotte and Hugh in their endeavor, she hoped Captain Wells would not be disappointed that his youngest daughter was in love with a fisherman. A sea captain and a fisherman would have much in common. They were both men of the sea, and that was nearly the same thing. Wasn't it?

————

THE EARLY WEEKS of fall were fading quickly into colder weather as the letters continued to arrive for Charlotte. Charlotte and Lydia had agreed that if anyone should ask, they would attribute the letters to a distant cousin in nearby Devon. Fortunately, neither girl had any reason to lie and so the fictitious story of the cousin was never told, almost to Lydia's disappointment, as she had invented the alibi.

Lydia could see that this friendship between Hugh Burton and her sister was not showing any signs of diminishing. In fact, it seemed to be flourishing, and now when her sister wanted to sneak to the harbor to see Hugh, she never went alone but was accompanied by her. Lydia would wander around the shops while the couple went for long walks, but she made sure that Charlotte was not left on the docks without a chaperone, although Lydia herself had spent a great deal of her life walking along the docks, alone.

Hugh's father, as Charlotte had described him, was a serious man who did not say very much or show any emotion. Lydia never noticed any change in his countenance; his frown, she assumed, conveyed suspicion or disapproval. Although his demeanor was in sharp contrast to that of his son, he had not been openly unpleasant. When he spoke, his accent was deeply Cornish, his English words occasionally mixed with his native tongue.

On a fall afternoon when Lydia and Charlotte were at the quay, Lydia was astonished when Hugh's father spoke to her. His son and her sister stood a short distance away, their conversation punctuated by laughter.

"Lass, your wee sister, she has taken to my boy."

"That she has, sir," Lydia answered.

He nodded. "And he is taken with her, something terrible."

Lydia wasn't certain what to say to the man who hardly ever spoke to her or Charlotte. She stood at his side on the dock, waiting for him to continue.

"Hugh's own ma would like you ladies to come to the house. It may not be much but you won't go away hungry."

Lydia answered quickly, "Yes sir, we would be delighted."

Half an hour later, Lydia was still shocked by the invitation. As she walked up the hill with Charlotte returning home, Lydia shared the details of the invitation. It was for the following Sunday, after church. They would need a good excuse to be absent from luncheon, but Lydia was certain they could think of some reason to be missing for an afternoon. Hugh would collect them from the dock and return them before sunset. It promised to be a daring adventure, as neither of them had ever sailed on a fishing boat before. Charlotte was excited to be meeting Hugh's family, and Lydia was always happy to see new places and meet new people.

Lydia didn't share with her sister what she thought the purpose of this meeting was to be. Hugh had not been so secretive about Charlotte, and neither had his father. Mrs. Burton must have heard about her, and wanted to meet the young woman who was spending time with her son. If Charlotte suspected that the invitation was more than an effort to be polite, she gave no indication.

Later that night, the two girls stayed up talking into the wee hours.

"For a girl who is supposed to be terrified of the ocean, you don't seem to mind riding in Hugh's boat. You must know it's small, and can tip over at the slightest wind."

"We are not going out to sea! I hope he doesn't intend to take us into very deep water with his boat."

"Shall I tell the fisherman you have fallen in love with and his family that you are scared to death of the ocean?"

"Don't you dare," whispered Charlotte in the darkness.

"Are you prepared for a life that revolves around the ocean, for worrying every day that your husband, like your father, may never come home?" Lydia asked, her tone serious.

"Lydia, that is a dreadful question to ask."

"I know; I don't know why I said it. I suppose I'm worried about Father; it's been a long time since we've had a letter or a visit."

"That's true. I forgive you. I have thought of that, but Hugh hasn't asked for my hand in marriage."

"Yet. I see it coming. All I can say is I hope you like fish."

"Do you truly think he is going to ask me to marry him?"

"Yes, he would be a fool not to. You're pretty, quiet, and ready to look after a house of your own. Socially, you are far better educated than any other fishwife I've ever met. That may be why he enjoys your company; he can talk with you. You do read admirably well and your writing is not terrible."

"You think he would accept my dowry?"

"It's large enough – more than what the average fish wife would have, I would wager, and your father is a captain."

"A sea captain whom we never see or hear from. What would happen if he does ask for my hand and then our father makes a sudden appearance? Our father could very well refuse to allow me to marry Hugh."

"He could, but I doubt he would. Hugh and his father have a boat, and neither seem to be starving. All of this is speculation... unless you are not telling me all of the facts?"

"What facts?" Charlotte said in a quiet voice.

Lydia shifted, adjusting her pillow. "Tell me the truth. Is there an understanding between you and Hugh? Are you promised to each other? Have you declared yourselves in love and plan to wed, without my or anyone else's knowledge?"

"No. Well, not in any way that matters."

"What does that mean?" Lydia asked. "In matters of engagement, every way matters."

"He did ask me to promise that I would be true to him, which I did."

"Go on," Lydia prompted her sister.

"He wants me to wait for him. He has a plan that will improve his prospects."

"I don't understand; what is he planning to do? What can the son of a fisherman hope to do to improve his situation?"

"He wants to become a sailor in the navy; more than that, he wants to be an officer."

Lydia didn't want to upset her sister, but she was forced to remind her of the requirements of the officer class. "My dearest sister, it is commendable that he wants to be an officer, but to do so requires money, references, and formal education if he has any hopes for a commission."

Charlotte answered in a whisper. "I know. Regrettably, he does not have any money of his own, all his references are in his own social class except for the vicar, and he has the simple education provided by the village school. He would have to serve on the crew if he were to enlist."

"I am impressed by the ambition of your young man. He has dreams, but I don't know how he can ever hope to make them come true. I don't mean to upset you, but the sons of fishermen – no matter how smart or witty they may be – do not become naval officers."

"I know of the difficulties that lie ahead for Hugh if he chooses to pursue his aspirations. I have assured him that I would wait for him, but there is no need to wait, not for me. I would marry him without a cent in his pocket."

"I suppose I should praise him for wanting to wait. He must want to provide a life for you that is far better than the one he is accustomed to."

"Yes, you understand him; I knew you would," Charlotte replied.

"If he chose to join the crew of a merchant ship, it may be possible for him to earn a decent wage; perhaps enough for a commission if he saved his money," Lydia suggested.

"Perhaps. I know so little of these things. It seems silly that I am the daughter of an officer in the navy; you would think I'd know more about these things."

"If you and Hugh Burton have an understanding you will quickly become accustomed to these things, very quickly, I should say."

"And what of this Sunday's outing? We are to meet his mother and his family. Have you any idea how to arrange that?"

Lydia sighed, her conscience weighing heavily. "I do have an idea but I must confess, I feel terrible about lying to Mrs. Peyton, to Cook, to Moira, and everyone here at the school. I know it's for a noble cause, but it does not lesson my discomfort with my part in the deceit."

"I am burdened as well, but for me it was far worse. There for a time I was lying to you, dear Lydia, and I have never lied to you – not one time. Perhaps God can forgive us, since this cause is a worthy one."

Lydia broached a question that had been on the tip of tongue these past weeks. "Charlotte, Mrs. Peyton's rules regarding the young ladies under her tutelage and their interactions with gentlemen are clear, that interaction with men is not allowed. Yet, you are no longer under her *direct* tutelage; your last classes can hardly place you in the category of the girls that I teach. Have you not considered telling her that you have a young man, a suitor?"

The question was met with silence as the cold wind began to howl, its mournful sound whistling under the eaves of the garret. Lydia tightened her grip on the blankets around her. She considered lighting the fire in the small fireplace in their tiny room as she waited for her sister to answer.

After many minutes of silence, Charlotte replied. "I know that I might have shared this happy news with Mrs. Peyton, but if you must know the truth, I was quite frightened to do so."

"Frightened? Of dear Mrs. Peyton? Why should you be?"

"It seems silly now to speak of it, but I was frightened that she would forbid me from ever seeing Hugh again."

"You are of the age when young ladies marry, why should she forbid it?"

"Hugh is but a fisherman. I don't mind his place in society, not in the least. I am not prideful when it comes to such silly ideas of rank and class – but I am all too aware of her rules regarding the quay and how she feels about us going about without a chaperone."

"That does not imply that she would forbid your young man from paying a call, only that she wants to protect the girls under her care. And rightly so, she has the reputation of this school to consider – and the reputation of the girls themselves."

Lydia did not impress upon her sister that there was another reason, a reason she knew far too well as she often walked alone along the quay. The sailors and crews did not come from the middle or upper classes of society. Their behavior and their manners were crude, and the women they often associated with at the public houses were not proper young ladies. Charlotte, in her youth, had remained innocent of this knowledge and Lydia hoped to keep her naïve to it for as long as possible.

"If we may keep my secret between us for only a little longer, I promise to tell Mrs. Peyton when it is the proper time. Will you promise?" Charlotte asked.

"Yes, my dear, I promise, but I would feel better if she knew of the understanding you have with the young man. Until that time, I have devised a plan for Sunday. You and I will go on a picnic among the hills overlooking the town. I shall say that we want to enjoy the last of the good weather before winter sets in. If we are fortunate, Cook may supply us a hamper."

"That's a lovely idea, but we must be careful. What if we are seen down on the quay?"

"That," Lydia answered, "is all part of the adventure."

————

SUNDAY CAME as it always did – with an early breakfast, and the donning of Lydia and Charlotte's bests dresses and bonnets. This was followed by an orderly procession of girls from the school, led by Mrs. Peyton and the other teachers, to an imposing stone church in the center of the town.

The service was lengthy this Sunday, lasting half an hour longer due to the honor of a guest, a bishop who gave a sermon far surpassing in time and substance any sermon that Lydia could recall. Ordinarily, Lydia would have been impressed by the orator, but not this Sunday. Begging God to forgive her, she found that she could not think of heaven, or the lesson from the bible or the pulpit. Her mind was far too engrossed in worldly matters, mainly a small boat and meeting the family who could one day be related to her by marriage.

As the bishop and then the vicar gave the last prayers of the service, Lydia added one of her own, that she and her sister should be safe in the journey by boat to Hugh's village, and that they should return without being caught. It seemed like a simple prayer and one she hoped the Almighty would approve.

Charlotte fidgeted through the last few minutes of the service while Lydia was praying, and neither one of them paid the slightest attention to the murmuring of *Amen* from the congregation. As they sprang out of their seats, Lydia wished there was some way for her to rush Mrs. Peyton and her staff back to the school. She didn't want to be late arriving at the quay, as she was excited to go sailing.

Despite her wishes, Mrs. Peyton followed her normal routine for a Sunday except with one-time consuming addition: rather than only speak to the vicar and half a dozen ladies from town, she added a lengthy discussion with the bishop regarding the upcoming holidays. Lydia did not think her dear Mrs. Peyton would ever leave the churchyard, until she was urged by Cook that it was past time for luncheon.

The procession back to the school was orderly and slow, much too slow for Lydia and Charlotte. At least they were closer to their goal of getting back to the school, quickly changing into less formal dresses and rushing down to the quay. It seemed like a good plan, and all was going well – until they were ready to leave for the afternoon, hamper in hand.

Mrs. Peyton stopped them as they were rushing out the door. "Girls, are you planning a lengthy walk this afternoon?"

Lydia answered, "Yes ma'am, we were planning to be gone until dinner. We hope to have one more nice day together, to take in the sun and sea air, since it does such wonders for Charlotte's constitution."

Charlotte added, "Yes, I feel better. The apothecary, Mr. Brewer, has spoken of the benefits of exercise and I believe he is correct."

Mrs. Peyton nodded. "Yes, I would agree that you do seem to be much rejuvenated these past months, but I do wish you would consider rescheduling your walk. There is tinge of damp in the air, and I fear you may be caught in a storm."

Lydia knew that Mrs. Peyton could insist they cancel their plans if she did not proceed with care. "Mrs. Peyton, I will keep a careful watch on the weather. If I detect a change I will shorten our trip and we shall return home at once. Charlotte has benefitted so much from our afternoons by the sea and strolls in the countryside that I fear her health may suffer greatly this winter without them. I consider it most important that she receive as much benefit as she can while the weather is pleasant; do you not agree?"

"I cannot argue with the benefits of exercise and salt air on a delicate constitution but I do wish you would reconsider your outing this afternoon."

Charlotte tried to help. "Mrs. Peyton, I know my sister would never allow any harm to come to me, and I beg you to permit us to take in the benefits of the good air in the countryside today. My spirits and my health are much improved. I have been looking forward to this outing all week and I hope you will allow us to go for a short time if we give you our word to be mindful of the weather."

Lydia watched in astonishment as Mrs. Peyton smiled at her younger sister and said, "If it means that much to you my dear, I don't want to tell you no, but be careful. The weather threatens to turn at any moment. It is my sincerest wish that neither of you become ill, but Charlotte, with your delicacy, I would never forgive myself if anything happened to you while you were under my care."

Charlotte smiled at the older woman as she nodded for Lydia to leave. "Thank you, Mrs. Peyton. I feel stronger than ever and I am grateful that you are concerned for my – for *our* –welfare. We shall see you when we return."

With a hamper of pasties and sweet cakes under Lydia's arm, they rushed down the hill towards the quay, taking care not to be seen by anyone from the school. Lydia was mildly impressed by her sister's expert handling of the situation that had nearly deprived them of their adventure. Charlotte was frail and sickly and surprisingly she had used those weaknesses to her advantage in a way that Lydia did not expect. Lydia could only conclude that the motivation was love.

Rushing down the quay, they raced past the enormous wooden ships of the navy and merchant fleet, past men who were recovering from their drunken escapades of the previous evenings. Sailors and crewmen lounged lazily along the harbor, and barely noticed the two young women who rushed by. At the end of the dock, Lydia could see the diminutive sailing vessel that belonged to Mr. Burton. Hugh was seated on a barrel, drowsing unhappily.

"I was about to set sail for home," he said, standing up.

Lydia answered before Charlotte. "We were delayed at church, please forgive us."

"I thought you had forgot about me," he replied to Charlotte.

"How could I ever forget about you?" she answered with a warm smile.

"If you had it would have been for the good, if not for my broken heart. The weather may not hold today. We shall have to keep an eye on it; the clouds are gathering in the west and I fear a real strong blow by sunset," Hugh said as he nodded towards the water.

"Mr. Burton, we must rely entirely on you and your judgment. Do you believe we'll be safe?" Lydia sked as she looked at the horizon.

Small white clouds drifted across the sky, and the weather was unseasonably warm and mild for autumn. Mrs. Peyton had warned of inclement weather in much the same way as Hugh, which gave her reason to worry not for herself, but for her sister.

"If we're careful not to stay too long, I don't think there is cause for worry," he answered.

The weather was not the only factor to be considered, thought Lydia, as Hugh assisted them into the boat. She didn't want anyone to see them leave the dock in a fishing boat when they were supposed to be hiking into the hills above town. She hoped that the other girls at the school were less like her and her sister, that they followed Mrs. Peyton's rules with more diligence, as Hugh cast off the lines and they drifted into the harbor.

Lydia, like her sister, was the daughter of a naval captain, but her experience upon the water was limited. She had never sailed on the ocean that she could remember, or spent any amount of time in any boat. The feel of the water under the fishing boat and the way the small vessel glided, yet was gently rocked by the waves, was both a source of interest and trepidation. She couldn't swim, and neither could her sister. If they should go overboard, or if the ship sank, she knew they would drown. It was a sobering thought and one that she tried to convince herself was part of the adventure. The adventures she read about in novels were always fraught with danger, and the very real fear of drowning made this adventure one she prayed she would survive.

As she worried about the safety of the little craft, she could see that Charlotte – who professed to be terrified of the water and all manner of sea monsters – looked at home upon the waves in Hugh's company. She was laughing in delight as a large wave broke over the bow, spraying salt water on the sails and the occupants of the cockpit. Lydia could only account for her original assessment, that it was love that had changed her frail and demure sister into a heroine as brave as any she read about in her novels.

Holding tight to the narrow wooden seat of the cockpit, Lydia tried to forget all her fears. She marveled at the swiftness of the boat under its sail, and the changing scenery of the shoreline. From the water, the world looked different, peaceful and beautiful in its own way. Gulls swooped along the waters, their wings outstretched as they glided near the waves. Seagulls perched along the docks or flew above the boat, their plaintive cries echoing in the quiet. The waves lapped against the side of the boat in a cheerful but subdued way that Lydia found delightful. She dared to lean closer to the water, to get a glimpse of light shimmering on the waves.

In that moment, when she forgot about her fear of dying, or her fear that her sister would fall overboard at any second, she found a beauty that she had never expected. The enormous ships in the harbor had always held a fascination for her, but it wasn't until this moment that she finally understood the hold the sea had on men like her own father or Hugh Burton.

She had always wondered how her father, or any man, could leave their families and go to sea. It was on this afternoon that she saw a glimpse of that passion and it gave her an understanding of the man her father was. Wiping a tear from her eye, she said a silent prayer for him and hoped that he would take her out in a boat when he returned, a dream she hoped would come true soon.

Hugh called out for Lydia and Charlotte to be careful as he steered towards a dock along the shore. The boom of the sail came around quickly, and Lydia ducked out of its way. She was thankful that their boat ride was coming to an end, grateful that they had made it to their destination safely, but she genuinely did not want to leave the water. Not now, when she found she finally understood that the beauty of being in a boat far outweighed the fear.

Hugh steered the boat into place at the side of the dock, a skill Lydia could see was honed to perfection by years of fishing every day for his entire life. The water along the shore was low; the tide was going out, which gave Hugh the opportunity to be chivalrous as he jumped to the wooden dock and helped each lady out of the boat, taking care to kiss Charlotte's hand.

With the hamper under her arm, Lydia maintained a respectful distance from Hugh and Charlotte as they walked towards the village. In her limited experience of people of other classes, she knew that tradesmen and fisher folk often lived in conditions that were crowded, in homes where the roofs leaked and the chimneys smoked. With this in mind, Lydia had prepared herself for a village of rundown cottages with sagging roofs, but she was pleasantly surprised to see clean but modest homes in a row. A few of the houses were facing a chapel in a kind of village square, while others were on the outskirts, along lanes lined with gardens and trees.

The village that the Burtons called home seemed idyllic. It was a small seaside village with nets staked out in the sun, fishing boats tied to the dock, and small rowing boats resting on a narrow beach. Smiling as they made way past a row of prim and proper wattle and daub cottages with thatched roofs, Lydia's opinion of Hugh's background brightened. As they approached a large house at the end of the row, a line of children ranging from very small to nearly as old as Charlotte came out of the house to greet Hugh and the visitors.

Lydia was charmed as two small girls toddled out after their siblings, followed by an older woman. The woman looked nearly as severe as Hugh's father, but she was shorter and thinner. She nodded at her son as he made the introductions.

Although short on words, the woman smiled faintly as she invited Lydia and her sister into the house.

Lydia curtseyed as she presented the hamper to the woman. "Mrs. Burton, it is a pleasure to meet you; Cook fixed pasties and sweet cakes."

"Thank you, miss," the older woman answered. "I was about to set the dishes out for tea."

"That would be lovely; a spot of tea would be just the thing," Lydia answered.

Lydia did not understand what the woman meant by tea, she was thinking a pot of tea and few sandwiches, but tea in the Burton household was an afternoon meal. Following the woman and her multitude of children into the cottage, she was pleased to see a long trestle table and benches by the fireside, a pot of stew, and plates of dark crusty bread set on the table. The aroma of the stew was heavenly, as she had not had a bite to eat since her toast and jam for breakfast.

Mrs. Burton directed her oldest girls to set the table as Mr. Burton took his place at the head, and the younger children climbed into their places. Hugh invited Charlotte to sit beside him at the end closest to his father while Lydia took a spot at the end closest to his mother. From her vantage point she was free to observe nearly everyone at the table, including the two sisters nearest Charlotte's age, who stared at Charlotte – one with a scowl on her face.

Lydia could not account for the scowling young woman as Mr. Burton began the prayer before the meal. As he finished his short blessing, Lydia thought of the parents' stern expressions, and decided that the scowling young lady must share their same joyless trait. It was a trait that seemed so at odds with Hugh's cheerful countenance.

Keeping largely silent, Lydia enjoyed the simple fish and dumpling stew, and the dark bread was the perfect complement to the lighter-than-air dumplings. Mr. Burton was right, she would surely not go away hungry from his house. Lydia complimented Hugh's mother as she observed that the woman, like the young woman seated at the table, was engrossed in everything Charlotte and Hugh did, every word they said, and every time they laughed together.

After the meal was over, Charlotte and Hugh left with the excuse of taking a stroll around the village. The children went outside to play quietly, reminded by Mr. Burton to be mindful that it was Sunday. Lydia offered to help clean the dishes, but the two young ladies were already clearing the table and wiping the plates clean beside Mrs. Burton. She sat by herself at the fireside as the young women whispered and Mr. Burton smoked a clay pipe.

Mrs. Burton soon left the dishes to her daughters and sat down beside Lydia. Lydia brought up the meal again and attempted to make polite conversation. "Mrs. Burton, the fish stew was delightful, I don't know when I have ever had dumplings so delectable."

"That is good of you to say, it was me own ma's recipe."

"I'm glad you invited us to tea this afternoon; I have enjoyed meeting your family."

"It was good of you ladies to come, I have to say, I didn't know if I wanted my Hugh to associate with ladies such as yourselves, with schooling. To my thinking, schooling isn't needed to sell fish and run a home."

"Yes, ma'am." Lydia didn't agree but she didn't want to appear impolite.

"Not for my girls, but your sister seems real nice."

"Yes, ma'am."

"I wanted to see her with my own eyes, to see if she is better than our Winnie."

"Better than your Winnie? I don't understand."

"Our Winnie. See the lass there with my own sweet Deirdre, the tall girl washing the soup pot? She is the eldest daughter of Goody Parker."

"Yes," Lydia answered, unsure where this conversation was going.

"She and my Hugh, well you see they're intended for one another

– have been since they were wee ones – but your sister is right nice with her school-taught ways and her fine how-do-you-do."

"Mrs. Burton, please understand, I'm not following you. You say that Hugh is intended for Winnie?"

"He is, but I don't mind if he keeps your sister company for a might longer, while Winnie grows up a bit. She's got another year before Goody Parker will part with her."

Lydia swallowed hard, her pulse racing. "You don't mind if your son is in love with my sister, and breaks my sister's heart when it's time to marry Winnie?"

"Why should he break her heart? They are passing the time together, there can't be no harm to it. Your sister is a fine girl but not the sort of girl for my Hugh. Winnie and Hugh will make a fine couple one day, mark my words."

Mrs. Burton called out to the young woman who was the topic of conversation. "Winnie, stop what you're doing there, Lass, and come over here and have a proper chat with our guest."

Winnie, of course, was the young woman who had scowled all through the meal. Curtseying, she replaced her scowl with a smile and sat down beside Hugh's mother. She wasn't a bad looking girl, thought Lydia, but the fact remained, this woman would be Hugh's wife one day, if his mother had her say in the matter.

Lydia sat in uncomfortable silence as Winnie and Mrs. Burton chatted between themselves, breaking into their native Cornish. Mr. Burton said nothing, and watched the fire. Lydia's mind was filled with confusion as she sat in awkward silence, which was suddenly broken by several of the Burton children rushing into the house at once. They crowded around the fire as they cheerfully announced that it was raining.

Rushing to her feet, Lydia ran for the door, her fear confirmed. With the first drops to fall from the sky, the storm Mrs. Peyton had warned them about had set in, and she and Charlotte were far away from home.

———

THE VOYAGE back to the school was not as pleasant or as peaceful as the voyage going to the village. Against the advice of Mr. Burton, and the imploring of Mrs. Burton, Lydia and Charlotte could not stay until the following morning. They had to go home, or they would face terrible consequences.

To add to Lydia's anxiety, she could see only two ways of returning to Falmouth. Walking could take hours over the hills and down winding roads; it was not an option. With Hugh's solemn promise to his father to be careful in the deteriorating weather, he rushed his guests down the lane of the village to the boat and cast off as the storm was setting in for the evening.

Lydia cradled the hamper on her lap as the rain stung her eyes, soaking her through her clothes. Charlotte was nestled beside her as Hugh had to give every effort to sailing the boat. The waves were growing high and the wind buffeted the little vessel as he fought to maintain the course. Lydia was glad, in a way, that the storm kept anyone in the little boat from having a conversation. At this moment, she had quite a few questions for Hugh, and they were far from pleasant.

Holding her sister tightly in her arms, she prayed that they would arrive safely at the quay. From there, they could make their way back to school and the warmth of the fireside, and explain to Mrs. Peyton how they were caught out in the rain far away from the school. Lydia knew she would be scolded but it was far better to be scolded for misjudging the distance of an afternoon's walk in the country than to not come home until the following day. The reputation of the Wells girls and the school would be compromised.

As angry as Lydia was at Hugh for failing to tell her sister about Winnie, she could not fault him for his masterful handling of the boat in unforgiving seas. The waves were building in intensity as the wind howled around the fishing boat, yet Hugh remained calm, his strong hands holding the tiller and tightening the lines of the sails. This was an adventure, Lydia thought to herself, as she tried to keep her sister from shivering as the temperature dropped with the worsening weather conditions.

Vowing to God that she would lead a life free of deceit if she and her sister could arrive safely at the quay, Lydia closed her eyes as the boat tossed and turned in the storm-driven waters. She wasn't sure how much time had passed when Hugh maneuvered the boat next to the dock, throwing the stern line over a wooden pylon.

Offering his strong and sure hands to Lydia and Charlotte, he helped them out of the boat. He embraced Charlotte as Lydia stood shivering on the dock, a damp hamper in her hands and her shoes ruined with water. With a cavalier wave, Hugh threw off the lines and sailed away as Charlotte stood motionless, crying in the rain, to Lydia's dismay.

"Come on," Lydia pleaded. "We have to get you out of this cold and wet. Mrs. Peyton is going to box my ears for this and I can't deny that I deserve it."

Charlotte was inconsolable. "Please don't make me feel worse than I already do; it's my fault we were caught in this storm and it will be my fault if anything should happen to Hugh. He's going back home in this weather – he could perish and it would be all my fault!"

"He'll be fine; mark my words. He is a capable sailor if I ever saw one, you saw how easily he handled that boat in the waves. But you, my dear, could catch your death and I would never forgive myself," Lydia said as she reached for her sister's hand.

"You believe all will be fine? That Hugh will get back home?"

Lydia could barely see in the rain that was growing heavier each minute as the wind sang in the rigging of the ships along the quay. "Yes my dear, I do. He will be fine, but you and I won't be unless we get out of these wet clothes soon."

"You wanted an adventure, and you got one; didn't you, my dear sister?"

Lydia smiled despite her chattering teeth. "Yes, I suppose I did.

Come along and don't tarry; you may have to run. Are you strong enough to keep my pace?"

"I will do my best. Thank you, Lydia, for coming today. I felt so at home there in Hugh's village. His family was very nice."

"We will talk all about it when we are sitting by the fire at home. Come on, we must hurry."

Lydia held the hamper tightly with one hand and her sister's hand with the other as she led her through the streets of Falmouth, climbing higher with every block. She didn't have the heart to tell Charlotte about Winnie, not when she was terrified that her young man would not survive the storm. She knew that Charlotte was right to be worried – that small boat was no match for the growing storm that sent the rain sideways in the streets and howled like a wild animal through the alleys.

She vowed as they saw the lights of the school in the distance, if she and Charlotte survived this adventure without illness, after Hugh sent word that all was well, then she would tell Charlotte the truth about his engagement to Winnie. Tonight, she knew would be terrible. Her sister would be shivering from fear as much as cold and Lydia would have to comfort her. They would have to face Mrs. Peyton, too. Lydia would pray that Hugh would survive. If he did, as she trusted that he would, she would be faced with an even worse tempest than the one that sent the rain whipping around them as they struggled to reach their home.

She would have to tell her sister the truth about Hugh, and that would break her heart.

CHAPTER THREE

Lydia was wracked with confusion and guilt. In the small hours of the morning after their return to Mrs. Peyton's, Charlotte lay in bed, pale and shivering. It was all Lydia's fault. If only she had listened to Mrs. Peyton and Hugh about the changeable weather, her sister would be in good health. Sitting beside Charlotte's bed in the garret, Lydia prayed that their adventure to Hugh's village would not be the cause of her sister's demise.

Yet it was not only guilt that Lydia felt, but a terrible confusion after the outing. Hugh's mother had all but assured her that her son was the intended of Winnie Parker, a local girl. Looking down at her sister's angelic features, her pale blonde hair and her fragile beauty evident even in her illness, Lydia wondered how any man could choose any other woman. If – and that was terrible word, if – her sister survived this sickness, Lydia would be compelled to tell Charlotte the truth.

The rain pelted the windowpanes and the storm showed no signs of abating. They had returned to the school and got a stern lecture from Mrs. Peyton, but concern and admonishment did nothing to deter Charlotte's illness. Lydia added another log to the fire and pulled a shawl around her shoulders. Returning to the bedside, she bowed her head, confessing, "Charlotte, how stupid of me to permit this folly. If you die, it will be all my fault."

Charlotte opened her eyes. "Lydia, you must not blame yourself, I wanted to go and I would have devised a scheme; you must know that."

"That does not remove my guilt in the matter. I ignored every warning; I saw the portents of bad weather and I insisted that we go. It was my folly that resulted in your illness. I allowed my own foolishness to supersede my knowledge of your frailty and weak constitution. It is my fault."

"Please, Lydia, for my sake, don't blame yourself – it will not heal me or change the circumstances. I chose to go. I would have chosen to go a thousand times over. If you must pray, pray for Hugh. I shall not rest or be well again until I know that he did not perish."

Lydia whispered, "About Hugh..."

"Yes? What is it?" Charlotte asked.

Lydia was torn. She felt she must tell Charlotte the truth about Hugh, yet she couldn't bear to do it. If her sister was as ill as she feared, the loss of a love might be too much to bear. Lydia feared that heartbreak would only hasten her sister's illness, destroying any chance that she might recover.

Lydia decided to keep the truth to herself for now, relying instead on her ability to cheer her sister with encouraging words. "You shouldn't worry about him; he was born to the water, and he's faced countless storms in his experience. I would be surprised if anything terrible befell such a capable sailor."

In her weakened state, Charlotte managed a faint smile. "You think he's home safe by his family's fireside, his boat tied securely to the dock?"

"Yes, Charlotte, I do believe it. He is undoubtedly concerned more for our welfare than his own, and I would not be surprised if he is writing you a letter detailing the saga of his harrowing journey home at this very moment."

"If only I had your confidence. I do not doubt Hugh's skills are formidable, but his boat was so small and the waves tossed it about as though it was no more than a leaf on the current. I do fear for him; I shall never forgive myself if I discover he has been killed because of me."

"Please don't say that," pleaded Lydia.

"If I should find that Hugh perished in this storm, I will no longer have any will left. Even now I fear my strength is fading."

Lydia had been at her sister's bedside many times; Charlotte's fragile state of heath was always a threat that lingered around her. Yet Charlotte had always found the strength to rally from each illness that laid waste to her diminutive frame. It terrified Lydia to no end that Charlotte spoke of her own will as being weak, her spirit lacking in strength. Without the desire to grow well once more, her fate may already be sealed.

"Charlotte, imagine how disappointed you would be to discover that Hugh is quite well and you have allowed yourself to slip away because you didn't have the will to regain your health. You can't allow that, can you? If you were to die and he survived, he would feel your loss most acutely and blame himself, would he not?"

"I suppose you're right; I cannot allow myself to despair."

"We shall both pray very hard, as I know Mrs. Peyton is, that you shall be quite yourself again."

"I'm tired and cold, is there not a fire burning?"

"There is." Lydia raised her hand to Charlotte's brow. Her sister was no longer cold to the touch but her face was flushed, her brow warm. "I shall give you the covers from my bed. I think you would benefit from a cup of tea. I shall leave you for just a moment, will you be quite all right in my absence?"

Charlotte did not give an answer. Her eyes were shut, her body shivering as her fever worsened. Lydia didn't to want to leave her sister, but Cook was undoubtedly asleep and Moira was snug in her bed. If there was to be a restorative cup of tea, it fell to her to sneak downstairs in the dark and procure it.

Kissing her sister's forehead, Lydia carried a candle and made her way downstairs, taking care not to make any noise. The steps creaked but the sound didn't attract any attention, being drowned out by the tempest raging outside. With each violent blast of the wind, she imagined that the brick walls of the school shook ever so slightly.

Lydia had lived through many storms in Cornwall. The peninsula stretched out in the ocean, and so was battered by weather in such a way and so frequently that it barely attracted her attention – but this storm was different. It was not weakening, and like her sister's fever, had only seemed to grow in ferocity throughout the night. The walls of the school were stone and brick, sturdy building materials chosen for their fortitude. Yet the wind made them seem as thin as paper, the relentless howling eerie.

Yes, Lydia thought to herself, a good strong cup of tea would warm them both. She strengthened her resolve to face whatever may come.

She hurried to build up the fire in the stove and find the tea. She hated to leave her sister all alone in the garret, ill and in this weather. As she waited for the water to boil, she watched the rain came down in sheets outside. Walking towards the window, she could hear the glass rattling in the windowpane, a testament to the force of the wind.

In her imagination she could see the waves in the harbor crashing over the quay, the ships tied to the dock bobbing and tilting in the wind. She had seen a terrible storm once in the daylight hours; it was awe-inspiring to witness the power of the sea, tossing enormous wooden ships about as if they were children's toys. In the dead of night, the storm outside sounded terrifying. Shivering, she opened the grate to warm her hands and gave thanks that the school was high on a hill, safely nestled above the shore.

The night promised to be a long one, which prompted Lydia to make a search of the kitchen for something to eat. Locating a leftover pie, she cut a large slice and slipped the plate onto a tray. She poured the boiling water into the teapot and quickly collected two cups. Carefully closing the grate, she hoped Cook would not mind that she had invaded the kitchen at so late an hour. Considering the dire circumstances, she was hopeful that Cook, and Mrs. Peyton, would understand.

Climbing the narrow staircase with the tray in her hands, she took care not to trip on her nightgown. Pushing open the door with her hip, she found the garret room was still snug and warm, and her sister was wrapped securely in a pile of blankets, her face flushed. Lydia set the tea tray down on the desk, and went to her sister's side.

"Charlotte, my dear, I have brought a fresh hot pot of tea and slice of pie. Do you feel hungry?"

Charlotte opened her eyes and whispered, "I'm not hungry."

"That's fine, let me fix you a cup of tea; it will help keep you warm."

Lydia poured a cup of tea for her sister. At first, Charlotte resisted the warm drink, but at Lydia's insistence, she was finally persuaded to drink some. Charlotte was too weak to hold her own cup, an alarming turn of events that Lydia could not ignore. It was becoming apparent that Charlotte's illness was beyond the administrations of her sister.

"Charlotte, I may have to leave you for a few minutes more. Rest and I will return with Mrs. Peyton; she'll know what can be done to make you better."

"No, Lydia, you can't ask Mrs. Peyton. She mustn't know about Hugh," Charlotte begged her sister in a weak voice.

"Mrs. Peyton is not going to interrogate you; she will only want to make you better. Never you worry, I will seek her out and that is the end of it. You must be better, what would I do without you?"

"Lydia, please don't leave me," Charlotte begged. "I'm scared of the storm."

"I have to go, but I'll be right back. And don't worry about the storm; it's only a little wind and rain." She didn't want to admit to her feverish sister that she, too, was afraid of the storm. "You lay here and I will be back before you know I am gone." Lydia pulled the shawl around her shoulders, and stifled her alarm at Charlotte's condition. She couldn't imagine her life without her sister.

Shivering from cold and fright, she ran downstairs to the second floor. Finding Mrs. Peyton's door unlocked, she crept inside the cold room. The fire was out in the fireplace, so she set the candle on the bedside table.

"Mrs. Peyton," Lydia said as she touched the woman's shoulder. "Mrs. Peyton. Please wake up! I need your help. It's Charlotte – she's taken ill."

Mrs. Peyton mumbled something unintelligible as Lydia continued to try rouse her. "Mrs. Peyton, please, you must wake up at once."

The old school mistress woke, grumbling about the candle light in her face. It was only after she recognized Lydia that she sat up, her eyes wide with fear. "Lydia, my dear! What brings you out of bed at this late hour?"

"It's Charlotte; she's gravely ill. I've done all I can for her...I'm scared, Mrs. Peyton."

"Hand me my robe. My word, is that the wind making all that noise? It really is a terrible night, is it not?"

"Yes ma'am," said Lydia as she found Mrs. Peyton's robe on a chair by the darkened fireplace.

"Has it been blowing like this all night?" Mrs. Peyton asked, her eyes drawn to the window. The rain was hitting the glass in a torrent as the wind howled through the chimney.

"Yes ma'am, it has."

"My word, no wonder your sister has taken ill, upstairs in that drafty garret. I have warned you that it is not a suitable place for you two young ladies."

"Mrs. Peyton, I assure that it's warm in our room – far warmer than your room, I daresay," Lydia replied.

"That may be true, but it cannot be good for your sister's constitution, you know of her frailty."

Lydia endured the woman's criticism; it was understandable. She had woken her up from her slumber and insisted that Mrs. Peyton leave the cozy confines of her warm bed to journey upstairs to attend to a sick woman.

"Furthermore, I warned you this would happen if you took your sister out in the weather today, did I not?" Mrs. Peyton asked as she wrapped a shawl around her shoulders. "Come, Lydia, we must not wait a moment longer."

Lydia held the candle as she led the way to the garret. Opening the door, she was relieved to see her sister was still breathing, her chest rising and falling under the covers, her cheeks still flushed.

"I must say you have it plenty warm in here; I give you credit for that. Close the door, don't let the heat out and the draft in or we shall lose her for certain," Mrs. Peyton admonished Lydia.

Lydia closed the door and watched Mrs. Peyton examine Charlotte. The wind and rain was much louder up here, the roar of the storm refusing to subside. Lydia understood why Charlotte was scared to be alone in this room while the tempest blew outside. Glancing up at the roof, she tried to calm her own fears that the roof was to be carried off at any moment.

Mrs. Peyton put her hand to the young woman's fevered brow. Charlotte's gaze fell on Lydia as she whispered Lydia's name.

"I'm here, Charlotte, I've brought Mrs. Peyton."

Charlotte murmured softly as her eyes closed, the fever overtaking her.

Lydia looked to Mrs. Peyton. "What should we do?"

"We must pray and fetch the doctor. You were right to come to me before her condition grew any worse. Wake Moira to fetch the doctor right away. If the doctor cannot come, send her for the apothecary, Mr. Brewer; he will know what is to be done."

"Mrs. Peyton, I cannot wake Moira and send her out in this storm – she has done nothing to deserve that. I'll go. I'm the oldest, and it was my decision that led to Charlotte's illness. I will go for help."

"I won't allow it; I cannot have you falling ill alongside your sister."

"I could never live with myself if Moira was taken ill. I cannot bear to think of Moira facing this storm because of my negligence to the weather conditions."

Mrs. Peyton eyed Lydia with a furrowed brow, her ordinarily cheerful face set in a deep frown. "If you do not want to wake Moira and send her as I have asked then so be it, you are a woman of an age to make your own decisions. No matter what my feelings are regarding your decision, the fact remains that your sister needs more help than I can provide."

"Then I shall go, if you will stay with her. I will bring back whatever help I can."

The old woman lay her hand on Lydia's. "God go with you, my child, mind the wind and the rain. This is no fall storm – no, this weather blows out of the ocean, a storm as dreadful as the ones that sink ships in the colonies. This is not a night for you to be taking a stroll, but it cannot be helped."

"Thank you, Mrs. Peyton, I will be careful; I give you my word. I cannot leave my only sister alone in this world, now can I?" Lydia asked as she reached for her hat, which would be useless, but made her feel better.

"If it weren't so cold and nasty I would say you would do better to wear one of those bathing costumes you girls like to wear in the sea," Mrs. Peyton managed a weak smile as Lydia gave a nervous giggle.

Kissing her sister's forehead, she could feel the skin was hot to the touch. Lydia knew there was no other way to save her sister's life; she had to go out in the storm. She prayed that her sister would still be alive when she returned.

———

Lydia was soaked; her coat, hat, and clothes were all drenched through and she sat dripping miserably beside the stove in the kitchen. In the late hours of the night, Mrs. Peyton had awakened Cook with clear instructions: heat the stove, boil water, and make broth from whatever she had on hand. The boiling water was to make tea for the doctor and Mrs. Peyton; the broth was for Lydia.

As Mrs. Peyton explained on Lydia's return to the school with Dr. Abernathy, she could not have both girls sick at the same time; it would not do. Lydia was ordered to the kitchen and Cook was in charge of seeing that she changed into a warm set of clothes and was given hot broth to drink.

"Miss Lydia, I have made you a cup of tea. Drink it down; you'll need to warm your bones," Cook said as she stirred the broth on the stove. Its aroma filled the room.

Lydia could not stop shivering. The cold and rain froze her body but the wind ripping at the town of Falmouth frightened her. She prayed with all her heart that no man was on the sea tonight.

Moira came bustling downstairs, her arms laden with clothes. "The missus told me how you wouldn't let anyone else go for the doctor. That was good of you, miss, it surely was. With my poor heart, I would have caught my death if I had to go."

Cook was an older woman, older than Mrs. Peyton, even. She had a name, but one ever called her by it – she was just known as *Cook*. She was as kindly as Mrs. Peyton, and every bit as stubborn when it came to the welfare of the girls in her care.

The old woman would not permit Lydia to freeze to death in her kitchen. "You come right here and stand in front of this stove where it's nice and warm. You need to get out of those wet things or we shall have to have the doctor for you, next."

"Yes ma'am," Lydia said, accepting the clothes from Moira.

"Miss, bless you," Moira said. "I pray that God will heal Charlotte and keep the sickness from you. You must have been very brave, to face this storm."

"Moira, take a fresh pot of tea to Mrs. Peyton. She and the doctor will be needing it," Cook said to the maid.

"Yes ma'am," the maid answered as she prepared the tray for tea, and left the room.

"That storm blowing out there is the worst I've seen these thirty years. Half of Falmouth will be under water. If the rain keeps up, I'll wager there will be people dying soon enough." Cook paused to taste the broth. "Needs a pinch of salt."

Lydia shivered as she removed the dripping clothes. Modesty fell away with the sodden pile at her feet. Reaching for the dry shift and robe, she asked Cook, "When can I go up and see my sister? Why has the doctor refused to let me see her?"

The old woman smiled as she reassured Lydia. "Miss Lydia, he sent you down to the kitchen to get dry and shore up your constitution with a cup of broth. No doubt he is worried about you falling ill, like your sister. You drink this broth and dry yourself by the stove, and you can see Miss Charlotte soon enough."

Lydia slid her feet into the warm slippers with a tiny moan of gratitude, and tugged her shawl around her shoulders. Looking at the kindly old cook, she said, "I'm glad to have your company; I don't know what I would do if you weren't here with me. I should be so unsettled in my thoughts."

"Miss Lydia, you are too good to me. Stay right there by the stove and warm yourself, and drink all that broth until there is not a drop left."

Lydia sat down by the fire as Cook told her tales of storms she remembered when she was younger, of the town being flooded up to the doorsteps of the church. Lydia did not have to imagine the terrible destruction of any historic storm, not when there was a real tempest blowing outside. She was worried, not only for herself and her sister, but for the inhabitants of the low-lying village that Hugh and his family called home.

"If Falmouth floods, what of the nearby villages? What becomes of them in these storms?" Lydia asked, afraid to hear the answer.

"My dear, the villages in all directions around Falmouth flood something terrible, same as the port and the town. I've seen the quay and all the shops flooded when I was a girl of your age. But you needn't worry about that; this school sits high enough on the hill not to ever be flooded."

Cook poured another ladle of beef broth into Lydia's bowl. "You keep drinking this broth; it will feed your blood. Don't worry yourself about anyone from Cornwall, we've been through worse than this storm. Drink that and warm yourself and then it will be time to see your sister."

Lydia did as she was told, and sipped. She prayed very hard for her sister and the village full of fishermen and their families – the Burton children being foremost in her thoughts. In all her prayers, she found there was room for Hugh. She was terrified that he'd been caught in this storm, but a part of her desperately clung to the knowledge that he was a competent sailor, a faithless man but a good seaman. Slowly, the warmth returned to her body; her fingers and face were no longer numb. The fire in the stove, the broth, and Cook's compassion worked as a powerful medicine to cure her of her cold and her fear.

She felt her eyes closing. She was so tired from the journey to fetch the doctor in the slashing rain, while the wind forced her to cling to doorways, fences, and anything she could find on the street that was stronger and heavier than herself. It was the will of God, she decided, that had guided her footsteps to the doctor's house, that brought the man out in the weather.

In the comfort of the warm kitchen, her aches and pains soothed by broth and kindness, she began to nod off. It was at this moment in the quiet, with Cook's soft voice recounting stories of old, that Moira reappeared. "Miss, the doctor says you may see your sister."

Lydia thought she read a sadness on Moira's face, but it didn't matter. She thanked the cook and Moira and climbed the stairs, ignoring with each step the agony in her muscles from the exertion of fighting her way through the wind to fetch the doctor. Gritting her teeth, she promised that she wouldn't allow either Mrs. Peyton or the doctor to see her in a pained or weakened state; she didn't want them to forbid her to be at her sister's bedside.

The last flight of stairs was excruciating but she found the strength to force herself up the steps, knowing that her sister needed her. Her legs shaking under her, she held onto the wall as she made her way down the darkened hallway to the garret. The soft murmuring of voices ceased when she opened the door. Her sister was reclined on the bed, the doctor and Mrs. Peyton sat together at her side, their heads bent in quiet conspiracy.

Mrs. Peyton walked the few steps across the garret floor to Lydia, reaching out her hand. "Lydia, your hand is still chilled, did you not take my advice and warm yourself in the kitchen? If you're not careful, you shall be as ill as your sister, and you shall be laid out in the bed beside hers."

Lydia shrugged off her own discomfort as she asked, "How is she? Has her fever improved?"

"There are no noticeable changes, my dear. Doctor Abernathy had administered medicine to her and we shall diligently apply his methods, but she is in God's hands now," Mrs. Peyton answered as she dabbed at her eyes.

"In God's hands? Whatever do you mean?" Lydia asked, looking from Mrs. Peyton to the doctor.

"My dearest girl," Mrs. Peyton explained, "I will not deceive you or give you false hope, your sister is very ill. I fear that we shall lose her. The doctor and I believe she is far too sick to be moved, her body is so weak from the fever. We must provide her with warm blankets, and medicine, and we must pray very hard."

Doctor Abernathy turned to Lydia. "You were right to come for me, even in this storm. I fear to think what may have happened if you had hesitated for even a moment. Her situation is grave, but take comfort that your sister is young; she may yet recover. All we can do is place the matter in God's hands."

Lydia was faint with apprehension for her sister. Holding onto Mrs. Peyton's hand, she asked, "Doctor, she can hear you. Do you think it's wise to discuss her illness so near to her? Will that not cause her to surrender to what may happen?"

Doctor Abernathy placed his thin hand on Lydia's shoulder in a way she knew was meant to be comforting. "Miss Wells, your sister is quite delirious, despite my administrations of medicine. She drifts in out of this world without any knowledge of her whereabouts, or much else, I presume. I doubt that she will recall this conversation or anything else about tonight."

"There's a blessing if ever there was one. This storm is the worst I have seen in many a year. Your sister is so frail, the poor dear, this storm would surely scare her out of her wits if she was awake," Mrs. Peyton held Lydia's hand tightly in her own. "Lydia, she needs your strength and your prayers. Go to her while I speak with the doctor."

Lydia walked to her sister's bed. Charlotte was only two years the younger, and she looked so small and frail. Her breathing was shallow, and with her eyes closed she looked as though she had already departed from this life. Kneeling beside her, Lydia reached for her hand, holding it in her own as she bowed her head and prayed. Unknown to Mrs. Peyton and Doctor Abernathy, Charlotte murmured the name *Hugh* in her delirium. It was barely a whisper, but Lydia heard it – and prayed that it would not be the last word her sister ever said.

CHAPTER FOUR

Falmouth was battered by the relentless storm for two days. The girls at the school huddled in their classrooms, too terrified to study as the rain fell in sheets, the wind driving it against the windows. Rivulets of water cascaded down the walls of some of the rooms, evidence of a roof that needed repair.

For two days, Mrs. Peyton's School for Girls seemed like an island. All of the inhabitants were like castaways – or so Lydia imagined as she spent her time in the tiny garret room. She kept a constant vigil at Charlotte's side. For two days she prayed, administered to her sister, and hoped for a miracle.

Mrs. Peyton offered comfort, reminding Lydia that every hour Charlotte lived was surely proof that she may yet recover. In those dark days as Charlotte clung to life, Lydia was grateful for Mrs. Peyton, Cook, and Moira. She would have fallen into despair without these women, this makeshift family, the only one she truly knew.

In the two days of her sister's illness, she didn't teach class, or even sleep for more than an hour at the time. Her mind unoccupied by her normal routine, she had ample time for worry and fear to seep into her mind like a poison. Hiding her terror that she may lose her sister, she remained strong, allowing herself silent tears when she was certain she was alone and her sister was asleep.

Of the fears that plagued her, she was still haunted by the question of what had happened to Hugh. He may be promised to another woman, but she didn't wish for him to come to any harm. The storm had confined the people of Falmouth to their homes; no one left their houses or went about their business. There was no news from anyone.

So to her dismay, she had no way of learning if Hugh was dead or alive, and no way of sending a letter or receiving mail. His fate, she knew, was tied to her sister's, and that frightened her. If Hugh was dead, she felt sure that her sister would surrender to the fever. As long as Hugh's fate remained unknown, Charlotte could take comfort in the hope that she would see him again. It was a powerful medicine that Lydia had yet to administer. Ravaged by the illness, Charlotte drifted in and out of consciousness, spending only brief slivers of time awake in the world of the living.

Hugh was not the only concern in Lydia's troubled mind. She was constantly reminded that Charlotte's fate hung precariously in a delicate balance. What was worse, Lydia harbored a selfish anxiety for her own future. What would become of her if her sister died, leaving her all alone in the world? Charlotte was her closest companion and her only real family. Somewhere on the world's oceans, her father captained a ship. He had been home so seldom that she hardly thought of him; he was like a stern but kindly distant relation.

These thoughts circled relentlessly as Lydia laid her head on her pillow. For now, Moira was at Charlotte's side, attending to her in the quiet hours of the night. Lydia rested, her body falling into a deep sleep. Her body was wracked with exhaustion, her head aching from mental anguish.

She woke in the eerie silence that followed the storm, Moira's gentle hand on her arm. "Miss, it's morning. I must attend to my duties; are you able to care for your sister?"

Lydia raised her head. The wind had stopped, and the quiet was eerie. "Moira, has the rain stopped?"

"It has stopped; I could hardly believe it myself. I wanted to wake you last night when it happened – it scared me something terrible. I was reading my bible by your sister's bedside, praying for her and for the good Lord to watch over all of us, when I noticed the oddest thing. The rain got quiet like, I could barely hear it, and then it stopped – like it just ran out. I tell you I was afraid, afraid of what would come after the howling and the rain. I wanted to wake you, but you were sleeping; I couldn't bear to disturb you, not as tired as you've been."

"Moira, thank you for all your help; how did Charlotte fare last night? Is she any better?"

"Slept like a babe, she did. She never woke, and didn't even cough or fuss. Mrs. Peyton left word for me to give her some broth but I didn't have the heart to wake her, not when she was sleeping so peaceful. I was thinking she was tired from being so sick. It may have been a trick of the late hours, of the dark playing with my eyes, ma'am, but I thought she looked like her old self. Her cheeks look rosy to me. I kept a close watch on her, I did. If you ask me, I think she's breathing like she ought to. See for yourself."

A glance in her sister's direction confirmed what Moira said; Charlotte did seem to be breathing without difficulty. Her face wasn't flushed, and it wasn't pale with illness. Gently placing her hand on Charlotte's forehead, Lydia turned to Moira. "Fetch Mrs. Peyton at once. I think she has taken a turn for the better. She is warm but she's no longer burning with fever. Oh Moira, I don't know what was in those prayers you said last night, but you have been the medicine she needed." Lydia embraced the maid.

"Miss, it weren't my doing; all I did was pray."

"Moira, if I am ever a breath from dying, I want no one but you at my bedside, praying. Hurry, find Mrs. Peyton."

Lydia was overjoyed. As the dim light of dawn filled the room, growing brighter as the sun rose, Lydia shielded her eyes. The room had been shrouded in darkness during the storm, but it was now bathed in warm sunshine.

"Charlotte, are you sleeping? The storm has passed."

Charlotte's delicate eyelids fluttered open. "Lydia, I had a dream that we saw Hugh, did we see him?"

"We did, but we can talk about that later. How are you feeling?"

Charlotte's voice was faint. "Tired. I have never been so tired."

"Rest, my dear. You have been very ill. Do you remember being sick?"

"Was I?" Charlotte asked as she closed her eyes and fell asleep.

Tears of joy fell from Lydia's eyes. Charlotte was showing improvement; she was not yet her old self, but her condition was no longer precarious. Laying her head on the bed beside her sister, she wept quietly, this time weeping out of relief and happiness rather than fear. It was in this state that Mrs. Peyton found Lydia when she rushed into the garret.

"Lydia, what has happened? Has Charlotte taken a turn for the worse? Do we need to send for the Doctor?"

Lydia lifted her head. Wiping her tears, she smiled at the sweet older woman. "Mrs. Peyton, come here, please. I must have your opinion; has Charlotte improved?"

Mrs. Peyton held her hand on her chest. "You scared me, child. You lying there crying by your sister's bed; I thought we had lost her in the night."

"I'm sorry, I never meant to scare you. Come, tell me that I have reason to hope. Is the worst behind us? Will she live?"

Mrs. Peyton felt Charlotte's brow and checked her pulse before listening to her breathing. "She is still ill. It is too soon; we mustn't raise our hopes yet. Your sister was never as strong as you. I knew from the moment I first saw her, when your father entrusted you both to me, that your sister was frail. I can still see you standing there with her, holding onto her, afraid you might lose her."

Lydia must have looked stricken, because Mrs. Peyton took her hand. "Lydia," she said, "there is reason to hope; there always is. Now that the storm has passed, I will send for the doctor to come and have a look at her. Take my advice – if she has improved, if he tells us that she will make a recovery – I want you to lay in your bed and rest. I have never seen you look so frail."

"When Charlotte is recovered, then I will rest, but not before."

"You must rest, my dear, or you shall make yourself ill. Do I have your word that you shall do as I instruct?"

Lydia nodded. Even though she had slept most of the night, she had never felt so tired. Her muscles ached and her head felt heavy on her shoulders. Mrs. Peyton was right, she could fall ill herself if she didn't take care. She couldn't permit illness to befall her. It was concerning to think of her own fate if Charlotte should die, but she shuddered when she thought of her fragile sister facing the world without her – all alone with no one to turn to, not even Hugh.

The sun streamed in the window, and the light shined on Charlotte's face, illuminating her features in an angelic glow. It also illuminated a greater problem that haunted Lydia. The storm was over, and she could no longer postpone uncovering the truth about Hugh. If Charlotte's health continued to improve, she would ask about him. Lydia needed answers about his fate.

———

WHILE THE CITIZENS of Falmouth picked up the pieces after the worst storm anyone could remember, Lydia maintained her vigil. Charlotte showed slow but steady signs of progress. She did not have an appetite, but she did manage to sit up in her bed without help and sip the broth Cook made for her. To Lydia, even in a weakened state, her sister was no longer in danger of succumbing to her illness, and that was all the encouragement she needed to feel content.

Cook and Moira were also attentive to their patient, doting on her with fresh tea and broth at any time of day. Mrs. Peyton looked in on her favorite pupil in between leading the classes that Lydia was currently neglecting due to her sister's illness. These women were

Lydia's only source of news from the outside world; her own world had narrowed to the frail woman confined to her bed in the small room.

Moira was the most reliable source for information although Lydia winced inwardly at the news she often told in Charlotte's presence. In the days following Charlotte's devastating sickness, the subject of Hugh had hardly been addressed. Lydia attributed that happy circumstance to Charlotte's delirium and weakness, more than anything else. As she was growing stronger, though, her faculties were returning to what they once were. Lydia feared for the conversation she knew was overdue, and the questions she would be forced to face regarding the fate of the handsome young fisherman.

On a bright but cold sunny morning, Moira came bustling into the room with a bowl of broth for Charlotte, a pot of strong tea and bread for Lydia, and the latest rumors from the town. Carefully setting the heavily laden tray down on the desk, Moira greeted the sisters and began her cheerful recount of the latest news.

"Miss, I know how you like to know of the goings-on in town, so I will tell you what I heard from the apothecary this morning."

Lydia glanced at her sister resting in the bed, her face turned to Moira. Charlotte appeared to be showing an interest in the news as well – news that Lydia hoped would not be tragic. "What have you heard this morning, Moira? I hope all is well with everyone."

Moira's expression was one of a woman who had stories to tell. "I wish it were so, but is not. After three days of rain, there was terrible flooding, terrible. And the sea came up over the quay. Mr. Brewer told me that he was lucky that his shop sits on the Hambridge Road, high above the flood line. He said the shops down on the lower end of High Street were flooded something terrible. Some of 'em had water up to the door frames, salty as brine. It was sea water, what do you think of that?"

"I think we were fortunate to be here at the school," Lydia replied.

"That's not all." Moira brought the broth to Charlotte, holding it reverently like it was a holy relic. "Here you are, Miss, that is some of Cook's best broth, her own recipe. Drink all of that and you will be feeling fit by Sunday."

Charlotte whispered, "thank you," and blew on the steaming bowl of broth, her eyes wide as a child listening to a bedtime story. "Moira, was anyone hurt?"

"I don't know about that, Miss, there are still people cleaning up what they can. Some pubs on the quay lost all of their spirits; I shouldn't be telling you ladies this. It's not proper to talk about, but it has been said there were barrels of beer floating down High Street from the pubs on the quay, barrels, furniture, chairs – and some say even people – but I don't know if that's true."

"People?" Lydia asked, glancing at her sister.

"Sailors, from what the talk is. A boat sank in the harbor, got loose of its moorings, or so I've heard. It sank right there, in sight of the town."

"Is that true? How horrid," Charlotte whispered.

"Don't know if it is or isn't, but that's the story Mr. Brewer told me. Said it to my face, he did."

"Those poor men; we shall pray for them," Charlotte said. "Was there anyone else hurt?"

"May have been, I can't say for truth. There has been stories of the sea taking back some of the land, taking back farms and houses."

Lydia hoped Charlotte wasn't paying attention, but from Charlotte's stricken expression, it seemed she had heard every word. Lydia decided that her sister had had enough of the local gossip. "Moira, how are the repairs going to the roof?" The sound of footsteps overhead had been going on all morning.

"Mrs. Peyton's got a man on the roof as we are here talking," she answered as she nervously gazed at the rafters overhead, "Don't know how he does it. I would be scared I'd fall off to my death. They couldn't pay me a month's wages to do it."

Lydia spread butter on her bread. "Nor I. Thank you, Moira.

Can you ask Cook to send up an extra bowl of that broth for me at luncheon?"

Moira was instantly concerned. "Are you feeling ill, Miss? Do you need me to fetch the doctor?"

"Oh no, Moira, I didn't mean to frighten you. It was a compliment to Cook; that broth smells delicious. After the cold, I could use a bowl of it to strengthen my constitution so I don't become ill. Just a prevention, you see."

Moira sighed. "We all could use of bit of it, if you ask me. The whole school is damp as a river from the leaks; the cold has set in and there's been sickness. We could all catch our deaths."

"Moira, you are a treasure, looking after us all. What would do without you?" Lydia asked, thankful that Charlotte was placidly sipping her broth, the crisis temporarily averted.

"That's good of you to say. Just see that you and your sister get well. We don't need no more illness, not with winter fixing to be upon us."

Moira left the garret, and an awkward silence settled between Lydia and Charlotte. Lydia ate the thick slice of buttered bread and drank her tea as her sister finished her bowl of broth. Lydia didn't say a word about the subject, but she was praying for Hugh and his family, that his village was not among those taken by the sea.

Charlotte was improving, and with her steady recovery, Lydia knew that she couldn't delay her errand any longer. She must find an excuse to go to the harbor. If she could locate anyone who knew the Burtons, she might be able to discover their fate.

That errand became paramount in her mind when Charlotte broke the silence. Her voice barely a whisper, she asked, "Lydia, you don't think Moira meant Hugh? Do you think he's still alive?"

Lydia had steeled herself for this very moment. Smiling her warmest (and she hoped most genuine) smile, she answered, "You can't trust idle gossip about these kinds of things. The Burtons have been fishermen for generations. They made it through this storm, as they have every one before it."

Charlotte was pacified, or so it seemed until she asked, "His family may be well, but we don't know about him, do we? I haven't received any mail from him."

"No one has received any mail; rest now. You will be receiving a letter in due time, it's only that he storm caused a delay in the post. I wouldn't worry."

Charlotte closed her eyes. Lydia felt guilty that she had spoken with such confidence regarding the fate of Hugh and his family, when she knew nothing of what tragedy may have befallen them. She had to go to quay, that very afternoon if she could manage it. Her words of comfort rang hollow in her own ears and would not placate her sister much longer.

———

THE QUAY WAS CONSTRUCTED of massive stone blocks, as were many of the buildings that lined it. The warehouses and public houses that stood on the quay were open, despite the recent flooding. Some of the public houses were doing a brisk business with little more than barrels for furniture, all their chairs and tables having been washed away.

Lydia held a basket gripped tightly in her hands. She had volunteered to come to the harbor for Cook, to see about fresh fish for dinner, if there was any to be had. The cold weather, Cook explained, was the perfect time for fish stew; she said it was just the thing to put the students at the school back in good spirits.

As Lydia walked past the large wooden ships, she was fascinated by the repairs being made. Sails had come loose during the storm, and the tattered and ripped canvas was being sewn on the quay. Masts, riggings, and railings were being fixed in earnest. She gazed out at the harbor for any trace of the ship that sank, but she could see nothing to prove that a ship had gone down.

Walking along the quay, she looked for fishermen. It didn't look promising, as many of their boats were beached along the edge of the harbor, the small boats tossed along the sand like children's toys after the storm. She was beginning to despair of finding any news about the Burtons or their village, and she might have to return to the school without the fish she'd promised Cook. At the end of the quay, she noticed two small fishing vessels, neatly tucked in behind the ships of the line. They seemed to be unloading their catch, and she quickened her step.

Lydia approached the men, happy to see they had a fine selection of fish despite the recent storm. "Excuse me, I was wondering if you might have a good price on your fish? I need a fat fish for stew; what do you have?"

A grizzled old man answered as he continued to unload fish from his boat. "You'll be wanting them stripers, in that barrel. They are freshly caught this morning and fat as houses."

"Stripers? Are they good for stew?" Lydia asked, trying to find the courage to ask about the Burtons.

"Best there is for stew. You making a stew, are ya? T'is fine weather for it."

"Yes, it is." She asked the price, and hesitated, realizing she had no idea whether it was fair or not.

The man smiled, seeing the problem. "I have a fair price, Miss, the best price you'll be getting today. There don't seem to be many fishermen about, so best not be too choosy."

As he filled her basket, she summoned her nerve. "Sir, I don't mean to be intrusive, but are you familiar with a fisherman by the name of Burton?"

"I am," the man said, frowning abstractedly at a fish that didn't match the others. He tossed it into a different barrel.

"If it's not too much trouble, do you know how he and his family fared in the storm?"

"Why ya asking about Burton?" he asked, nonplussed. "What's a lady like yourself care about an old fisherman?"

Lydia swallowed. "I usually buy my fish from him and his son;

they seem like nice people. I...I was hoping they came through the storm without too much trouble."

"That I cannot say, Miss. There was a lot of places under the water, a lot of boats lost, and it's rumored some people drowned. I don't know no more than you."

"Thank you, sir, and thank you for the fish," Lydia said as their transaction was concluded. Trying to hide her disappointment, she bid him good day. Returning back up the quay, she eyed the pubs and considered stopping inside one and asking about the Burtons. From what she knew of Hugh and his family, they seemed like hard-working people, not the sort to waste their earnings on drink. Still, she decided it was worth a try to make a few inquiries.

Pulling her bonnet down around her face as much as she could, she found the courage to inquire with some of the men serving beer and whiskey inside, and occasionally outside, their flood-damaged establishments. No one could tell her anything but rumors and gossip about the flooding. As she left the waterfront, she had to face the truth – she knew nothing more than she had before. Rumors and gossip could hardly be relied upon. She would have to tell Charlotte to be patient, that only time would reveal the truth.

Returning to the school, she was greeted by Cook who commended her on her choice of fish. Stripers, she said, were made for stew, and these were the best-looking ones she had ever seen. She set to work preparing the fish for the stew pot. Lydia sat in the kitchen watching Cook work, feeling dejected. She wished there was someone she could confide in about her dilemma, someone who might be able to tell her something she could believe, some scrap of news that was reliable.

"Miss Lydia?" Cook asked as she gutted a fish in several well-practiced strokes of a knife. "Are you unwell? I was that worried about you going down to the harbor after your sister has been so sick. The cold and wind are not good for you. You sit there and let me make you a cup of tea."

"Thank you," Lydia said with a sigh.

"What's wrong, Miss? Are you feeling poorly? Did the broth not help that I sent up for lunch?"

"The broth was wonderful, and I feel better from having a bowl of it. I was just thinking about all those people lost in the storm, how terrible it has been."

"My dear, you mustn't worry yourself. You've been listening to tales told down at the harbor, haven't you? Fisherman and sailors are terrible for that, for spinning a yarn. A lot of what they say don't mean anything."

Lydia prayed that Cook was right as she sat in the warmth of the kitchen, preparing herself to walk upstairs without a scrap of good news for her sister. Cook hummed to herself as she cut and sliced the ingredients for the stew, taking time to make a cup of tea for Lydia. Lydia drank the tea, still despairing, although the strong brew helped ward off the chill from the harbor.

Finishing the tea, Lydia rose and with a deep breath, left the kitchen. She would have no choice but to tell Charlotte that she would have to be patient. Lydia had never been in love but she saw love shining in the Charlotte's eyes every time she spoke of Hugh. Patience was almost all she had left – patience, prayer, and hope that her sister would not find herself brokenhearted when they finally had news.

She met Moira in the hall at the top of the narrow stairs, her face pale, a look of fear on her features. "Miss, you must come see your sister! I'm scared she is ill, taken leave of her senses, she has."

"Whatever can you mean?" Lydia asked as she heard a sound coming from the garret. It was an unearthly sound, a wailing and crying that gave her chills. It sounded like the screeching she heard in the rigging of the tall-masted ships before a storm – a sound that foretold of tragedy. Rushing to the room she shared with her sister, she pushed open the door to find her sister sitting on the bed, her face in her hands, her body shaking.

Moira tried to explain. "I don't know what came over her! I brought her the mail, you know how she likes to read letters, it always brings a smile to her face. I don't know what it was; it must have been bad news."

"Charlotte, what's wrong? What's happened?" Lydia asked, as she sat down beside her sister in the bed.

Charlotte looked up, her face red, tears streaming down her cheeks. "This," she said as gave Lydia a crumpled piece of paper, wet from her tears. "Read it, oh Lydia!"

Expecting the worst, Lydia unfolded the paper, which was hardly a scrap. Reading the message, she could scarcely believe what she saw written in the familiar hand. A wave of relief washed over her as she read the words once more.

Moira stared intently. "What is it, Miss? Bad news? Is someone dead?"

Dropping the letter in her sister's hand, Lydia stood up and embraced the maid, to the maid's astonishment. "No, my dear Moira, it's not bad news. It's good news."

"Good news, is it? I'm glad of it for your sister's sake – she had me scared, she did. I was going to fetch the doctor if you hadn't come when you did."

Lydia smiled at the kindly maid. She wanted to scream to the rafters and laugh and dance, to express her joy at the news. Hugh was alive. The message was brief but he and his family had survived the storm. For that afternoon, Lydia could rejoice with Charlotte; the man her sister loved was alive and well. Yet, in the back of her mind, Lydia could not escape the truth – she was going to have to tell Charlotte about Winnie Parker. But that news could wait. Today was a good day, and Lydia did not want anything to cause her sister to fall ill once more. She, like Moira, hoped she had seen the last of illness for a long time.

CHAPTER FIVE

Spring, 1816
Falmouth, Cornwall

LYDIA WAS CONTENT; she was reading a book as her sister sat nearby in the garden. Charlotte's sketch pad and pencils lay on a table at her side, and a group of girls from the ages of ten to thirteen gathered nearby, all with sketch pads of their own.

It was late March. An early spring warm spell had beckoned Lydia, her sister, and several of the students outdoors. The winter had been long, with ice and snow, and no chance for escape from the school. Lydia was sure she was not the only one happy to be outside after being confined inside the school for the seemingly endless winter months.

The sun warmed her face and the garden with its rays. Robins heralded the change of season as they flitted in the grass, searching for food among the first buds of early daffodils that sprang from the ground along the stone paths. The girls laughed and sketched, while

Charlotte seemed to be preoccupied with a letter when she was supposed to be critiquing the sketching of the students. Lydia knew without having to be told who the letter was from. From the intense look of concentration on her sister's face it was obvious that Hugh Burton was the author.

Waiting for her sister to fold the letter and slip it back into the envelope, she considered the weight that bore down on her conscience. She had still not told Charlotte about the conversation she'd had in the fall with Hugh's mother, the conversation about Winnie Parker. For four months, she had witnessed her sister regain her health, slowly build up her strength, and every day come a little closer to a full recovery. At no time had it seemed appropriate for Lydia to disclose facts about Hugh that could prove detrimental to her sister's recovery and break her heart.

After months of living with this terrible secret, Lydia wished she knew more about the situation, because Charlotte was surely going to have questions. She could not recall her sister saying a single word about Winnie, nor did she seem to know about Hugh's plans for marrying the girl. As she watched her sister reading the letter, she realized that her sister was still not discussing plans for her own nuptials, either.

Hugh, according to her sister, wanted to be an officer in the royal Navy. He aspired to a better life than being a fisherman. His ambition, Charlotte explained, delayed any plans to wed – or so had been said last summer. Lydia could not help but wonder if that was still the case, or whether Hugh was planning on getting married, all right – just not to Charlotte.

"You're watching me. I know you are, I can feel it," Charlotte said as she looked up from the letter, folding it carefully as she spoke.

"Am I?" Lydia answered with a smile.

"Yes, you are. You have spent the better part of the winter watching me. I suppose I should be flattered that you think so much of me that you are worried for my health. Do you suppose it's your careful observation of me that has kept the fever at bay?"

"You must be feeling better; you have your humor back. I have been watching, and what is the matter with that? You're my little sister, and I have to keep a careful eye trained on you at all times. You may fall ill or run away with the slightest provocation."

"Run away?" Charlotte asked, "Where would I run away to?"

"Not where, with whom," Lydia answered.

"I assure you, nothing could be farther from the truth. There is positively no chance that I will be running away anytime soon," Charlotte said, exasperated.

"Are you quite certain?" Lydia asked, peering at her sister.

"Quite. You are aware of the circumstances that prohibit me from planning my future, at least for present time."

Lydia glanced at the girls nearby, and kept her voice low. "I am aware. So he has not changed his mind regarding his plans?"

Charlotte shook her head. "Regrettably, he has not. There is nothing to be done but be patient, I suppose."

Winnie Parker would not be eligible to be married until the fall, Lydia mused. Was Hugh stalling? Did he really intend to marry Charlotte, or was he telling her that they must wait because he knew they could never be wed? She wished there was an answer to this dilemma that did not include upsetting her sister, but she couldn't see one.

Charlotte seldom saw Hugh. Their village and their fishing boat had sustained considerable damage during the storm last autumn. He and his father had spent the winter repairing what they could, and facing enormous hardships in the bitter cold. In these last weeks, his time was occupied by fishing. It was necessary to work long hours to earn money to pay back the loans his family was forced to accept to feed themselves when they could not earn a living from the sea.

If Charlotte didn't see Hugh, then Lydia didn't see him. In the rare moments when they met she had not had a chance to speak to him alone, and a delicate matter such as Winnie Parker was not something to be discussed casually. This would take time to handle properly – time, and a few minutes away from Charlotte. Lydia considered writing to him, but she wanted to see his face, to study his countenance for signs of deceit when she mentioned his promised bride. A letter would not allow her to divine his sincerity.

"Lydia, you look cross. Are you vexed?" Charlotte asked as she resumed her sketching.

"Do I look cross? How strange. I do not feel vexed in any way," she answered, although she was cross, if the truth be told – cross with Hugh Burton for placing her and Charlotte in this terrible position.

Charlotte returned to her charges, making suggestions on their technique and use of shadow as Lydia attempted to concentrate on the pages of the book in her hand. But her mind was far from focused on the characters depicted on the page. If she was being entirely honest with herself and her sister, she had more to think about than Hugh Burton. There was also the dilemma of what to do about her future, and her sister's. She had served as a teacher at Mrs. Peyton's school for two years. With the anticipated completion of her studies this spring, delayed by her illness in the fall, Charlotte would be in want of a position, or marriage.

Lydia shuddered to think of leaving the only home she had ever known. Mrs. Peyton had been like a mother to her, and her school would always be regarded as her home, but she knew that she and her sister couldn't continue to live as they had when they were students. Mrs. Peyton had not said that it was time for them to make their way in the word, but they couldn't both be teachers at so small a school. Their father paid for their tuition, but even that would be coming to an end, according to the solicitors who arranged for the funds to be distributed.

Longing for adventure, Lydia had dreamed of the day when she would leave the port town of Falmouth and journey to see the ends of the world. She had pored over books, longing for the chance to see new places, hear languages she didn't know, and eat exotic foods. From the window high atop the school in the garret, she'd observed the ships in the harbor, wishing she could be on one of them bound for ports far away...but that had changed.

Charlotte's illness had shifted something deep inside her, had shown her how easily her only family could be snatched from her grasp. Once content to dream of the day she could leave Falmouth, she now dreaded it. She didn't want to be apart from her sister, and she had to admit that she didn't want to leave Mrs. Peyton, Cook, or Moira, three women she held dear to her heart.

If she could be sure of Hugh Burton's intention to marry her sister, she would feel better about the future. If Charlotte's future was secure, then Lydia could sleep at night knowing her sister was happy and well, and she might find the courage to venture from Falmouth, (but not too far), to find a position of her own. Or she might remain at the school, teaching for all the years to come.

Later it would seem odd to Lydia that she had been thinking about the future at the moment when Moira came running into the garden. "Mrs. Peyton," she said, as she grasped her chest, her face red from exertion. "Mrs. Peyton needs to see you ladies right away."

Lydia closed her book with a snap and jumped to her feet. "Moira? Are you unwell? Has anything happened to Mrs. Peyton?"

"No, Miss, I don't know what it is. I would be telling tales if I said I did, but she said she needs to see you, the both of you. It can't wait, she said."

"Girls, take your sketch pads and return to your rooms," ordered Charlotte. Her words were met with groans from the students as they reluctantly followed her instructions.

Lydia knew something terrible had happened; she could feel it in her bones and sense it in the way Moira looked away, avoiding her gaze. Yes, Moira knew what was going on, but whatever it was, the maid did not want to be the one to tell her.

Charlotte was as pale as she had been during her fever. Lydia prayed that whatever awaited them, it would not be bad enough to send her sister into a relapse. Wordlessly, she walked behind her sister through the school as they made their way to Mrs. Peyton's office. Mrs. Peyton did not smile; her face was wet with tears as she invited them to be seated. But it was when Mrs. Peyton closed the door that Lydia knew her worst fears were confirmed. Something had happened – something so terrible that Mrs. Peyton did not want anyone else to hear of it.

Reaching for Charlotte's hand, Lydia steeled herself for whatever the news may be. Mrs. Peyton was trembling, wringing her hands. On her desk lay a letter. Lydia didn't know what was about to be said, but she knew her life was never going to be the same.

———

Mrs. Peyton urged Lydia and Charlotte to remain strong in the face of such news, not for her, she pleaded, but for the young girls in the school. Some of the girls were barely old enough to be students, whose fathers, (like Lydia and Charlotte's) were career naval officers, on ships far away, facing countless dangers. Lydia did not consider Mrs. Peyton's request to be selfish or unfeeling. On the contrary, she knew the fears the girls faced in the school, the nightmares that some tragedy could befall their fathers, leaving them destitute.

That was the nightmare that came true for Lydia and Charlotte. For Lydia, it was worse than all the ones she ever conceived of as a child. When she was a young girl, she went to sleep every night praying fervently that God would protect her father. When she lay in her bed at night, she would keep herself from falling asleep, terrified to face the dark images inside her head.

As a young girl, she had believed that the monsters of mythology roamed the oceans, just like the ones on the mariners' maps, guarding the unknown waters of the world. Serpents larger than Falmouth, whales that could swallow ships whole, and toothsome sharks swam in her imagination with whirlpools, ferocious storms, and waves higher than mountains. It was a dangerous world beyond the port of Falmouth, yet it was a world that entranced her with adventure and carried her father as he captained his boat upon the sea.

With tears in her eyes, Lydia could still recall his assurances that the *Thames* was too large a boat for even a whale to sink. He described the sturdy oak used in her construction, the masts made of tree trunks that could withstand the worst winds nature could throw at her. To hear Captain Wells describe this boat, it seemed like the safest boat in the world, the best built, a testament, he said, to good English shipbuilding. He had journeyed across oceans in service of the crown, and the *Thames* had always brought him home to his daughters safe and sound.

His stories of the sea were not like the terrifying monsters that stalked her dreams. He would tell of faraway lands, of people who lived differently, of animals she thought were fanciful. He told of mermaids and lost treasures beneath the waves, of pearls the size of melons, guarded by the denizens of the deep. For a man as stoic as Captain Wells, as stern as he appeared, he always had thrilling tales for his daughters – especially his eldest, or so it seemed to Lydia.

His visits were rare events but they seemed in Lydia's memory to be more like holidays than social calls. He would arrive on the doorstep of the school, looking like a great explorer in his navy uniform with his plumed hat upon his head. He would be carrying boxes and gifts wrapped in paper for his daughters, each gift a delight. He always brought back candies and exotic fruit from his travels, a treat that Lydia welcomed almost as much as the clothes, hats and trinkets he gathered from around the world. It was his generosity, and his love for her and her sister that made this nightmare worse than she could have imagined – that, and the terrible uncertainty. In her nightmares, her father met his fate fighting heroically but losing his life. In the nightmare she was living, the one she never saw coming, he was missing. Reports were that the ship had sunk off the coast of Spain with all hands feared lost.

Her father was missing, Mrs. Peyton said, as was his ship and her crew. It was feared she had been caught in a sudden storm on the rocky coast, that the ship had sunk in high seas, or broken up on the rocks. Mrs. Peyton tried to remain optimistic, reminding Lydia that her father was not declared dead. He may still be alive, but it was a hope that waned a little with each day that passed without further news.

The fate of *Thames* and her crew was unknown, according to all official reports, and it was unknown whether there was a single survivor. The word *unknown* was terrible, but *missing* was a cruel word, thought Lydia. *Missing* meant that her father may still be clinging to life, floating at sea. He could be dead; no one knew, and that made his legal status and the distribution of his small estate impossible.

Lydia did not care for the money her father had left in trust upon his death for her or her sister. She was never greedy, never one to be concerned with material wealth. What money there was, it wasn't much, as her father was a sea captain and not a wealthy man. His missing status impended his solicitors from any action. When he was declared dead by a British court, she was assured that the estate could be dissolved – but not until that time. That could be a long time, they warned, perhaps more than a year, depending on the circumstances. The only money that could be negotiated were the small sums set aside for dowries but those was only accessible in the event of marriage. In the current circumstances, there were no funds for Charlotte and Lydia – no money available for their continued support, the last of the school funds having been spent in the autumn.

Lydia as not entirely without means. She did have the teaching position at Mrs. Peyton's school, but it was not enough to secure a living for both her and her sister. Mrs. Peyton was generous, a loving woman who promised the girls that no decision had to be made, that Charlotte could continue to live at the school for as long as was required – but Lydia felt the sting of it acutely. She did not want to burden Mrs. Peyton with any unnecessary financial burden, and neither did Charlotte.

This worry plagued her sister, and Lydia wished there was some way she could ease Charlotte's fears. Charlotte, as frail as she was, had begun to offer her services in the kitchen and around the school. Mrs. Peyton tried to persuade that such actions were not necessary, but Charlotte would hear none of it. She assisted Cook and Moira despite their protestations. Hugh Burton, to Lydia disappointment, was not spurred to action by the announcement that Captain Wells was missing. He did not seem to be overly concerned with altering his plans to include a wedding, even though such a wedding would have given Charlotte security, albeit as a fisherman's wife.

Lydia found Hugh's lack of action to be irksome, compelling her to make arrangements for Charlotte and herself. An idea had formed in her mind, despite the burden of grief that she carried. Something had to be done. As the eldest sister and the head of their small family, Lydia knew it fell to her. Shouldering her responsibilities, she approached Mrs. Peyton with her plan and was pleased to find that Mrs. Peyton was in agreement with it.

She had decided to conceal the plan from Charlotte; she didn't want her sister to share her burden. She still feared that Charlotte would weaken and slip into illness once more. With her mind set on the scheme, Lydia sent out correspondence, letters of inquiry, and combed the newspaper. With Mrs. Peyton's assistance she was soon able to turn all her attentions to her plan, a plan she hoped would soon come to fruition. Mourning the loss of her father, she grieved but she diligently worked to secure a future for herself and for her sister.

CHAPTER SIX

Midsummer, 1816
Falmouth, Cornwall

LYDIA REREAD the letter once more, worried that she may have missed some detail, something of importance that would delay her journey. Her plan had worked marvelously, so well, in fact, that she had been unprepared for the swiftness its success. She already held the letter that would ensure the security of both her and her sister. Folding it, she slipped it inside her purse.

Charlotte wept quietly. "Do you have to go? Lydia, it doesn't seem fair that you should be the one to leave! It was your post, your position as teacher that I've inherited. It's not fair that I should have it, that you gave it up for me."

Sitting beside her sister in their garret room, Lydia's heart ached. She longed to stay in the room they had called home for so many years. She reached for Charlotte's hand, holding it tightly with her own. This was the last time they would be together here, in this school, apart from visits. A part of Lydia was dying from grief that she had to leave it all behind, but another part of her felt the stirrings of adventure within her soul.

"Charlotte, this was my plan all along. I have to be the one to go. How could I have been so selfish as to stay here in the school, and send you out into the world, far away from your Hugh? What kind of person would I have been to do that?"

"You didn't even ask me! You sacrificed your position for me and you never asked."

"My dear sister," Lydia began, "I'm the oldest; it's my responsibility to take care of you. Besides, I intend to be an old maid, you have to stay here and marry that young man of yours." Lydia suppressed the usual twinge of unease as she teased her sister.

Hugh Burton was still no closer to marrying her sister than he had been in the spring. It was disconcerting to Lydia to be leaving her sister in such an uncertain state: promised, but with no wedding date in sight. To her shame, Lydia had not been able to discover Hugh's true intentions – in her search for a position, she'd had no time to spare for him. She could only hope that he was an honorable man, that her first impression of him was true.

"Why couldn't you have stayed and both of us taught here at the school?" Charlotte asked, petulant as a child, her cheeks wet from tears.

"You know that Mrs. Peyton has all the help she needs. She didn't need an additional teacher and we are out of money for room and board. By resigning, I made a place for you on the staff. You can stay here with Mrs. Peyton, keep her from being too lonely without us, and I will be in Plymouth at my new post."

Of course there was another reason not related to money or position that Lydia has chosen to leave and not asked Charlotte to go out into the world. Charlotte would be at the school in Mrs. Peyton's care, who would be as diligent as she always had been, keeping a watchful on Charlotte and doing everything in her power to keep her healthy. Cook and Moira also doted on Charlotte, mindful of the weak state of her health. It made leaving easier for Lydia, knowing her sister was in left in capable and loving hands.

"I am in dreadful need of cheering up. Tell me again about your exciting new position."

Lydia would be leaving by stage to Plymouth, there to be employed by Sir Michael Hartford, son of the baronet. He served as a colonel in the war, and had returned home safely. While he was away, his wife had died – leaving his two little girls in desperate need of a governess.

"It will not be very exciting after teaching classes filled with giggly little girls, as you will soon discover for yourself. You shall have more excitement than I shall."

Charlotte smiled, "These two little girls sound a lot like us, don't they? Their father is a colonel, their mother is dead...how providential you should end up with them. It will be a comfort to know I've lost you to a family who has need of you. Maybe you can do some good for them, poor dears."

"Maybe so, and Plymouth is not so far away. It's not like I'm leaving you and journeying all the way to Yorkshire," Lydia said. "I can come see you any time I like."

"Promise?" Charlotte asked.

"I promise. If I get a single report from Mrs. Peyton that you are not behaving as a young teacher ought to, I can be back here to set you straight, and don't you forget it."

"I never misbehave," Charlotte answered.

Laughing, Lydia said, "Never misbehave? What of the handsome Hugh Burton? You have been known to sneak around the harbor associating with all sorts, just to see him. What shall you do when I am not here to act as your chaperone? I dread to think of what will become of your reputation."

"Lydia, how can you be so shocking? I hardly see him and when we do find a way to see each other, it's always in public."

"So, you've told me. Mind you behave or I promise you, I will drag you away to Plymouth."

"You wouldn't!" Charlotte said with mock indignation.

"I would, so you'd best behave while I'm gone."

Charlotte's smile faded. "Lydia, promise me – give me your solemn vow – that nothing will happen to you in Plymouth. After losing Father, I could not bear to lose you, too."

"I promise nothing will happen to me; you have my word. If you need anything, you have Mrs. Peyton, Cook, and Moira, and you will always have me."

Mrs. Peyton knocked on the door, wiping her eyes with a handkerchief. "Lydia, it's time. The carriage is waiting for you; your trunk has already been loaded. If you don't hurry you will miss the coach at the Wyvern Inn. It leaves in half an hour."

Lydia embraced her sister. "Promise to write to me every chance you have. I will be lonely without news."

"You as well. I'd better receive a letter every week," Charlotte sniffled, and her chin wobbled.

Lydia reached for her purse as she took one last look at the garret, at her sister, and Mrs. Peyton. Mrs. Peyton held out her arms and Lydia fell into her embrace, like she had when she was a girl. "Mrs. Peyton, I will miss you; you have been like a mother to me."

"My dear girl, hush your crying. You can always come and see me, anytime you like. Promise you will write to me now and then? Tell me how you are faring in the world?"

"Yes, Ma'am," Lydia sniffed, as her mind was flooded by second thoughts. "Maybe I..."

Mrs. Peyton wisely interrupted. "Your trunk is on the carriage. Go to Plymouth; see how you fare. If you aren't happy, you come home, do you hear me? Remember, you have a strong spirit in you; you always have. You're a woman now, and you will be a fine governess. In Plymouth there are two little girls who need you, who need your strength and your love."

Lydia embraced Mrs. Peyton and Charlotte one last time. Saying goodbye, she rushed out of the garret and down the narrow steps, afraid to look back. If she looked back, she knew she would see two reasons to stay. The part of her that longed for adventure urged her forward. Wiping away the tears, she lifted her skirt and raced down the steps, there was a carriage waiting and after that, a stagecoach to Plymouth and her new life.

PLYMOUTH, England

LYDIA PEERED out the carriage window, her heart beating wildly. Seated on the edge of the velvet carriage seat, she abandoned all pretense of ladylike behavior and pressed her face against the glass of the window. She was all alone and glad of it, because she was behaving like a schoolgirl who had never been anywhere – which, in fact, was true. She had never known a home other than the port town of Falmouth. She had spent almost her entire life at a small, well-run school for girls – which did make her a school girl, she supposed with a smile.

It was all very different, a sharp contrast to the small world she knew in Cornwall. She knew from the geography lessons she'd taught at the school that Plymouth was large, but she'd never seen it with her own eyes until now. It was enormous compared to Falmouth – its churches were larger, their steeples rising high above the surrounding buildings. The port was immense; a vast number of tall-masted ships were moored at the docks. The buildings and shops were plentiful, lining the streets for blocks. She'd never seen so many people in one place, or so many tall buildings.

When she'd arrived in Plymouth at the White Goose Inn, a carriage bearing a regal crest was waiting for her, and *only* for her. She had never had a carriage all to herself, much less a carriage as luxuriously equipped as this one. The seats were lined with well-cushioned soft velvet, and a carpet was available, folded neatly in case she should take a chill. The driver was polite, seeing to her comfort, offering to wait for her to take tea if she required refreshment after her long journey from Falmouth.

Sitting in the carriage, she felt like a queen, not just a governess. With her eyes turned to the changing scenery outside the window, she was surprised when the carriage did not stop at one of the row of modern townhomes, where she might have expected a colonel to live. The carriage passed the residences of wealthy Plymouth residents as well as the poorer parts of the city, but both faded from her memory as the journey continued on a tree-lined road that led out of the town. With eyes wide and a smile on her face, she watched with anticipation as the crowded streets of Plymouth gave way to the green lawns and fields of the houses and estates that perched like spectators on the hills above the town.

Soon, the carriage turned onto a private drive, and Lydia sat back in amazement. The grand house that sat back from the road, high above the town, took her breath away. The house (although that word failed to truly describe the imposing edifice) grew larger with every step of the horses. Constructed of grey stone, it was larger than any building Lydia had ever seen that belonged to one family. It was over three stories high, with tall windows and large rounded towers at the corners – like a castle. Lydia glanced around, half looking for knights dressed in shiny armor, holding lances.

The grounds were extensive, with long expanses of green, well-kept lawns, hedges, and ornamental bushes. Tall oaks towered overhead; by their size she was certain they must be as old as the house itself. As she drew closer, she wondered if there might be a mistake. Had she taken the wrong carriage, to the wrong place? This house was far more grand than she had expected.

Taking a steadying breath and wiping the dampness from her palms, she decided that she was being silly. The driver knew her name and clearly would not have made a mistake. This house, this enormous castle above the town of Plymouth, was to be her home. She had not anticipated that being a governess to a small family would be quite this exciting.

Lydia looked down at her simple muslin dress, the unadorned short blue jacket, and her purse, which was as plain as the rest of her attire. She knew she should be wearing black; she should be in mourning. Yet mourning didn't feel right, somehow. How could she be in mourning for someone who might be alive, as unlikely as that was? Her father was missing – not confirmed dead – and she could not accept a position if she was in mourning, by the strictest sense of the word. And she needed to take this position.

A moment of doubt swept over her. Even in her best afternoon dress she was so plain; her clothes were clean and pressed but they were clear evidence of her modest upbringing. Would she be mistaken for a maid, she wondered, as the carriage came to a stop at the side of the house just as the deep rumble of thunder filled the air.

The driver helped her down and a footman met her at the door. The entrance of the house was as impressive as the exterior, and she clutched her bag with both hands to stop them from shaking. The floor was marble, the walls were covered in dark wood panels, and a display of swords and cutlasses hung above an enormous fireplace at the far end of the room.

At the sound of the rain beginning to pound down outside, she shivered. Did she belong here? Would the colonel find her unqualified to teach his children? She was just a young woman, a captain's daughter. Did she have enough education and cleverness to recommend her? Self-doubt had never plagued Lydia before she arrived at this grand house, but now she found herself questioning everything – her clothes, education, her own ability to be a governess.

A woman in her late twenties came down the staircase smiling, her stride confident. "Miss Wells, allow me to welcome to you Dartmoore Park. I am Mrs. Tumbridge, the housekeeper."

Mrs. Tumbridge was shorter than Lydia, and her light hair was pulled back in a lace cap. Her somber-hued dress was conservatively styled, but was clearly made of a higher quality material than any of the dresses Lydia owned. The woman was plump with a round face and bright eyes, a genuine smile, and a cheerful personality.

"I'm Lydia. It's a pleasure to meet you."

"We're the ones who are pleased that you are here. Miss Elizabeth and Miss Sarah have been in state since their mother died, God bless her soul."

"Has it been very long since she passed?"

"The poor dear died this winter, while the colonel was still away in France. He was serving with Wellington, overseeing some of the provinces in the occupation when he received the news. He has recently arrived home to be with his daughters."

"I look forward to meeting them."

"I am certain they look forward to your arrival as much as the rest of the staff. They have been without a mother or governess all these months."

"Mrs. Tumbridge, do you mean to say they have not had any education since their mother passed?"

"Yes, that is correct. The colonel sent explicit instructions that nothing was to be done to secure a governess or make plans for the girls' education, not until he came home and could oversee the matter personally. He chose you from the among all the other candidates, and a great many there were. He will want to meet you before you're introduced to his daughters."

The prospect of meeting the man who owned this magnificent house – a colonel who served with General Wellington – made the breath catch in Lydia's chest. It wasn't like her to feel inadequate to a purpose. In Falmouth, she'd known who she was; she was the reliable young woman who cared for her sister, who taught at Mrs. Peyton's school, who could be counted on by her students and staff alike. She had only just arrived here in Plymouth, and already she felt like she didn't deserve the position. She certainly was not prepared to meet a man whom she was suddenly certain would find her lacking in ability.

"Miss Wells? Are you unwell?" the housekeeper asked. "Your color has quite gone from your face."

Lydia smiled. "I am a bit tired from the journey, nothing more. I am unaccustomed to travel. I shall be quite restored when I have had a cup of tea."

"You have journeyed a great distance, have you not? I shall see that you have a cup of tea and something to eat waiting for you after you have met the colonel in his study."

"He wants to meet me now? Right now?"

"Yes, by all means. He was most insistent that upon your arrival – before your things were unpacked – he should meet you and approve of you. I wouldn't worry, Miss Wells, not at all. I'm sure you will find him to be a most agreeable man."

————

FOLLOWING Mrs. Tumbridge through the corridors, Lydia wished desperately for a delay. She needed some time to compose herself, some time to think.

All the correspondence about the position had been between her and Mrs. Tumbridge, and she'd assumed it was the housekeeper who would be in charge of her employment. After all, the father was a military man, and absent like her own father – except he really wasn't like her own father, was he? Her father had installed them with Mrs. Peyton, and scarcely taken an interest in them since. And not to say that Mrs. Peyton's school had been inadequate, but this man sounded like he was rather more particular. Surreptitiously, she plucked at the front of her dress. She was sweating, and hoped nobody could tell.

Mrs. Tumbridge moved surprisingly quickly for a woman of short stature and round figure; Lydia, with her longer legs, struggled to keep pace with the diminutive housekeeper. Concealing her breathlessness, Lydia knew she had far more important thoughts to occupy her mind at the present. At any moment, they would be arriving at the door of the colonel's study, and she was entirely dependent on his approval. If he didn't like her, she would be sent back to Falmouth, and forced to make other arrangements.

She dreaded to consider that as a possibility. This position suited her needs perfectly – it was close to Falmouth, and the salary was generous. Also, she thought she would like to stay in Plymouth and explore the town. If the colonel sent her away... she quickly tried to dismiss that line of thinking as Mrs. Tumbridge stopped at a tall, wooden door at the end of a hallway.

Her heart beat wildly as Mrs. Tumbridge knocked on the door and was given permission to enter the room. Lydia had never felt so foolish or so terrified, except perhaps when she'd thought she and her sister might drown in that terrible storm, when Hugh Burton risked everything to see them safely home. What, Lydia wondered, was happening to her? She had never been afraid for her own sake, only for her sister and her father. She was positively lightheaded.

Willing herself to calm down, she took a deep breath as she was escorted into the study by the housekeeper. The study was like the rest of the house, an opulent testament to the prestige of its master. Bookcases and oil paintings of famous battles lined the dark, wood-paneled walls. A globe sat on the corner of a desk so large that Lydia wondered if it could be used for a dining table. As impressive and intimidating as the study was, the man standing behind the desk was the most daunting part of the room.

Lydia could only assume the gentleman was Colonel Michael Hartford. He stood a head taller than her, she estimated, which was impressive as she was considered tall for a woman. His dark hair and equally dark eyes complemented his olive complexion. From the slight graying at his temples, she placed his age to be a little older than Mrs. Tumbridge. He had a strong jaw, and his features were rugged, but not unattractive. On the contrary, she thought he was rather handsome, even if he was frowning distract-edly at her.

"Colonel Hartford, may I introduce Miss Lydia Wells, the new governess?" Mrs. Tumbridge said with a smile. "She has just arrived from Falmouth."

The colonel did not offer polite words or a welcoming smile. He continued to stare at Lydia, his brow furrowed, his dark eyes narrowed. He opened his mouth, and then closed it again. After a pause, he raised an eyebrow and asked, "Do you always slouch?"

"I was unaware that I was slouching," Lydia answered, her voice sounding quiet and unnatural to her ears.

"Speak up, woman. If I am to conduct this interview, I must be able to understand you. Is mumbling also one of your weaknesses?" the colonel asked.

"Colonel, if I may, she has had a long journey without rest or nourishment," Mrs. Tumbridge said.

"Mrs. Tumbridge, your opinion is noted but it will not affect my own. You are dismissed." Lydia was certain he used the same tone to order his troops.

Mrs. Tumbridge nodded and left the room. As the door closed behind her, Lydia felt a weakness in her knees and wondered if she might faint. She gathered her strength and made sure she was standing straight. She wished he would ask her to sit down, but it soon became obvious that he would not. Shivering, and disappointed that this interview was going so poorly, she concentrated on not bursting into tears of frustration. She was accustomed to walking great distances around Falmouth; she could not account for her sudden weakness or the anxiety which threatened to send her into a crying fit.

"Miss Wells, you seem pale and weak to me. How am I to expect that you shall have the stamina to see to my daughters' education when you have a sickly constitution?"

"I am not sickly, sir, it's only that I have traveled a long way."

"Are you not? Your voice is so quiet I can barely hear it; your coloring is pale indeed, and you are shaking. You are to be a role model to my children, a woman they can respect and admire. How can I allow them to be instructed by a woman who is prone to feminine anxiety? Do you suffer from the ailment of feminine hysterics, or is it fear?"

"Fear?" Lydia asked in a high-pitched voice.

"It *is* fear. Indeed, you are giving me no reason to think you worthy of a position in this household. Do you have anything to say that would change my mind, before I send back to Falmouth?"

Lydia could hardly believe what she was hearing. Ordinarily, she would have dealt with the man in front of her as she did any person in Falmouth, with confidence and wit. Intimidated and alone, she could not seem to find her usual strength. Searching for a response that would garner his approval, all she could do was express her frustration.

Swallowing, she stared at him, her own eyes narrowing as she replied, "I am not fearful. I have never left Falmouth, yet I journeyed all this way, unaccompanied, to take this position in a house filled with strangers. Does that sound fearful?"

He dismissed her remark. "There is nothing remarkable about your journey, nothing at all. I have commanded thousands of brave young men who have journeyed across the continent far from their homes here in England. If that argument is all you have to recommend you then I see that this interview is concluded. See Mrs. Tumbridge regarding the arrangements for your journey back to your home. I shall pay for your lodging at an inn this evening and your fare for the trip. Good day."

Her eyes wide with shock, Lydia's mouth gaped open. She stared at the colonel, unwilling or unsure whether to believe him. In fewer than five minutes he had decided she was unsuitable for the position, and he hadn't even asked her any real questions. Mrs. Tumbridge had said that Colonel Hartford was a "most agreeable man." He certainly was not – or at least not to *her*.

Fighting back the urge to cry, she instead found her voice. "Sir, I don't mean to be impudent, but are you dismissing me based on my posture and your perception that I am afraid?"

Glancing up from his desk, he said, "You do not meet the criteria; is that so difficult to understand? There is nothing more to be said. Go and find Mrs. Tumbridge, she will listen to whatever nonsensical remarks you want to make. Good day."

His statement that she didn't meet the criteria angered her, hitting on the source of her anxiety, echoing her own fears. It was true that she didn't have extensive references or long experience. She was aware that her teaching was limited to Mrs. Peyton's school, but she was as capable as anyone – and better, she reasoned, than most other women her own age. While her education had been complete over two years ago, she had not been content to stop learning, and continued to advance her studies in the languages and literature. Even more frustrating was the inability of this man to see past her fatigued condition, her weary posture, and other mysterious criteria that he judged her upon without giving her a proper opportunity to champion her own cause.

Standing her ground, she astonished herself with her response. "Nonsensical? This entire interview has been a wasted journey for me. You have neither asked me about my education, nor my ability to teach students. I meet or exceed all the criteria specified in the advertisement for the job."

"I will not repeat myself. Good day, Miss Wells.

"Good day? That is all you have to say to me? You'll dismiss me as though I was barely worth your notice? You have decided I am quite without merit, even though I meet your criteria, but I wonder if *you* do. Can you play music, or read it? Are you well versed in French? How is your knowledge of math and literature? Very well, Colonel Hartford, I bid you good day but before I leave, I would have you know..."

Lydia's declaration was interrupted by the colonel's outburst. "You would have me know what? You are as presumptuous as you are unqualified. Leave my study at once before I order you out of my house without a penny for your troubles."

All trace of fatigue and nervousness were gone. Lydia was livid, and she saw neither the class divide, nor her own vulnerable position. "I would have you know that even if you were to double my salary I would not work for you – not now, or ever. I *am* qualified, but your daughters will not have the benefit of my care. I shall not be staying in this house a minute longer than is absolutely necessary. If you will excuse me, I shall be on my way."

Lydia stormed out of the study, her heart racing, her face burning red with indignation. Storming down the hallway, she went to find Mrs. Tumbridge and arrange for her immediate departure. She was entirely sincere about her promise not to stay in the colonel's residence, not for a king's ransom.

Mrs. Tumbridge was not far away; she was in the hall of the house supervising the footman as he carried Lydia's trunk up the stairs. "See that placed in the apartment on the third floor by the nursery, the second door along the hallway to the left."

"Mrs. Tumbridge, you may ask him to bring my trunk downstairs. There is no need to carry it up, as I shall not be staying," Lydia said brusquely.

The little housekeeper's eyebrows shot up. "Oh, my dear, what is the matter? I've had tea brought to your room, and your trunk is going up now."

Fighting back tears of hurt and anger, Lydia answered bluntly despite being in the presence of servants. "There is no need to send my trunk upstairs; your master has decided I am unsuited for the position due to a peculiar set of circumstances which have nothing whatsoever to do with my abilities."

The housekeeper glanced at the footmen standing in the foyer. "Come, we can discuss this matter in your room, where we will not be overhead," she said quietly.

"Overheard? It matters not, I cannot bide another minute in this house. Please make arrangements for my trunk to be brought outside, and if you would be so gracious as to arrange my travel back to Plymouth, I shall find my own way from there."

Mrs. Tumbridge stared at Lydia as though she did not comprehend what she was saying, but Lydia noted a thread of stubbornness in her deep gray eyes. "I can certainly not arrange your travel back to town; in this weather the roads to Plymouth will be a mire of mud that will be treacherous for you and our horses. Please, come upstairs, Miss Wells, you are overwrought."

The slightly older woman left Lydia with little choice but to follow her up the stairs to the room the housekeeper had selected. It was enormous compared to the garret Lydia had previously inhabited with her sister. A four-poster bed with an embroidered curtain stood on one wall, a desk was positioned by an enormous window, and a fire burned brightly in a fireplace flanked by two cushioned chairs. The room was as handsomely furnished as the remainder of the house, but Lydia was in no frame of mind to appreciate it.

A gaunt woman with pale hair pulled tight under a cap was the sole inhabitant of the room. She curtseyed to Lydia as she spoke to Mrs. Tumbridge. "The fire is lit, and tea is on the table, Mrs. Tumbridge."

"Thank you, Hannah, you may go." Once the servant had scurried out, the housekeeper shut the door firmly. "Miss Wells, we are in our own company now, with no concern for maids or footmen. I do offer my sincerest apologies that I cannot accommodate your request to leave so quickly this evening, but the weather will not permit it. Have a cup of tea and settle in. The fire will warm your bones. If you need anything, just ask." She hesitated, and seemed about to leave, but turned back. "What happened, if I may ask?"

"Your master has decided that I do not fit his criteria for a governess," Lydia replied.

Mrs. Tumbridge sat in one of the chairs, looking thoughtful. She motioned again for Lydia to sit as well, and began to pour out the tea.

"That doesn't sound like him. Are you quite sure you understood?"

Lydia could see that she was not leaving the Colonel's house on that stormy evening. Resigned to her circumstances, she sat. Mrs. Tumbridge poured tea into two identical china cups, and handed one to Lydia.

Lydia took it with a hand that still seemed inclined to shake. "I did, quite. He determined that I have a weak constitution, I am prone to hysterics, and I slouch," Lydia explained.

Mrs. Tumbridge frowned, but there was something knowing in her expression. "That sounds odd; did he ask about your references? Or your extensive knowledge of literature?"

"You know more about my accomplishments than he does, and yet it is he who was to be paying me, if he had chosen to honor the offer of employment that was made to me."

Mrs. Tumbridge frowned into the fire, and then glanced at Lydia, seemingly having made a decision. "Don't let this trouble you; there must have been a misunderstanding. The colonel I know is a kind man of few words, but he treats his staff fairly. Rest tonight; you look as though you could use a good sleep. I will send Hannah up with your dinner, and then tomorrow morning we can get you sorted. I must say I'll be sorry to see you go so soon; the young misses were looking forward to having a governess."

"Thank you again, Mrs. Tumbridge. I am sorry too that I shall be leaving – at least for girls' sake."

Mrs. Tumbridge stood, smoothing her dress. "Well, my dear, if you are quite settled for the night, I have to be leaving. Dinner is in an hour; I will send Hannah up with a tray for you. I wish you a good night. You have journeyed far today." The housekeeper closed the door behind her, leaving Lydia all alone in a strange room in a house that was grander than her dreams.

In the morning she would be leaving this place. Tonight, she had to decide whether she was staying in Plymouth, or return to Falmouth as a failure.

CHAPTER SEVEN

Opening her eyes, Lydia did not immediately recall where she was. The large four-poster bed was unfamiliar, and she sat up, blinking and surveying her surroundings. The morning was bright, and a small fire burned sullenly in the fireplace. Stretching, Lydia remembered every detail of the previous day – the journey from Falmouth, her arrival in Plymouth, and the horrendous behavior of the master of the house.

The terrible weather of the previous evening was a memory, as she hoped all of this would soon be. Recalling her own ill temper and lack of decorum in regards to the housekeeper, she winced. It was not in her nature to speak to anyone as candidly or disrespectfully as she did when she stormed out of the colonel's office. Soon, she would be dressed, and all of this would no longer matter.

Searching inside the trunk that rested at the foot of the bed, she had every intention of dressing quickly and searching for the house-keeper. If she was fortunate, she may find Mrs. Tumbridge and be gone from the house before breakfast was served to the master. Inspired by the overwhelming need to leave this grand manor, she was not expecting a knock at the door at such an early hour.

"Miss Wells, I see you are awake. How did you rest?" Mrs. Tumbridge asked as she walked into the room, her expression warm.

"I am happy to see you; I was afraid I was going to have to search this house for you. Thank you for your hospitality. I found the evening I spent here to be restful."

"I am glad to hear it; your color seems much improved."

"So is the weather, I see. I expect the roads will be in a passable state this morning? I should like to arrange transport to Plymouth as soon as I am dressed."

"Transport to Plymouth? Yes, about that...it will have to wait."

"Again? Mrs. Tumbridge, are you certain? I have no wish to linger in the house. I don't want to seem ungrateful for your kindness, but I have to find another position and I cannot do that here."

"I understand, but the master wished for you to remain a few more hours; it is a small request. He would have liked to arrange an appointment with you before breakfast, but that has proven impossible. He has expressed an interest in speaking with you this morning. You see, Miss Wells, it is as I suggested – you have misunderstood the master. Come now, a few more hours shall be no trouble to anyone, especially as he has generously offered to supply you with the cost of your passage back to Falmouth."

Lydia sighed and narrowing her eyes at the housekeeper, who pretended not to notice. "If he had not treated me so terribly there would be no need of passage back to Falmouth. I am certain I did not misunderstand him, Mrs. Tumbridge. Can I not leave before breakfast? I would like to make my departure within the hour if I may." Lydia really didn't want to see the colonel again.

"You may leave now if you wish, but he has informed me that he shall only pay for your transport if you remain until after breakfast."

The truth was that Lydia could barely afford the passage, and she didn't want to spend the money unless it was entirely necessary – especially since she was now without employment. If she stayed a few more hours as Mrs. Tumbridge was asking, she would not have to spend her own money. She could save it for lodging and food if she chose to stay in Plymouth to look for another position.

"I suppose I could remain for the morning, but you assure me that I can leave at any time? I am not being kept as bird in a cage?"

Mrs. Tumbridge laughed. "If you were a bird, can you think of a better cage than this house and the gardens of Dartmoore Park? My dear, dress and I shall have Hannah bring your breakfast. May I suggest a stroll around the gardens this morning? It is far too beautiful a day to remain in this room."

From the garden outside her window, Lydia heard the birds singing. Yes, she would stay, have breakfast, and then perhaps she would enjoy the air outside, but that was all. By midday, she vowed to herself, she would leave – even if she had to walk back to Plymouth.

As promised, Hannah appeared with a tray containing tea, bread, butter, and jam, and links of sausage with an egg. The food was delicious and the tea, strong. She ate every crumb and drank the hot beverage, to fortify herself for whatever adventure awaited her upon her departure later in the day. With breakfast finished, she was anxious. She checked that her trunk was packed and waiting by the door of her room.

Gazing out the window, Lydia was transfixed by the beauty of the walled garden. The expanse of the garden was laid out in a series of rooms, as it were, with arbors, trees, and elaborate knot patterns of hedges and flowering bushes. The view from her room was breathtaking, so she went out to see the gardens up close before she left Dartmoore Park forever.

Careful to avoid the staff and the master of the house, she made her way down the staircase, using her best judgment to find her way to the back of the house, and the doors that opened into the garden. Once outside, she enjoyed the sunshine on her face. She tightened her bonnet around her chin, and tilted her chin up.

The scent of dozens of varieties of flowers blooming all at once was enchanting as she walked around the manicured paths, taking in the beauty and tranquility of the setting. She longed for her sketch pad or a set of watercolors to capture this morning, but she would just have to try and remember it later, when she was at leisure to make a record.

She sat down on a bench under a majestic tree as birds sang their cheerful song, flitting from the bushes to the trees in the arbor nearby. Yes, she had to agree with Mrs. Tumbridge – this would be a delightful cage to be in if she was a bird – but she was not, and she would not stay longer than noon. Although she was reluctant to leave such beauty behind, she could not stay in a house ruled by such a tyrannical master.

As her mind turned to the colonel she saw to her displeasure that he was striding towards her. She hoped that he was simply talking a stroll, perhaps for his morning exercise, but she soon discovered this was not the case. She cringed, and worried that he would continue in the same vein as yesterday.

As he drew closer, she steeled herself for any cruel words he might say. She vowed that she would be away from him soon, and that she would not embarrass herself with any more outbursts of temper.

Seeing him now in the bright sunlight, she thought she wouldn't have believed him capable of the treatment he had given her yesterday. She blinked and looked away as he sat beside her on the bench.

"Miss Wells," he began. "May I offer you an apology?"

Dignity and decorum, she reminded herself silently. "You may offer any words you wish, sir, and then I shall arrange my departure as soon as possible."

"My behavior was reprehensible, and I am sorry for it. I understand why you were reluctant to stay here unless I compelled you with payment for your time, as I have arranged with Mrs. Tumbridge."

Lydia made a face that revealed her feelings about that bit of manipulation, and gave no further answer.

After a pause, the colonel cleared his throat and continued, looking at his hands, which were loosely clasped between his knees.

"Miss Wells, I should like to speak with you concerning the matter of the interview yesterday and my treatment of you. This is the reason I've asked Mrs. Tumbridge to wait on arranging your travel arrangements. I have no intention of keeping you against your will, but I do wish to give you time to familiarize yourself with the house and grounds. Perhaps the beauty of this house shall prompt a change in your perception of your prospects here, and if I do say so, allow me the opportunity to offer my sincerest apologies."

"Perhaps these grounds and this house can entice another woman to accept the position of governess. If you are finished, I have my trunk packed and waiting."

"Miss Wells, what I said to you was unjust. In truth, I doubt I will find a more suitable person to fill the position. Please reconsider. Perhaps this afternoon we can talk again? If you do not find my offer of apology or my invitation to stay to your liking, you may leave at first light."

Lydia did not reply or acknowledge him when he left.

Confused, she watched him as he grew distant, his form disappearing from her view as he turned a corner in the garden. He was very handsome when he spoke kindly, but she could not forget the man she had met within minutes of arriving at Dartmoore Park. She could not erase her vision of the man who had criticized her without provocation.

Which man was the real Colonel Michael Hartford, and did she care to find out?

———

"I've chosen the drawing room for our meeting this afternoon. The study seems too cold, too steeped in business and matters of finances. I...I wish to speak to you as acquaintances, if I may be so bold," Colonel Hartford explained as he greeted Lydia.

Walking slowly, carefully navigating her way past upholstered chairs, card tables and sofas arranged for social gatherings, Lydia was escorted by the colonel to chairs arranged beside the fireplace. It was a warm day, but the large rooms of the old house were prone to drafts, making fires essential even in the summer months.

"Shall I stand?" She eyed the comfortable chair at her side.

"There is no need to stand; you are not a soldier. This is not a formal interview. Please sit down."

"Thank you, sir," she said as she curtseyed, slowly lowering herself down in the chair.

"I did you a great disservice yesterday," he explained. He hesitated in case she should make some comment, but she did not. "I've been an officer in His Majesty's army for a great many years. I'm afraid the habits of the battlefield and the military encampment are quite strong, and sometimes I am too harsh with the people around me."

Lydia narrowed her eyes at the colonel, her brow furrowed. "You treat your staff as you do your soldiers?"

"Occasionally I do, and this is not always inappropriate. At times it is required."

She sniffed. "That does not excuse your behavior towards me. You did not take into account that I am a woman deserving of your respect. You may be an officer, you may own this fine house, but I am the eldest daughter of an esteemed captain. My father commands a ship of the line. I am not without pride in my family, my father, and in my own abilities."

"Your father is a captain in the navy? How extraordinary," the colonel said with an approving smile.

Lydia swallowed. "Well, yes. But...he's missing at sea."

"Is that so? Since when?"

"Since the spring," she said quietly, rearranging her hands in her lap.

"And do you have other family?"

"Just my younger sister. She...well, she is sometimes sickly, but she is feeling quite well right now."

Colonel Hartford examined her face for a moment, and she felt her color rising in her discomfort.

"So," he said softly after a time, "your sister is depending on you for her care and upkeep."

Silently, she nodded.

His features cleared somewhat, and he sat back in his chair. "I can see that you would bring a unique understanding of my daughters' current conditions – they've lost their mother and are without me for extended periods of time. Mrs. Tumbridge was quite right; you are singularly qualified to take over their care. Again, I ask you to forgive me. Please accept this position, Miss Wells."

He was quite charming when he wanted to be, Lydia thought. She was sorely tempted to accept his apology – and his offer of employment. In the space while she formulated her answer, he spoke again.

"You are quite correct," Miss Wells. "I should have treated you with respect, as you are a woman of good character."

"Thank you for the sincere apology," Lydia replied. "I should be pleased to accept the position, and I hope we may proceed with a better understanding of one another."

The corner of his mouth quirked, and the ghost of a sad smile passed over his face.

"What is it?" she asked.

"You'll be unaware, of course, but standing in my study yesterday, you bore a remarkable resemblance to my late wife."

Lydia raised a brow at that. "And this prompted your...conduct?"

He shook his head and shifted his shoulders uncomfortably. "I was...unnerved. When you walked into my study, I was overcome with the impression that I was seeing my wife returned from her earthly rest. The sight of you, your dark hair, the way you looked at me, the lilt of your voice caught me unaware. I was prepared to ask you to leave my presence at once; I could not bear to gaze upon the face of someone so dear to me, to my daughters."

Discomfited by his familiarity, she looked away. "Say no more of it, then. I cannot alter my appearance, and perhaps it is inappropriate, or too uncomfortable, for me to stay." She made to stand, but he halted her with a gesture.

"I've embarrassed you, and that was not my intention. I presume too much on our acquaintance. I do not wish to burden you with this, but I do not wish to portray my actions as anything but what they were – the regrettable deeds of a grief-stricken man. It is not your fault that you resemble my wife, that I could not bear to look at upon your face, or that your very presence angered me because you are not her."

"I sincerely wish you good fortune, but surely you cannot expect me to stay."

"What will persuade you to remain, to consider the position?" He looked directly at her, his dark eyes gazing into hers.

She could see the pain in his eyes. She understood these emotions, but she was not prepared to hear them described by a man of rank who now shared them with her after a day's acquaintance. He was complicated, and she suspected his moods would always be as changeable as the weather. She thought of his daughters, hurt and mourning for their mother, their loss even more painful than the colonel's.

"Your daughters," Lydia said. "*If* I stay, I shall stay because they need a governess."

His smile was relieved. "Thank you, Miss Wells. You may understand them as no one else will, and I cannot hope to find another young woman who is your equal in independence or bravery. You have cared for your sister and taken responsibility for her. That is the type of bond I hope my own daughters shall always have and one I know you shall be able to foster."

Lydia frowned, wondering about the colonel's sudden change of heart. She had believed him to be a terrible, unfeeling man, but this man who implored her to stay and care for his daughters was not the same person she had met in the study. This was the side she glimpsed in the garden, the side of him that perplexed her, for this man was not so easy to loathe.

"I would like to stay and teach your daughters, but to be honest, I'm still hesitant. I cannot accept the position if I do not who I shall be working for; your nature is changeable, and you have shown me that you are entirely unpredictable in your treatment of me."

"What do you mean?"

"I mean that you have shown me two sides of yourself, and neither one is like the other. I do not know which gentleman I would serve – the one from the study who treats everyone as soldiers on the battlefield? Or this man I am addressing today, this gentleman who now sits in front of me, this man who cares for his daughters, who has shown me kindness? Who is the colonel? To whom would I owe my loyalty if I should accept your offer?"

The colonel stood and walked to the fireplace, restless. She knew her question had no easy answer, but she needed to ask. Everything in her life depended on whether or not she accepted this offer, and she could not afford to make a rash decision.

Finally, he turned back to her. "I have freely admitted that my behavior in the study was terrible, and it was. However, I am a military man, and I expect I always will be. So in answer to your question, I am both men that you have encountered. Although I try to be generous, I try to be the man you see before you today, I will always be the colonel first and foremost."

"Thank you for your honesty. I see that I have a decision to make."

"Yes. And as you consider, I would mention one caveat. I do have reason to be concerned about your independence, and your opinionated nature. I have seen your ability to defend your position as honorably as any man I have commanded. Your sharp tongue and your reprisals of my behavior – unseemly as it was – have not gone unnoticed."

Lydia raised her eyebrows, surprised. "You think I have a sharp tongue?"

He smiled ruefully. "Tell me, Miss Wells, have you done anything else to prove otherwise to me?"

"Has your training in the army not hardened your heart and your sensitivities to all manner of insult or criticism?"

"Is that how you see me, as a cold stone of a man who is incapable of feeling?"

"How am I to see otherwise? As you have said, it is part of your nature."

"So, it is. Very well, I shall be forced to endure your scathing criticism, is that your warning?"

"You have warned me of your propensity for treating the staff as soldiers, can you not allow for my 'sharp tongue,' as you call it?"

"If you accept this position, you shall be a member of my staff, and you shall treat me with the proper respect – withholding that wit of yours when we are in view of others."

"I am respectful of you, but yes. I shall take pains to retain my opinion of you and your conduct to myself."

"It sounds like you have chosen to remain."

"I would stay for the sake of your daughters; they have lost their mother. It is a pain that is surely too terrible to be endured at their tender ages. I do not relish leaving the little girls with a governess who cannot help them as they grieve. I came here to teach them, and I would still like to do that."

"Good. I shall not subject you to a fit of temper or treat you as a soldier, if it can be helped. Allow me the respect of my rank, do your best by my daughters, and we shall find this to be a very agreeable arrangement for both of us."

"I shall begin tomorrow," Lydia replied.

"Very well. Rest well this evening, Miss Wells, you shall need it. As you'll soon discover, my daughters are lively, healthy, and strong. They have been indulged by the staff and are quite wild and unruly."

"I hope they are! Being unruly shows a strength of spirit, an independence that I shall endeavor to encourage."

"Encourage? Miss Wells, are you not here to see that they receive a proper education and become young ladies?"

Lydia answered, "Oh they shall be proper young ladies, but they can still benefit from knowing their own minds."

He gazed at her thoughtfully, the ghost of a smile hovering on his face. "I expect they shall. Until tomorrow then, I will say good afternoon."

———

Colonel Hartford hardly spoke of his wife again after the interview in the drawing room, and if he did it was a rare occasion. Lydia had been at her post for several months, and now felt a small pang of guilt when she recalled their first meeting. He was a widower, and now that she knew him better she was more inclined to think he was deserving of her compassion. Since that time, she had settled into her new position and become part of the household as easily as if she had always been there.

Mrs. Tumbridge, although younger than Mrs. Peyton, was of the same friendly disposition, helpful, caring, and at times stern with the staff – but always motherly in her attention to any ills or problems. Hannah, the maid, was a thinner version of Moira, expressing many of the same religious notions, and as excitable. The remaining staff were friendly to her in a courteous way, as in her position as governess she ranked higher than the maids, servants, and cooking assistants – equal to the housekeeper and butler.

The children in her charge were much like her and her sister, with some differences. Both girls had dark hair and eyes with a catlike slant. The eldest child, Elizabeth, was nine years of age and quite reserved. The younger of the girls, Sarah, was seven. She had a mischievous nature that reminded Lydia of the fairies she'd learned about in the superstitions of Cornwall. It was as though fate had switched Lydia and her sister in age and nature.

She met the challenges of teaching and entertaining the children as she had in Falmouth. She filled their days with a combination of proper exercise, art, languages, math, and grammar, and then music to fill any gaps in their schedules.

The girls, she soon discovered, had different talents, as sisters often do. Beth, as she was known by her father and Mrs. Tumbridge, adored music. Her sight was weak, but she seemed to play by ear, a compensation Lydia encouraged. The youngest was as likely to climb the trees in the garden as she was to play pranks on the staff; her interests were not musical or academic, except for the rich stories of English history – particularly the bloodier chapters involving wars and uprisings. To Lydia's amusement, the child was enraptured by tales of King Arthur's court, and she imagined herself to be a knight. The little girl often paraded around the house, charging the furniture and the servants with a makeshift lance she fashioned from one of her father's discarded walking canes.

Both girls were delightful, and they wanted to share their memories of their mother with Lydia, since their father did not speak of her to them. Lydia obliged them in this as she obliged them in their other indulgences, sometimes privately chiding herself for spoiling them, as the staff had done. When she looked at them, with their hair hanging in ringlets, their perfectly pressed dresses and cherubic faces, she was struck by the resemblance they both had to French dolls, their future beauty clearly present at a young age, a trait she could only assume they inherited from their mother.

Their mother, Lydia discovered, was a beautiful woman with long dark curls and the same cat-like eyes of her daughters. There was a portrait of her hanging in a place of honor in the gallery, a portrait of a woman who reminded Lydia of her sister – a woman of fragile constitution and delicate beauty. Beth and Sarah liked to visit the portrait on their way to the schoolroom every morning. The little girls curtseyed and bid the woman in the painting good day, Beth wiping away tears and Sarah chatting away about her adventures as though the portrait was listening. Often Lydia turned away, to hide her own emotion.

Mrs. Tumbridge spoke to Lydia about the girls' morning ritual, suggesting that she try to discourage it when she felt the time was appropriate, as she did not want the children growing up led by their imaginations. Lydia took the woman's advice into account, but did not feel compelled to act upon it. The girls had lost their mother at a tender age, and then they were without a parent for many months until the colonel returned from France. They could hardly be expected to have overcome their grief in such a short time.

The colonel was the one detail of her new position that Lydia was unsure of; he was the one person who did not naturally or easily envelope her into the household. The candor that marked his admission of Lydia's remarkable resemblance to his wife, and the kindness he showed to her for his daughters' sake were not repeated. He was a busy man; the business of his estate was time consuming, and his management of his holdings required travel away from his home and long hours in his study. There were weeks when neither the children nor herself saw him, but his appearances were always marked by elation in the school room, his arrival and the gifts he bore were welcomed with joy by his daughters.

To Lydia it seemed that history was once again playing itself, like a novel read twice or more. The father, absent from his children, arrived with gifts. It always seemed that the gifts were compensation for his absence. Beth and Sarah were like Lydia and Charlotte had been with their own father. These young girls were accustomed to his absence, never knowing of his return, and overjoyed to see him once more.

Lydia never knew what to expect from the colonel when he arrived. Would she be meeting the military man, or the man she knew he could be – the compassionate, kind man who spoke to her as a friend? It was a mystery upon every departure, which man would return. Regardless of his mood, she endeavored to be respectful and kind, but there was always tension. Would he be chilly, keeping her at a distance, or would he invite her to dine with the family and take tea in the drawing room? It was always uncertain, and she tried to prepare for both, but she usually failed. Uncomfortably, she realized that her disappointment revealed the feelings she was developing towards him.

It was late autumn, and Lydia observed the changing of the season with no news of a wedding from Charlotte, or news regarding her father. All was the same in Falmouth and seemed to be in Plymouth as well, the only change that of the colder weather. At Dartmoore Park, she encouraged the children in her charge to make the most of the final days of sunshine, as she could feel the cold creeping in at night. Soon, she warned them, they would be unable to take their daily walks or enjoy carriage rides around the estate.

Early one Monday morning, as she led the children through the garden to collect the colorful fallen leaves for study and to decorate the school room, she was met by Hannah, who came running towards her from the house, her face red from the exertion. Lydia braced herself for any news that may have warranted the maid to run to find her. She had only her sister, Mrs. Peyton, Moira, and Cook to care for now, and she steeled herself for any terrible tragedy that may have befallen them.

"Miss Wells, you must return to the house at once. The master has sent a messenger ahead that he is on the way home. He arrives within the hour," Hannah said between breaths.

"Of course, we shall be in the school room," Lydia said as she breathed a sigh of relief. This announcement she could handle; no one she loved was dead or ill, it was only the notice of the arrival of the master.

"No ma'am. He wants you and the children to meet him in the drawing room, dressed suitably for company."

"Very well, Hannah. Will you help me?" Lydia asked.

"Yes ma'am, I shall attend to the young misses if you need to change your dress."

"I do, thank you," Lydia said as she rounded up the girls who were only momentarily disappointed that their time outside was cut short. Upon hearing about the arrival of their father, they were once more smiling and laughing, their excitement infectious. Even Lydia felt happy that Colonel Hartford was returning.

Lydia followed Hannah and the girls inside, her thoughts of the colonel and his arrival. She was overcome with her usual nervousness when she thought of him, not out of fear, but of her self-consciousness. How did she look? Did she sound intelligent, and was her conversation entertaining? These thoughts were not like her, but they were commonplace when she thought of spending any length of time in the colonel's company. Somehow, over the summer, her opinion of her employer had changed. She now found that she sought his approval and even more strangely, his company.

An hour did not seem enough time to change her dress and fix her hair. In the first weeks of her residency at Dartmoore Park, she would casually change dresses, tucking her dark curls into a simple bun at the back of her head without much care. Now, she tried to select the best dress for the occasion, taking care to fix her hair in an attractive hairstyle. Today she selected a new dress, a small indulgence from her generous salary. The dress was a simple style that was not expensive, but the color was becoming, a shade of blue that complemented her eyes.

As she waited in the nursery for the girls, she looked down at her dress, hoping it would meet with the colonel's approval. He wouldn't comment, of course, but she hoped that one day that would change. Lydia had never considered herself a beauty; her sister was often referred to as the handsome Wells sister, a beautiful frail flower. Lydia was too tall, her looks to plain for any comment (either good or bad) from anyone at her old school or the townspeople of Falmouth. It hadn't mattered to her before; her appearance was something she had never given much thought to until she arrived at Dartmoore Park. Now, she wondered if she could ever be considered handsome or even modestly attractive, or was she doomed to be plain?

This sudden interest in her appearance was disturbing, she realized, as she watched Hannah finish tying large silk ribbons in the ringlets of the young ladies in her charge. Was this vanity, or something else? Why did she seek the colonel's approval, and why did his opinion of her outward appearance matter? It was all very strange, her seeking comments from a man she had only known since midsummer. Her employer, at that.

"Come on Beth, help your sister; she has misplaced a glove. Hurry, Sarah. We do not want to keep your father and his guest waiting," Lydia urged the girls as she noted the anxious expression on the maid's face.

The girls were far too excited to be of much help, so she selected a new pair of gloves for Sarah. Once they were both dressed, their hair arranged in cascades of ringlets held by enormous bows, their shoes matching and gloves on their small hands, Lydia led them from the nursery to the drawing room.

"We shall behave as ladies. We shall be quiet and still, and smile. Sarah, remember to curtsey to the guest. Beth, remember to smile and be pleasant."

"Yes, Miss Wells," the girls answered in unison as they walked down the stairs.

From the staircase, Lydia could hear the faint sound of masculine laughter coming from the direction of the drawing room. There was the deep sound of the colonel's laugh, so rarely heard, but there was another man in his company, a second voice she did not recognize.

As they approached the drawing room, she whispered to the little girls. "Beth, Sarah, remember to walk in slowly. No running; you are ladies."

The girls did as she commanded, one on each side of her as they kept pace, walking in a slow deliberate fashion, the way a proper lady enters a room. Lydia was so focused on the behavior of her charges, (particularly the youngest one who was prone to running everywhere she went), that she did not see the gentleman whose voice she'd heard on the stairs.

Smiling as she watched Sarah's deliberate attempted to be a lady, she looked up to find the colonel watching her. Even with the weight of his gaze on her face, Lydia's attention was drawn to the gentleman at his side. This man was slightly shorter, his shoulders were wider, and his sandy brown hair was worn in waves to his shoulders. He was not as handsome as the colonel, but he looked at Lydia in a way that made her feel like she was dazzling.

"Miss Wells, Beth, and Sarah, may I introduce Captain William Poole; he served with me in France."

The girls at her side curtseyed gracefully, and Lydia replied, "Captain Poole, it is an honor to meet you."

"Miss Wells, it is indeed a pleasure to meet you."

Lydia bowed her head as she waited for the colonel to invite her to stay or to dismiss her. She hoped he would not dismiss her today, as she wanted to speak with this dashing young captain. Was he married, or engaged, she wondered, as she stole a surreptitious glance at him. He appeared to be not much older than her, and he smiled at the young girls. She noted that he had dimples, and his laugh was infectious as Sarah whispered a secret to him.

His charm and warmth made him seem approachable, as though she could, like Sarah, tell him anything. Standing still, she waited for the colonel to decide her fate, as a footman brought in tea.

"Beth, Sarah, would you like to join me and my guest for tea?" the colonel asked.

"Yes, Father, we would love tea, we haven't eaten since breakfast!" announced Sarah.

"Very well. Miss Wells, you may leave the girls in my charge while we take tea," the colonel said, dismissing her.

Lydia hid her disappointment, and curtseyed with dignity. "Yes sir."

"Colonel, are we to be deprived of such lovely company? I have only just arrived from France; I would enjoy the sound of my own language spoken by a charming English lady," the captain said as he smiled at Lydia.

"Of course. Miss Wells, if you have nothing else planned for your afternoon, you may stay."

"Thank you, sir," Lydia replied as she took her place on the couch by the fireplace. The girls sat on tufted stools at their father's feet, and the captain joined Lydia on the couch. When he smiled at her, his dazzling green eyes sparkled in the light of the fire.

"Thank you," whispered Lydia to the captain when she was certain the colonel was distracted by his daughters. "I was feeling hungry; the kitchen staff here at Dartmoore make the best cakes you have ever eaten."

"I am glad I could help; I can't remember the last time I enjoyed a cake that was not made of flour and sawdust. Miss Wells, I hope I didn't sound too forward when I called you charming. Do forgive me for sounding less than respectful," the captain whispered to her.

"Not at all, I appreciate the compliment. As a governess, it is not often said that I am charming."

The captain was very pleasant. She soon found herself engaged in conversation with him, no longer caring if the colonel was distracted or not. They chatted about all manner of things, from state of the Empire to the latest novels. It was not until the colonel cleared his throat that she realized she had not drank a sip of tea or touched a bite of the delicious cake.

"Miss Wells, it is good that you and Captain Poole are forming an acquaintance."

Lydia turned her attention to her employer. "It is, sir?"

"Yes. He shall be here at Dartmoore in my stead when I am away on business, so it is important that he become acquainted with the staff."

"You'll be here? At Dartmoore?" Lydia asked, belatedly realizing she should not seem so enthusiastic about it.

The colonel laughed. "Captain Poole, have you not shared the news of your new position with Miss Wells? Have you kept our governess unaware of whom she is addressing?" he teased.

"We have just been introduced, there has not been time," the captain replied.

Colonel Hartford smirked. "You two seem to have discussed

every subject of importance, but surprisingly not the most significant one of all."

"If you insist. Miss Wells, what the colonel has hinted at is my new position, upon the resignation of my commission. He has offered me employment as the estate manager to Dartmoore Park and the tenants and farmers within the confines of the property."

"Estate manager?" Lydia asked, resisting the urge to smile.

"Yes, Captain Poole served under me with distinction in France; his cool head and resourcefulness regarding our supplies are traits I can put to good use," the colonel boasted.

"You think too highly of me," the captain laughed before turning to Lydia. "He does. He has only offered me the job so that I will have gainful employment."

"Gainful? That may be, but I expect you to run my estate with the same efficiency you ran the regiment. I expect my coffers to be filled with rents and profits, but that is business and we don't want to discuss it in front of Miss Wells or my daughters," the colonel said as he turned his attention back to his girls.

"I am pleased beyond expression that I made your acquaintance today. Colonel Hartford has promised me a house of my own on the property. I know my duties will consume a great deal of my time, but I hope to see you in the garden. Perhaps we could meet for a stroll, or tea?" Captain Poole asked as he smiled at Lydia.

Lydia smiled back at him, her mind leaping forward to walks along the garden paths, to lengthy conversations at tea, maybe even sharing a kiss under the arbor. She blushed. "Yes, Captain Poole, that would be lovely."

Looking up, she saw the colonel staring at her. His expression was impossible to interpret, but he wore a faint hint of a frown on his face. She was curious about why he was giving her such a strange look, but she didn't have time to dwell upon the source of the Colonel's displeasure. The captain was telling a joke and Sarah climbed into the colonel's lap. When she looked back at the colonel, he was speaking with his daughter, and the moment had passed.

CHAPTER EIGHT

Early Winter, 1816
Plymouth, England

LYDIA HAD NEVER EXPERIENCED the sensation that was growing inside her. She'd thought she felt the first stirrings of romantic feelings for the colonel, but she quickly realized by comparison that she did not feel anything for her employer – not like what she felt for Captain Poole. He laughed at her jokes, and he spoke to her as an old friend, as though they had known each other for a long time. It was odd to think that she should have feelings for a man she didn't really know, aside from his rank in the army, his name, and his new position. He could have a wife or be engaged; he could have a terrible temper. There were so many things that she didn't know, but one thing she did know with certainty. In the moment when she met Captain Poole, something inside her changed. Something shifted within her that she did not think could ever be altered back to its original form.

When she closed her eyes, her head was filled with the captain, with images of his handsome face smiling at her, his laugh, the wave of his brown hair. Her heart beat wildly in her chest at the mere memory of him, and she smiled when she recalled his voice. She didn't know what had come over her, but she suspected that she was stricken with the same ailment that plagued her sister. She had fallen in love with Captain Poole as Charlotte had fallen in love with Hugh Burton. This love, this feeling of desire that coursed through her, was more powerful than anything she had ever felt. It filled her waking thoughts and her dreams. As she lay in bed at night, she could not sleep for thinking of it.

Walking to the window of her bedroom, she shivered in the cold but did not feel it. She was consumed by thoughts of Captain Poole as she stared out of the window. She wondered if he was asleep or whether he thought of her too. Was she being silly, or did he feel what she did? Was he in love with her, as she was with him? Gazing through the glass, she could see the garden and if she let her imagination stretch further beyond, she knew his modest stone house sat in the village just beyond the walls.

Snow fell outside as winter settled in. Shuddering from the cold, Lydia still kept her nightly vigil at the window. The faint blue of the snow on the ground, the moonlight filtering between the snowflakes – it was a romantic winter landscape as magical as any fairy world she could imagine. It was in this world that she and Captain Poole enjoyed an occasional sleigh ride or a hot cup of tea when he visited the house to discuss business with the colonel.

Lydia was startled by a sudden loud knocking at her bedroom door. She did not know what time it was, but by the silence in the house, she thought it must be quite late.

Reaching for her robe, she wrapped her hand around the doorknob as the frantic knocking continued.

"Miss! Miss, please wake up!" a familiar voice said on the other side of the door.

"I am awake," Lydia answered as she opened the door to reveal

Hannah, her expression strained and a piece of paper held tightly in her grip.

"Miss Wells, there is a messenger arrived here from Boscombe Hall in Cornwall. He insists that you read this; he is waiting for your answer."

"A messenger? Are you certain this is for me? I know no one at Boscombe Hall."

"Quite certain, miss. The man won't listen to a word I have said. I told him you were asleep, but he insisted that I wake you. It's urgent, he said. He arrived in a carriage, miss."

"Thank you," Lydia said as Hannah handed her the message.

Straightening the crumpled paper, Lydia felt faint after reading the first line. By the second and third lines of the letter, she needed a chair and strong cup of tea.

"Hannah, is this true?" Lydia whispered.

"Is what true? I did not read your message, that would have been improper."

"Hannah," Lydia whispered as she tried to collect herself. "My father is alive, it says in this message that he is at Boscombe Hall. He is unwell, but he is alive!"

"Yes, miss, that is good news," Hannah replied.

"Tell the messenger I will be ready in an hour. My father needs me; it's urgent that I go to him at once."

"Shall I help you pack, Miss Wells?"

"Yes, tell the footman to bring my trunk. I don't know why my father is at Boscombe Hall, but if he is alive I shall go anywhere to be with him."

Cornwall, England

LYDIA READ the words of the letter over and over. She could hardly allow herself to believe that her father was alive. Since the spring, she'd feared the worst – that he'd drowned with all his crew when the ship he had captained, the *HMS Thames*, went down off the coast of

Spain. In her hand was a missive declaring that he was in England. She could scarce believe it.

Your father is alive. He requests your presence at Boscombe Hall, Cornwall. Come at once. He is unwell; do not tarry.

Your servant,

James Finnigan

Folding the brief letter, she held it gently, reverently, and then slid it into her reticule. She didn't want to damage what would surely become a cherished memento. He was alive! It was more than she could ever hope for, especially with only three days left until Christmas. Charlotte would call this news a Christmas miracle.

Charlotte! In all the excitement of packing her belongings and saying goodbye to those she cared for at Dartmoore, she'd completely overlooked what the driver had said about her sister. Charlotte was already at Boscombe Hall, collected from Falmouth two days before.

Poor Charlotte! Lydia thought about her younger sister. Charlotte had never traveled more than a few miles from Falmouth...and in the cold! Charlotte must have been anxious, thought Lydia, as she imagined her demure, retiring sister all alone, heading for a part of Cornwall she had never been to, in a carriage as fine as the one Lydia found herself in at present.

On the softly tufted seat, Lydia had never known travel to be this comfortable. Yet it was the crest on the door of the carriage that was the most puzzling. The crest, a large design boasting a knight's helmet and a full coat of arms, was in the name of the noble house of Wharncliffe, a name she did not recognize. It was as unfamiliar as the name signed to the letter. She had never known a person by the name of Finnigan, much less one who would know of her whereabouts and her circumstances.

And her circumstances were perplexing. Her trunk, containing all her belongings, was strapped to the back of the carriage. She didn't know if she would ever return to Dartmoore Park, although she wanted to very badly. Colonel Hartford's daughters, Beth and Sarah, had become very dear to her in her short tenure as their governess.

Yet it was not only the daughters of the colonel that made her sigh with remorse for her sudden departure – Captain Poole would also be greatly missed.

He had shown her a friendship that was so warm that she scarcely knew how to contain her feelings for him. In Captain Poole, she'd had her first real taste of romance. She'd read about the sentiment in novels and seen how her sweet sister was transformed by the emotions she harbored for Hugh Burton, but Lydia had never known the powerful feeling until she met the captain. Despite the early hour, he came to say goodbye to her, and his distraught reaction to her sudden departure was what she knew a man in love ought to feel. He'd promised to write, and to continue their correspondence until she knew what was to become of her.

The colonel, in contrast, had reacted coldly.

Recalling the scene in the hall with perfect clarity, she could see Hannah and Mrs. Tumbridge offering their prayers for her father's recovery as Colonel Hartford said she may use his name as a character reference. But his eyes had been cold, his demeanor stony as she promised to write of her circumstances as soon as they became known. She didn't know what lay in store for her, she'd explained. She didn't know if her father would need her at his side to help him recover from whatever injury he'd sustained, or whether all was lost, and she was being called to his side to hear his last words. She would know nothing else until she arrived at Boscombe Hall.

Boscombe Hall. She recalled how the colonel said those two words with respect and reverence. Yet he did not elaborate when he asked her of her connection to the house and the family that owned the residence. It was, as she told the colonel, a mystery to her and one she knew would soon be revealed. Wishing her a safe journey, he had left her in the presence of his crying housekeeper and maid. She thanked them for their friendship and left Dartmoore.

The scene that tore at her heart more than any other was her memory of the little girls crying and begging for hugs. They had already lost their mother, and now she was leaving them. This pain threatened to her break her heart more than leaving Captain Poole, but she promised to see them again. They had stood uncertainly in front of her in the nursery, holding their dolls as they sniffed and met the news of her immediate departure with tears. They did not understand why she had to leave them and begged to go with her, but she explained to them that their father needed them to be brave. They promised in the earnest way of children and sent her away with kisses.

As the carriage rumbled into the countryside of Cornwall from Plymouth, she had the distinct feeling that this adventure had only begun. At the end of this ride, her sister and her father waited for her at Boscombe Hall, with a gentleman by the name of Finnigan who may be able to explain why she was being transported in a carriage grand enough for royalty and owned by a family called Wharncliffe.

Leaning back in the seat, she pulled the fur carriage rug up around her waist; the weather was cold and snow fell outside the window. The countryside of Cornwall was starkly beautiful, covered in white. The driver had told her before leaving Dartmoore that Boscombe Hall was an enormous, grand old house overlooking the ocean. She had lived near the water her entire life, from Mrs. Peyton's school at Falmouth to her position as a governess in Plymouth. And with her future so much up in the air, it only seemed fitting that she should be traveling to a house that sat on a cliff.

She remembered how she had felt upon her arrival to Dartmoore, her concern for her clothes and her plain but sensible wardrobe. If the carriage she was riding in was any indication, she was on her way to a place that would surely make her feel like a pauper. But what was important was that her father was alive, and she would soon see him and her sister again. At Boscombe Hall, the owners of such a magnificent place must surely make allowances for the poor daughter of a sea captain, a woman whose only life experience consisted of teaching at a school for girls and being a governess to a colonel.

Her life, once so orderly, had become with that single letter chaotic and uncertain. There were far too many other pressing matters than to be worried about her wardrobe and her station. After she learned of her father's fate, if she was free to go, then she could plan a hasty return to Dartmoore and hope to secure her position and the regard of the handsome, charming Captain Poole.

Captain Poole was more dear to her than she ever thought a gentleman could be. His wit, his laugh, and thinking about the way he looked at her with such respect and admiration made her long for him. Would she ever see him again? And if so, when would it be? Of course she didn't regret leaving him or anyone else for the sake of her father, but she did long to know when, if ever, she would find herself on this road, going back to Dartmoore, to her new friends, her darling girls, Captain Poole – and strangely enough, to Colonel Hartford. She knew she would not soon forget the colonel, and she wasn't sure if that was a good or bad thing – to be haunted by the specter of the man she could not hope to understand.

———

DARTMOORE PARK WAS the grandest residence Lydia had ever seen outside the pages of book. That house stood in her mind as the paragon of architectural achievement – until she beheld Boscombe Hall. The name of the building was not fitting, she decided, for the magnificence and the enormous size of the imposing structure that sat, exactly as the driver described, on a lonely road, past a tangle of low brush and forest, on a cliff high above the sea.

It was late in the afternoon when they arrived. Lydia was fatigued from the journey and cold, as she imagined the driver to be in his fine livery, exposed as he was to the elements. From the road carved into the green hills approaching the edge of the cliff, she saw the house from a distance and watched with fascination as it loomed larger and larger in the window.

The building was more recent than the name suggested. A hall, to her way of thinking, was an ancient building, perhaps a medieval hall in a castle. This place sat high above the crashing waves of the ocean, three stories tall, with thick colonnades and a wide stone staircase at the entrance. In the center of the highest peak at the entrance, the house boasted an enormous coat of arms that matched the crest she'd observed on the door of the carriage. It looked like a royal palace, a home built for a king.

She felt a flutter of nervousness as the carriage slowed to a stop outside the main entrance. Why was her father here, at this grand residence? She could not fathom how he was connected to this place. As nervous as she was, she was very excited to see her father.

The footman escorted her up the main stairs and opened the grand door. She did not have an opportunity to observe her surroundings, other than to see they were richer than her wildest dreams. Her attention was demanded by a young, pale woman who stood near the marble staircase.

Lydia was still wearing her bonnet, coat, and scarf when she was greeted in a flurry of embraces and tears by her sister Charlotte the moment her feet touched the interior of the house.

"Lydia! Thank heavens you're here; I prayed you would come! Isn't it wonderful? Father is alive! I can scarcely believe it to be true, it's more than I could have ever hoped for," Charlotte babbled. She was full of high emotion and energy, which was unlike her.

"Charlotte! My dear, you are not like your old self. Who is this woman who stands before me speaking in such a rapid fashion? Do I know her?"

Charlotte smiled as she embraced Lydia again. "Oh, how I've missed you, but that doesn't matter now. We must hurry and go to Father at once. I have ever so much to tell you –just wait until you hear all the news. First you must see Father, and then more wondrous news awaits you."

Lydia was whisked upstairs so fast she didn't have time to see to her trunk, freshen up, or do much else. Charlotte was animated, and the excitement she exuded was contagious. Despite Lydia's fatigue from the journey and curiosity about the regal home she was now invading, she wanted to see her father. Charlotte pulled her along from the second story landing along a gallery of paintings in a blur, holding her hand tightly, urging Lydia ever faster. Lydia's heart was pounding as they reached the end of a hall so grand she had never seen, or even imagined, its equal.

Without knocking or announcing her entrance, Charlotte turned the knob of a tall carved oak door, and opened it to reveal a bedchamber fit for a king. The chamber was cavernous, its muraled ceiling high overhead. A four-poster bed sat at one end, a formidable structure in its own right. Two couches and table were arranged in front of a blazing fire.

Lydia's heart stopped beating for a moment as she beheld a wondrous sight. Reclining on a couch by the fire was a man she remembered, a face she recognized. Her father, reclining under quilts.

She hurried to his side, and his smile was broad and sincere. He had the same salt and pepper hair and smooth-shaven face that she remembered. His frame was thinner, his features were more pronounced and his cheeks were hollow, but he was Father.

"My dear Lydia," he said as she fell to her knees by his side, kissing his hand as he reached out to touch her.

"Can this be real, are you truly alive and not a ghost?" She wept silent, joyful tears at the reunion.

"I am alive; it is true. You may trust your eyes," he whispered as he embraced her.

Lydia wept as Charlotte joined them in an embrace that encompassed the whole of the Wells family. Lydia was so relieved that her father was alive, and that her sister was with her at his side. Questions about future and the mysterious Boscombe Hall didn't matter as she fell into childlike wonder and joy. She felt like she was once more transported back in time to her girlhood, and her delight every time her father arrived at the doorstep of Mrs. Peyton's.

The bliss of this moment was fleeting, being interrupted by a knock and the entrance of a tall man who wore somber clothing that matched his demeanor as he greeted the captain. The man stood like a soldier, awaiting orders. With his brown hair and gray eyes he was not handsome, nor was he plain, but he appeared to be determined that his duties be carried out diligently.

He spoke in a voice that was low, with the pleasant lilt of an accent Lydia did not recognize as he bowed to Captain Wells. "My Lord, the doctor has returned. May I show him in, or shall I ask him to wait?"

"Ask him to wait, Finnegan. I will be a moment," Captain Wells replied absentmindedly.

"I shall do so; may I ring for tea?"

"No. That will be all."

The man nodded, leaving Lydia with one question answered. This was the mysterious Mister Finnegan, who had sent a message and a carriage to Dartmoore. However, she still had many more questions. For instance, she wondered, why had Finnegan called her father *My Lord?*

"Lydia, did I not say there was much news to tell?" Charlotte asked with a smile.

"My dear Lydia, Charlotte has told me of your bravery, how you saw to the security of her position and your own in my absence. I am so proud of you that I cannot express it as I might, but I have much to discuss with you after I have seen the doctor. I know you've journeyed far to arrive here and you must be cold, tired, and hungry. The housekeeper, Mrs. Sloane, will see to you. I look forward to spending the remainder of this evening in your company."

Lydia nodded and embraced her father once again before she and Charlotte left his side. At the door she paused, struck with a sudden worry that if she went through it, he might vanish like a dream. Looking back, she saw his face, his eyes twinkling in the firelight. He was alive. She could rest knowing that her family was reunited again, in this magnificent house by the sea.

CHARLOTTE SAT in silence with a sly smile on her face as Lydia drank a hot cup of tea in a less than ladylike fashion, gulping it down as soon as it became cool enough to drink. She was thirsty, and ready for the answers that her sister was refusing to provide.

"Charlotte, this is ridiculous. You must tell me, you must!" Lydia pleaded between bites of a sandwich.

"Do you like your room? I selected it for you; it has a view of the ocean. It reminds me of our garret room at Mrs. Peyton's," Charlotte replied as she gestured to the tall window behind Lydia.

The room was, like her father's chamber, enormous by Lydia's standards. She sat on a silk upholstered chair beside a fireplace with her sister, enjoying tea from a service that was so delicate she was nearly afraid to touch it. The bed was a tall four-poster that held up a canopy of cream-colored material embroidered with flowers, which matched the bed curtains that were lined in green and pale pink silk. A writing desk and a seating area completed the room's furnishings, but they were paled by the view. The window faced the ocean, stretching for as far as the eye could see, a view she could have spent hours observing – but not his afternoon.

"Charlotte, this room is lovely, but you must tell me, is Father gravely ill? Why are we here? I have yet to be introduced to our host."

"Father is ill, yes, but not gravely, or so I have been told. *Ill* may not be the correct word; he has been injured but he will tell you about that when we see him this evening."

Lydia breathed a sigh of relief, but her questions were unanswered. "And the rest of my inquiries?"

"I long to tell you everything, I truly do, but I wonder if our father should be the one to tell you the news," Charlotte replied.

"Perhaps you can tell something of what you know, and save the details for Father to tell me? Is that agreeable? You did promise to tell me all the news when I first arrived, remember? On the staircase, you said that."

Charlotte sighed in mock resignation. "I suppose that is agreeable. Forgive me for making such promises; I was so excited to see you that I spoke without any thought. I shall tell only a little and then Father can tell the rest."

"A little will have to do, I suppose," Lydia resigned herself to be patient as she reached for another sandwich.

"You asked about our host."

"I did; this house is far too grand and well maintained not to have a master."

"Oh, my dear sister, it does have a master," Charlotte said with a smile as she sipped her tea.

"The master...does he have a name, may I meet him? I've seen the name Wharncliffe, is that the name of the family that owns this house?"

Charlotte set down her teacup as her eyes widened with excitement. "Lydia, put your sandwich upon your plate and listen very carefully. You shall not believe it, as I did not at first but every word of what I am to say to you is true."

Lydia did as she was commanded, placing her sandwich on the small, fragile plate, and setting the plate on the table beside the now empty teacup. Steeling herself (for what she was not sure), she whispered, "I'm ready, you may tell me."

"Our father is the master, or he may very well soon be its master."

Lydia was vaguely aware of the passage of time as she sat still, silent in that moment of surprise. Her astonishment was tempered by the words she recalled spoken by Mr. Finnegan, *My Lord,* he had said. *No,* she thought. *This can't be right.*

"No, Charlotte you are mistaken, our father is a naval officer."

"Yes, he is that; you are correct. But he is the lord of this manor."

"He cannot be, we have no money but our meager dowries and the small amount he set aside upon his death for us. He cannot be the master of such a place as this, and we be nearly penniless."

"There is much to be explained, and he shall disclose the details that I fail to fully comprehend, but you may rely upon my word. Our father is the master of Boscombe Hall, as far as the staff is concerned."

Frowning, Lydia considered that as terribly farfetched as it may seem, it was possible. She and her sister had never met any of her father's family, or her mother's. Their mother died when they were far too young to ask about relations, and their father was never home for very long. When he was home, he was busy preparing the ship for the next voyage, journeying to the naval office in London and visiting with them as much as he could be spared from his duties. He was a captain at a time of war and he was dedicated to the service of His Majesty. His time was a precious commodity

She recalled meeting with the solicitor in Falmouth after the news that her father's ship sank, and the solicitor had not been forthcoming with details of any surviving family. Lydia had assumed that there were none and that she and Charlotte were alone in this world. As she glanced around the room, she came to the realization that obviously, if Charlotte was correct, she did have a relation or two she hadn't known about.

"How is this possible?"

"You must hear that from him; he shall explain it all. In the meantime, I have to tell you about Hugh!"

Lydia didn't really want to hear about Hugh Burton, the fisherman her sister adored. In their last conversation regarding the handsome, ambitious Hugh, her sister was still waiting patiently for him to find a way to become a naval officer. Lydia remembered his attachment to a daughter of his mother's closest friend, and held her tongue as she listened to her sister recount every meeting and every letter they'd exchanged during her months at Dartmoore. There was still no hope of a wedding, but Hugh had not become married to anyone else either – *or so he led Charlotte to believe*, thought Lydia cynically.

Lydia longed to ask Charlotte more questions about the house, Finnegan, and the name of Wharncliffe but she could see that until she spoke with her father she would get no more information from her sister except about the subject of a certain young fisherman.

As Lydia resumed drinking her tea, she felt like her head was spinning. So much had happened, it was nearly too much to take in.

An hour later, Charlotte had exhausted every story regarding Hugh, Lydia had eaten every scrap of food on the plate, and the teapot was empty. The sun set, prompting a maid to arrive in the chamber to light the candles and replenish the fire. A second maid arrived to request the presence of both Lydia and Charlotte in their father's chamber after dinner. The maid, a woman a little older than Lydia but not much, offered to help the young ladies dress for dinner, which was to be served downstairs in an hour.

Despite eating a lot of sandwiches, Lydia found she was still surprisingly hungry for food – and for knowledge. She could hardly hide her impatience to visit her father and learn how he survived a sinking ship and became master of Boscombe Hall.

CHAPTER NINE

Lydia sat beside her sister on a couch facing her father, as they had done many times when they were young, both attentive to his calm, steady voice as he recounted a tale of his adventures. The captain was a gifted storyteller and Lydia was always amazed at his ability to hold her attention. Tonight, she felt the same thrill as she sat in silence, her eyes turned towards her father.

"Charlotte has already heard what I am to tell you, but I doubt she will offer any objection," Captain Wells began. "I start by offering you and your sister an apology."

"An apology? Father, I don't understand," Lydia said.

Captain Wells nodded. "I know you don't, and that is entirely my fault. I must begin a few years ago, if you will be patient. I assure you that all will be made clear by the end."

"Many years ago, when I was a young man, I was the second son of the tenth Earl of Wharncliffe. I grew to manhood on this estate, and in this great house. My father was a man who, like his own father, was severe, unyielding, and tethered by tradition, as one might expect from a noble lineage as esteemed as his."

Lydia didn't how to react to her father's admission. It was far too much to accept, but she listened with rapt attention.

"My eldest brother, George, was the heir, and as heir he behaved much as my father did, imperious, demanding, and oblivious to any life outside of the running of an estate. I was not like them in nature or temperament. I did not consider myself to be unfortunate in my birth as many other second sons of nobility might. I would not inherit great wealth or title, but what I did stand to inherit was my independence and small amount of money with which to begin a career. My father preferred that I assume a place in the clergy, but I had other plans of a more adventurous nature."

Captain Wells reached for a cup of tea, sipped the steaming brew, and continued. "I was born in this house and raised here. The sea called to me from an early age. I cannot remember when I didn't feel the tug of it upon me. As a child, I longed to go to sea; I read tales of pirates and adventures, sagas of old, and naval battles. I longed for a life upon the ocean, but my father would not hear of it. He didn't approve of the sons of noble birth wasting away as officers in the navy or army. He insisted on the church, and would not be moved."

"He forbid you to become a naval officer?" Lydia asked. "Why would he do such a thing? The navy is a respected profession."

"So it is, but not to my father's way of thinking. He was immovable in his belief that men of great houses and lineages were not to spill their blood in times of war, that they must endeavor to preserve the institutions of church and state by their leadership, not by their lives. He threatened to withhold the small amount set aside for my living unless I chose the church as my profession. My mother was more sympathetic; she promised that she would assist me in any way she could. She had no wealth of her own – her money and property were attached to the estate – but she arranged the private sale of a brooch her mother gave to her. The sum, she gave to me in secrecy for my commission, if I should ever need it."

"You mother and father, are they still alive? May we meet them?" Lydia asked as Charlotte looked down, her expression sad.

"My mother is not, and my father is not himself. That is where this tale takes a turn that has led us to this moment. My mother died when I was seventeen, leaving me with no one in this house who believed as I did, that I was suited for the navy. My brother George sided with my father and they both condemned my choice of profession. I was threatened with disownment if I did not journey to Oxford to begin my studies in theology. I remember well the last conversation I had with the two of them. My father was so angry, and he told me I was no longer his son. My brother did little to advance my cause, offering his own scathing opinion of my prospects. They threatened to cut me off, financially.

"I left this house that very evening, with only the suit of clothes on my back and the money from my mother in my pocket. That money, and my own good name, was all I had to recommend me in this world."

Charlotte leaned close to her sister and said in a whisper, "Does Father remind you of a young man we both know, a man who longs to be a sailor?"

"I suppose so," Lydia agreed as her father coughed and then continued his story.

"I became an officer. The money from my mother purchased my commission, and references from my circle of friends supplied my character. I left this world behind and became my own person, independent of will and free from the constraints of my family's name. My father was as good as his word, never once rescinding his disownment of me. It was many years later that I learned of my brother's death, of the dissolute habits that led to his untimely end, but I shall not share those details with either of you, they are not for a lady's ears. By the time I heard of George's passing, I was no longer a young man. By then I was married to your mother, a fine woman, herself the daughter of an officer. We lived a simple, quiet, and content life and I gave no thought to my place here at Boscombe Hall despite knowing that I was rightfully the heir. My father had made his wishes understood, and I could not imagine a life away from the sea, in this richly decorated cage.

Your mother suspected that I was not the son of a minor baronet or knight. I concealed my lineage in marriage as I did in my life because I feared our happiness, simple as it was, would not survive if she knew that I chose to live as I did rather than better my situation or improve our lot. To her credit, she was not avaricious, and she never pried into my past. In our short time together, she was never certain that I was more than a captain. To her credit, she never asked me, and I did not discuss it, for that part of my life was over and I did not mourn its passing. When your mother died, I set aside what money I had remaining of my mother's small gift and your mother's dowry. I instructed my solicitor in Falmouth to pay your school fees and set your dowries in trust. He did not know of my noble connection and I don't suspect anyone else in the port of Falmouth did, either. Only a few of my superiors knew my true origins, and of course the admiralty was aware of my lineage upon my commission."

"Father, if you were disowned, how are you sitting here? Why are we here?"

"I was coming to that part of the tale. Many years passed since my brother George died, and I did not have a scrap of correspondence from my father. I could only assume that he had done as he promised and disowned me. I knew of cousins who might stand to inherit Boscombe Hall. I wished them well, and I continued my life upon the ocean, with you two as my sole responsibility in the world, aside from my crew and ship.

"I spent the years of the war, as you both know, serving the king. My ship was a good one; how I miss her and her crew, God rest them. We were called to serve all over the known world. We served with honor and fought battles over the years. All of my men were experienced sailors, the ship a capable vessel. At last we have come to the part of the tale that pains me the greatest – our journey home last spring.

"We were ordered to set sail from the Greek islands. We left the

Mediterranean heading north; the wind was with us and we were advancing at a terrific pace. I was pleased that the ship and crew were performing so well, and it was then – in my moment of pride – that the disaster that awaited us made its first appearance. We rounded Gibraltar and had reached the coast of Portugal when several members of the crew were taken ill with a mysterious malady. When I wrote about it in my log I was not concerned. In my years as captain I had seen that maladies similar to those of the tropics are commonplace in the Mediterranean.

"As we sailed up the coast of Portugal, the illness passed from the crew and infected several of my officers. Even though no one had succumbed to the illness, I did not think making port was a wise decision. Many ports would be closed to a ship carrying illness and I did not want to lose the winds that carried us home. I consulted with my officers, and we chose to continue on, ever watchful for any changes to the crew or the officers from the ravages of this illness.

"After a week, the illness seemed to have taken its course, but most of the crew were weakened by it. The pilot, a Master Young, had served with me for a great many years, and his judgment I would trust, even now. He knew the routes, the bays, and the coastlines of all our routes. He had been sick, but he said he was well enough, and so I trusted him with the fate of our ship as we headed north from Portugal into the dangerous waters near the Spanish coast.

"Mr. Young was serving with a lieutenant of many years' experience on watch on a night as clear and unclouded as any I have ever seen when I went below to bed. In the late hours I did sense a change in the weather as a storm blew in from the east, as often happens at that time of year. The boat tossed among the waves, but I felt no cause for alarm, until I was awakened by a sound so loud and terrible that I do not want to ever hear the like again.

"There was a crashing noise, accompanied by the sudden halt of all momentum. I was tossed from my bed by the violence of it. The boat shuddered as though a great hand held it from under the waves. I dressed quickly and went on deck and was dismayed by what lay before me. The rain pounded against us as the waves and wind thrust the ship, my ship, against the rocks that lay like great sleeping monsters under the waves. Mr. Young had, through error or depletion of his faculties from his recent illness, failed to alert the officers at the helm of any danger from his charts. It sounds as though I am laying the blame for this wretched circumstance at his feet, but I cannot, I am merely recounting the details of the disaster which befell us. In my report to the admiralty I took all responsibility, as is my right as captain. To my regret, the admiralty has not accepted my report, instead considering me to be blameless."

"Captain Wells' voice trailed off into silence as he stared into the fireplace, his eyes fixed upon a point that seemed farther away than the walls of the fireplace. Lydia glanced at her sister, horrified.

"Father, do you need to rest? Shall we hear the remainder of your story tomorrow when you are better?" Charlotte asked, her voice soft in the silence of the enormous bedchamber.

Captain Wells turned once again to face his daughters. "No, I want to continue to tell you what happened aboard the *Thames*, but it is difficult to speak of. I am no coward, and neither were my men, but the events of that night were terrible, and I wish them on no man.

"We were unable to free the Thames from the rocks; her keel and hull were badly damaged when she struck upon them. The wheel and rudder were of no use, with the wind dashing us against the unseen monoliths beneath the waves. I was powerless to save my men or my ship, and I gave the order that all captains dread, to abandon ship. I knew that many of my men were not able to swim, and abandoning the ship was as sure as signing a death warrant for them, but there was no other choice.

"I remained on board until everyone was gone. I was the captain and I was going to go down with my vessel. I thought of you, and prayed for each of you as the ship was dashed to pieces, and I along with it. I was washed into the cold, stormy water, bleeding and broken."

Lydia had never seen her father so emotional as he was now,

speaking of the demise of his ship and its crew. She wiped away a tear as she thought of that dreadful night when he was forced to make the decision that doomed his crew. She wanted to reach out to him, but he seemed to be steeling himself for her and her sister, so she remained firmly rooted in place on the couch beside her sister, reaching out to Charlotte instead.

With a sigh that sounded as though it rattled his chest, Captain Wells continued. "I shall not recount the details of that night, of the men who didn't last the night, of the crew that drowned. I will carry those sights and sounds with me for the rest of my days. I myself did not expect to survive. I had been thrust into the rocks and pulled down beneath the waves, and I held onto a wooden beam with one arm while other dangled broken at my side. I must have passed out from the shock, grief, and pain. At dawn, a fisherman found me and my second mate, Jones, and pulled us on board. He also saved one other – a young man named Charlie White, who was only fifteen. We were carried back to the fisherman's village on the coast."

"Father, what happened to delay your journey home?" Lydia asked, overcome by curiosity.

"The village was a small place, with only a few families, all living in deplorable conditions. They cared for us as best as they could, but they did not speak English, and my Spanish was rudimentary. Jones and White were not as badly hurt as I was, and they were soon patched up and well. I lingered on, in and out of this world. My wounds were infected, and my bones needed setting. The fisherman and his wife cared for me as best as they could, but they could do no more than bring me water and food, which I could not eat. What was left of my crew decided to seek help.

"They left the village and journeyed to a larger town, where they found a priest who knew some English and was sympathetic. I was brought to his church and cared for by the priest and a local apothecary with some knowledge of medicine. Jones and White feared for my life, as I was in such terrible shape that the priest performed last rites. Yet I lingered in a fevered state, in pain from my broken bones and a breath from death. White and Jones stayed with me until I was well enough to order them to find a way back to England. They reluctantly left on foot, and I stayed behind under the care of the priest, Father Enrique Costello.

"In their absence, I survived. I grew stronger, until I could move with the aid of the priest and using a crutch. When Jones and White returned in the summer, my leg was still infected and lame, but I was no longer in danger of death. They had news to tell me – they had found a way from Spain into France along an old pilgrimage road. If we could get to France we would find English officers in the occupation forces, or so we hoped, as we had no money to buy our passage back to England. We were paupers, but the priest once again proved to be a true man of God. He donated a donkey cart for our use and blessed us on our journey.

"It was many weeks before we were in France. We begged by the side of the road, accepted meals at churches with beggars and occasionally scrounged for fruits and vegetables. I am not proud of how we survived, but we managed to reach France as the weather began to turn colder. In France we were met with either hostility or hospitality, depending on the village. It was difficult traveling as we did but we were able to find our forces in the late autumn and were given a passage home aboard a naval vessel.

"Upon our arrival, I was sent to London to meet with the admiralty. I sent letters to you in Falmouth from France, but of course now I realize that you did not receive them. In London, I did not know what I was to face for the loss of His Majesty's ship and all but two of her crew. I did not send another letter because I didn't want either of you to be concerned. Had I known that you did not receive my other letters from France, I would have written immediately.

"In London, I was not forced to face a tribunal. Instead, I was given the privilege of a standard inquest, which was ruled in my favor despite my protest. It was also at the admiralty that I learned my father was alive. There was an urgent request for my immediate return home as he was considered to be dying, having episodes robbing him of his speech and his ability to move.

"My thoughts were of you two, my darling daughters, but I was compelled to attend to this business with my father. Despite my misgivings about returning to Boscombe Hall, I could not deny a dying man's final wishes. I rushed here and upon my arrival learned that he has suffered several episodes, the last of which has paralyzed him. His secretary, Mr. Finnegan, who penned the letters to both of you, informed me that upon his first episode many months ago, my father reinstated me as his heir, despite his vow to the contrary."

"Father, what of your own health? The letter I received said you were gravely ill, are you not?" asked Lydia.

"Lydia, my dear, I am injured. My leg was broken too severely to be fixed by a simple splint. I shall be lame all the days of my life, but I have suffered an infection in that leg that pains me and does not heal. When I arrived, the infection was inflamed by the cold and damp of the journey. Mr. Finnegan was concerned that I may succumb, but he was mistaken. If the infection does not heal soon, the doctor may have to operate on my leg. That may leave me without the use of it for the rest of my life, but there is no other danger. Mr. Finnegan was being cautious, as you both shall soon become ladies, members of the aristocracy. He was doing as a secretary to an earl might, securing the lord's family at a time of crisis."

Lydia was struggling to take in all her father's words. He was alive, he had survived a terrible wreck, and he was injured. She was thankful he was alive, and for the loss of the crew and ship, she would say prayers. Yet there was more to his story than the tragedy. If she had heard his words correctly, their family was in upheaval. He was also to be Lord Wharncliffe upon the death of the present earl. Trying to grasp the event that led to her rise to the aristocracy, she asked, "Your father disowned you. What led him to change his mind; did he suddenly accept your decision to defy him?"

"When my brother died, my father was determined to run the estate until his own death, and then leave it to the next male relative in the line of inheritance, a distant cousin from Kent. This cousin proved to be as dissolute in his habits as my brother. I have just learned that my brother did a great deal of damage to the finances of the estate under his management, as my father has been in declining health these many years. My father, despite his pride, does not shrink from his responsibility to the lineage of the Wharncliffe title and the people in the villages and farms of the estate. He could not bear to leave it all to a man who would ruin the good name of the Earl of Wharncliffe and the lives of so many. It was with reluctance that he chose to reinstate me as his heir. And it is with the same reluctance that I accept. But with my leg as it is, I cannot sail any longer. And if I am able to save the livelihoods and preserve the way of life for our tenants, I shall come back to Boscombe Hall."

Lydia sat as though she was in a trance, her mind whirling with all that she had learned. Her father was the next Lord Wharncliffe, an earl. She was to be a lady, and so was her sister. When she left Dartmoore, she was but a governess, nearly penniless, and an orphan. How quickly her fortunes had turned, and how quickly she was thrown into the chaos of deciding what to do. Yet, for tonight, she was content to sit by the fireside with her father and her sister in this grand old house. In the morning, she decided, she would try to make sense of everything that had happened. By the dawn, she would be able to think clearly, she hoped, as tonight she was unable to accept any of the events that were unfolding. Her father was alive, and she was soon to Lady Lydia Wells. She could be a governess no more, and to that end, she wondered what she would do about Caption Poole.

———

CHRISTMAS ARRIVED at Boscombe Hall with all the pomp and tradition befitting a great house. The servants decorated the great hall of the residence with greenery festooned with ribbons. A yule log larger than Lydia was brought in on a sleigh and carried to the enormous fireplace to burn during the season. Food for the tenants of the estate was prepared, and set out on long tables in the hall as musicians played carols. This was traditional, but completely new to the Wells girls, who sat at the head table, and greeted people shyly when they were approached.

For the family, Christmas was a quiet time. They had a dinner on the eve of the holiday, then a breakfast and the exchange of pleasantries. In the rush of the sudden departure to Boscombe, there had been little time to be concerned with gifts. There was an exchange of small items, such as a pair of mittens and a matching scarf Lydia had knit for her sister, and Charlotte had saved money to purchase a novel from a bookseller in Falmouth for Lydia. For both girls, Christmas was more about the joy that their family was reunited, shadowed only by a dim sense of trepidation as her grandfather – a man she had just met – lingered on in his diminished state. His body was paralyzed, and his speech greatly impaired. He languished in his chambers as removed from the celebrations of the hall as though he had already passed.

It was during this season that Lydia began to think about all that becoming a titled member of the aristocracy might entail. For Christmas, her father surprised her and her sister with news of their generous dowries, and allowances for clothes befitting their new station in life. They were both to have wardrobes, and lessons in deportment beginning in the new year. It was at her father's announcement of their gifts that Lydia began to really understand that these changes in their lives would have far-reaching consequences.

One evening, as she lingered in the drawing room with Charlotte, Lydia was thinking about these changes and her romance with Captain Poole, and this prompted her to remind her sister of the expectations that now defined their lives.

"Charlotte, have you written to Hugh to tell him of your change in title?" Lydia asked as she set aside the novel, the Christmas present from Charlotte.

"I have written to him, but I am still waiting for an answer. We are on the other side of Cornwall, a day's journey from Falmouth, and yet it seems we might as well be across the world."

"Have you given much thought to how different your life and prospects are, now that you are no longer a teacher at a girls' school? Although, even then, you were above the Burtons in station."

"Lydia, how can you say that? You know that I adore Hugh and he loves me. You gave me your blessing in our father's absence that I should pursue the matter of matrimony with him. You didn't seem to be concerned at that time with the difference in our class when we had very little ourselves," Charlotte declared with a pained expression.

"I don't mean to be callous or unfeeling, but you must listen to me. You're a lady now, or soon will be. You can't marry a fisherman, not when he has shown little inclination towards matrimony when you were nearly penniless. Suppose he suddenly alters his interest in marrying you, suppose he should suddenly find no impediment to your marriage now – would you not doubt his intentions were driven by greed and your much larger dowry?"

Lydia wondered about her own romance with Captain Poole. Would he be an acceptable husband for the eldest daughter of an earl? Would she ever be able to trust his motives, now that she was wealthy? As her thoughts drifted to the romance she'd left behind, she was afraid to know the answer.

Charlotte's irritation with the line of questioning regarding Hugh soon became apparent. "If he did want to marry me, why would that be any reason to question him?" she retorted. "Has he not been the only man I have loved, or will ever love?"

"You can't know that. I hope for your sake he is as honest as his word, as you think him to be, yet I cannot account for his delay in asking you to become his wife. He has had all these many months to ask you for your hand in marriage, but he has left you in a state of uncertainty."

"He is waiting until he can join the crew of a naval ship!" Lydia exclaimed, her face red with anger.

"If only that was true. Charlotte, there is more to your Hugh Burton than even you know. I don't suspect him for any reasons that are base or low, and I do not find myself to be above him because of rank – but I have always doubted his sincerity."

Lydia realized that she had said more than she intended when she saw the stricken look on her sister's beautiful face. Regretting her choice of words, she hoped that Charlotte was not aware of the full scope of meaning in her statement about the man she loved.

"You doubted his sincerity? Since you became the daughter of the next earl of Wharncliffe, or when you were but a girl like myself, living in a garret?"

"Charlotte!"

She and her sister were not prone to rancor. But now Charlotte was truly vexed with her, and she was full or remorse.

"Please, I spoke in haste. I'm tired; it's late. I must be overwrought from all that has transpired since we arrived," Lydia explained, hoping that Charlotte would accept her apology.

Charlotte seemed to soften, and her frown dissipated as she replied, "There has been much that has changed for us in a short time. I did not mean to question you. You have been a true and good sister to me. You have cared for me all our lives. If you are over-wrought, I should do all that I am able to ease your troubles. Hugh Burton is a subject best left for another time when the hour is not so late."

Lydia breathed a sigh of relief that her sister would accept her poor excuse. She hadn't been lying when she'd said she didn't think Hugh was sincere. She knew that there was another woman in Hugh's life, or at the very least one whom his mother had chosen to be in his life. The question was, and had always been, whether Hugh was in love with Charlotte, or Winnie Parker? Could he be married to the other woman already, and Charlotte unaware of the arrangement?

Charlotte returned to her needlework as Lydia picked up the book discarded at her side, staring blankly at the pages. One day, she would have to tell Charlotte about Hugh, especially if he decided when he heard about her new, enormous dowry, that he could not live another day without marrying her. She had wanted to tell Charlotte so many times before this night about Hugh, not to break her sister's heart, but to establish the intentions of the man she loved.

If what she suspected was true, Hugh would want to marry Charlotte as soon as possible, and then Lydia knew she would have no other choice but to tell her sister the truth. The only question was whether Hugh wanted to marry Winnie Parker. If he was innocent of that, she didn't know how well Charlotte and a fisherman would get along with the sudden alteration to Charlotte's circumstances. If Hugh was guilty, then Lydia was in danger of losing her sister's regard and her trust for keeping a secret from her.

Although Captain Poole had no Winnie Parker waiting to become his bride, Lydia wanted to believe that he treated her as he did because of genuine affection. When she told him about her newfound wealth, would he also grow more amorous?

With the thought of Dartmoore, she remembered her promise to the girls, Beth and Sarah, and to the colonel, that she would write as soon as she had news of her father's condition. They would be expecting a letter from her, advising them all of her plans to return to Dartmoore. These were letters that were pressing, weighing heavily on her mind. What was she to say to them all? The children would miss her, and the news would be received as a tragedy if she was not able to return to her small charges.

Lydia tried once again to concentrate on the book but found her mind was distracted by other thoughts. She was concerned about the captain; did that signal a lack of trust or a cynicism borne out of practicality? He had never given her a reason to doubt his intentions, but she had never known what it was like to become attractive for more than her wits. Soon, she found her mind drifting to the colonel.

The colonel was a man of cold temperament, his moods varied and his manner distant. He treated her with respect at times and with disdain at others, yet she could not help but wonder what his reaction would be when she wrote to him that she and her family outranked him? Would he be impressed, or would he fail to register an opinion of the matter, as though she was of little consequence? She was anxious when she considered what he would think, and worried that he would regard the news as he often did her, with little reaction. With a chill, she wondered if that was how he truly felt about her, and found herself wishing that he was not so unmoved.

She decided she would write the letters to Dartmoore in the morning. With her grandfather nearing death and her father's insistence that she and her sister become educated in the etiquette and manners of the upper class, she did not see a way to get back to the position of governess. A governess would not require a new wardrobe, or lessons on how to be the daughter of an earl. In the morning before she wrote, she promised herself she would ask her father about her previous circumstances, but she was confident he would want her to remain at his side, as he did Charlotte. If he was to become an earl, they were to be ladies, and a lady would be terribly out of place teaching the children of the son of a baronet.

CHAPTER TEN

Winter, 1817
Cornwall, England

"STAND perfectly straight as you enter the drawing room at the end of dinner. Walk gracefully; there is no need to make haste. Heads up, movements slow and regal!" the woman demanded as she clapped her hands to a slow, methodical beat.

Lydia felt silly. At her age she was being taught as though she was a child with a governess. But her father insisted that she and her sister learn the proper behavior of young, aristocratic women, instruction they would never have been given at Mrs. Peyton's. The woman he chose for the job was the unmarried daughter of a viscount who was experiencing a financial setback. Miss Caroline Perry was the third daughter of the Viscount Hayworth.

The woman, a tutor in all matters of deportment, was a decade older than Lydia, shorter than her, and plump, yet she had a bearing befitting her station and a pleasant voice – when she was not screeching orders. She was pretty, and wore her auburn hair in a halo of ringlets on either side of her round face. Lydia suspected that the woman was hired not only as a tutor but also as a companion and chaperone. These duties also seemed to be cheerfully accepted by Miss Perry, despite her father the viscount's misfortune. She seemed pleased to be at Boscombe Hall, in a position that did not require the education of young, unruly children, as she occasionally remarked.

On a Monday morning in mid-January, Miss Perry began her instruction, as was becoming the custom of the days at Boscombe Hall. Lydia and Charlotte attempted to do as they were told so as not to earn reprimands. Lydia already found herself prickling under the instruction. It was not due to Miss Perry; on the contrary, Miss Perry was an amiable woman with a serene nature. But Lydia wondered how her father could insist that they change how they behaved in order to be socially acceptable members of the aristocracy. It was this concern that nagged at her as they prepared for their debut and presentation in London in the spring.

It was a mystery to her why her father would insist on such a fundamental change in his daughters' behavior and way of life when he himself had run away from this world to become a naval officer. Why would he not consider allowing them the same independence? She did not mind Miss Perry's presence, but the endless hours of instruction were a source of annoyance to Lydia, who was accustomed doing things her own way and dictating her own schedule. She had not questioned her father's intentions, and she had not mentioned her romance with Captain Poole. In the days following Christmas, she wondered if her sister had brought up her promise to marry Hugh Burton the moment he proposed.

"Lady Lydia, you are not paying attention. Again, enter the room as though you were a queen!" Miss Perry insisted, using Lydia's future title, though her grandfather was still alive and the title of earl did not yet belong to her father.

Lydia concentrated on doing as she was told as she tried to catch her sister's eye. Charlotte was better at being a lady than Lydia was, but that was no surprise. Charlotte was naturally serene and graceful. Manners and a regal bearing seemed to suit Charlotte, who had joked that she would, one day, put her regal bearing to good use as the wife of a sailor. As Lydia practiced sitting, maintaining perfect posture, and holding her head up all at the same time, she found herself thinking about a letter she had received from the captain the previous week.

He congratulated her on the alteration of her rank and her father's good prognosis. He said he missed her. He proclaimed his admiration and esteem for her, as he optimistically insisted that a way could be found to become reacquainted at the earliest possible convenience. It was a charming letter, and a romantic one. It was written conveying everything she longed to read from a man who held her in the highest esteem, but it was not his letter she read and reread, trying to discern the true meaning of the words.

The colonel wrote back to her in a manner suited to his personality. He congratulated her and wished her a long and healthy life, if he was unable to see her again. Yet, he wrote, he sincerely wished that would not be the case, for his daughters missed her terribly. He invited her to come and see them at any time. His letter was brief, but she was drawn again and again to read those few lines, as she tried to discern his feelings. Was he solely concerned with his daughters' feelings? Was he as cold as she considered him to be, unmoved by her departure and her permanent absence?

Lydia's mind was drifting to this subject when once again she was chastised by the ever-observant Miss Perry. "You must pay attention! You are the daughter of the noble house of Wharncliffe, all eyes shall be fixed upon you and little else. If you are shown to be lacking in manners, you will find every door to you in London shut to you."

"Very well, let them be," Lydia grumbled.

Miss Perry stared at Lydia as though she was an unruly child in the midst of a tantrum. "My Lady," the woman began in a tone that implied a mild degree of frustration, "you do not yet understand the importance of manners and deportment in society. You may be the daughter of a plowman, but if you carry yourself well, observe all the rules of decorum, you shall be more welcome than the ill-behaved daughter of a duke."

"A plowman? Surely, you're jesting," Lydia suggested with a derisive snort.

"Am I? The ladies of your class and rank shall have been born to their positions. They have been learning their skills every day since they could hold a teacup. Your father has explained that you have not been raised with those advantages. I do not mean to be impertinent; I am here to assist you."

Lydia felt a twinge of guilt. "I apologize, Miss Perry. This is quite a change from the life I thought was to be mine. I feel overwhelmed this morning. If you do not mind, I shall resume our studies after luncheon."

"Very well," Miss Perry replied as Lydia slipped from the drawing room, leaving her sister in the company of the pleasant tutor.

In the corridor, Lydia breathed a sigh of relief. She'd bought a few minutes of freedom from the daily regimen of the Wharncliffe schedule. Breakfast was served promptly at half-past eight, and instruction with Miss Perry lasted for the hours of the morning. Luncheon was served at noon, or half past if there was an alteration to her father's appointments in the morning. Musical instruction was after lunch and for many hours of the afternoon. Tea was in the late afternoon, and then she was dressed for dinner which was served after sunset, at seven. After dinner, it was off to the drawing room until she retired for the evening. There was little time for walks or reading, or much of anything. Lydia longed for a few hours to be free to write letters and collect her thoughts, but that was not the routine at Boscombe Hall.

The schedule was not the only thing that weighed heavily upon Lydia. There seemed to be a shadow over the house and all the inhabitants, a shadow of darkness and gloom that made people whisper and speak in hushed tones. The shadow was her grandfather, the Earl of Wharncliffe, a once formidable man with a vaunted title. She had gone to his chambers to introduce herself and to visit with him, but she not confident that he knew she was there. He remained immobile in his bed, his eyes either shut or staring, unblinking. His breathing was raspy, and he did not acknowledge the presence of servants or relations. He lingered on, his body and mind ready to seek his eternal rest, but his soul firmly rooted to his life here on Earth. Between this dark specter and the confines of her schedule, she was not adjusting to her new life as well as her sister was.

She hurried down the hall. In the heady burst of freedom, she smiled and thought of going outside to the garden. Standing at the doorway in the great hall, she saw with disappointment that the snow was falling heavily upon the wintry landscape outside, and the wind was biting. Abandoning the idea of taking a walk along the cliffs, which she had been wanting to do since she arrived, she decided instead to take her few minutes of unchaperoned time to explore the library.

She knew the way to the library. It was past the drawing room, the dining room, and the music room on the first floor of the residence. She had had the good fortune to spend an evening in the library when she'd first arrived, but had not found the time to return. A large heavy oak door opened with a satisfying creak when she turned the latch. The library was not cold, as she expected it to be, but warm, with a fire burning in the fireplace and candles lit in sconces along the bookshelves and on tables. The walls were lined with dark wood bookcases that stood three or four times her height, accessible by a ladder positioned at the end of the row on each wall. The room was larger than the dining room and the drawing room, the collection of volumes held within its walls, enormous.

Her gaze was drawn to the myriad books and papers catalogued in an impressive display of knowledge she was hungry to explore, but her attention was captured by the quiet presence of a man seated on a chair beside the fireplace. He was focused solely on the book in his hand, a cup of tea steaming hot but ignored on a table at his side. She recognized the profile of the lanky man; this was Mr. Finnegan, the Earl of Wharncliffe's secretary. Studying him, she quietly assessed the arch of his brow and the line of his jaw as he read, quite oblivious to her presence. She hesitated to interrupt him, so she carefully backed out of the room, disappointed that her own exploration would have to wait. She did not know why she was willing to give up her own use of the room to a member of staff, but somehow she felt that he was in need of the respite more than she, a feeling she could not account for as her hand fell on the latch of the door.

This time the hinges creaked louder than before, emitting a sound that echoed through the room. Wincing, she hastily tried to slip through the opening, but her plans for departure were quickly ended by Mr. Finnegan.

"Lady Lydia," he said as he rose quickly, the book in his hand dropped to the chair.

"Mr. Finnegan, I did not mean to disturb you. Please continue with your reading," Lydia replied.

He picked up the cup of tea and the book as he left his comfortable chair beside the fireplace. His tone was sheepish. "I apologize, I do not mean to sound impudent, but I am not used to sharing this house with anyone but the earl and the staff. I fear that I may have been overindulged in my freedom. This library is now yours, and so is this house. I should not have the run of it as though I was entitled to enjoy its many wonders. If you will forgive me, I shall return to my duties."

Lydia was struck by his humility. "Mr. Finnegan, please sir, you have no cause to apologize. I implore you, don't leave on my account. Please, I insist that you set your tea down and return to your book. It is I who have intruded upon your time, which must be limited. I have only just escaped from my governess and I understand the respite of a few minutes of freedom."

For the first time since she'd met Mr. Finnegan, she watched as a smile spread across his face. "Your governess? If I may be so bold, I thought you were too advanced in age to require the hiring of a governess."

Lydia rolled her eyes. "I thought the same. Apparently, I do not behave as a lady ought, as evidenced by my father's hiring of Miss Perry."

"If I may make an observation, if you were to act properly as a lady, we would not be having this discussion," he replied with the same smile, his gray eyes twinkling.

"No, we wouldn't. Please sit once more; I do not want to deprive you of a few minutes respite."

"No, I really must be going, His Lordship and your father will be in need of me. I take my lunch in here most days, and I have tarried far too long. If you had not arrived I would surely have been late in returning to my work."

"You take lunch at this time? But breakfast has hardly been over for an hour."

"I arise at dawn, and take my breakfast early. My luncheon is also early, as the afternoons are inevitably consumed with correspondence and other such work that I hesitate to discuss, as the details are surely tedious."

"On the contrary, Mr. Finnegan. I long for the details of employment other than lessons in deportment, as I long to once again be permitted to take a walk outside."

"Perhaps that can be arranged, m'lady."

"Perhaps, but you are mistaken in one aspect. I am not a lady yet."

"If I am mistaken, forgive me. The title may not be yours but I consider you to be nothing less than a lady, even if you don't follow all the rules."

Mr. Finnegan nodded to her as he slipped out the door, balancing the book and the teacup in the same hand, an act of coordination that delighted Lydia in a small way.

She was now alone in the library. Thousands of books awaited her perusal, and all she could think of was the secretary – a man who in a few minutes' conversation impressed her with his candor and his disarming charm. She was certain that according to the strict rules of class and decorum, he should not have spoken as he had to her, as though they were equals in rank, but she didn't mind. She'd enjoyed the dialogue with a man who was her equal before her rise, and in her way of thinking, still was. Rankling at the matter of title and class, she wondered if she would always be hampered in forming new acquaintances by her status. Would she be forced to only associate with other aristocrats? Would she be compelled to leave behind those she adored, such as Mrs. Peyton and Captain Poole?

Standing in the library of Boscombe Hall, she decided that the time had come to speak to her father about the subjects she had been reluctant to seek clarification about. The time had come for her to ask the questions she dared to know the answers to. She could not continue to live as she was, with a part of her still the daughter of a sea captain, and the other part becoming the next lady of Boscombe Hall. There was no way for her to find contentment in her new role until she knew the expectations of her new life, unless she heard them from her father's own lips. It was time to have the conversation she'd been dreading, and one she knew was necessary. As she glanced at the leather-bound editions lining the walls, her mind drifted to Captain Poole, the colonel, and suddenly to her surprise, Mr. Finnegan.

———

"Lydia, I have the most wondrous news; I have had a letter from Hugh!" Charlotte announced as they entered the dining room

She made that announcement in front of several footmen, prompting Lydia to remind her that they were not alone. "Charlotte, my dear, lower your voice. We may speak of this later," Lydia replied as she glanced at the footmen in their fine livery, their faces expressionless.

"Oh, I don't care about that. I am so happy I could burst!" Charlotte exclaimed.

Lydia was relieved that the subject of Hugh Burton had come up naturally, as she was apprehensive recalling their last dreadful conversation regarding the fisherman. It was only this morning that she had decided that she needed to discover the expectations of her position with her father. His schedule for the day was as daunting as her own, with only dinner and the hours remaining afterward free to discuss important matters with his daughters. With the arrival of a letter from Hugh, Lydia was glad that they would now be able to broach the matter of marriage with their father.

Their father was not in the dining room; he sometimes took meals in his room, depending upon the state of his injured leg. Lydia made her way to the long table with only two place settings. The candles were lit in tall, silver candelabras along the entire length of the table, and the room was lined with footmen waiting to serve the two young women who were the only attendants of the formal meal. It seemed to Lydia like a waste of time and money to provide her and her sister with full courses when a bowl of stew and a piece of bread would do.

"I must tell you what he said. It is too exciting for me to wait until we are alone," Charlotte gushed quietly as they sat down at the table. The footmen mobilized into action, pouring wine and serving the first course.

Sighing, Lydia realized that being alone in a great house such as Boscombe Hall was nearly impossible. Even in the bedchambers or the recesses of a closed study, maids and footmen were always present, going about their duties. It was a part of this life she would have to become accustomed to. She lowered her voice. "What news, then? If you cannot wait, I know it must be important."

Beaming, Charlotte spoke in a rapid succession of words. "Do you recall that conversation we had one evening in the drawing room at Christmas? You told me that Hugh would ask for my hand in marriage? You were right, how could you have known? He has proposed! After so many months of waiting, the joyous day has arrived. He has asked me to be his wife!"

Clearly, Charlotte was choosing to interpret Lydia's prophecy of a marriage proposal as an optimistic wish for the future, and not the warning that it had been. And now it was coming to pass. Hugh, who had long kept Charlotte waiting for a proposal without much hope, had proposed after learning that her prospects were greatly improved. It was terrible that he was living up to Lydia's worst opinion of him.

"Lydia, are you not happy for me? Do you not share my joy? He has finally asked for my hand! It is everything I ever dreamed of, and it has arrived. Are you not glad?" Charlotte asked, her eyes searching her sister's face.

If Lydia was truthful, she had to admit that she was stunned Hugh was behaving this way. Why had he not proposed before Charlotte sent him a letter announcing her rise in rank and wealth? Why had he not asked for her hand before now? Sighing, Lydia tried to think of the words to say that would cause the least amount of pain. She was no longer able to conceal all that she knew about Hugh; the time had come to speak her mind. As she gazed at her younger sister's face, so hopeful in her happiness, she thought of her father. Perhaps he could put a stop to this marriage until she was able to ascertain Hugh's true intentions, a task that was long overdue.

"Charlotte, I'm happy that the man you love has proposed, although I question his intentions. Yet, this is not a matter for me to decide or comment on until we speak to Father after dinner. Let's discuss this with him, and then we may know how to proceed."

"Oh, I hadn't thought of that. I haven't told Father about Hugh. Have you spoken to him about Captain Poole?" Charlotte asked as the second course was set in place by the footmen.

Lydia replied, "I have not spoken to him yet, but the arrival of this letter may be the best time for both of us to ask him about our future prospects."

Charlotte seemed content with that answer, and she continued to talk of Hugh Burton throughout dinner in the warm, flowery tones befitting a woman in love. There could be no question in Lydia's mind that her sister was besotted by the man, a man who was handsome, smart, and ill-suited to remain a fisherman the remainder of his days. After the dessert was served, Lydia's own apprehension grew as she stood up from her seat at the dining table and walked with her sister up the grand staircase to their father's room.

Mr. Finnegan was walking down the hall, his hands full of papers. As he nodded to them, Lydia thought she detected a hint of smile, but she was too consumed by what lay ahead of her to dwell upon that detail at the present. A knock on the door announced their arrival, and their father greeted them warmly.

"How are your studies with Miss Perry?" he inquired as they settled into their customary places on the couch, across from him by the fireplace.

Charlotte answered, "Very well. My playing has greatly improved since she has arrived. Perhaps I can play for you one evening?"

"Certainly. And what of you, my dear? Do you find her instruction to be useful?" he asked, directing his question to Lydia.

"I do; she is well informed in her subject and her instruction has been valuable," Lydia replied.

Captain Wells regarded his eldest daughter thoughtfully. "Although I fear you have not been given the proper amount of time to devote to taking in the air and your independent studies. I shall speak with Miss Perry regarding an adjustment to your schedule, if you would find that agreeable?"

Lydia smiled. "Yes, very agreeable. I have missed taking the air since my arrival. I fear my health may suffer for it." *Or my sanity*, she added silently.

Fleetingly, she realized that Mr. Finnegan must have mentioned her concerns to her father. She would offer him her heartfelt thanks upon their next meeting, she decided, as Charlotte cleared her throat, her voice trembling as she began speaking to their father.

"Father, Lydia and I were just talking about something very important at dinner. You see, I have a letter from a man I knew in Falmouth," Charlotte stated, her voice strained.

"There, there, Charlotte. There is no need to be anxious. You may always speak to me about any gentleman of your acquaintance, provided they have good character and are worthy of you. Now, take a moment, gather your strength, and tell me about this man you know from Falmouth."

Lydia watched her sister collect herself and with a look of expectation, began speaking, "Father, you have yet to meet him. His name is Hugh Burton. He wants to become a naval officer and he has proposed to me."

It was done; Charlotte had told her father. Now Lydia watched, waiting for his reaction. Turning towards him, she watched his expression change from a warm look of love to cold stone as he asked, "This man, when did you receive this proposal?"

"The letter came today, in the afternoon post."

"I see," Captain Wells replied. "What is his present profession?"

"He is a fisherman, the same as his father. They are such good people."

"A fisherman? A literate, presumptuous fisherman has proposed to you, the daughter of the next Earl of Wharncliffe?"

"Yes, you see, I met him in Falmouth over a year ago." Charlotte explained, her smile unwavering.

Captain Wells, continued, "Did he offer his hand at that time? Did he ask you to promise yourself to him?"

"No, he wanted to become an officer in the navy before he proposed."

"Yet, he has changed his mind now. *Is* he an officer?" asked Captain Wells. The room seemed to drop several degrees with the tension.

"No, he is not an officer...he has yet to apply for a commission as he has not the money or the references," Charlotte explained in a voice that was barely a whisper.

"Surely, something must have changed to give him the impression he may ask for your hand? Could it be your sudden ascension to nobility?" Their father asked, mirroring Lydia's sentiment.

"No, Father. He loves me, he has spoken of his feelings for me on many occasions!" Charlotte replied, her eyes welling up with tears.

"He loves you, but he thought no better of proposing to you until you had something to offer him," snorted Captain Wells. "A fisherman hopes to wed my daughter, a lady? I forbid it. You will forget this foolishness. You are to journey to London before Easter. There, you may meet a gentleman who is more suited for your station. Until then, I forbid you from having anything else to do with this fortune hunter."

Charlotte was silently weeping, her face wet with tears as she looked stricken. Without saying a word, she leapt from her seat and ran from the room, the door slamming loudly behind her. Lydia had never heard harsh words from her father before now. In the past, his visits were pleasant and short, yet this evening he was authoritarian in his orders, his demeanor cold and distant. As she stared at her father, she hesitated to mention her own romance with Captain Poole.

Perhaps, she decided, it was best not to ask any questions about her prospects tonight. From the response poor Charlotte received, Lydia was certain she had the answer she was searching for about her own future. They were journeying to London, and her father expected her and her sister to marry gentlemen. Captain Poole, she feared, would not meet that criteria, and neither would Mr. Finnegan. Sighing, she quickly realized that more than her own schedule had changed. Her independence and freedom to make her own decisions were rescinded from the moment she had stepped into Boscombe Hall.

CHAPTER ELEVEN

Early Spring, 1817
Cornwall, England

THE SNOWS of winter were gone but the air was still chilly high upon the cliffs overlooking the ocean on the grounds of Tintagel Castle. Lydia shivered despite the warm, fur-lined muff and hat she wore, which matched the pelisse she'd chosen for this outing. Inside the warmth of her room at Boscombe Hall, the outfit had seemed sensible. Outside on the windswept plain of Tintagel, she felt underdressed. The cold wind whipped around her ankles despite the length of the carriage dress, and her cheeks were nearly numb from the frigid wind. The air was damp and certain to cause illness, but she didn't care. She was free for the afternoon, and away from the strict regime of Boscombe Hall.

The waves crashed on the rocks far below. The view was breathtaking from here, near the ruins of the castle. It was a view she wished to enjoy for many hours before climbing back into the safety of the carriage to return home. The smell of salt carried on the air; she closed her eyes and drew a long breath. How strong the sea sounded as it pounded against the shore. From somewhere in the distance she heard the call of a gull, and from beside her, the voice of a man she had come to regard as a trusted acquaintance. The man who had invited her to come on this outing.

"Lady Lydia, I do not mean to disturb you, but we should tour the castle before the hour grows much later," the tall, serious man said.

"Mr. Finnegan, you don't have to call me Lady Lydia. Not when we're alone," Lydia replied, opening her eyes..

"That is your title, since your grandfather His Lordship passed," her companion explained.

"I know it is, but I was not born to this world of titles, ranks, and nobility. I am still the simple girl from Falmouth, the one who served as a governess," Lydia said, staring at the ocean. "That is who I am, and who I will always be. As a governess, I am your equal."

Turning back to her companion, she caught the rarest of events as Mr. Finnegan smiled.

"That may have been the ways of things before, but we must accept the way of things now. Society will not view us as equals, and neither should we. I have known you as the eldest daughter of His Lordship, and that is how I must treat you."

"Not when we're alone. I command you to call me Miss Wells, or Lydia, which I prefer. I shall call you Mr. Finnegan, or as I prefer, James."

"M'lady, at the risk of seeming impertinent, I cannot permit myself to observe such a breach of decorum. I would prefer to be Mr. Finnegan, and you shall remain Lady Lydia. Now, if you accompany me, I would be honored to show you the ruins of the castle."

To say Lydia was disappointed would be understating how she felt. Turning away from the ocean, she replied, "It is unfortunate that you feel as you do. I apologize for the embarrassment I have caused, and I humbly ask for your forgiveness. I misunderstood your kindness to mean...well, I was rather hoping that we may be considered friends. Among ourselves, at least."

Mr. Finnegan was quick to answer. "I did not intend to cause you any discomfort. You honor me with the high regard which you place upon our acquaintance, but I am a secretary to your father, and that is all I am."

"I will not hide my disappointment, even though I know Miss Perry would scold me. She would tell me that I should conceal my feelings behind a veneer of grace and poise at all times, but I am not the lady she believes me to be. I am a girl from Falmouth who is accustomed to speaking her mind and hiding nothing. I assumed from the arrangement of this outing that you must have regard for me that goes beyond the feelings of a servant for his mistress, or a secretary for his lord. I see I was mistaken," she said, and walked past him.

Mr. Finnegan was silent as they walked towards the rambling stones and crumbling ramparts of the castle. The roof of this once-imposing structure gone had long ago, and the walls fell apart over the years of storms and neglect. The large blocks had fallen down onto the ground, and lay in piles of gray stone. The doorways remained, leading from one enormous space to another. Inside the ruins, the wind did not chill Lydia as much, but now she was cooled by a different feeling, a feeling of profound sadness.

Breaking the silence, Mr. Finnegan spoke quietly in a long narrow room that suggested the remains of an ancient hall or chapel. "M'lady, I did not mean to offend you or upset you. I was merely stating that we must observe decorum in private as well, if we are to observe it as expected in the presence of others. I did arrange this trip for you because I share your interest in history and adventure. Perhaps you do not know the legend of Tintagel Castle?"

Lydia's feelings were still wounded, but she could not argue with his reasoning. If he wished for more than a relationship based on rank and position, then he would have to be the one to speak of it. Lydia resigned herself to never again suggest a familiar understanding between them. His rebuff was the only answer she required to show her that she had only imagined that he felt more for her than just regard.

Returning to her role as Lady Lydia Wells, she answered, "No, Mr. Finnegan, I am not familiar with the legend. If you would be so kind as to share it with me."

With a gleam in his eye, he explained. "Tintagel Castle is thought by the residents of this part of Cornwall to have been the seat of power for King Arthur. This very castle is also considered by many scholars to be none other than the court of Camelot. If that is true, then we are standing where Arthur himself may have stood. This room, all that is left of the hall, may have held the round table, and his knights may have assembled here – in this very place – centuries ago."

Lydia was familiar with the legend of King Arthur, who had long been a hero of hers. The tragedy of his ill-fated marriage, the quest for the grail, the knights and their chivalrous deeds all swirled in her mind as she reached out to touch the rough stone of the walls with her gloved hand. The sense of wonder she felt almost made her forget about her repudiation at the hands of Mr. Finnegan. Almost.

"What is your opinion, Mr. Finnegan? What does a gentleman such as yourself believe about these local legends and stories? Are they true? Do you accept that there was a King Arthur who shall return from the island of Avalon one day?"

"I cannot say what is and is not true. I was raised in County Meath, in Ireland. In my childhood, I was acquainted with tales of heroes and kings, all of them true – or so I was led to believe. I traveled to the hill of Tara, the fabled hill of kings, to determine whether I came from noble blood, if I could be king of all Ireland."

"What did you discover, are you noble born?"

"Sadly, m'lady, I learned that I am James Finnegan, and that is all."

"I didn't realize you were from Ireland," she said, as she thought about the lilt in his manner of speaking, and his accent, which was not heavy to her ears like the Cornish brogue.

"I am from Ireland, but I am more English than Irish. My father was headmaster at a school for boys, and my mother's family owned land in Meath. I left Ireland to attend school in Birmingham when I was a young man. I have lived in England ever since."

"Do you miss your home? Are you able to return to Ireland often?"

Mr. Finnegan spoke quietly, with a faraway look in his eye. "I return when I can, although it is never often enough for my liking. I take comfort in the countryside of Cornwall, because it reminds me of the wild green hills of home."

"It's interesting that you have remained in England."

"Is it? My father is English, so therefore I suppose I am. England is as much my home as Ireland in that respect. My father wanted to me to return home to assume duties as the next headmaster, but I am not content to leave my post in His Lordship's employ. As much as I miss the beauty of my home, I have grown attached to the peace and solitude of Boscombe Hall."

They walked from the large empty space that once was the hall into the ruins of the other parts of the castle. Mr. Finnegan did not elaborate about Ireland, his family, or much else. Lydia wondered if perhaps he was aware, as she was, that he had already shared a great deal with her. He had disclosed more than a staff member ordinarily would have shared with the eldest daughter of an employer. Walking in silence, she did not press the matter further, but she enjoyed the companionship, the thrill of exploring the ruins and the breathtaking view of the ocean that was only rivaled by the view from Boscombe Hall.

Why would he share such personal details of his boyhood if he did not regard her as more than his lady? Mr. Finnegan was proving as difficult to read as a book written in an unknown language. Her feelings, like Mr. Finnegan, were confusing. Glancing at him as they strolled through what remained of the castle, she reaffirmed her belief that if he had any inclination towards her of more than a secretarial nature, he should be the one to say so. She would not make that mistake again.

The wind whistled through the cracks in the outer wall of the ruins as Mr. Finnegan urged Lydia to return to the carriage. She had enjoyed the tour, but she was frozen. Climbing into the warmth of the waiting carriage, she looked back at Tintagel Castle and the ocean beyond it. This place was not far from Boscombe Hall. She quietly made a promise to herself to return in better weather.

———

LYDIA RETURNED to Boscombe Hall to find Charlotte concluding her musical instruction with Miss Perry. Charlotte was thin and frail these days, and her mood had been erratic since she received her father's ultimatum that she cease all communication with Hugh Burton. Lydia knew that Hugh Burton was not gone from her sister's thoughts, or her life. As she strode upstairs, she thought of her own confused state. Captain Poole wrote to her, but without the sense of urgency in his letters that had once dominated his writing. She suspected that he was now content to remain friends, that his ardor may have cooled. Either way, she was no longer sure what she felt.

She'd once dreamed, rather girlishly, that perhaps she could become Mrs. Poole. That dream was impossible now, with the distance and her father's insistence that she and her sister find husbands in their current social class. She could not foresee a way to pursue marriage, even if Captain Poole insisted, which she wished he would. It was heartbreaking that a change in geography and rank could alter the man's feelings for her. Was the experience of their former happiness only perceived as romantic by her? When she was alone she was in the habit of reading his letters. She was certain, or perhaps *almost* certain that she was not imagining that once, when she first arrived at Boscombe Hall, he had been in love with her.

In the quiet of her room, she removed her bonnet and sat beside the fire, slipping her gloves off as a maid brought a pot of tea and a plate of cakes from the kitchen. The tea was especially good on a chilly day, as was the fire. She was nearly comfortable again when a sudden intrusion into her room disrupted her thoughts. Her sister arrived in a rush, nearly knocking over the maid as she marched into the room, throwing herself onto the couch across from Lydia.

With a curtsey, the maid left as Charlotte began lamenting her current situation. "Lydia, I cannot go on, not anymore, I tell you. If I am not allowed to marry Hugh I shall perish!"

Lydia rolled her eyes, although not where Charlotte could see. Hugh Burton was not a topic that would ever go away on its own. Charlotte was frustrated by the actions of their father, the former Captain Wells, who upon the passing of their grandfather during the winter, became His Lordship the Earl of Wharncliffe. At the time, Lydia considered his pronouncement forbidding Charlotte from marrying a common fisherman to be draconian. Now, she thought of the secret she was still harboring about Hugh Burton and wondered if her father was not right to deny her sister the association.

As she watched her sister crying about her lost love, she fought with herself about whether she should tell Charlotte the truth or not. She had hoped that with time and distance Charlotte would forget her feelings for Hugh, but with each passing day that seemed more unlikely. She wondered if she should give up the secret she had been hiding since she left Falmouth.

"Charlotte, my dear, I wish you would reconsider your feelings for Hugh. I know you love him, that you have convinced yourself that there can never be another man to rival him. But—"

"I do love him, Lydia. We were meant to be together."

Lydia set the teacup down on its delicate saucer as she tried to think of any other way to help her sister overcome her attachment for a man she would never be allowed to marry. Aside from the unfortunate piece of information that Lydia had kept secret, she liked Hugh. He was handsome, brave, and a skilled sailor. When she thought about telling her sister about his betrothal to another woman, it felt like she was betraying not only her sister, but Hugh as well. This was not a feeling that Lydia relished but one she thought maybe necessary if her sister was ever to be happy.

Fighting the urge to tell her sister everything she suspected about Hugh, she tried to change the subject. "Tell me, have you heard from Hugh? I know you are forbidden to write to him."

"He has written. He wishes, as I do, that we could find a way to be wed. I have wished that every day since I first met him."

"I don't see how you will ever convince Father to change his mind. You are Lady Charlotte of Boscombe Hall, and not just Charlotte Wells any longer."

"I shall always be Charlotte Wells and nothing more. I don't care what anyone says."

"You *should* care. You are what a lady should be, beautiful, graceful, and far more accomplished than I will ever be in music."

"What does that matter if I am not allowed to choose for myself how I shall live my life? What is the reason for my study of music or much else, if my life shall be planned for me? When we had nothing but ourselves to depend on, were we not happier?" Charlotte asked with a frown.

"Happier? I suppose we were, but we were poor. We no longer have to concern ourselves with employment, or much else, these days," Lydia replied.

Charlotte answered wistfully. "How I miss those days when we lived in the garret at Mrs. Peyton's. We had so little money, but we were content. I had Hugh and that was enough."

"Hugh," repeated Lydia as she stared into the fire.

"Yes, Hugh. I would trade this great house and all of my fancy clothes for a life with him."

"Would you? Even when we lived in Falmouth, your life was never going to be one of ease and contentment with Hugh. You would have lived as the poor wife of a fisherman, barely able to afford the niceties you had in your time as teacher at Mrs. Peyton's."

"Niceties? I do not care for such things. If I have love in my life, what need do I have for much else?" Charlotte asked with a sigh.

Lydia could see there was simply no way of breaking the spell that her sister was under. Charlotte was in love with Hugh Burton. She would continue to love him when they went to London, and for how much longer after that? There was nothing to be done but to try to break the spell before Hugh Burton did it himself. How much longer would he wait for Lady Charlotte, if Lady Charlotte would be penniless? Would he withdraw his proposal after Charlotte had sunk into ruin or been disowned?

Lydia could find no other way to justify waiting to tell her sister about Hugh. Vowing never to regret her decision, she looked at Charlotte. She studied her sister's pale, delicate, face and decided that she must be told the truth.

"Charlotte, did it not seem the slightest bit strange to you that Hugh was content to have you wait until he joined the navy before he asked you to marry him?"

"No, that seemed rather sensible. He wanted to be in a better position to marry than just a fisherman."

"Did you not think to question his insistence that you wait for him to find the resources and the references to become an officer – an event that in all likelihood would never have taken place? Did that not strike you as a method used to sustain your affection for him with no true promise that anything should ever come of it? How many times did you long to be his bride with no concrete indication that would ever ask for your hand – until you became rich?"

Charlotte narrowed her eyes at her sister. "Why would I question his word? He never gave me cause to question him or anything he said. He loves me."

Lydia cringed. She hated the thought of telling Charlotte anything unpleasant. But if she didn't tell her sister the truth, Charlotte would be unhappy indefinitely.

Deciding on a course of action, she continued. "He wanted you to wait for him to alter his life, a noble idea, but one that was quite impossible. Yet, he proposed to you the moment your fortunes were altered. Has that not struck you as strange?"

"Why should it be strange? My absence was more than he could bear. He told me so in his letters. You've read them; does he not say so?"

"Yes, my dear sister, he does. But I wonder now if he was at liberty to propose to you at all."

The quiet settled between them as Charlotte stared at Lydia, her face stony.

"Lydia, I do not understand you, not at all. What are you implying? I wish you would just tell me."

"Very well. What do you know about Winnie Parker? The young woman who was friends with Hugh's sister, whose mother was his mother's closest friend? Are you well acquainted with her and her family?"

"Winnie Parker? Heavens, no! Why would I be acquainted with her? I have no reason to be."

"Perhaps it would be better if you were."

"Lydia! Stop this intolerable discussion at once. You are not making sense, not at all. I am unable to understand you, please tell me what it is you wish to say to me."

Lydia looked at her sister. Her voice, like her gaze, was unwavering. "Charlotte, think of while we were at the Burton's, the day of our visit. You remember the day of the terrible storm? I sat with Hugh's mother while you strolled outside with him. She told me that he was engaged to be married to Winnie Parker, and had been for some time."

"Winnie Parker?" Charlotte said as she shook her head slowly. "That can't be."

"I'm afraid it is true. Mrs. Burton told me, I heard her quite clearly."

"You must be mistaken," Charlotte replied.

"No, I'm not. I wish that I were. I have often wondered if he kept you waiting for him because he was promised to her. A promise that he may not have been able to escape. He may be wed to her already."

Charlotte cried out indignantly, "That can't be, he can't be wed to her, he just can't!"

"Charlotte, before you left Falmouth, were you in the habit of going to see him in the village? Or did he come to see you?"

"He came to see me, of course. It was impractical for me to go to the village. It was far easier to meet in Falmouth."

Lydia tried to temper her words, to soothe her sister. "Then, if you don't mind me saying this, you have no way of knowing what his circumstances may have been at his home in the village. I cannot tell you he is married, or that he's deceived you, but I know what his mother told me. I also know that he showed not the slightest intention of marrying you until you became wealthy. I wish I was wrong about him, but he does not seem to be the man we both mistook him to be."

Charlotte was standing in an instant. Accusingly, she said, "You're wrong. I know who he is! Hugh loves me, he wants to marry me, and I believe him. I don't care if it was after I became a lady that he asked for my hand, or that he was engaged to Winnie Parker! The only thing that matters is that he loves me!"

Lydia had known her sister would be angry, but still she recoiled from her frail sister's ire. "I did not intend to hurt you; I was trying to help you forget about him. Please, Charlotte, we have never been at odds with each other. Say you are not angry with me!" Lydia pleaded.

"Of course I am angry. I am vexed with you in the utmost. What is this rot that you have told me? Did our father put you up to this trickery? Is that what this is? An attempt to discredit the man I love? Well, you are both wrong. Nothing you or anyone can say can ever make me stop loving Hugh!"

"Charlotte, please listen to me! I do not wish to discredit him, but I am concerned that his intentions are not as you imagine them to be. I am your older sister, and I have cared for you all our lives. That is my only concern, my care for you."

Tears ran down Charlotte's face. "If you truly cared for me, you would help me convince Father to grant his permission that I may marry Hugh. I can see that you have no intention of doing anything but trying to ruin my only chance at happiness!"

Lydia was stunned, speechless. She'd anticipated that her sister would be angry and hurt, but she did not anticipate that Charlotte would hold her responsible for the situation, or suggest that she was trying to destroy her happiness. It was a ridiculous notion, when Charlotte's happiness was all that Lydia ever sought. Before she could defend herself against her sister's baseless accusations Charlotte left the room, her cries echoing through the corridor as Lydia brushed away a tear. She had told her sister the truth, knowing it was a truth her sister did not want to hear. As she turned back to the fire, she prayed that Charlotte would forgive her, one day.

CHAPTER TWELVE

Spring, 1817
Plymouth, England

THE ROAD from Plymouth was as Lydia remembered it. The town below was just as idyllic, and the ships docked at port were just as mesmerizing as they ever were. After the quiet of Boscombe hall, Lydia longed for the traffic and activity of the ports, the markets with their merchants and customers, and the sailors strolling the streets dressed in the uniforms of the Royal Navy. In Plymouth she could recall when she was younger, with far more on her mind than the perfect ballgown or which fork to use for her fish course. Leaning back in the carriage, she thought of Dartmoore Park and how much she longed to see her former charges Elizabeth and Sarah.

She'd been very surprised to get a letter from the colonel, inviting her to Dartmoore for Elizabeth's birthday celebration. Since her arrival at Boscombe she had received several sweet letters from the daughters of Colonel Hartford, each letter breaking her heart once more with the childish wishes that she return to be their governess again. The heartbreak from missing these darling girls was nearly as painful to endure as the one she suffered at the hands of Captain Poole. She wondered if she would see him again, and if so, would he be as distant as his letters had become.

She had thought the whole of Dartmoore would be moving on now, and forgetting her, hence the shock she'd felt upon receiving the invitation to go there. She was to be a guest of the colonel, an unusual request that her father was obliged to permit. He was acquainted with the record of Colonel Hartford, who was well regarded among the ranks of officers of the navy and the army. Although Lydia was scheduled to leave for London in a fortnight, her father generously allowed her a sennight away from Boscombe Hall, an indulgence which proved to offer some respite from the rift that had formed between herself and Charlotte.

Lydia was surprised to be allowed to journey alone with only a maid for a companion, an indulgence she suspected was only granted because of the proximity of Dartmoore to Boscombe Hall. The maid, a shy woman named Nola, was hardly an adequate chaperone, but Lydia did not object. She would prefer to have no chaperone at all, but a quiet one who was barely noticeable was not a terrible burden upon her freedom.

Traveling over the tree-lined drive leading to Dartmoore Park, Lydia thought about the word *freedom*. She used to have freedom to do what she wished when she wished it, but those days were no more. Of course, she did have to admit that having the liberty to work as a governess, to do as she pleased when she chose, was greatly curtailed by a lack of funds and a constant concern for her sister's and her own welfare. As a lady, she was wealthy, far richer than she could ever have imagined, but with that wealth came enormous expectations. She was no longer free to do as she pleased, or even speak to whom she chose. As an aristocrat, she was mindful of class, rank, and title in a way that never had any meaning to her when she was a teacher or a governess.

This world of privilege was such a strange one that she feared she may never grow accustomed to it. So far it seemed to her that it was a lonely world, at least at Boscombe Hall, far away from other people who were of her social class – the only people she would be permitted to know as equals. The carriage, with its crest emblazoned on the side, the team of four matching horses, a driver, and a maid were in service to her for the length of her stay at Dartmoore Park, a change from the way she had arrived when she was a governess.

As the carriage neared the rambling edifice, she remembered how her heart had beat wildly the first time she saw it. Her heart beat quickly within her chest now, but the cause was different. She wondered how Captain Poole would receive her, and how the colonel would treat her. Would he be dismissive, as he once was to a governess? Would the housekeeper, Mrs. Tumbridge, and the colonel's daughters have to curtsey and call her *my lady*?

The weather was warm and bright as Lydia stepped down from the carriage. The sun shone on the house, giving Dartmoore a welcoming glow, as though Lydia was visiting an old friend. The servants stood on either side of the door, a change that her status necessitated. The colonel himself stood with his daughters, his expression as stern as ever. The girls were barely able to contain their joy.

Mindful that she was not permitted to run towards the little girls and scoop them up as she wished, Lydia walked – regally, as Ms. Perry would have said – to the colonel. A slight raise of his eyebrow, accompanied by a bow, reminded her that things had changed.

"Lady Lydia Wells, it is an honor to welcome you to Dartmoore Park," the colonel said, without a hint of a smile.

"The honor is mine, Colonel Hartford. I am pleased that you invited me."

"My daughters are delighted that you have arrived safely from Boscombe Hall."

Elizabeth and Sarah curtseyed and smiled, unable to remain still. A young, plain woman standing on the steps beside Mrs. Tumbridge nodded her head. The new governess, Lydia surmised. Tears threatened to well up in her eyes as she remembered her time spent as governess at Dartmoore, her camaraderie with the housekeeper, the love of the children, and the companionship of Captain Poole. Captain Poole was not there to greet her, and she wondered where he could be as Mrs. Tumbridge showed her to a luxurious guest bedroom and sitting room located in the opposite part of the house from where her room once was.

The footman brought her trunk to her room, and Nola began to unpack it at once. Mrs. Tumbridge stared at Lydia and shook her head slightly.

"My lady, it is a surprise to welcome you back to Dartmoore as a lady, if I may say so," the housekeeper replied.

"It is as much a surprise to me as I am sure it is to you. I did not expect the colonel to send an invitation to Boscombe Hall."

"Miss Elizabeth was beside herself with grief when you left, and so was Miss Sarah. It tore my heart to pieces to see those girls missing you so badly."

"My dear Mrs. Tumbridge, why did you not write to tell me of their grief? If I had known it was so terrible I would surely have found a way to come and see them before now."

"I know you would have, but who was I to make invitations on behalf of the colonel? You know how he can be if his orders are not followed. The young misses were terribly sad you were gone, but Miss Powers has done much to help them. She is the new governess. She is not as pretty as you, and she keeps to herself more than you did, but the young misses are taken with her."

Lydia smiled as she replied, "How well I remember the colonel and his way of ordering us all about. He was always one for the strict rules and regulations of his army days. I daresay he would find an ally in my father, the sea captain! He orders me and my sister around as though we were crewman on his ship!"

"He may order you about, but you're pleased to have him alive and well, my lady."

"Mrs. Tumbridge, how right you are. How I've missed you! How is everyone? The girls, the colonel, Captain Poole?"

"We are well enough, I suppose. If there is anything you need, I shall do all that I can to see that you have it."

"Mrs. Tumbridge, I greatly appreciate that, but you haven't told me how everyone is faring. Colonel Hartford seems well and so do Elizabeth and Sarah. What of Captain Poole? I did not see him when I arrived."

"Was he not there? I didn't notice," Mrs. Tumbridge replied as she fussed with the placement of a pillow on the enormous bed.

"Mrs. Tumbridge, you forget yourself. I know you. You oversee every detail of this house with such attention that it would prove impossible for anyone to do anything under its roof without your knowledge."

"My lady, you flatter me with your praise."

"It's not flattery if it's true. Where is Captain Poole? I sent him a letter regarding my visit to Dartmoore."

Mrs. Tumbridge did not answer. Lydia could see that the conversation was making her uncomfortable. Mrs. Tumbridge would not meet her eye, and it was obvious that the housekeeper did not wish to say a word about the man.

"Mrs. Tumbridge, I do not wish to intrude or embarrass you in any way. I just wish to know what has become of Captain Poole. If you have no wish to tell me, I shall not trouble you. As you may recall, he and I were acquaintances during the brief time I was governess at this house. As a woman, you must understand why I'm insistent in my questions."

"I do understand, and that is why I have no wish to tell you anything you may find unpleasant. You are a lady now, but I still see you as Miss Wells, our own dear governess. It is because of my loyalty to you that I dare not say a word about Captain Poole."

Lydia searched her old friend's face. "Is he well? He has not written that he is ill or that any calamity has befallen him."

"He is well enough. There is no illness or injury that has befallen him, but you may not find him to be the gentleman you remember. That is all I can say about the subject. If you will forgive me, I must see to the preparations for dinner. It is not every day that we entertain the daughter of an earl here at Dartmoore."

"Very well, Mrs. Tumbridge. I shall not trouble you about it anymore. You have always been good to me. I know you have much work to do. Perhaps we can have tea while I am here?"

"Perhaps, although I do not need to remind my lady that it would hardly be fitting."

"No, it would not, but I would welcome it. We shall not tell a soul."

"As you wish, my lady," Mrs. Tumbridge replied.

Nola was going about the business of unpacking the trunk as Lydia decided that, since she was a guest at Dartmoore and a lady, there was no reason she should remain hidden away in her room. There was the garden, the library, and the school room, which beckoned to Lydia. It troubled her that she could not discover why Captain Poole was absent from welcoming her to Dartmoore. Perhaps she could stave off her curiosity about his whereabouts by visiting the children.

————

WALKING through the halls of Dartmoore, she remembered the way she had once looked at the house in awe. The gallery with its oil paintings and ornate furnishings did not seem as intimidating as it once had. She had become too accustomed to the wonders of Boscombe Hall, a house even more luxurious and magnificent than Dartmoore. It seemed strange that she should view anything about Dartmoore as though it was commonplace.

In the corridor outside the school room, she hesitated before knocking on the door. She knew that the governess was inside, busily instructing the daughters of Colonel Hartford. She may not welcome an intrusion into the schedule by a stranger. Yet, Lydia reasoned, she was not a stranger, not to the children and their father. Raising her hand to the door, she knocked before opening it.

The governess was, as Lydia had noticed earlier, a plain young woman dressed conservatively, her hair pulled back in an unflattering style, her face gaunt. She was neither plump nor thin, and her hair was a nondescript shade of brown, but she did not seem to be an unpleasant person. Elizabeth and Sarah forgot to curtsey and address Lydia by her title as they jumped from their desks to greet her. It was a slight that Lydia scarcely noticed, but Miss Powers was quick to point out.

"Elizabeth, Sarah, we have a lady in our midst. What do we do to greet her?" the governess reminded her charges.

Elizabeth stepped back and quickly performed a curtsey as she said, "I'm sorry, Lady Wells."

Sarah remained where she was, her arms wrapped around Lydia's legs.

"It is no matter. We are old friends, so there is no need for formality amongst us," Lydia said in a cheerful voice.

The plain woman answered, "Yes my lady. It is an honor to have you in our school room."

"The honor is mine. I apologize for the intrusion; it has been far too long since I was last here. As we have not been formally intro-duced, I am Lady Lydia Wells, daughter of the Earl of Wharncliffe."

"I am Miss Augusta Powers of Devonshire."

"Pleased to meet you, Miss Powers," Lydia replied as she embraced the two small girls.

"If you would care to visit with the children, there is some corre-spondence I should attend to at my desk," Miss Powers explained.

"For just a few minutes, if I may."

Sarah reached for her hand. "Miss Wells, I have a kitten. Father bought it for me, shall I tell you about it?"

"That would be delightful!" Lydia replied as she listened to the children tell her of their adventures and the news since she had gone away. In their letters they were not as expressive but in person they were overflowing with the details of their lives, from the goings on of their dolls to the subjects they were studying. Lydia lost track of the time as she sat in rapt attention to the girls, who reminded her of her sister and herself so many years ago. It was with great reluctance that she tore herself away from the school room.

She missed the days when her schedule consisted of instructing the Hartford daughters in their subjects. It was a simpler time then, and she had been happy. She decided to take a stroll in the garden.

Aside from the children, the garden was undoubtedly one of the things she missed about Dartmoore. She missed the beauty of this place, the birds singing and the butterflies flitting from one flower to another. This garden was a place she was always sure to find happiness. She missed it so very much, almost as though it was a member of the Hartford family. She missed the ancient trees and brick and stone walls, the blooming flowers and bushes in the vivid colors of spring. As she walked along the paths, she recalled the bench she'd shared with the colonel. How imposing he'd seemed to her when he was her employer. Now that she was a lady, the colonel may seem intimidating, but he was not likely to dismiss her, and she was in no danger of repercussions from his displeasure.

The colonel, while he'd been there to welcome her when she'd arrived, was conspicuously absent. She wondered if it was commonplace to leave an important guest to her own devices, but she suspected it was not. From the instruction provided by her own Miss Perry, she was aware that when houseguests were present, it was the duty of the host and hostess to see that the guests were never bored. Whether that meant cards, music, carriage rides, or other entertainment, it was expected. Lydia, however, did not mind being left on her own. She relished the freedom to explore Dartmoore as she once had, but she did consider it rather odd that the colonel, like the captain, was not present.

In the garden, she could forget her cares. Her worries drifted away as she examined the cool water of the pools. The water reflected the colors of the garden blooming and bursting in the warmth of the sun, and it also reflected the house. From her vantage point, she could see the window of her old room. From that window she could almost see Captain Poole's residence, or she'd imagined that she could.

Her thoughts drifted back to the first time she was introduced to the captain, how handsome he was, how he wore his wavy, sandy brown hair. The way his green eyes sparkled when he'd said that he hoped to see her in the garden for a stroll. She was in love with him then, and she wondered if she still felt something of that emotion as she stood in the garden thinking of him. This time, she was alone. There was no Captain Poole to talk to, or take a stroll with among the boxwoods and rosebushes.

She wondered where he could be, but her imaginings were quickly brought to an end by the appearance of the colonel. Somehow, Lydia mused, he always seemed to find her in the garden. She was surprised to find that she was still nervous. For reasons she could not explain, she found herself wondering if she'd chosen the right dress and bonnet for the afternoon. Was the color becoming, and how did he find her appearance after the winter? Shrugging off these questions that seemed to wander into her mind while she watched Colonel Hartford approach, she smiled pleasantly for her host.

"Colonel Hartford, I want to convey my gratitude to you. Your invitation could not have come at a better time. After the doldrums of winter, to be back here at Dartmoore for the spring is such a pleasure."

"Lady Lydia, I must apologize. I have been a terrible host; there were matters which required my attention that I could not neglect. If you will forgive me."

"Forgive you? Colonel Hartford, may I say something shocking?"

Colonel Hartford was a handsome but chilly person. His face, like his muscular build and imposing nature, was strong and manly. He was the model of a gentleman, masculine and not prone to the display of his emotions. Lydia's pronouncement was met with the slightest, nearly imperceptible raised eyebrow before he returned to his normal façade of unreadability.

"If you insist. As a military officer, I believe you will find me difficult to shock."

Lydia smiled. "I know I should not be telling you this, but I have rather enjoyed the breach of decorum your neglect has caused. Not since I arrived at Boscombe have I enjoyed a few hours to call my own. Here at Dartmoore, I have been at liberty to recall my once unbound life. The feeling of being tethered to my new title has never been more pronounced than this afternoon, here in the garden. I have visited the school room and strolled alone among the fountains, and I have enjoyed it. There, are you shocked?"

"Should I be? I suppose no lady born to the title would ever admit that the life of a noblewoman is as confining as a cage is to a songbird. I am astonished, not by your admission, but that you chose me to hear it."

"Colonel Hartford, how well I recall our conversation in this very place. You were honest with me then, as I am with you."

"I recall the conversation. We had it while sitting on a bench under a tree. Lady Lydia, you were leaving. I recall I was trying to impress upon you the need to stay."

"You must have done a fine job of it. I recall staying. There are many days I wish I had never left."

Colonel Hartford did not attempt to fill the quiet between them with unnecessary words as was the custom of polite small talk. They walked along the path for few minutes before he spoke again. "My daughters feel the same way. They, too, wish you had never left Dartmoore. I do not think they are alone in their feelings."

"You must be referring to dear Mrs. Tumbridge. Does she miss me?"

"I was not referring to her. Although I have no doubt that she finds Miss Powers a worthy replacement in her office as governess, I don't believe she finds her temperament and society as pleasant as yours."

Lydia half wondered if he might be speaking of Captain Poole, but she could not imagine why, if the captain missed her, he was not at Dartmoore to greet her after her prolonged absence. She was about to ask about the captain when Colonel Hartford continued with his own shocking proclamation.

"You may find it astonishing, but I have missed your presence here in my house."

Lydia was unsure how much time passed as she tried to fully comprehend what the colonel's intentions were in telling her something as personal as his last statement. She decided to proceed slowly. "While I was here as the governess, I did not notice that you were aware of my presence. In truth, I cannot blame you for that. I was a poor girl from Falmouth who barely deserved your notice at all."

"I thought you to be a smart woman in possession of a sharp wit and intelligence, but I wonder how you failed to see my obvious attempts to make you feel welcome."

Lydia stifled a decidedly unladylike snort. "Welcome? Colonel Harford, you were as quick to dismiss me from your presence in the drawing room as you were to invite me to stay. How keenly I was aware of the difference between our classes, by your manner. By no means do I hold you responsible for my feelings; you were acting as a man of your rank and status ought to act towards a subordinate."

"Thank you, Lady Lydia, for ignoring my failings. As you were made aware when you first came to work for me here at Dartmoore, you do possess an uncanny resemblance to my departed wife. I cannot continue to blame that for my discomfort around you, but I did find myself often unsure of the feelings I possessed. I was compelled to question whether they were for a memory of how I felt for her, or the beginning of a regard I felt for you. I regret that I did not convey that sentiment to you as I should."

"Colonel Hartford, I must admit I was unaware that you held me in your regard as anything but a member of your staff."

"I was foolish. I should have spoken, but it was not in my nature to pursue a woman who sought the attention of another gentleman."

Lydia began to understand what the colonel was trying to tell her. "The other gentleman is Captain Poole, is it not? Was I so shameless in my actions that I appeared to be forward?"

"I cannot bring myself to describe your actions as forward. On the contrary, you behaved as any young lady who is enamored with a gentleman. I did not consider your behavior a poor reflection on your character."

"The appearance of my character does seem to be a casualty of my judgment. I must have seemed rather foolish to be enamored of a gentleman who did not share those same feelings."

"Lady Lydia, I cannot speak for Captain Poole, but I do not consider you to be foolish."

"Thank you, Colonel Hartford. It would pain me greatly to be considered foolish in the opinion of a man such as yourself," Lydia answered.

She was holding back from the question that was bothering her, gnawing away at her from the moment she'd arrived. Where was Captain Poole? Why was he not at Dartmoore to greet her? After the conversation with Colonel Hartford, she could not bring herself to ask about the gentleman's whereabouts. She did not want the colonel to believe that she'd come to Dartmoore for any other reason than to visit her former charges and to make a child's birthday complete by her presence.

Elizabeth and Sarah were so young. They'd lost their mother, and then she'd left them to become a lady. It broke her heart to think of these girls, alone in their great big house with a father kept busy by his affairs, and only a governess and the servants to dote on them. No, Lydia thought to herself, she did not want the colonel to think her motivation was anything other than Elizabeth's happiness. The answer to her question would be revealed. Until then she would be patient.

———

THE CONVERSATION in the garden set the tone for a visit that would prove to feel very strange to Lydia. Colonel Hartford had said that he'd missed her. That, to her, seemed like an odd admission for a man of the colonel's rank, particularly when he was discussing a time when he'd far exceeded her in class and title.

For the remainder of her time at Dartmoore, she thought of his words and wondered why he had not written to her about his feelings, or made them known before she left for Boscombe Hall. During her days as the governess to his daughters he did have ample opportunity, but he chose not to say anything to her. The reason he'd given, while understandable, hardly seemed adequate, that he was aware of her interest in Captain Poole.

It seemed rather remarkable to Lydia how quickly her time at Dartmoore passed. Elizabeth's party was a delight with acrobats, musicians, and children from the prominent families of Plymouth in attendance. Colonel Hartford was a gracious host, and the party was a success. Her own present of a doll and a silver locket was met with appreciation and happy tears. Sarah was not forgotten, as she too received a small cross of her own from Lydia, and she was as pleased as her older sister.

The colonel was attentive to his guest, but at no time was an explanation for Captain Poole's absence provided.

When she had first arrived, Lydia had spent much of her time looking into rooms and peering around corners, thinking she would catch a glimpse of the man she'd shared correspondence with. That was not to be, she soon discovered. He was conspicuous by his absence, and the more so because nothing was said about it, except in that short inquiry with Mrs. Tumbridge. In the days following, she had ceased to look for him, feeling disappointment that she could not ignore, despite the attentiveness of her host and the joyful reunion with his daughters.

Hannah, the maid, was the only person in the house to reveal that Captain Poole may have had other interests occupying his time. Nola was Lydia's personal maid, charged with the keeping of her wardrobe, arranging her hair, and seeing to her every need. Hannah was a maid on the colonel's staff. She was charged with seeing that the rooms of the guests and family were kept immaculate. Securing a moment alone with this woman, whom she knew from her time employed at Dartmoore, was not difficult. What proved to be more difficult was convincing the maid to speak to her about Captain Poole. Hannah was not a gossip. She was a good woman who believed strongly in keeping the tenets of the bible. After some degree of friendly cajoling, Lydia learned that the captain had been called away on personal family business rather suddenly, the morning of her arrival. It seemed unusual to Hannah, but it was not in her nature to question the motives of others.

This discovery that Captain Poole was suddenly called away was remarkable to Lydia, but only in its convenience. Had he been unable to leave a note? If his absence was so easily explained, why was it not? Colonel Hartford did not offer a reason for it, and Mrs. Tumbridge was far too uncomfortable to speak about it. Yes, Lydia decided, it was suspicious. She was certain now that she was the only one to have felt anything other than friendship in her short acquaintance with Captain Poole.

On the morning of her last day at Dartmoore she sat in front of the mirror as Nola arranged her hair, pinning it into place in a style that was becoming. She was far too preoccupied by the chaos in her mind to answer Nola when she asked about the choice of dress for her last dinner at Dartmoore. She was so deep in thought that she was unaware that Nola was standing idly behind her, having finished Lydia's hair.

Lydia was reminded of how irrational her sister had been about Hugh Burton. Charlotte had been thrown into despair, anger, or delight, all depending on the circumstances surrounding the handsome fisherman. Could she say the same about her feelings for Captain Poole? By any measure, her emotions were far less powerful than those of her sister. Did that mean that she did not *feel* them as strongly, or were they simply not as strong? Was she the more sensible sister, or had she not yet experienced a love like Charlotte felt for Hugh?

This was the question that consumed her thoughts as she realized rather self-consciously that Nola was patiently waiting.

"Nola, I should like to wear the blue dress this afternoon for tea, then the crimson dress for dinner."

"Yes m'lady," Nola replied, leaving Lydia to ruminate as long as she wished.

Alone in the richest suite of rooms at Dartmoore, she slowly walked across the floor towards the window. It was still early. The mist hugged the shrubs of the garden as Lydia gazed on the outside world. At this time of morning, very few ladies of her rank would be awake. The schedule of late dinners and socializing into the evening dictated a later time for breakfast. Lydia was all too aware, as Miss Perry had reminded her on more than one occasion, that she kept servants' hours. In London, she was told, she would fall out of her habit of rising early.

This morning, Lydia was glad she was not still asleep in her bed as other upper-class women may be. The garden, waking from night, proved far too lovely to miss and her mind was preoccupied with important matters. On this morning, her mind was firmly rooted in the idea of love. Love was something she was not sure she would ever experience in the way her sister felt it. She had thought she'd loved Captain Poole (and maybe she had), but the distance and his neglect of their budding romance did much to dampen her expectations of their relationship. His odd disappearance did little to restore her faith in her feelings for him. When she thought of the captain, she also thought of Mr. Finnegan's insistence they remain as distant as their class differences dictated.

Mr. Finnegan – how odd to think of him at Dartmoore. Lydia was confused by him. She felt some inclination towards the man who was largely responsible for any freedom she had at Boscombe Hall. If he didn't care for her as more than the eldest daughter of his employer, why did he do so much to ensure her happiness? It was a perplexing problem. It was very much like the mist below her window, soon to be burned away by the warmth of the day, but for now it obscured every-thing in sight, blurring the lines between dream and reality.

Her thoughts drifted from Mr. Finnegan to the colonel. His actions were as mysterious to her as the captain's absence and Mr. Finnegan's taciturn manner. The gentleman who played host to her during her stay seemed to be the same man she once knew, but there was much changed about him. He smiled more, he engaged her in conversation, and he had said he missed her. *He missed her.* How those words resonated inside her mind. It hardly seemed possible that he should notice her absence. And yet.

The captain, Mr. Finnegan, and the colonel flitted through her imagination as lightly as butterflies in the garden as she gazed at the scene below her. Did she have time to take a stroll in the mist before breakfast? Looking down at her new shoes, she wondered if the dew from the grass would ruin them. As she resumed her vigil of the garden, her mind on matters of the heart, a movement down below captured her attention.

The motion that stole her attention from her ramble of confused thoughts was not the rapid activity of a squirrel or rodent, nor was it the morning hunt for bugs and worms conducted by the songbirds of the hedgerows. This movement was unquestionably the gait of a person. Peering through the glass of the window, she saw the governess, Miss Powers, moving deliberately through the garden towards a figure who emerged from the white haze. *That* figure was unmistakable. Lydia gasped as she recognized the man. Captain Poole was at Dartmoore, and Lydia could see as the mist evaporated that he was not alone. He was the object of Miss Powers' attention.

Lydia wanted to turn away, but she was rooted to her spot as a tree is rooted to the ground. She was transfixed and could not, would not, turn away. Here was the man she had taken great pains to convince herself did not matter, that he had merely been an infatua-tion. She watched him greet the governess, and then embrace her. It was at that moment that Lydia recalled his words to her, his promise to see her, his continued correspondence. Forcing herself away from the scene in the garden, she felt the sting of rejection. His ardor for her had cooled in his letters, she had known that for some time, but she did not suspect the reason was another woman. If he was in love with Miss Powers, why did he not tell her or make an end to their acquaintance?

The pain she felt in her heart, was it truly heartbreak, or was it her pride being wounded? Lydia was under no illusion that she was a beauty. Her appearance, while not unpleasant, was not ideal. It was at times like this when she wished she had her sister at her side to share her pain and her troubles. Charlotte was miles away, on the other side of Cornwall. The way she felt about Lydia after their argument, Lydia doubted she would have found the companion she sought.

She questioned whether or not Captain Poole had ever left Dartmoore. Was she being lied to by everyone, or had he returned that morning? Regardless of the circumstances, this sudden weight of emotion brought tears to her eyes and made her think of Charlotte. Lydia may not have loved the captain as Charlotte loved Hugh, but the pain was still acute.

After witnessing Miss Powers in the captain's embrace, Lydia did not think she could bear to be at Dartmoore a minute longer. She was due to leave that day. Would anyone miss her, she wondered, if she left that morning? She wanted to be by herself to cry, and to mourn the loss of her optimism when it came to matters of the heart. She was in no mood to converse or play cards, while a man she'd thought had feelings from her hid from her sight.

She stood still, unable to settle on what to do. If she left at that early hour, she was running away. Running away was not in her nature, but her mind and her heart were reeling from the scene that had played outside her window. Latching on the one course of action that ensured that she would not have to see Miss Powers or Captain Poole, she made a decision. Yes. She decided that there was nothing keeping her from going home.

During her brief time at Dartmoore, she'd enjoyed visiting with Elizabeth and Sarah, but she could not return to the girls now without seeing Miss Powers. She was grateful she'd had the opportunity to renew her friendship with Mrs. Tumbridge, and surprisingly, the colonel. There was nothing delaying an early departure. Reaching for the bell pull, she pulled it. She could not bear to hide her emotions behind smiles, or happen upon the cause of her pain. If she was being truthful, she suspected that the colonel and Mrs. Tumbridge knew of the relationship, but perhaps Hannah did not. Yet Hannah had come the closest to being honest. How could she remain in a house where those she trusted would not tell her the truth?

Nola, her maid, came running into the room, a stricken. "Lady Lydia, are you unwell? Your face is flushed; shall I send for a doctor?"

"No need for a doctor. I am well, but please pack my things at once. Alert the driver of my carriage that I wish to leave at once. Tell him to ready the horses for our journey back to Boscombe Hall."

"Yes m'lady," Nola answered as she raced out of the room.

Lydia walked to the desk, from which she withdrew a small stack of thick sheets of paper. Sitting down, she penned a letter to Elizabeth and Sarah. She then wrote one to the colonel, and one to Mrs. Tumbridge. The last one she wrote was to Captain Poole. With a few well-chosen words in a language not often used by ladies of her rank (but used frequently by sailors along the quay at Falmouth), she explained to him that she would no longer burden him with her attentions as he was doing quite well without them. With the last of her letters finished, she allowed Nola to help her change into her carriage dress and bonnet. The colonel protested her sudden departure, but she would not be persuaded to stay a minute longer. With tears in her eyes, she said goodbye to Dartmoore Park.

The carriage ride from Plymouth gave her ample time to cry for the loss of her Captain Poole, and to lament the difficulties of finding love. Love, she decided during the lengthy journey, was not an emotion she cared to pursue after her disappointment with Mr.

Finnegan and her rejection by Captain Poole. In the future she would not think of love.

Her reception at Boscombe Hall was as to be expected. Mr. Finnegan was reserved in his satisfaction that she arrived safely. Her father was pleased to see her home, and her sister was still not speaking with her. The big house seemed empty by comparison to the warmth she'd found for a few days at Dartmoore in the company of Elizabeth, Sarah, and occasionally the colonel. But all of that was over. Now, she had her future as Lady Lydia Wells to consider. In a sennight she would be leaving for London, a city she had never seen, to meet other people like herself who had titles, rank, and wealth. She was apprehensive about the reception she would be given among members of society.

She took consolation in knowing that in a place like London, her wealth would be more attractive than her appearance. For that she was grateful. Love, she decided, was of no interest to her any longer. In London, she was certain to find what she needed to distract her from the disappointment in her attempts at romance. Love was best enjoyed by those without imagination. What she needed was adventure, and she was sure to find in it London. The halls of Boscombe were quiet and the schedule curtailed her freedom, but she was not going to let that – or Mr. Finnegan's reserve, or her sister's distance – deter her from dreams of the glittering world of the capital of the British Empire.

———

LYDIA WAS AWAKENED by the soft squeaking of the hinges of her door. It was the faintest of sounds; normally such a noise would have hardly captured her attention. The door was often opened in the early hours by a scullery maid whose job it was to ensure that her fire had not gone out during the night. On this night, only days after her return from Dartmoore, she was awake in her bed, unable to sleep.

Lying motionless, she heard the door open, and then footsteps across the floor.

In the darkness of her room, she could not see the intruder, but she did not recognize the gait to be that of the scullery maid. Sitting up in her bed, she called out to the person who had come into her room.

"Who's there?" She asked as the shadowy figure stopped only feet away from her bedside table.

There was no answer as Lydia shoved her covers aside and stood, her heart beating wildly in her chest. Was someone in her room to rob her, or cause her harm? She reached for the bell pull and hissed, "I don't know who you are, but I am summoning help this instant unless you reveal yourself to me!"

"No! Please!" a familiar voice cried out from the shadows.

"Charlotte? Is that you? What are you doing sneaking around in my room at this hour?"

"I wasn't sneaking," Charlotte said. "Please don't pull the rope!"

Lydia lit the candle at her bedside. Her sister was dressed in a coat and her bonnet was tied around her neck, hanging down her back.

"Charlotte! You'd better explain to me what is going on or I will pull this rope, and then I will tell Father. Why are you dressed at this hour? Are you going somewhere?"

Charlotte looked defeated. "I came to give you a letter. We haven't been on the best of terms and I didn't want to leave without thanking you for all you did for me. I should have mailed the letter to you, rather than leaving it for you to find. Please, Lydia, let me go."

"Let you go where? Are you running away to marry Hugh? Father won't give you a pound if you do that."

"I know. I wasn't running away to marry Hugh...well, not exactly. I was running away to find out if it's true."

"If what is true?"

"If what you said is true."

"Charlotte, I have no reason to lie to you. I want you to be happy."

Charlotte frowned. "I don't mean whether you lied. I want to find out if *Hugh* lied to me. If I go to see him without announcing my arrival, then I will know, won't I? If he's married or not."

Lydia wanted to scold her sister, but then she compared Charlotte's desperation to her own recent misfortune with love. She did not feel half as strongly for any man as her sister did for Hugh. It was easy to dismiss her sister's feelings as girlish infatuation when she had no understanding of them. But after her recent experiences at Tintagel Castle and Dartmoore, she was far more sympathetic, a change that was reflected in her next statement.

"Charlotte, let me help you. If you steal away into the night without a chaperone, a carriage, or our father's permission, you will regret it. You could be harmed or robbed by highwaymen. It's not safe and it's not worth the harm to your good name if you succeed."

"Lydia, if you stop me tonight, I'll keep trying until I do succeed. You can be certain of that!" Charlotte replied defiantly.

"I know, which is why I'm asking you to trust me. Remember how it was at Mrs. Peyton's. Did I not help you see Hugh? Let me help you, and together we shall discover the truth about Hugh Burton. I hope his mother was mistaken. I pray that I am wrong about his intentions. I would be the happiest of sisters if he proves himself to be the young man you believe him to be."

"Do you mean that?"

"I do. And what's more, I will do all I can to help you convince Father."

"Oh, Lydia! Would you do that for me?"

"I would, but you have to promise me, no sneaking away. You have to accompany me to London, as Father has our short season arranged. While we are in London I shall make plans to see Hugh. You must not tell him of our scheme."

Charlotte exclaimed, "I don't want to go to London! There is nothing for me there."

"Father expects you to go. He has paid Miss Perry to teach you how to be a lady. You will go much further to convince him if you follow his orders."

"I hadn't thought of that, but what about Hugh?"

"Charlotte, If Hugh Burton is a man of good character, he will wait for you. If you behave as a lady in society, that will go far to convince Father that you are mature and ready to decide for yourself whom you should marry. If you are resistant, he may regard your actions as impertinent, and childish. You won't convince him to let you marry Hugh that way."

Charlotte sat down on the bed beside her sister. "Lydia, I was angry at you for telling me about Hugh. I didn't want to hear anything bad about him, not after Father insisted he won't let me marry him. I'm sorry for how I behaved."

"All is forgiven. Go back to bed; we can discuss in the morning, if you're still here."

"I will be. If you're going to help me, I know all is going to be well."

"For you, maybe it will be," Lydia replied, thinking of her own dismal prospects at romance.

"Before I go back to my room, I want to know what we're going to do about Hugh."

"I don't know yet, that may take some time. I give you my word, though, that I shall plan a way for us to discover the truth," Lydia answered.

"Time? That is another reason I was hurt by you, Lydia. You knew about Winnie Parker for a long, long time. Why didn't you tell me about her?"

Lydia knew the question was not to be avoided. There was no partial answer that would satisfy her sister's need for an explanation. Meeting her sister's direct gaze, Lydia replied, "I didn't tell you because I was hoping I was wrong. There never seemed to be a good time to tell you, not when you were so happy. I didn't want to take that away from you."

"What happened to alter that?"

"Hugh, that's what. When he decided to ask for your hand after your sudden change in fortune, I suspected the worst of the man. I know I had no proof of that, but I have come to terms with how much our lives have changed; you may have to face that as well. I told you about Winnie Parker hoping to ease the hurt and pain that finding out he was a scoundrel would cause. How would you feel if he only wanted to marry you for your wealth?"

"I pray he loves me, as he has always claimed. I don't think he's a scoundrel."

"I know, I hope he isn't. Do you forgive me for not telling you?"

"Lydia, you have been my only family for our whole lives. How could I harbor any resentment towards you in my heart?"

"Thank you, Charlotte. You're my sister, we have always looked after each other, and nothing will change that. Come with me to London, we shall have fun, meet a few people, and I will have time to think about a plan. You have waited this long for Hugh, I think you can wait a little longer to learn the truth about the man you want to marry."

"You're right. I don't know what I was thinking. Running away with a few pieces of jewelry? I was terrified to do it, but it seemed like the only way. Maybe I knew there was a better way, maybe that's the reason I came in here to give you this letter. Yet, when I search my heart, I knew that I could not leave you without your forgiveness. It's the only reason I didn't get away from here tonight. I could not bear to part with you in anger."

"Charlotte, I'm glad I caught you sneaking around. If I hadn't, we wouldn't be going to London together."

"We're going to be miserable in the city with all the noise and people."

"Miserable? How could we be any more miserable than we are here at Boscombe? In London we can attend balls and teas, and we can buy whatever we want! Doesn't that sound delightful?"

Charlotte smiled, "If you believe it will be delightful, I suppose it will be. I cannot think of a single reason I should adore London more than Falmouth or Boscombe Hall."

Lydia replied brightly, "Just you wait, Lady Charlotte Wells, as beautiful as you are, and with your grace and poise, you will be the toast of the town!"

Lydia said those words in earnest, trying to cheer up her sister after her unsuccessful attempt to run away. She didn't know as she sat on her bed that evening, that Charlotte would not be the only Wells sister who was soon to be received in the grandest houses and among the wealthiest members of society. Lady Lydia Wells, the former governess at Dartmoore Park never dreamed that in London, she, with her plain appearance, would be considered a wit and her sister a belle. Their lives were on the cusp of a great change that neither one of them could foresee that spring night in Cornwall.

CHAPTER THIRTEEN

Early Summer, 1817
London, England

THE SOCIAL SEASON in London was nearly over, but Lydia was not sad. Her first season, even though it was far too brief, was a success. Despite her background as a governess, which no one in London knew about, and her occasional lack of polish and imperfect comportment, she was indulged in her peculiarities because of her enormous wealth and her title. Under Miss Perry's continued tutelage, conducted surreptitiously, Lydia blossomed, as did Charlotte. To a casual observer, they appeared to be three high-born ladies spending the season together, as friends often do in the fashionable neighborhoods of London. No one suspected that Miss Perry was a paid companion to the Wells sisters, or that her main job was to keep them from embarrassing themselves or the earl, who was unable to join them in London due to the enormous responsibility of overseeing his late father's immense business interests

In London, rank, status, and title opened a great many doors —
but Miss Perry reminded her charges that their behavior as perfect
ladies kept the invitations coming their way. It would be disastrous,
she assured them, to be without a full social schedule. By conducting
themselves as ladies at all times, the Wells sisters were ensured the
attention of eligible bachelors and inclusion into the *ton*, as the top
tier of society was known. With Charlotte's serene beauty and handsome frail countenance, and Lydia's keen observation and skill in
challenging anyone at the card table, they were always in demand at
balls and dinners.

Their father's ascension to the rank of earl was a thrilling tale
known to many of society's prominent families. The tragedy of his
experience was never mentioned, and the upbringing of his daughters
was left to the imagination of whoever was telling the story. It was
thought that Charlotte and Lydia were educated by a series of private
tutors. Rumors abounded about Charlotte and her musical talent. It
was whispered that she was taught to sing by the choir director of
Westminster, and to play by an exiled court pianist for Napoleon. To
Lydia, all the stories and rumors were a source of entertainment, and
a warning. She did not want to discover how she would be treated if
anyone suspected she'd lived in a garret in Falmouth for many years,
or that her sister, the beloved Lady Charlotte Wells, was in love with
a fisherman.

Privately, her feelings about her past were unchanged. She still
wrote to Mrs. Peyton and Mrs. Tumbridge. She did not intend to
forget about them even though there as a growing rift between them
in rank and life experience. It was the same feeling she had about the
colonel. The colonel was the son of a baronet, barely an aristocrat, as
far as titles were concerned. His rank and reputation were based on
his estate and the popularity he enjoyed as a hero of the war.

In London, war heroes, particularly young, handsome ones, were
prized guests at social gatherings, as novelties. As the daughter of a
man who made his own living in the ranks of His Majesty's navy,
Lydia did not agree with the rise in status of these officers as mere

curiosities. She knew that these men deserved to be praised and not be seen as ornaments. Yet, she did not observe any of the heroes of the day being misused, because of their connections with the higher ranks of nobility. Many of these men were the younger sons of viscounts, barons, and occasionally earls themselves. Fame and popularity did not hurt their individual causes, and it helped to further their own futures.

Unlike the dinners and balls hosted by many of her new acquaintances, Lydia did not add war heroes to her invitation lists as a nod to fashion. She included them as a gesture of her respect. The daughter of the Earl of Wharncliffe, a former captain of His Majesty's navy, did not have to rely on a fad to assure her continued success among the ton, an acceptance that was surprising to Lydia.

Growing up in the small port town of Falmouth, far away from the ranks of the glamorous, wealthy members of the British upper class, she had no knowledge of this closed circle of social elites until she'd arrived in London. It was not until a certain Lady Hilda Breakridge invited her to tea that she learned of its vaunted existence. Lady Hilda was herself one of the guardians of this clique of fashionable and affluent members and a patron to *her girls*, as she called the Wells sisters.

It was Lady Hilda who often sat beside Lydia on pleasant days in the drawing room of the earl's London residence. Lady Hilda and a retinue of her distinguished friends would often assemble to enjoy a good gossip and talk of nothing but the final ball of the season, to be given at Lady Hilda's residence. She said it was an honor to be hosting the last formal event of any season. She assured Lydia and Charlotte that they would do well to wear their finest gowns, as there would be many young men of good family and wealth at the ball.

Lydia did not object to being referred to as Lady Hilda's girls, although there were times when she felt like she had become the pet project of a bored, wealthy socialite. Lady Hilda was a prodigious woman, whose own children were grown, wed, and on their own. She had no one to occupy her time, except *her girls*. With her nearly constant meddling and matchmaking, Lydia was often exasperated by the acquaintance as much as she benefited from it. Yet, she could find no other reason to reproach Lady Hilda, and so she and Charlotte chose to go along with many of the lady's schemes.

On the evening of the ball, Lydia and Charlotte rode in their gilded carriage to Lady Hilda's immense London residence, located a few blocks from the Prince Regent's palace. Miss Perry was unable to accompany them, having a last-minute stomach complaint. This left Lydia and Charlotte alone, an opportunity they did not mind in the least. Tonight was the last ball. Tomorrow, they would pack their trunks to return to Boscombe Hall, and after that, they would discover the truth about Hugh Burton.

"Lydia," Charlotte reminded her, "What are we going to do about Hugh? You promised me that if I accompanied you to London, you would help me find out about him."

The carriage rumbled through the streets as Lydia nodded, nearly afraid to move her head for fear of ruining the elaborate hairstyle and silken turban that was pinned to the top of it. Reaching up, she felt the soft feathers and wondered how she would ever keep from looking a mess. "I have not forgotten my promise. I do have a plan. We may have to enlist Miss Perry's assistance."

"Miss Perry? She is a darling woman, but can she be trusted?"

"I don't know. I have not told her anything about my plan. I have considered bribing her, if I must," Lydia explained.

"Bribe her if you have to; we must know the truth. I don't think I can meet another young man or stomach the attention of any more eligible gentlemen. I want Hugh Burton! Until I know the truth, I shall remain loyal to him."

"Never you mind about Hugh. I promise, I have an arrangement in mind. Tonight, we shall dance and behave as ladies. Tomorrow we shall scheme and plan as thieves, if we must!" Lydia said with a gleeful smile.

"I just know we shall learn the truth, but yes, we have one more night in London to call our own, and without a chaperone!" Charlotte replied in delight.

The carriage arrived at the residence of Lady Hilda and was met by a footman dressed in a white wig and formal livery. Light blazed from every window of the tall, red brick mansion as Lydia and Charlotte climbed down from their carriage. On a night like this, with so many beautiful, fashionable people to meet, music playing and dancing to be enjoyed, she could forget that she had not heard from Captain Poole since she'd left Dartmoore, and only received a few short missives from the colonel. Tonight, she could imagine that she was never unlucky in love as she carefully climbed the steps and entered the marbled foyer of Lady Hilda's home.

The music was lively, as were a hundred conversations around her, as Lydia and her sister moved through the crowd. Lydia felt the weight of the turban on her head and wished she had chosen a less fashionable outfit than the crimson ballgown, the yards of expensive matching silk on her head, and the tall peacock feathers. She was certain she was among the best dressed of the ladies in attendance, but she was unable to enjoy the company – or much else – as she settled herself against a windowsill.

Charlotte was dancing with a middle-aged gentleman, a cousin of the Duke of Lindingham, as Lydia surveyed the room. Dancing was not her favorite pastime, but she did enjoy a lively reel from time to time with a skillful partner. Tonight, Lydia feared that there would be no reels for her, not with her terrible choice of outfit. She was mulling the decision to remain in the ballroom or seek a card table in the drawing room, when she observed the hostess coming towards her across the crowded room. It wasn't the hostess that shocked Lydia, so much as the gentlemen who accompanied her.

From across a room of aristocrats and well-dressed lords and ladies, Lydia recognized the unmistakable silhouette of a gentleman she knew from her not-so-distant past. Her eyes were locked on his handsome features as her face flushed bright crimson. He knew who she was, and all her secrets, and he was walking next to Lady Hilda Breakridge.

Steeling herself for the embarrassment that she was certain was coming when Lady Hilda announced that she knew of Lydia's common history, she stood tall, preparing to meet her expulsion from society with grace. She was the daughter of a captain and an earl; she could be honorable even in disgrace.

"My dear Lydia, there you are! I have been searching for you for an hour!" Lady Hilda exclaimed.

"Have you? I'm sorry you were unable to find me," Lydia answered as she looked into the face of the man who would be the cause of her imminent ruin.

"I would like to introduce you to one of our finest heroes of the war, Wellington's trusted advisor, Colonel Michael Hartford of Plymouth."

Lydia replied, "Colonel Hartford, what a pleasure to meet you."

"The pleasure is mine."

Lady Hilda continued to smile at the young couple in her midst. With a saucy wink, she said, "There, now you are introduced, I shall leave you two alone to decide what you shall do with the acquaintance."

"I would be honored if you would accompany me in the next dance," Colonel Hartford said with a sparkle in his dark eyes.

Lydia did not say anything as she walked beside him, her worries about her turban erased from her mind. The colonel had never looked more regal or handsome than he did that night. Dressed in a black tailored coat and crisp white waistcoat, he was a striking man. He'd tricked Lady Hilda into providing an introduction that he did not require. For what reason, Lydia could not ascertain, but she intended to find out.

As the music began to play, she took her place in the line of ladies on one side of the dance floor. She faced a man she knew very well, and wondered why he was in London, and why he wanted to dance with her. His smile as the music began made her tremble with anticipation, but she didn't know if she could trust him. Could she bring herself to trust any man, she wondered, as she gazed into his eyes and found herself reluctantly drawn into their depths. Yes, she vowed, she would find out what he wanted and why he'd lied to Lady Hilda. But that could wait until after Lydia enjoyed this dance with him.

———

"Colonel Hartford, you owe me an explanation," Lydia said as they stood on the veranda outside the ballroom.

"I do. It was not my intention to place you in an awkward position by not revealing our acquaintance," he answered. "I was motivated by loyalty to you and your family."

Lydia studied his features, staring into his dark eyes as she tried to make sense of his answer. "I'm not entirely sure I understand. What motivation compelled you to misrepresent yourself, and by extension, me, to Lady Hilda?"

"In Plymouth, my name is enough to ensure me a place among the highest-ranked members of society. In London, I am only an officer. My title is worthless among a sea of earls and dukes. I had heard of your acceptance into the ton, and the mystery surrounding your past. I did not want your patroness to be aware that we have met previously. I feared it would lead to questions of how the eldest daughter of a wealthy earl came to be introduced to the son of a baronet. It is not often that we would be invited to the same parties, I'm afraid."

"Lady Hilda has taken an interest in Charlotte and me. If your rank was not considered equal to my own, I wonder why she would have introduced us?"

He cleared his throat awkwardly. "I'm considered heroic and I'm wealthy, which is thought by many to be an asset. She may have introduced not because of rank, but because of my wealth," he explained.

Lydia nodded thoughtfully. "How kind of you to consider how our former acquaintance would have been viewed by a woman like

Lady Hilda. I often wish to tell all of these grand ladies how I was really raised; do you think they would consider it shocking?"

Leaning close to her, he answered, "I *know* they would consider it shocking. What do you suppose they would do if they had any indication that a member of staff, a mere governess, was among them tonight, dancing with their sons and brothers? Do you believe they would be able to survive the shame of admitting you and your sister to their society?"

Lydia could not recall a time when she had stood this close to the colonel. His eyes sparkled in the soft light of the torches and candles, and his lips were close, close enough to kiss. Surprising herself with her impulse to lean towards him and kiss him, she blushed.

Her response did not go unnoticed. "You're blushing. I should not have reminded you of your previous position in my household."

"No, I'm not blushing because I used to be a governess, I'm blushing because..." to her horror, she realized she had been about to admit the truth. Quickly she scrambled for a reason, any reason, to explain her reaction to him. "I'm embarrassed because of Captain Poole."

Now it was the colonel's turn to look uncomfortable. "Captain Poole? You are embarrassed because of your previous...correspondence with an officer?"

Lydia realized much too late how her poorly planned comment could be construed. Did Colonel Hartford now believe that she considered any connection to officers to be beneath her? Struggling to rectify her misstep, she used her own mistake as a reason to inquire about a troubling matter.

"I am not embarrassed by my connection to an officer. As the daughter of a captain, I welcome the connection. Since we are now speaking about Captain Poole, I have a question I would like to ask. I do not wish to seem ungrateful after you concealed our former acquaintance to Lady Hilda, but there is a matter which has caused me some distress."

"I fear I may know the substance of your question. My only

answer is that I did not wish to intrude upon your feelings for Captain Poole. As I explained at Dartmoore, my own regard for you has been muddled by the memories of my departed wife. Being here in London, away from the house that serves as the temple for all my memories of her, I find I am no longer as confused as I once was. My introduction tonight was my way of reacquainting myself with you as a man who wishes to make his bid for your regard known in a public manner. If you still harbor feelings for Captain Poole you need only say that you do, and I shall trouble you no more."

Lydia had not expected this admission. The red in her cheeks darkened and she stood gaping, overwhelmed. There was a panicked feeling in her stomach, a tingle of excitement that raced through her as her heart beat wildly. What should she say? How should she act? In the silence, she compared how easily she'd spoken to Captain Poole, and how little she censored her speech for Mr. Finnegan. She may be a lady now, but she was still intimidated by the colonel. She still felt like she was the governess to his daughters, that he held a power over her.

"Perhaps I am mistaken. I should not have told you of my intentions," he said as he turned away.

"Colonel, please." She reached for his arm.

"It is Captain Poole, isn't it? You have an understanding with him. If that is so, merely say it at once. Know that I did not mean to disregard your connection to him. I assumed, perhaps incorrectly, that your connection with him was severed."

Lydia sighed. In this she could be honest, at least. "My connection to him is severed. I no longer harbor any affection for him. I wonder if I ever did. My question to you – and I shall ask to be rid of any specter of him – is this, did you know of his understanding with the new governess? Is that why he was absent during my visit, or was there another reason other than the one I was given? Once you answer, we shall never speak of him again."

Colonel Hartford shifted uneasily, but he met her eye. She saw the truth there long before he answered. "There is an expectation of loyalty between officers, which troubled me. But above all, I wished to avoid causing you distress."

"You have not answered my question. I saw him with the governess the morning I left Dartmoore. Yet you supposed I might still feel an attachment, so it seems you were unaware that I knew the truth. At what point would you have been honest with me? Would you have allowed me to make a fool of myself?" Lydia glanced over her shoulder, uncomfortably aware that her temper was rising, and so her voice might be, as well.

"No," he answered softly. "I knew your attachment with Captain Poole would come to nothing, because I would have spoken to prevent it. I only wished to avoid seeming to slander the man in order to further my own case."

"You didn't tell me about him because you wanted to protect me? Did I not deserve to know the truth about him? A word of warning from you would have been sufficient. Now, I am left to wonder if your loyalty to a fellow officer outweighs your loyalty to a me, a woman you have admitted you hold in high regard."

The colonel's face was as hard as stone. His features, once soft and handsome in the moonlight, were now set in a frown. The conversation had taken a decidedly dark turn. Lydia was confused about her own feelings. She was indignant that the colonel had been loyal to Captain Poole. She was embarrassed that she was drawn to the colonel, her old employer, in a way she could not explain, and she was still unsure of his intentions.

"Lady Lydia, I did not wish to cause you any offense. If I have done so, I humbly apologize. My loyalty to my men, and my officers, is the habit of my former position. As the daughter of a celebrated naval officer, I expected you to understand the fealty of the battlefield. Regarding my statement of intention towards you, that has not changed, although I am now left wondering if I spoke hastily."

Under the burdensome silk, Lydia's head was spinning in confusion. She heard his rebuke, and yet she was being asked to consider him as a potential husband. Leaning against a column, she looked down at the stones under her feet, gathering her thoughts.

Lifting her head, she readjusted her turban, which was slipping, as she admitted, "I feel we have stumbled our way through this evening. I thank you for the dance, and for your candor."

The colonel's frown was still in place, but it seemed less severe. "What is it that leads us to disagreement? I sincerely hope you understand that I am motivated by my truest feelings for you. I assure you, I am not moved by your rank or wealth. I apologize if I have spoken rudely. As you know, I am unaccustomed to maintaining decorum in a drawing room. I am far more accustomed to the field."

"Are you suggesting that we have this conversation in a setting you find less taxing?" she asked with a smirk.

"Do be reasonable. You no more belong on a battlefield than I do inside a drawing room, but that is where I fear this is leading. Shall I pay a call on you tomorrow? Since we have been formally introduced, perhaps I may expect an invitation to tea so that we may discuss my proposal to you."

Lydia's eyes were wide with excitement at the word *proposal*, but she maintained a calm demeanor as she spoke. "Yes, Colonel Hartford, please come to tea tomorrow afternoon. We shall speak no more about this tonight. We are at a ball, the last of the season. Perhaps our time would be best invested in lighter subjects that do not lead us to discord."

"Thank you, Lady Lydia, for the invitation. I look forward to tea with you. If I may have the honor of the next reel, I would be delighted," he said with a return to his previous state of carefully measured good manners and unreadable countenance.

Lydia knew the colonel as a former employer, the father of her previous charges, and her host at Dartmoore, but she could not say she knew the man who stood before her any better now than when she first made his acquaintance. He was enigmatic, with his combination of cold military manners, his mask of emotionless stone, and his occasional gestures of generosity. There were a great many things about him she did not understand, but she learned that night there were many things she desired to know about him.

Not only did she wish to know him, she wanted to understand herself. Why did she want to feel his lips on hers? Why did he spark anger, indignation, and a whole roster of emotions she could scarcely understand? As he led her back inside the ballroom, she caught the eye of her sister. A knowing glance passed between them as Lydia realized that sometime later that evening there would be a lengthy conversation about the man who had stayed at her side the rest of the evening.

———

"Colonel Hartford is a handsome man, is he not?" Lady Hilda beamed at Lydia as the other ladies in her retinue nodded their approval.

Lydia could feel the eyes of the small party fall on her as they waited for her answer. She suspected they were watching her reaction to discern the true nature of her feelings for the man she'd supposedly met the previous evening. Lydia wondered how they would react if she told them she was very well acquainted with the colonel, and that he'd paid her salary before she ascended to the rank of lady.

Lydia cleared her throat before answering. "I barely noticed his countenance." Charlotte stifled a giggle.

"Barely noticed? Those words seem empty indeed! You must have barely noticed his ease in conversation, and his lightness of foot as you danced two reels with him as your partner!" exclaimed Lady Hilda.

"I cannot deny that I found him to be amiable," Lydia said as she attempted to bring the matter to a conclusion. "Regardless of how amiable he may have seemed, the season is at an end. We shall soon be leaving London."

"We may be leaving London, but I do not think that my ball will be the last you shall see of Colonel Hartford! I am sure that I was not the only person at the ball to note the mutual admiration between you. You seemed to be – in my opinion and I'm sure my word shall be universally upheld – well matched. You shall have me to thank for your good fortune if a happy union results," Lady Hilda answered, beaming at her success.

"What if no happy union results?" asked Charlotte in her diminutive voice.

Lady Hilda wore a look of profound disbelief. "Why shouldn't it result? I have selected the perfect match for your sister. It is not an easy thing to match the eldest of daughter of an earl to a gentleman man who deserves her notice. Charlotte, my dear, I do not mean to speak so brashly, but you are equipped with beauty, and your musical ability is unparalleled. What of your sister? She is a wit and a demon at the card table, but what other attributes does she possess?"

Lydia chafed to hear her qualities reduced to wit and her talent for card games. Still she offered no response as Lady Hilda expressed her opinion of the matter.

Placing her hand on her chest as though she was a dramatic actress on the stage, Lady Hilda, unrebuked, spoke to her audience. "As you have no mother to place either of you girls in situations best suited for meeting eligible gentlemen, I have taken it as my task to do so. I shall see both of you married well."

Charlotte did not respond to Lady Hilda's proclamation, but Lydia once again found her voice. "We appreciate your efforts on our behalf, yet I do wonder if we should rely on our father's counsel in the matter of finding suitable husbands."

"Your father should be grateful that I have chosen to champion his daughters. Never you mind about his opinion. If I have selected a gentleman worthy of notice, he will be pleased," Lady Hilda answered in a smug tone.

With the discussion at an end, Lady Hilda returned to a subject she preferred to matchmaking. Speaking about herself, she continued for many minutes before rising to announce that she was due at another address. Her entourage of sycophantic ladies rose in chorus. With the usual wishes for a good day, they left Lydia and Charlotte to receive other less notable guests (in the opinion of Lady Hilda). Lydia was reminded once again that she should be honored that her home was the first to be visited that day by Lady Hilda, and that such an honor was rarely bestowed on unwed ladies.

Lydia thanked Lady Hilda for her regard, but she knew her title and her admittance to the ton was not the reason for Lady Hilda's insistence she be seen first the morning after the ball. This prodigious woman wanted to be the first to gauge the success of her romantic enterprise. Rising early, she was dressed and found her way to the Wells, nearly bursting with curiosity. Her curiosity satisfied, she was free to discharge Lydia and Charlotte to the remainder of their day and carry herself and her followers to their next expected visit.

Lydia was relieved that Lady Hilda had chosen the morning for her visit, and not the afternoon. Colonel Harford was due to arrive after luncheon, a meeting Lydia hoped to conduct in private. Her reason for wanting to be alone with the colonel was not embarrassment at the connection or any reticence that her name be linked with an officer. On the contrary, it was simply because she was not sure of her feelings, and she did not want rumors spreading that she was engaged before she ever returned to Boscombe Hall. Gazing out the window at the carriages disembarking from her house, she feared that this particular gossip was already let loose upon the wealthy neighborhoods of London. The harbinger, Lady Hilda, would use such speculation as entertainment for all the ladies she visited that day.

Now that they were alone in their opulent drawing room, Charlotte spoke without reservation. "Lydia! You don't look pleased. Lady Hilda has given you and the colonel her blessing; isn't that delightful? It does make me wonder how she would receive Hugh. Do you think she would demand that he be removed from her house or send him downstairs to the kitchen to sell fish to her cook?"

"Charlotte, if Lady Hilda or anyone else in society knew of Hugh, *you* would be sent to the kitchen. If they knew I was once a governess and you a teacher at a girls' school, we would both be swiftly expelled from their company."

"I wonder if I wouldn't prefer to be expelled," Charlotte replied.

"Charlotte, you are the darling of society. You have become the belle of London this season. It is a wonder you have not had a great many gentlemen clamoring for your hand. Lady Hilda has admitted that she intends to see us both married to rich men."

Charlotte laughed. "It is a wonder, indeed. I have found a way to dissuade them."

Lydia looked at her sweet, demure sister as though she no longer knew her. "How have you managed to dissuade them? The sister I know is far too honest to be deceptive; have you used a magic spell?"

"No, it's not magic, but it works remarkably well, although I have found that I must alter the practice ever so slightly each time I use it."

"Charlotte, what is this? You must tell me at once."

"I will confess but so must you. Do you agree to answer any question I pose?" Charlotte asked, her innocent face pursed in a serious expression.

"Very well, you have my word."

"It is simple. These men see me, and I venture you as well, as ladies with large dowries. If the gentlemen are the second sons of lords, I lament the fact that my dowry is much reduced recently due to the failings of my father's estate. If they are the heirs to a title, I include the addition of an understanding with Mr. Finnegan."

Lydia was shocked. "Charlotte! You have been spreading these stories about our family, about yourself? I hardly know where to begin. You have told gentlemen that our fortune is lost – what must they think about our father? It is no wonder Lady Hilda regards us as her personal charges. She insists on finding us rich husbands because she believes us to be nearly poor! As if that is not stinging, you have told these man that you have an understanding with our father's secretary? What could have given you such motivation to tell these wild stories?"

"If I was given permission to choose whom I shall marry, then perhaps I would have been more careful with our father's reputation. It is his fault that I have been subjected to proposals from men who only wish to marry me for my dowry. The men I would choose if I had never met Hugh would not meet with our father's approval. Regarding the story of the secretary, you must see yourself in that tale. Did you not realize that I have seen how Mr. Finnegan acts when you are near? The glances you have exchanged?"

"I do *not* have an understanding with Mr. Finnegan, and neither do you. While I admit that I have found him to be an amiable companion, his insistence that we remain entrenched in our social positions has removed any possibility that we could ever be more than an employer and a staff member. Why would you tell such a story?"

"I tell these stories to dissuade the more persistent men. Oh Lydia, is there so much difference between the small tales I tell and the lies that Lady Hilda and the women in her circle tell? What harm am I truly causing, except to father's reputation – which he deserves for forbidding me to marry the man I love. Who can inquire whether I am at liberty to marry? Since Mr. Finnegan is far away in Cornwall, there can be little danger that anyone shall search for the truth of my statement."

Lydia sat still and gazed at her sister incredulously. "Charlotte! You have shocked me in a way I could not have anticipated. How did you come to be this treacherous? Was it the time you spent at Mrs. Peyton's when I was at Dartmoore? Did you begin to lie to see Hugh? How have you perfected the art of duplicity in London society?"

Charlotte no longer seemed weak; her voice grew stronger as she declared, "Do not underestimate me because I am frail or because my constitution is weak. Since I have met Hugh, I have perfected a talent for deception by necessity. If society, if our father, would accept him as an equal then perhaps I would not have had to rely on deceit. I love Hugh, and I want no other man for my husband. I am not proud of my lies, and I seek forgiveness to God for that, but I was justified in every wrong I committed. God knows my heart, and he knows the guilt I feel, but I have had no other recourse."

"I understand wanting to lie to deceive dear Mrs. Peyton so that you may steal a few hours with Hugh, but what of these men here in London? Do you truly have a desire to ruin our father's good name?"

"It is true that I have sometimes enjoyed the attention of these gentlemen, and I have even found some of them to be charming. Yet to me there could be no one as charming or as lovely as Hugh. If I was allowed to speak of the man I adore, to say his name, to plan our wedding, then I would not have had to discourage these men. I would be married, and not forced to endure them. You should be applauding my efforts as I have also removed any hope that the mercenary among them may induce me into matrimony."

Lydia was forced to admit that her sister, her once sweet sister, had become a cynical woman behind the perfect complexion and the diminutive figure. Was is the brief time spent among society that also played a part in the transformation, as Charlotte claimed? Was her sister influenced by the machinations of these women like Lady Hilda, who used their influence (and any other means) to do as they pleased? Had she acquired this skill when Lydia encouraged her to lie to Mrs. Peyton? Lydia felt chilled.

"Charlotte, when we arrived in town, you were understandably upset about Hugh. I promised you that we would resolve the matter. I have not forgotten those words."

Charlotte smiled. "I recall what you said, and I believe you will help me as you have promised. You hold the colonel in much the same regard that I do Hugh, is that not true?"

"You know very well from our conversation last night that my feelings for the colonel are not clear. I am not sure whether he truly sees me, or if he thinks of me as his wife, a version of the love he lost. If only I understood what he hopes to gain, I could be sure of my feelings for him."

"If you loved him you would not have to wonder about your own feelings. They would be as clear as mine are for Hugh," Charlotte observed.

"I suppose you may be correct. I do not know what is to be done."

"You are clever, more than I ever hope to be. You shall find a way to resolve this dilemma for yourself. Anyway, I have answered your question as to the contents of my magical elixir for banishing suitors, so you must now answer my question. What is your scheme for determining Hugh's true intentions? We are nearly at the end of our season. We shall be leaving for Boscombe Hall within the week."

Lydia knew this conversation could no longer be avoided, but she'd hoped that she would know better what was to be done when the time came. With a deep breath, she answered her sister as honestly as she could. "I have been attempting to devise a solution. We shall have to rely on Miss Perry's cooperation to manage without Father finding out about our venture. I do not have a detailed itinerary, but I would like to visit Falmouth before we return home. If we go to Mrs. Peyton's, we shall have time to pay a visit to Hugh Burton and his family in the village."

"Miss Perry will cooperate, I am sure of it! She must!" Charlotte answered, seeming satisfied with Lydia's plan.

"If she does not, I fear we shall have to abandon the entire trip."

"She is still confined to her bed from weakness brought on by her ailment. I pray she is ready to travel soon. I long to see Hugh again, and our old friends at Mrs. Peyton's."

Lydia was suddenly struck with an idea, a part of the plan she had been lacking. "Charlotte, what if we were to leave before her? She is a member of our staff. We may explain that it is necessary for her to remain behind to oversee the closing of the house. What if we were recalled to Boscombe Hall, or you were overwhelmed with homesickness, what do you suppose she could say? She would have the use of our other carriage; her safe travel would be assured."

Smiling, Charlotte answered, "Do you think she would agree? I could be ready to leave in the morning."

"We once went about as we pleased without concern for anyone but ourselves. We are ladies; we may do as we wish."

"Yes, we may. If Father is displeased we shall beg his forgiveness. I would rather suffer his displeasure than not see Hugh. If I could only learn the true nature of his feelings for me, I could happily accept any condition."

"But Charlotte, when we have returned home, do I have your word that you shall never deceive anyone or speak terrible lies about our father, or anyone else?"

"You have my word. You are making too much of it; everyone lies in London."

"Perhaps, but we don't have to. We never did when were poor, and we shall not do it now."

"What about Miss Perry? Are you going to tell her the truth?" Charlotte asked with a smirk.

"I shall speak to the staff and Miss Perry. If she will not stay behind to see to the house as I shall order, then perhaps I will tell her the truth and swear her to secrecy, although I hope she doesn't ask for any explanations."

"And if she doesn't bend to our wishes as you say? What then? You did say that we would abandon the venture if she will not help us."

Lydia spoke with determination. "I have thought about it. I thought we would have to abandon our plans if Miss Perry is against us, but if we are willing to face our father's anger, then what have we to fear? We shall make ready to leave in the morning. I will send a letter ahead to Mrs. Peyton."

Charlotte reminded Lydia of her own romantic attachment. "What of the colonel? If we leave London early what shall you do about him?"

Lydia sighed. Leaving London meant she wouldn't see him for a long time. It was a terrible price to pay, but it was the only way she and her sister could return to Falmouth and, if they were fortunate, learn the truth about Hugh. As she gazed at her sister's face, a woman who was no longer the innocent young girl she once was, Lydia knew that she had to remove Charlotte from London. She was becoming tarnished by the city. If she could return to the quiet life at Boscombe Hall, she would be better for it.

It pained her to think of the duplicitous woman her sister was becoming under the influence of society. The machinations of the members of the ton, with their relentless pursuit of rank and status, had influenced her sister long enough. Once they knew the truth about Hugh, she prayed that her sister would return to her old self.

This afternoon she would see the colonel, she hoped he would understand the necessity for her hasty departure. He was a man who understood loyalty, and so Lydia prayed that he would recognize her loyalty to her sister. If he was unable to support her decision to honor her word to Charlotte, then perhaps she did not need to consider his petition for her hand in marriage.

CHAPTER FOURTEEN

The conversation with Miss Perry was not as difficult as Lydia feared it might be. When she knocked on the door of Miss Perry's room after luncheon, she found the woman sitting in bed, wearing her dressing gown. She looked tired and drawn, but did not seem terribly ill. When pressed for an answer to Lydia's request that she remain behind in London, Miss Perry expressed concern for her charges to be traveling unaccompanied by a chaperone. Lydia assured her that there was no need to be troubled, since Lydia and Charlotte would be traveling together. With the slightest degree of hesitation, Miss Perry agreed to act as agent, and oversee the closing of the house. Lydia was greatly relieved.

As Charlotte packed her trunks. Lydia waited in the drawing room for the colonel. She thought about her censure of her sister for lying. What a terrible habit to have acquired, and one that cast a decidedly dark shadow on the season. Lydia was the first to admit that she found London to be far more enjoyable than she could ever have imagined. She had flourished (and so had Charlotte) in the exclusive circle of the ton. It would be tragic to never grace the hallowed halls of the theater or the ballrooms of London ever again.

When she reflected on her activities in London, she came to the startling realization that every week, every day had been filled with a series of teas, dinners, and dancing. She could not remember the last time she had gone for a walk in the garden, keeping her own company. Surrounded by every possible luxury, she thought of Falmouth. She missed the accent of the fisherman along the quay, the colorful attire of the sailors who came into port aboard great ocean-going vessels. She nostalgically wished for a time when a few yards of material from a distant land were a cherished gift. She wished to once again be the girl who took pleasure in the simple things such as invigorating walks along the harbor, or a flock of sea birds on the wing.

She was lost in this world that once was her own, remembering with longing the garret she'd shared with her sister when the footman announced the arrival of the colonel. Colonel Hartford strode into the drawing room as handsome as he had been the night before, his posture as tall, his eyes as dark, and his features set in a smile.

Lydia was not prepared for the surge of emotions she felt when she looked at him. These feelings did not rely on her understanding of his heart. Perhaps, she decided, it was because of the nostalgia she was indulging in before his arrival? Colonel Hartford was as much a part of her past as being a governess or taking long walks on High Street in Falmouth. He represented a time in her life when she knew she and her sister were innocent.

"Lady Lydia, I am honored you invited me to tea. I do not see anyone else in attendance, are we to be alone?"

"We are alone. It may not be proper to receive you without a chaperone, but this is my house, I shall do what I wish if it shall please you, Colonel Hartford."

"It pleases me very much. We have not enjoyed the benefit of a truly private conversation since you left Dartmoore. It is strange to recall how we act as ourselves at my home. In London we are forced to wear masks. You must play your part as a high-born lady and I am to be the celebrated hero. Neither of these masks fits us very well."

Lydia was struck by his candor, and his assessment was correct in ways he could not know. "Colonel, there is much truth in what you have said. If I were to be honest, I would have to tell you that I agree with every word you have uttered. I, too, tire of the necessity of appearing to be anything other myself. I long to be and do as I wish, to speak as I choose. I long to tell each member of the ton that once, I was a governess. I wish for so much more than I can explain."

"I, too, wish to be entirely honest. I see now that I should have walked across the ball room at Lady Hilda's house, I should have bowed before you despite the wagging of tongues and the rumors that would come of it. Yet, I did not. I preferred to act as one protecting another, to allow Lady Hilda the belief that she was making the introduction at my request."

"You did that for me, didn't you? And I was angry because of your fealty to Captain Poole. How I regret that. Since we spoke last night at the ball, my own loyalty to someone I care for has caused me to be duplicitous, a trait I abhor."

"Who can be the cause of such an alteration to your character? Have I done anything to warrant the necessity of lying? Am I the cause?"

Lydia could not face him as she answered and I feel that my confession of lying has weakened your esteem for me."

He gave her a wry look. "I have moved in society on occasion when I was not at war. I find it to be tedious, and the nature of those who move in it is not entirely honest. I cannot fault you for doing what has been required to endure the company of these people."

"I fear once you learn the cause of my deception, you will wish to know me no more."

"I cannot imagine a time when I should wish to renounce you. Unless you have an engagement or a previous understanding, I shall not be deterred."

"My loyalty to my sister prevents me from disclosing the details, but my sister has a connection to gentleman of low birth. So low that he was nearly unsuitable when she was a teacher and I, a governess.

If you are shocked by what you have heard and have no wish to remain in my acquaintance I beg you not to speak of it to anyone."

The colonel looked at Lydia for a long moment. She recalled her sister's penchant for telling gentlemen outright lies to escape their proposals. She hoped that the colonel would not think her guilty of anything as dishonorable. She felt his gaze upon her face, strong and steady.

"This man, is he a gentleman? Is he honorable?" he asked.

Lydia was struck by his words. "He does behave admirably, although I fear he may be promised to someone else."

"Do you approve of him? Do you want to see your sister become the wife of this man? That is the question that must be answered."

"I don't know how to answer your question. You're not bothered that he is socially inferior in every way?"

"I am the son of a baronet, but I am also an officer. I have met a great many men who were born under inferior circumstances and brought honor to themselves on the field of battle. If he is honorable, I would feel no shame in acknowledging the connection. If he has behaved dishonorably, I should not invite your sister to Dartmoore."

"You are far more reasonable than my father. I think he forgets he was a captain. As an earl, he demands that we find gentlemen who are equal to us in rank and wealth. I have been introduced to many fine gentlemen during my season, they are as alike in opinions as they are in appearance."

"Would your father be content to settle his eldest daughter on a colonel, a knight of the realm?"

"I cannot say," Lydia replied, her voice distant as she sat in disbelief that not only could the colonel accept an acquaintance with a man of inferior birth – but that he felt the sting of the difference in rank himself. Perhaps, she wondered, that may account for his tolerance of others not born to the upper class.

"If your regard for me warrants a meeting with your father, I welcome it. You have not disclosed your feelings on the matter. Shall we speak of it now?"

Lydia did not know what her feelings were. The colonel, who was as imposing a gentleman as ever, who valued loyalty and honor above all other emotions, was far more tolerant than she'd ever dared hope. She examined his features, his stern expression, which was now softened by the romantic nature of their conversation. Why couldn't she answer? She held him in higher regard than any other gentleman in her acquaintance; she yearned for his notice and his esteem. She was pleasantly surprised by his independent mind, but she was still unsure of his intentions. Why did he want to marry her?

Lydia nervously glanced at him as she answered, "My feelings? If we are to continue the practice of being honest, then I beg your indulgence that I may speak candidly.""

"You shall always speak as you wish. I do not care for ladies who say only what is proper. I welcome your honesty in these matters and all future discussions."

Lydia looked down as she gathered her nerve. "Colonel Hartford, I am flattered by your attention, and that you wish to become my husband. Although you have not formally proposed or spoken to my father, I feel there could be an understanding between us, if we are equal in our regard."

"That was my intention. I have wanted to become more to you than the master of Dartmoore. Captain Poole, I fear, was far more appealing to you than me, a war weary old colonel years older than yourself."

"Captain Poole is of little consequence. I was naïve when I foolishly considered his attention to me to be anything other than a few hours divertissement. The morning I left from Dartmoore, I was hurt by his callous disregard for me. A gentleman would have written that he no longer cared for me, but Captain Poole did not choose to behave as a gentleman. Despite the sting I felt keenly from the slight, it was your part in the matter which wounded me gravely. You are the master of that great house. I cannot imagine that you did not know of his deliberate attempt to avoid my presence and the reason for it. I was injured by your actions then, and by your confession of loyalty to him last night."

"I explained to you that the expectation of loyalty merely gave me pause, and that I wanted to protect you from the pain the revelation of his churlish behavior would bring. I witnessed the affection between you and him grow while you were a governess in my employ. I observed it with some reservation, as I suspected Captain Poole's nature. My suspicions were proved, yet I wished to spare you that pain."

"Yes, I understand your actions far better today than I did last night, as I have said regarding my sister. Yet it is not Captain Poole, as you have suspected, which has given me cause for hesitation regarding any understanding between us. It is you, Colonel Hartford."

He left his seat, finding a place beside her on the settee. He did not move towards her in a romantic manner, but his sudden appearance at her side suggested that he wanted to be close to her even if she was to reject him. Lydia could barely breathe. Her feelings, like her thoughts, were muddled by his nearness. She wished to reach towards him, to touch his hand, but she dared not allow herself to be so forward. Clasping her hands in her lap, she turned to look at him, mesmerized by his eyes.

"What is it?" he asked softly.

"When I was a governess in your house, you behaved as was customary for your station and mine. You were cordial, distant at times, and aloof. I longed for your approval, any indication that I was worthy of notice. Sometimes, you were generous to me, and sometimes you seemed to take no notice of me at all. You said that I reminded you of your dear departed wife. Am I to be a living representation of her to you and your daughters, or do you care for *me*? Why do you seek my hand?"

He sat back a little, and looked at her keenly. "I understand why you ask me these questions. I have treated you without constancy. When you arrived at Dartmoore the resemblance between you and my wife seemed very marked. Your mannerisms at times recalled her own, and your smile was hers. Seeing you made me miss her very much, and I cannot deny that I was torn by this conflict.

"With your interest in Captain Poole, I was able to measure your temperament and independent nature in the manner of an observer. It was in these moments when I feared I had lost you to another man that I truly came to know you, not as a version of my wife, but as you are, as the brave woman who cared for her sister as she did for my daughters. I found your wit, your opinions, and your laugh to be entirely your own. I mourned for the loss of my wife, and I rankled at the suggestion that I should marry again, to replace her in any way in my heart to my regard. When I realized I had begun to wonder whether I may find happiness with you, I was consumed by guilt. As I came to this conclusion, I was unable to speak to you about my feelings, which grew each day, because of the presence of Captain Poole."

Lydia was moved by his words, and her face burned red with embarrassment at the memory of the anger she had expressed, and the frustration she felt because of his actions. How terribly misunderstood he was; her heart ached to soothe his sorrows, to comfort him. Deep inside, moved by more than compassion, she desired to embrace him, to feel his arms around her. She wanted to know him, to care for him, to spend hours listening to his voice.

Wiping away the faint glisten of a tear on her long eyelashes, she sighed as she looked at the man seated beside her. "Colonel, I am at a loss. I am the worst of women, to have chastised you for your coldness, to have berated you for your inconstant behavior. Please forgive me for questioning you or your motives."

Hesitantly, slowly, he raised his strong hand to her face. Wiping away the tears, he answered, "I have failed in my task. I have brought you sorrow when I sought to bring you happiness."

She closed her eyes. Leaning towards his touch, she reached for his hand, holding it as she rested her cheek on his palm. Opening her eyes, she gazed at him with such tenderness that she saw his eyes glisten as hers did.

"You have not failed. You have moved me to tears with your confession. How was I ever so callous, so terrible to treat you as I have, to demand explanations from you?"

"You deserve every explanation I can give to you. I want you as my wife. I have seen how my daughters have responded to your presence, how you treated my staff, as you have treated me. When you arrived as a guest for my dear daughter's birthday, I watched you with great interest. You did not behave as a lady, and by that I do not mean offense. You treated each of us as you always had, with respect and with compassion. I feared your title and wealth would spoil the independent spirit I fell in love with when you were a governess. When I arrived at the conclusion that nothing had changed about you, you were unaltered, I was delighted, and I was fearful. I was delighted that you were as I remembered you to be, and fearful that you still harbored feelings for Captain Poole. I was afraid that even if you should be at liberty to give your heart, I would not be free of the terrible guilt to accept it."

"What changed for you?" she asked breathlessly.

"Your sudden departure from Dartmoore set a chain of events in motion that I scarcely understand myself. I found your withdrawal from my home pained me more than I could have known possible. When you were with me at Dartmoore, I may not have conveyed my pleasure at your presence, but I anticipated every game of cards, every dinner. With your sudden departure, I was reminded once more of what I had feared lost to Captain Poole. With many weeks to feel the sting of your withdrawal, I decided that I could no longer bear to be without you. My guilt was at an end, and it was finally overcome by some words of wisdom by Mrs. Tumbridge. She saw me suffer through pain of regret and my guilt. Not one to hold her own feelings thoroughly in check, she reminded me that she, too, felt your loss, and so did my daughters. What right, she scolded me, did I have to deny my own happiness and the happiness of the whole household?"

"Dear Mrs. Tumbridge, she said that? How forward you must have thought her. I wonder you did not dismiss her for her boldness."

"I cannot dismiss such a person as Mrs. Tumbridge. Dartmoore would fall into chaos," he smiled as he held her hand in his.

"So, it would, dear lady. How I long to thank her for her words," Lydia replied.

"I assure you, she has received my gratitude. Have I addressed your hesitancy? If I have not thoroughly assuaged any concerns you may have as to my inventions, I beg you, tell me what you find objectionable. I shall fix it."

"Colonel Hartford, there is no need to alter anything. Say that you care for me, that you wish me to be your wife, and I will accept you without delay."

"Lady Lydia, I wish for no other woman than you to share my life. I care for you, I long for you to be my wife."

"Then I shall say yes without hesitation or a moment of delay. I accept you, but you must grant me a request. I implore you to forget about propriety and decorum."

"What is the request? Whatever it is it shall be yours," he asked as his dark eyes twinkled.

"Grant me this," she said as she leaned close to him. "Grant me a kiss, that I may know you are as enamored of me as I am of you."

He leaned close to her, his eyes gleaming, his mouth set in a smile fixed firmly on his face as he caressed her check, drawing her face towards his own, tilting her chin up. Lydia closed her eyes as his lips met hers. She could not recall a surge of emotion before like the one that swept over her body and her heart. His powerful arms wrapped around her trembling frame, and her heart beat furiously.

A knock at the door brought the scene to a quick end. The intruder was none other than Charlotte, who found her sister and Colonel Hartford only inches away from each other, seated on the settee together.

"Lydia, I did not mean to...I am terribly sorry for the interruption," Charlotte exclaimed as she froze in the doorway.

Colonel Harford rose, bowing to Charlotte as Lydia inquired about the reason for Charlotte's intrusion.

"Charlotte, my dear sister, what brings you to the drawing room?"

"My trunks are ready; the coachman wishes to know our itinerary. There is much to be planned for the journey. I confess my ignorance or else I would not have bothered you."

Lydia regained her composure. "Tell him I will speak with him after tea."

Charlotte nodded before hastily rushing from the room. Lydia realized that she had failed to tell Colonel Hartford of her immediate plans to leave for Falmouth. She did not want to be apart from him for even a day. The certainty of this revelation struck her as being unlike any emotion she had ever known. This must be love, this feeling that coursed through her body and her mind, united by her beating heart.

Turning to the colonel, she said, "I fear I have news which I failed to impart to you upon your arrival. I did not seek to deceive you, I was merely swept along in the current of your proposal."

"What is it you wish to say, confess anything."

"We, my sister and I, shall be leaving London in the morning. We are journeying to Falmouth on the way home to Boscombe Hall. We have business there which concerns the gentleman I spoke of earlier. I dread the journey, not because I have no wish to revisit the town I once knew as home, but because I have no wish to be parted from you."

He gazed at her with such depth of feeling that he seemed to radiate patience and understanding. As he kissed her hand, he said, "Have no fear for my opinion of your travels or your obligations. I shall mark the separation with sorrow, but I too must journey from London. My estate requires my attention. I have an errand in a fortnight which is of great importance to us both."

"Will you seek my father's approval?" she asked.

"Yes, I shall be journeying to Boscombe Hall. There, I shall speak to him as one officer to another, an equal who deserves a chance to make his daughter happy."

"Shall I speak of our plans to him? Shall I tell him of what has transpired between us?"

"No, my dearest. I fear his rebuke before he has yet to know me. For now, I ask that you remain as you are to him, unencumbered by any engagement."

"Kiss me again, kiss me goodbye, it shall be far too long before we see each other again."

Holding her in his arms, he kissed her, making her forget anything else existed except for the two of them. If she had not been so distracted, she may have noticed that she and the colonel were no longer in private. From the door, left ajar after Charlotte's departure, someone surreptitiously observed the tender moment between Lydia and the colonel.

CHAPTER FIFTEEN

Falmouth, England

"Lydia, Charlotte, let me look at you! My, how you have changed since I last beheld you!" Mrs. Peyton beamed as she embraced her former students. Lydia breathed in the fresh scent of the air in Falmouth, a trace of salt in the breeze. It felt delightful to be back at Mrs. Peyton's School for Girls.

"Oh, dear me, what am I doing? You are both ladies now!" Mrs. Peyton exclaimed in horror.

"Oh no, Mrs. Peyton, here in Falmouth we are still ourselves. There will be no m'lady this and m'lady that here, do you understand?" Lydia replied.

"Very well, but it's not proper, and it's not how I taught you," the older woman pretended to scold them.

"It feels like old times, does it not?" Charlotte asked as she stood beside Lydia outside the gilded carriage.

From the windows of the school, the faces of over a dozen girls looked out at the scene below, marveling at the arrival of two fashionable ladies in their carriage. The team of four horses, all milk and dapple in coloring, matched handsomely in power and presence. The coachmen and driver in their livery were unlike any men seen on the streets of Falmouth. Lydia observed the disruption their arrival caused to the neighbors, as people she knew from her childhood stood about in doorways gaping at the display of wealth in front of their eyes.

Moira rushed from the school to greet the visitors, her face as transfixed by the sight of the carriage and the team of horses as any of the students of the school. She swallowed many times before curtseying. "My ladies," she whispered.

"Moira! You dear, sweet woman. How delightful to see you!" Charlotte exclaimed as Lydia rushed to greet her.

"Shall I help with your trunks?"

Charlotte answered, "No, you shall not. Our coachmen will see to them."

Turning to the woman who'd raised her, Lydia inquired, "Mrs. Peyton, I fear that the stabling of our horses and the rooms for us and our men may be asking too much of your hospitality. Shall we seek rooms at the inn?"

Mrs. Peyton looked appalled. "I will not hear of it. I have made arrangements for your men, your horses, and yourselves, although I am ashamed that your old room is not furnished in accordance with your rank."

"What a joy to sleep in our old quarters once more! Promise me, Mrs. Peyton, that you shall always make that room available to us whenever we come to visit."

"You may count on it. Come now, we have prepared a tea the likes of which no one in this school has ever seen. Cook was keen to demonstrate her skills for you fine young ladies."

Lydia and Charlotte were shown into the small drawing room as Moira led the coachmen up the narrow flights of stairs to the garret. She seemed to enjoy the task of ordering liveried coachmen about as Lydia and Charlotte enjoyed tea with Mrs. Peyton. The drawing room was simply furnished, the wood floor worn from generations of young students who had walked across the boards. The same thread-bare rug lay beside the grate of the fireplace, the same plain teapot with blue flowers was sitting on the table beside the cane-backed chairs.

Lydia breathed in every detail as she savored the cake, a simple recipe that she had not had since she left Falmouth. From the hall-way, she could hear the twittering of girls who fought for position to see the fashionable ladies in the drawing room. Their giggles were hushed several times by Mrs. Peyton, who good naturedly attempted to restore order.

Charlotte, Lydia noticed, was anxious, unable to make herself comfortable as she ignored the cup of tea and cake placed before her. Lydia knew why her sister was agitated. Her discomfort was caused by the nearness of Hugh Burton, and the questions about him that would soon be answered. In a small port town the size of Falmouth, Lydia knew that news of their arrival would travel swiftly from High Street to the quay. If they hoped to find out the truth about Hugh, they would have to leave after tea.

Nodding at her sister in a conspiratorial manner, Lydia drank her tea, feeling much revived from her journey by the simple fare of cake and sandwiches. Expressing her interest to pay a call on an old friend, she thanked Mrs. Peyton for tea, and promised that they would be back before dinner. Mrs. Peyton assured them a dinner of their favorite dishes would be waiting for them upon their return. It warmed Lydia's heart to know that Mrs. Peyton was still as she ever was, and so was the school. Nothing had changed in Falmouth, except for them. They were now ladies and in an hour by carriage they would discover if Hugh Burton would be forever altered in their estimation.

Anxious to learn the truth, Charlotte hastened Lydia out of the drawing room and into the carriage, her mood wildly changing from exuberant to terrified. This was the moment they had both been anticipating and dreading. Charlotte nervously stared out the window as Lydia signaled the driver they were ready to depart.

With the turn of the great wheels of the carriage, the horses pulled it from the streets of Falmouth out into the countryside. The view changed little as the sea was ever present in the near distance. There was silence in the carriage as Lydia noted her sister's agitation was increasing. How long had it been since she last saw Hugh? How many months was it since they were together?

Her sister's unease was caused, she assumed, by the knowledge that she may learn that Hugh Burton was not as he seemed to be, that he was a scoundrel. What would be the toll if he was married? Lydia longed to comfort her sister, but for the moment there could be no consolation. The only way to offer Charlotte any comfort was to unearth the truth, no matter what that truth may be.

In the distance, Lydia saw the tendrils of smoke rising over the trees. Even in the summer heat, the people of the village still lit fires to cook and heat water. Her own heart beat faster. She feared for her sister. She prayed that all was as it should be with Hugh Burton, not only for Charlotte's sake but for her well-being. Charlotte may have learned the practice of deception in London, she may act as a stranger at times, but she was still frail and weak. A disastrous outcome to this venture could send her into illness.

The young children of the fishing village were the first to greet the carriage as it jostled slowly along the rough-hewn road. The road, such as it was, was a narrow path barely large enough for an ox cart, let alone a carriage and four. From the excited reaction of the village children as they ran alongside the carriage, yelling and laughing, Lydia suspected they were not accustomed to receiving visitors.

Charlotte was pale as milk, the color drained from her face as she gripped the tufted material of the seat as the carriage came to a stop. A coachman climbed down from his position beside the driver, and opened the door for his mistresses. In an uncharacteristic act of impertinence, he spoke to Lydia.

"M'lady, forgive me for speaking out of turn, but I must insist you remain in the carriage. This place is not safe for you ladies. These people have a rough look to them. Tell me your business here; I will consider it an honor to do your bidding."

Lydia was taken aback by his boldness, and stared at the man. It was not the practice of coachmen to offer their opinions or speak first. Normally she would have noted his impertinence and dealt with it upon returning to Boscombe Hall, but she found his concern to be well placed. His loyalty overrode his fear of losing his position.

"M'lady, forgive me," he said once more as he bowed.

"There is nothing to forgive; I appreciate your concern for our welfare. Be at ease, I know this village. Despite their rough appearance, these people mean us no harm. They are fishermen's families, not ruffians."

He bowed once more as he held open the door of the carriage, assisting Lydia as she stepped down onto the dirt of the road.

Charlotte was apprehensive. "I have waited for this day for so long, I am terrified what I may find."

"Be brave, this is why we came here – to learn the truth."

"Brave? I was never very good at being brave. You were the bold one, never me," Charlotte proclaimed as she climbed out of the carriage.

The children of the village swarmed around the ladies as though they were in the presence of fairytale creatures. They reached out with grubby hands to touch the fine azure and pale pink material of the dresses worn by Lydia and Charlotte. They danced about them merrily, as though they were fairy folk.

Lydia looked at the village laid out in front of her. There was the row of tidy houses with their thatched roofs. Women were outside in the sunlight, drying fish and mending nets. Grizzled old men stared at them from under the eaves of the houses. At the docks of the village, Lydia saw the outline of many small boats.

Charlotte stood at her side. Her eyes wide with anticipation, she held Lydia's hand, gripping it as she said, "It's been so long since we were here; it's been so long since I saw him."

"I know, but you have to know the truth before you decide what to do," Lydia replied as the children danced around them. "If the boats are in for the afternoon, Hugh should be here. Let's go to his house and inquire about him."

They left the carriage behind on the roadway. There were no roads among the low stone houses of the villagers. Charlotte released Lydia's hand as she walked slightly ahead, her gait more certain as they approached Hugh's home. Lydia could see the change in her sister as they drew near to the house overflowing with children. Hugh's younger brothers and sisters rushed around them, greeting them as they walked towards the wooden door.

Mrs. Burton appeared in the doorway, a baby on her hips, her face gaunt and her hair under a cap. She had not changed in appearance since they last saw her many months ago. At first, she did not recognize Lydia or Charlotte, but as they drew near, she narrowed her eyes at them. "What business do you ladies have here?"

"I have come to see your son, Hugh. I'm Charlotte, this is my sister Lydia. Do you remember meeting us?"

"I remember you well enough. You won't find him here. He's at the Parkers' these days," she said with a nasty little smile.

"The Parkers'? Do you mean as in Winnie Parker?" Lydia asked as Charlotte looked stricken.

"That's what I said; he's at the Parkers'. If you're looking for him you can find him there, when he's not fishing," the woman said as she abruptly shut the door.

"Oh Lydia, how am I to bear this?" Charlotte asked as she steadied herself against the stone wall of the house.

"You will bear it. We have to find the Parkers' house," she replied.

"I know where the Parkers live," a small girl said as she tugged at Lydia's skirt.

Lydia recognized him as one of Hugh's little sisters. Producing a coin from her purse, she handed it to her as she said, "My good miss, can you take us there?"

The little girl held the money in her hand in wonder, turning over the shiny coin as she nodded. She dashed away at a surprising rate of speed as Lydia dragged Charlotte behind her. They kept up with the child as they hurried past chickens, small children, and a pen of pigs. Lydia would have laughed at the spectacle they presented if she wasn't so disappointed in Hugh Burton. He was at the Parkers', just as she feared.

The little girl ran to the door of cottage, which was smaller than the Burtons'. She knocked loudly on the door as Lydia stood firmly in place and Charlotte looked as though she might faint. The door opened to reveal an old woman who was short, stout, and missing several of her teeth. She stared at the child then at the two well-dressed young ladies at her door.

"Goody Parker, they came to see you!" the child announced, and then in a flash, she was away once more, leaving Lydia to explain what she was doing in the woman's front yard with her sister.

"You do not know us; we have not been introduced. I am Lady Lydia Wells, this is my sister Lady Charlotte Wells, of Boscombe Hall. We are looking for Hugh Burton, is he here?"

The old woman stared at them. She did not curtsey or greet them as their title demanded. Instead, she yelled inside the house, "Winnie, you and Hugh come here. There's some ladies looking for you!"

Lydia wished she had something to steady herself against, such a chair, a door, or a wall when she saw Winnie Parker emerge from the cottage. Her belly was much rounder than when she last saw her. She was with child, a condition that her thin summer dress did little to hide. Charlotte gasped as Hugh Burton appeared behind her.

"Miss Parker, perhaps you don't remember me or my sister. We were introduced at Mrs. Burton's home. It is good to see you again, and you Mr. Burton, how well you look," Lydia said as she glanced at Winnie, then to Hugh.

Hugh was as handsome as she remembered, although he appeared to be suffering from a case of astonishment so profound that he didn't say a word. Charlotte's face had taken on a distinctive pallor as she whispered, "Hugh?"

Winnie Parker rubbed her swollen belly as she smiled beatifically at the ladies. "I'm married now; I'm no longer just Winnie Parker. Won't you two come in by the fire and have cup of tea? Hugh won't mind, will you Hugh?"

Lydia reached for her sister as Charlotte stumbled. Moaning, she looked faint. There was nothing more to see; Winnie was pregnant and married and Hugh was undoubtedly her husband. If Lydia could have been wrong, she would have given anything to have found Hugh lonely and pining away for her sister. Instead she found him cozy and snug with Winnie Parker.

As she struggled to hold her sister upright, Lydia scowled at Hugh. "Thank you, but my sister has taken ill suddenly."

"Poor girl. Come inside; I can see to her," Winnie suggested.

"Thank you," Lydia said, "but we can manage."

Holding her sister up, Lydia struggled to keep her moving towards the carriage. Hugh overcame his shock as he moved towards them, finding his voice. "Lydia, let me help you."

"No, Mr. Burton, you have done enough," she said as Charlotte stared blankly ahead.

"Charlotte!" he begged. "Please look at me; have you come to give me an answer?"

Charlotte dug her nails into Lydia's arm as she stood as tall as she could manage. "An answer? Mr. Burton, there is no need of an answer. I shall give you one even though you do not deserve it. The answer is no, of course not! I knew your mother wanted you to marry Winnie Parker. I should have taken it as a warning, but I insisted that you loved me. How foolish I have been," Charlotte replied as she once again fell into the arms of her sister.

"Charlotte, please, hear me!" he exclaimed.

The coachman, who had been waiting by the carriage, saw Charlotte faint in Lydia's arms. He rushed to their aid, brushing Hugh aside with a gruff command. "Out of the way."

"Charlotte!" Hugh called out. "Lydia, please wait, you don't understand!"

Lydia was no longer interested in hearing what Hugh Burton had to say. Helping the coachman lift her sister into the carriage, she ordered the driver to leave the village in haste. Looking through the window, she saw Hugh standing on the road, his head in his hands.

———

CHARLOTTE WAS NOT ILL, but her spirits were low. She was roused from her fainting spell by the jostling of the carriage along the road. She wept as pitifully as she had when she thought Hugh was dead during that terrible storm so long ago. She repeated that she had been a fool to love him, as Lydia did everything she could to comfort her on the carriage ride back to Mrs. Peyton's.

Lydia was not pleased that her suspicions about Hugh were well founded. The devastated look on her sister's face as she cried was heartbreaking to her, causing her pain as if she had herself experienced a terrible loss. Hugh Burton was the only man Charlotte had ever loved, or was likely to ever love again. Finding him in the company of Winnie Parker, discovering the worst about him, did not ease the burden of heartbreak Charlotte would carry for many months, and perhaps her entire life.

As the carriage approached Mrs. Peyton's school, Lydia knew something had to be done. Charlotte could not walk into the school in this state. Between Mrs. Peyton and Moira, they would have a doctor called and Charlotte confined to her old bed for days, fearing illness.

"Charlotte, we shall leave for Boscombe Hall tomorrow, but for now I have to insist that you manage to be strong, to appear as though you are well."

Charlotte wiped her tears as the carriage came to a halt. "How am I supposed to appear as if all were well? Do you know what you're asking me? I will never be well ever again. Hugh was the man I loved, that I will always love. There can never be anyone else but him. How am I supposed to live now?"

"You must find a way. You may cry as much as pleases you tonight. Dear Mrs. Peyton has prepared our old room for us; she and

Cook have made a dinner for us that they worked hard to prepare. I know what I am asking is very hard. I know I am being cruel, but we cannot treat Mrs. Peyton as though she does not matter. She loves you as much as any woman could; she has been a mother to us both."

Charlotte waved a hand weakly, looking bleak. "I know every word of what you're saying is true, but I don't know if I shall be able to sit at dinner and be pleasant. How can I do that when Hugh is gone from me forever?"

Lydia held her sister's hand. "You must be stronger than you ever were before. You must be brave. Show Mrs. Peyton that all is well, and then we shall be on our way home in the morning. I am not asking for me, I am asking for Mrs. Peyton. Do not give her any cause to be worried about you."

Charlotte wiped her eyes with the back of her hand. "How do I look? Do I look terrible?"

"You look terrible, but if you rush upstairs, wash your face, and return to the drawing room, you may be presentable," Lydia reassured her.

"I'll do as you say, for Mrs. Peyton."

By dinner time, Charlotte did not seem happy, but she did seem less tragic. She attempted to eat the food offered to her by Mrs. Peyton as Lydia nudged her from time to time to remind her of Cook's hard work preparing the sumptuous feast. The other teachers of the school were invited to sit with Mrs. Peyton and her guests at dinner as they enjoyed dishes rarely seen except for special dinners such as this one. Lydia made every effort to keep Mrs. Peyton and the other ladies engaged, telling them about the balls she'd attended and the fashions of London. She entertained their questions about every manner of dress and what fashionable ladies wore in the evening.

As she regaled them with stories and funny anecdotes, she tried to conceal her sister's lack of participation. Charlotte appeared dejected, her face set in stone as she stared at her food with a trembling lower lip. Lydia feared her sister would cry at any given moment. Holding her head up, she pressed on with the evening, hating herself for subjecting her sister to socializing when her heart was broken. She also detested Hugh Burton for causing the heartbreak in the first place.

After dinner, Mrs. Peyton enjoyed nothing better than sitting beside the fire in the small sitting room that served as a drawing room. She often indulged in needlework or reading a novel, when she wasn't engaged in lively conversations about the news of Falmouth. Her habits had not changed, to Lydia's delight, as she sat in her old place by the fire. Mrs. Peyton gathered her needlework as she asked Lydia about her afternoon, with a glance towards Charlotte, who was till obviously despairing. Lydia was trying to formulate an answer when a banging on the front door piqued the attention of everyone in the room.

Moira bustled by in the hallway as Mrs. Peyton stood, her needlework forgotten. "I hope it's not bad news. No good news ever comes at this hour."

Lydia watched in horror as Hugh Burton appeared, out of breath, in the door of the sitting room behind Moira. His clothes were disheveled and his face was red from exertion. He looked as terrible as Charlotte.

"This man says he's here to see Lady Charlotte," Moira announced.

Mrs. Peyton stared at Hugh. "What business do you have here, sir, say it at once before I ask you to leave. I give you lot alms and food when I can; what can you want from this lady?"

"I am not a beggar. I don't seek charity or food," he declared.

"Are you not? Then what is your business? State it, and leave," Mrs. Peyton demanded as she stood before him.

Hugh quickly answered, "I have come to ask her to marry me, proper like, not in a letter, but as I should."

Mrs. Peyton gasped, as did every other lady in the room except Lydia and Charlotte. Rousing from her stupor, Charlotte exclaimed, "Hugh, leave me alone. I never want to see you again."

"You have to listen to me," he pleaded as she rushed past him into the hallway.

Charlotte was furious. "No, I never have to listen to you, or anyone else. How can you ask me to marry you, humiliate me in front of my sister, and the ladies here at this school?"

Mrs. Peyton stared at Lydia. "Do you know this man? It is not proper for an unmarried man to be paying a call at this hour in a girl's school. He shall ruin me!"

Lydia acted quickly. Inserting herself between Hugh and her sister, she demanded, "Both of you, come with me. Hugh, if you want to talk to my sister you shall do what I say. Charlotte, he has come a long way to see you, hear him out so he can go on his way."

Hugh and Charlotte complied and followed Lydia downstairs to the kitchen. The kitchen was empty and dark, the only light from the lamps on the table. In the dim room, Lydia stood at the stairway as she waited for her sister to be finished once and for all with Hugh Burton. She could hear every word exchanged between them, as if she was standing in the room. In her sister's frail state, she did not want to leave her entirely alone as she listened closely for any sign of trouble.

"How can you stand before me asking me to marry you? You are already married!" Charlotte declared.

"No, I'm not married."

"Then it's worse than I imagined. Poor Winnie. Do you intend to marry her? Your mother said you were promised," Charlotte spat angrily.

"Our mothers made that pact when we were children. No one else has mattered for me since I met you. Winnie was never the woman I wanted for a wife, and I was never the man she wanted for a husband."

Charlotte cried, "Why would she say she was married? Why were you at her side, and her with child?"

Hugh pleaded, "I know how it appeared, but you are mistaken. I love you. I am not, nor have I ever been married to Winnie Parker.

Yes, she is married, but not to me! Her husband is a man I know well, a sailor in the merchant fleet. He is gone to the Caribbean. I look after her and her mother when he is away."

"Hugh, how can I believe you?" Charlotte asked, her voice stained.

"You can believe me, and you can believe the church record. Winnie was married here in Falmouth at the church. If you don't believe me, ask the vicar."

"So...you and Winnie aren't together, and the baby..."

"Is not mine, Charlotte."

"Oh, Hugh." Lydia heard her sister's voice break. "Forgive me."

"Forgive you? There is nothing to forgive you for, I know how it must have looked."

"It did, but Hugh, that is not the only reason I came," Charlotte replied. "Why did you wait so long to ask for my hand? You waited until I was wealthy to ask me to marry you. Why did you wait until then?"

"Do you want to know the truth?" he asked.

"I deserve to know the truth," she answered.

"I was afraid you would meet a fine gentleman, a man of property who could give you everything I cannot afford. I wanted to wait until I had my commission, but I did not think you would wait for me."

"Hugh, if you love me and no one else, I would wait as long as you wanted me to."

Lydia sighed contentedly as she leaned against the staircase. Her sister was happy once more, and Hugh was not the scoundrel she'd feared him to be. As Charlotte appeared with Hugh from the kitchen, Lydia was the first to congratulate them.

Mrs. Peyton marched down the stairs, her manner impatient as she stared at Hugh. "I am asking you to leave. Single gentlemen have no place here, no place at all!"

"Mrs. Peyton, he isn't single any more, he is engaged to my sister," Lydia explained.

Mrs. Peyton's anger turned to astonishment as she looked from

Charlotte to the young man who stood sheepishly in front of her. Her attention on Charlotte and Hugh, Mrs. Peyton demanded, "Is this true? You are engaged to...who are you, if I may ask?"

Charlotte proudly introduced Hugh. "This is Hugh Burton, he is a fisherman and I shall be his wife."

"He's going to be an officer in the Royal Navy," added Lydia.

Mrs. Peyton closed her mouth, which had been hanging open. "An officer, did you say? Well, that changes things, doesn't it? Congratulations seem to be in order."

"Yes, they do, congratulations," repeated Lydia as she smiled at her sister and the man she loved standing side by side in the basement of a girls' school.

She wondered if any other daughter of an earl had ever announced her engagement in such a way. Finding the question comical, she smiled. This was a joyful outcome to the day and one she wished would last forever. Yet, she knew her father had forbid this match and soon, Charlotte would have to choose between her father and the man she loved.

CHAPTER SIXTEEN

Summer, 1817
Cornwall, England

CHARLOTTE LOOKED TREMENDOUSLY happy as the carriage drew closer to Boscombe Hall. Her smile was as beatific as a saint's, thought Lydia as she gazed at her sister. Lydia smiled and made every effort to conceal her true feelings about the matter of matrimony. She had much to consider – she was secretly engaged to Colonel Hartford, her sister was engaged to a fisherman, and they were due home by the afternoon.

Of the two of them, Charlotte's need was the more immediate. Lydia knew that her sister would not want to wait to be married. She had waited for too long already, as Charlotte had repeated more than once on their journey across Cornwall. However, there were big problems with Charlotte's marriage to Hugh, and Lydia couldn't help but be preoccupied by them, even if Charlotte was somehow able to put them out of her mind. Hugh was a fisherman, far below the Wells family in social ranking. What was worse, Lord Wharncliffe had already forbidden the match – in no uncertain terms. Lydia was very worried.

What would her father's reaction be to the discovery that his orders were being blatantly disregarded? There was no question; he would be furious.

Still, there was hope. Hugh sought a commission into the ranks of officers of the Royal Navy. If he could obtain the money he needed and the right references, perhaps he would find a way to be admitted, even though he lacked the rank and title that were customary.

Lydia wondered how Hugh would accomplish such a feat. Fishermen, and other men without a family connection or education, stood little chance of bettering their standing in society unless they married well. Would a marriage – rejected by Charlotte's father, an earl and illustrious naval officer – help Hugh to rise to the rank of officer? If he was the second son of a lord, or even the son of a solicitor or doctor he may find acceptance, but a fisherman without sponsorship, self-educated and engaged in a romance with the daughter of an earl, would hardly have any chance at all.

As Lydia silently considered the details of her sister's prospects, Charlotte seemed willfully ignorant of any detriment to her happiness.

"Lydia, where shall I be married? The church in Falmouth? Oh, that would be a lovely spot. It feels far more like home than the chapel at Boscombe Hall. I would like to invite Mrs. Peyton and every one of the staff and our remaining friends at school. Do you think they would come?"

"Yes, I think they would. If you invited them, they would surely be with you to celebrate your marriage to Hugh," answered Lydia.

"My marriage to Hugh, how fitting that I should be married to an officer, since I am the daughter of one," Charlotte mused as she played with the ribbon on her bonnet, gazing out the window of the carriage.

Lydia did not wish to spoil her sister's happiness, but she knew it would be in tatters when they arrived home. From the moment Charlotte told their father of her intentions, the same terrible retribution she had received before they left for London would be brought to bear on her again. There was no doubt in Lydia's mind as to what would happen when they got home.

"You may have been the daughter of a captain, but now you are the daughter of an *earl*, and that is the problem, dear Charlotte. Father will not receive the news that you have become engaged without his permission very well. I fear that he will punish you severely," Lydia reminded her sister gently, although she hated herself for saying it.

"I am no longer concerned with that, not at all. If Father chooses to disavow me, to bar the door to me, what have I lost? I will have lost my father but gained a husband. Father may be angry, but he will come around. I know he will, when he understands that Hugh is no mere fisherman but wants to become an officer."

Lydia frowned. "Think about what it is you're saying. Without Father's blessing to the marriage, Hugh will find his path to becoming a captain blocked at every turn. What manner of man marries an earl's daughter, reducing her rank and status and garnering her father's ire? An officer must be educated. He must have the proper background, the connections, and the references to recommend his character. Hugh is lacking in nearly every requirement for a commission. If Father banishes you, Hugh will surely bear the blame."

Charlotte's smile evaporated and she sat still, her features becoming unreadable as the brightness of her mood disappeared. Lydia felt terrible for destroying her sister's girlish dreams of wedding the man she loved, but it was necessary.

"Charlotte," Lydia continued, "I do not wish to discourage you or dissuade you. It was I who planned for you to meet with Hugh, to learn the truth. It is I who have been your champion, and will always be. I know that you love him, and he loves you. I wish only for your happiness, but we cannot immediately tell Father of your plans. We must find a way to assist Hugh with his commission. If he is already an officer, even one of low rank, it is far more likely that Father will accept him. His sense of honor and brotherhood to be shared with a fellow officer of the Royal Navy would surely sway his opinion. Even if Father doesn't give his blessing, if Hugh is already an officer, your life will be one of ease and contentment. The life of the fishermen and their families is difficult. There is no romance when there are no fish in the nets to be sold, or bread on the table to eat. You would fare so much better as the wife of an officer."

"All, right," Charlotte agreed softly. "I know I once threatened to run away to seek out the truth about Hugh, but I had not given that scheme very thorough consideration. I knew that I could bear the sorrow of being disowned. I lived without seeing Father for so long when were girls at Mrs. Peyton's that just knowing he is alive in his grand house is enough to sustain me. I did not consider my life, or Hugh's, without the blessing we so desperately need. What can be done?"

Lydia replied, "I do not know what is to be done, not yet. Write to Hugh, tell him the need for references is dire. He must find a way to strengthen his suit to become an officer, or abandon your love altogether."

Charlotte's mood did not remain dark for long. After a few moments of silence, she raised her chin. "I will do as you suggest. I know that he has the reference of the vicar at Falmouth, perhaps if he can arrange other references of similar gravity, he may be accepted."

"He will need very strong connections indeed. Perhaps better than the vicar, although a vicar's reference does much to recommend his character. We shall see what may be done," Lydia answered, not wishing to abandon her optimism, although it was weakened.

"What of your own plans?"

"My plans?" asked Lydia.

"Regarding Colonel Hartford? Your engagement will be met with a better chance of acceptance than my own."

Lydia had sworn to the colonel that their engagement would be a secret, but there were few secrets between sisters. She was less concerned with her own match than her sister's. Colonel Hartford was a wealthy and respected man; any slight upon on him could only be measured in the difference in rank, not character or property. She knew that the colonel was not concerned with any falling out between her and her father. Her dowry and her title were of little consequence to him. He had known her as a governess, and had loved her even then.

However, she did want her father's blessing very much. She wanted to be received at Boscombe Hall, to be the daughter of a man she greatly loved and admired, a man she once grieved to think was lost at sea. After so many years apart, she did not wish to sever the connection that existed between her and her father – or see her sister reduced to such a circumstance.

The carriage, led by a team of strong horses, made its way along the road leading to the great house that sat upon the edge of the sea. Gulls and other birds of the ocean flew above the vast green lawn as the house came into view. Lydia hoped that her bribery of the coachmen and driver with a substantial amount of money would be sufficient to purchase their silence regarding the trip to the fishing village. A trip to see an old acquaintance such as Mrs. Peyton could hardly raise an eyebrow, but an errand to see a forbidden paramour would surely have grave consequences. As Charlotte was already consumed by her own set of worries for her future happiness with Hugh, Lydia did not mention her anxiety that their father would find out where they'd gone.

———

For two blissful days, Lydia and Charlotte basked in their father's warm welcome. He had missed his daughters and wished to hear of their adventures in London, paying special attention to the mention of any young men suitable for marriage. Charlotte spoke of the great kindness of Lady Hilda and the gentlemen she'd met in the drawing rooms and at balls. Lydia was pleased by her sister's performance, even as her own anxiety grew.

In London, Colonel Hartford had vowed to pay a visit to her father in a fortnight. The time was nearly at hand when he be would be arriving at Boscombe Hall. This happy peace among her family would be at end then, Lydia feared. When the colonel arrived, her own engagement would come to light, followed swiftly by her sister's announcement. As the hours drifted away like seafoam, Lydia's apprehension strengthened, her certainty for her future and her sister's diminishing.

Mr. Finnegan had not seemed at all pleased to see her since she had returned from London. His severe and often stern countenance had become even less amiable since the last time Lydia saw him. She recalled with embarrassment her heartfelt confession at Tintagel and his polite rejection of her. Was his coldness simply a result of the discomfort he felt in her presence now? How she wished she could assure him that she no longer wished to be anything other than his friend, or in this case, his employer.

As he rushed about the Hall, always on business for her father, she was unable to catch his eye. Determined that she would see an end to the chill that had emerged between them, she decided that at tea that afternoon, she would find a way to speak to him alone. If he did not think her behavior was proper or fitting, so be it. She had too many other concerns on her mind to go about her own house being frowned at by a secretary.

Tea in Boscombe Hall was a formal affair and often taken by Lydia, Charlotte, and Miss Perry in the drawing room. Since Miss Perry was still journeying home from London, tea was between the two sisters. Lydia and Charlotte were free to converse without fear of being overheard.

"Lydia, when shall we tell Father about Hugh? I know it's only been two days since we returned, but I am impatient to be married," said Charlotte as she nervously glanced at the door.

"I don't think we have any reason to fear being overheard. The footmen have retired to the hall, and the door is closed. We are alone," replied Lydia.

"I know we are, but I never feel as though we can talk in this house – especially with that great dark shadow lurking about every corner."

"Dark shadow? Who do you mean?" asked Lydia.

"Mr. Finnegan, who else would I be suggesting? He is like a dark cloud on a sunny day. He was never warm, but he has become positively mournful in our absence. I have not heard that he received bad news since we were last home. What do you suppose can be the cause? It seems that he and his sad face are there, wherever we are, lurking in doorways."

"Lurking in doorways? I had not noticed," said Lydia. "You must be exaggerating."

"I'm not, but I would prefer not to speak about him anymore. I want to talk about Hugh." Charlotte stirred her soup and tapped the spoon on the edge of her bowl. "How long do I have to wait?"

Charlotte's observation of Mr. Finnegan's strange behavior reinforced Lydia's own opinion that something should be done about him. She had no wish to cause trouble for him by approaching her father, but she knew that her decision to speak to him was the right one. If Charlotte, so in love with Hugh and filled with dreams of being a wife, noticed Mr. Finnegan's behavior, then surely Lydia was right to want to speak to him.

"Lydia, you haven't answered my question," insisted Charlotte.

"I know I haven't. Forgive me, I was preoccupied. You have to be patient. You have done very well these last two days, but you must continue to be as you are now. Do not make a mistake and say anything to Father about Hugh. Not yet. Until his commission is secure, Hugh needs you to be silent about your engagement."

Charlotte pouted. "I have no wish to be silent; I want to be a bride. I have waited far too long. I know that your plan is the proper way to do things, but I wish there was another way. I would gladly give up all my fine new dresses and these great houses, if I could be wed to Hugh."

Lydia nodded in understanding. "I know you would give up everything for him, but let him have a chance to become an officer. We have spoken many times about this. Please don't be hasty; carry on as you are. Do I have your word?"

Reluctantly, Charlotte agreed. "Yes, you have my word. If only there was a way to hasten his commission."

"Have faith that all will be as it should. Hugh is a good man; his family is hardworking and honest. There must be other educated gentlemen in Falmouth who can provide a reference for his character."

Lydia silently prayed that Hugh would find references, but she knew that it would be difficult. Who would stand for a fisherman who had little more than a village school education and the indulgence of a vicar with a small library? When she thought of the tremendous amount of luck he would need to secure a commission she was nearly brought to despair. But she did not share her sentiments with her sister. Instead, for the remainder of tea, Lydia listened to Charlotte planning every aspect of her life with Hugh.

After tea, Charlotte excused herself to the music room, wishing to play for an hour or two before dinner. Lydia welcomed her departure, as she had a particular plan she wished to implement.

As Charlotte's melodies wafted throughout the house, Lydia lay in wait for the secretary. It would soon be time for dinner at Boscombe Hall. Mr. Finnegan's work would be ending for the day; she just had to catch him as he left her father's study, or as he rushed about on business. Feeling apprehensive and a little guilty for her own surreptitious behavior, Lydia determined that Mr. Finnegan was in the study and so she waited for him, staking out a place away from the notice of the footmen in a small sitting room.

Nervously, she watched, waiting for him to appear. She knew she would have to be quick as he moved with surprising speed, a trait of an efficient secretary. At last, he was emerged, his arms laden with correspondence and papers. Lydia leapt up from her seat, waiting like a predator to pounce.

When Mr. Finnegan was safely away from the study, she followed him along the corridor. He noticed her immediately, and turned around to speak to her.

With her hand raised to indicate he should stop, she whispered, "Mr. Finnegan, please don't say anything. I must speak with you."

He glanced over her shoulder towards the study and spoke quietly. "My lady, what do you wish to say to me that you must whisper? There can be no secrets from His Lordship."

"In general I do not disagree, but this business does not concern him."

"If it does not concern him than I cannot be a party to it, for my work solely concerns him and no one else in the residence," he said in a haughty fashion.

Lydia had not expected Mr. Finnegan to be uncooperative, so she immediately explained the situation clearly. "Yes, I believe you, and I hope he does too, when my sister – whom he adores – tells him of your unsavory behavior as of late. She fears what you must be planning if you must haunt this house like a specter, leering at her from corners."

"I have never leered at her from corners! I beg your pardon My Lady, I do not wish to question the word of His Lordship's daughter, but that is not an accurate account of my behavior."

"Perhaps, you should agree to speak with me, then. You can explain your odd activities so that I may determine if my father needs to hear about it?"

With a defeated look, and his haughtiness gone, Mr. Finnegan answered, "Very well. I will speak to you, although it is not proper that we should have no chaperone."

Lydia was exasperated. "I sincerely doubt that my vesture or your good name are in any danger if you deign to speak to me, the daughter of your employer. Shall we adjourn to the library?"

"Yes, Lady Lydia."

Inside the library, Lydia did not wish to waste any time with pleasantries. "Mr. Finnegan, if I were not so consumed by your troublesome behavior since my sister and I returned from London, I should be offended that you would hold yourself in such high esteem that you should be anxious regarding my intentions. What have to say for yourself? Do you wish to insult me?"

"That was not what I wished to imply. I spoke hastily, m'lady."

"You did speak with haste, but I shall forgive you, as I must also speak hastily. What is the cause of your behavior? You have behaved rudely to me, and you are causing my sister to become nervous."

"M'lady, I don't know what to say," he stammered uncharacteristically.

"Do not try to deny your skulking about and scowling at me. If this pertains to our conversation during out outing at Tintagel, then I assure you, sir, you have no reason to let that be a concern to you."

His face reddened at the mention of the ill-fated discussion, but he did not relent his position. "No Lady Lydia, if my behavior has been less than courteous, it was not a result of our conversation."

"Then why is my sister concerned that you are listening to her words, and watching her from dark places? Why do you frown in my presence as though I am distasteful to you?"

He looked down at his shoes, and slowly answered the accusation. "If I have behaved badly, I humbly request that you forgive me. It was never my intention to make your sister anxious or to behave without decorum in your presence. From your description of me, I should tender my resignation rather than spend another day in this great house."

"Perhaps you should, but I do not wish it. My father relies on you, and his trust has been well earned. You have done much to assure the success of his endeavors and I have no desire to see you abandon your post. All I require from you is an answer. Why have you behaved so abominably? If you fear that I shall behave towards you as anything other than proper, you are mistaken."

"You have misunderstood me, but I cannot blame you for your

mistake. I can only offer you an answer that may not be all that you wish for: I am not at liberty to discuss a confidential matter that has arisen."

Lydia felt her own face redden with the implications of what he had said. What confidential matter was he referring to? Did the coachmen or the driver betray her confidence? Did her father suspect the truth about Charlotte? If he did suspect the truth, how was her father being so jovial if he knew his daughters defied him?

Willing herself to remain calm, she asked, "To what confidence are you referring? If there is a matter that pertains to a member of this family, then any confidence that has been shared with you should be disclosed to me at once."

"I wish I were at liberty to disclose the matter to you, but I am unable to speak about it."

"Do you dare to refuse me?" Lydia asked, her desperation rising (as was her anger) that Mr. Finnegan was refusing to tell her the truth.

"I have no choice."

"Shall I divulge your behavior to my father? Shall I have Charlotte explain how you have scared her? If that is how you wish to be known in this house, to have your character questioned, then I shall not hesitate."

Mr. Finnegan squirmed, his face betraying his discomfort. "All I can tell you is that I have discovered news of great interest to me, but it was not something I can discuss with your father. If I have behaved poorly towards you or your sister by watching you, it was not my intention. I do not have designs upon you or your sister that are less than honorable in any way."

"You confess that you've been watching, then. What news have you discovered that would warrant spying on the daughters of your employer?"

"I cannot tell you, m'lady, although it pains me to hide it from you. All I can say – and I fear this may be too much – is that I am your father's secretary. I am privy to his correspondence and any

news he may receive. If you are able to understand what I am implying, then you shall understand my behavior."

"Father has received correspondence which has caused you to
spy on me and my sister? On whose orders are you observing us? Are
you acting on his behalf?" Lydia asked, afraid of the answer.

Her mind was awash in a thousand possibilities, all of them terrible. What news had her father received, and why did that warrant
the concealed observation by his secretary? What did her father
know? She shuddered to think upon it as she waited for Mr.
Finnegan to answer.

"It would be easy for me to lay the blame for my actions on His
Lordship, but I am not deceitful. I am not acting on his behalf, but
simply in my own interests. This news pertains to me as well,
although His Lordship cannot know that. I observed you and your
sister with the hopes of either confirming or refuting what I suspect
to be the truth."

Lydia was growing weary. Her nerves were frayed as she considered all the different ways that her engagement (or her sister's) could
have reached her father's ears. Pressing Mr. Finnegan, she made a
suggestion. "Shall we dispense with the formalities? Shall we enter
into our own confidence? Would it not be far simpler to ask me what
it is you suspect? Shall it not be easier for me to discover the news
that has lead you to behave as you have?"

"I cannot. I have given my word. Know that I am driven by an
emotion so strong that I dare not say its name. I only acted as a man
who is guided by his heart and not his mind. If I caused your sister
any reason to suspect that I was dishonorable, or to give you a
moment's discomfort, I apologize. I am tempted by your offer, but I
must decline it, even though your answer may bring me great
comfort. If you will excuse me, I have much work to do this evening.
Unless you insist that I resign?"

Lydia was only more confused now. Why would he be led by his
heart? Why would his emotions affect his behavior? Whose confidence was he keeping? She could see that he was not willing to say

any more about the matter. What was he hiding, and why wouldn't he tell her?

"Very well, Mr. Finnegan, you may go about your business without fear of reprisal or retribution. I have no wish to see you leave Boscombe Hall although I am disappointed that you have not revealed a matter that is most pressing."

"M'lady, I should not be troubled if I were you. If the news is as I suspect, then you shall discover it before long, of that I am assured. May I go?"

"Of course you may go. I shall speak to my sister, and you shall not be reported."

"Thank you, m'lady," he said with a bow as he nearly lost the papers he was clutching. He left her in the library, alone in a room where she often sought comfort. This afternoon, comfort was not to be found even in this familiar space. She was afraid of what news the secretary was concealing, and why he was assured she would soon discover such news for herself.

CHAPTER SEVENTEEN

On the third day after the girls returned to Boscombe Hall, all peace and contentment were destroyed. It happened so suddenly and in such a manner that she scarcely could have imagined her world changing as it did. After the conversation with Mr. Finnegan, she had grown even more anxious. She was worried that a coachman may have spoken about the trip to the fishing village, or that perhaps a letter had been intercepted from Hugh. Could an acquaintance in Falmouth, or someone she knew from Mrs. Peyton's school, have written to her father?

Her own secret engagement was a source of concern, but she did not suspect anyone knew of it except for Colonel Hartford and her sister. That engagement would soon be known anyway, upon the arrival of Colonel Hartford, and so it did not trouble her as much as Charlotte's promise to Hugh. For what other reason could Mr. Finnegan be concerned with observing Charlotte, except if her engagement was known?

When she finally found out what was happening, she was astonished that she had never suspected events to unfold as they did. It began as any other day at Boscombe Hall. The kitchen staff had worked diligently since dawn to prepare meals for the family and the enormous staff. The maids and footmen went about their duties, serving meals, tea, and seeing that the rooms were kept impeccably clean. Mr. Finnegan was employed in his usual duties, seeing to the formidable correspondence required of His Lordship. Lydia and Charlotte were planning the menu for the dinner to be served in honor of a viscount who was visiting in a week.

Miss Perry's return from London that afternoon was hardly any cause for excitement or fanfare. Lydia and Charlotte were pleased to see their tutor once more, as any lady would be to see an esteemed member of her staff. Lydia thought nothing about Miss Perry's return except to ask about her journey and the closing of the house in London. Miss Perry answered her queries cheerfully, and begged leave to refresh herself. Lydia paid little attention to the conversation until after tea. She and her sister were summoned to their father's study, in a most insistent manner by Mr. Finnegan, who appeared stricken.

Fearing the worst had happened, that their father had learned about Hugh, Lydia urged Charlotte to keep Mr. Finnegan's pace as they approached the study. Standing as a sentinel at the door, he did not walk into the room with Lydia and Charlotte, but a swift glance at Lydia alerted her that something was amiss. His eyes were wide, his face set in stone, his expression grim.

Lydia was not certain what she expected, but finding her father with Miss Perry seated beside him was not it. Miss Perry's perfect posture seemed even more perfect, her head raised in a slight tilt, her stare unwavering, her plump features set in a smirk. Lydia could not discern why her tutor would be seated so familiarly beside her father.

Her father was not smiling; his face was red, and his lips were set in a tight frown. Lydia recognized the look – he was furious. His narrowed eyes conveyed a fury that she feared would overcome her and Charlotte. Reaching for Charlotte's hand, she felt her sister's smaller one trembling in her own.

"My dear, will you wait for me? This will not take long," said Lord Wharncliffe to Miss Perry without glancing towards her.

"Yes, m'lord, as you wish," Miss Perry replied with a sweet smile that barely concealed an air of intrigue that made Lydia fear what circumstance could have led to her father calling her tutor *dear*. As the door closed behind Miss Perry, Lydia thought for a brief moment that Miss Perry seemed to want to stay, that she left reluctantly despite her acquiescence to Lord Wharncliffe's wishes. All these thoughts were soon supplanted by more pressing concerns.

Charlotte tightened her grip on Lydia's hand as they stood side by side under their father's stern gaze. Neither woman spoke or moved, understanding intrinsically that remaining still was preferable to being singled out in his attention. Charlotte could not account for Miss Perry's gloating manner or her father's anger except that something must have happened. Perhaps her fears were not unfounded. Did Mr. Finnegan know what was going on? Why did he not try to warn her?

Closing his eyes, their father appeared to be attempting to contain his fury. Finally, he broke the tense silence. "To say that I am disappointed in you both is the epitome of understatement. I do not know what has come over the both of you, except that you have deceived me. You have dashed my trust in you as though it was nothing of importance."

Lydia's heart was pounding. She had known there would be a reckoning for her part in Charlotte's secret engagement and her own clandestine match with Colonel Hartford, but she had not expected her father to be this angry when the truth came to light. Somehow, she had never imagined his fury to be this terrible. Willing herself to endure the brunt of it, she stood stoically, hoping that his rage would be quickly spent.

"I have been informed that there exists a secret engagement, made without my consent or my knowledge," he spat.

Charlotte opened her mouth to speak, her only words, "I can explain..." she said in a whisper.

Charlotte was immediately silenced her father. "There is no need for you to speak in your sister's defense. I have been made aware of her lascivious behavior under my own roof in London. Entertaining men without a chaperone, engaging in acts of lewdness, agreeing to be married! Such shamelessness shall not be borne!"

Lydia swallowed as she listened to her own behavior catalogued this way. When had she ever acted without regard to her good name or virtue? The accusation regarding the engagement was true, but it was to a gentleman. How she longed to defend herself, but she could see that her father was far from finished.

"I am shocked, Lydia, by your grievous behavior – and in the same house as your sister. Have you no care for her prospects? Have you no care for your own reputation? I have been told that you have paraded with men of no account, and that I would be shamed if I should show my face in London again. Your engagement to a disreputable gentleman who preys upon your naivety for your fortune is terrible. The disrespect and shame you have brought down upon your head, your name, and your sister is truly without equal. You were trusted to be responsible for Charlotte, to take care that neither of you encouraged gossip, and yet you have behaved as a woman of ill repute, and in my own house!"

Lydia could bear the accusations no longer. Risking his fury, she mounted a defense, "What manner of rumor have you been told? If you were to speak with Lady Hilda—"

"I have no intention of investigating this report of your behavior. I should like to think the good members of society shall forget your transgressions, as long as I do not make inquiries to freshen their memories and confirm their suspicions. Dragging a woman like Lady Hilda Breakridge into your sordid affairs – a woman of good reputation – is beneath you. If I had known of your deceit, your low behavior, I would not have welcomed you at all back to the Hall. I should have sent you away, back to your life as a governess, or married to his man who dares to raise my anger. Who is he? A commoner of ill repute, no doubt. A man without honor or character!"

"The man you speak of so callously is none other than Colonel Hartford, a well-respected hero of the war and my employer when I was a governess. Have you no recollection of him? He has no need to fear you, as he is not a commoner. Think what you will of me, but I will not have you speak about a man of his character in such a manner." Lydia's own anger overcome her fear. She was furious about her father's insistence that she had behaved abominably in London, and his refusal to hear her defense.

"Colonel Hartford? If such a thing were true, he should be unlikely to wed a woman who has behaved as you have during your time in London. When he discovers your behavior, he shall not wish to marry you, of that I am certain. When he finds that you have no dowry settled on you, we shall see where you stand in his esteem."

The last of Lydia's fear vanished in her anger. "How have I behaved? I wish to know who stands as my accuser. I should not have to produce character witnesses for my own father when I know I have behaved with honor. Say the name of my accuser and let me know where this evil story began."

"Miss Perry, your tutor and my trusted confidant, has told me of your behavior – behavior she desperately sought to correct. She told me how she was rebuked while you played about in your merry ways, leading your sister into equally objectionable behavior. I have it under her council, Lydia, that you encouraged your sister to publicly claim that my estate and my business ventures were failing. Yes, indeed! I have also heard that you stole Charlotte away on some perilous unchaperoned journey – to what ends I dare not imagine. I am heartbroken that my own daughter would seek to discredit me and cast suspicion on her sister's reputation."

Gasping, Lydia stared at Charlotte. Charlotte's eyes were wide, her face streaked with tears as she cried, "Lydia did not tell me to do any of that or steal me away; it was of my own devising."

"Charlotte, you shall not lie for your sister. Your heart is too pure to deceive me in such a grievous manner. Miss Perry adores you as I do, and she only wishes for your happiness. If that means that we have no choice but to separate you from Lydia, then we shall."

Lydia was undeterred. "We? You speak about me as though I was a convicted criminal, yet your only evidence is that gained from Miss Perry. Tell me, Father, is there some reason you have chosen to hear her words, believing them without hesitation, while my words fall silent on your ears?"

"Lydia, I had hoped that you would learn our news under better circumstances, but as you will not be present for the announcement, I shall make it known now. Miss Perry and I are engaged. She will become Lady Wharncliffe at Christmas. I can only hope that her influence will halt the tide of terrible choices that might well keep your sister from marrying a man of good fortune."

Lydia was in shock. Miss Perry had not only lied about her to her father, but had used her influence to worm her way into his heart. The news that the woman would become the next Lady Wharncliffe was almost as horrid to Lydia's ears as hearing the details of her own banishment. Her face pale, her voice temporarily silenced by horror, she listened as her sister – her sickly, weak little sister Charlotte – stood to her full height and bravely faced her father.

"You say that Lydia has influenced me, that I will not find a suitable husband because of her. How wrong you are, Father. How wrong Miss Perry is. The terrible reputation you speak of was *mine*, if any reputation existed at all, which I doubt. Lydia did not see or speak to any gentlemen except for Colonel Hartford. I was the one who spoke to gentlemen, telling them that you had lost your fortune, so they would not seek my hand. The journey that Miss Perry spoke of was for my advantage, and on that journey I became engaged to a man I met a long time ago, when you were still at sea. You say that I have been corrupted, that I have been influenced, but you're wrong. If this is how you treat the best of us, my sister, who has cared for my happiness, who has seen me through the days when we had no one to provide a living for us, then I shall stand by her side, and by the side of the man I love. You shall not have the concern of choosing for me. I have already chosen my husband, and so has Lydia."

Lydia was astonished by Charlotte's speech, and regretted that her defense made it necessary. Her sister was sobbing but she was still standing her ground, as did Lydia. Lydia tried to think of what to do; her own banishment could be borne, but not Charlotte's. Moving to protect her sister, she found her voice yet again. "Father, do not listen to Charlotte. She seeks only to protect me. I am responsible for all of it, for any crime you and your bride-to-be are capable of imagining. If that is what you need to hear to absolve Charlotte of any guilt, then so be it. Banish me, but I will not let you banish her."

Charlotte would not be protected, and rounded on her sister. "I know full well what I have said and what I have done. I don't regret a single action, unless you must pay the cost of my folly." To her father she said, "I cannot know why your bride wishes to sow discord, but she shall not do it between me and my sister, not when I owe my life and my happiness to Lydia. Who but Lydia cared for me in your absence, when we thought you were lost?"

His anger no longer so palpable, Lord Wharncliffe, the old captain of the sea, stared at his daughters aghast. Speaking slowly, he said, "I do not know you, Lydia. You have become a stranger to my eyes. Miss Perry was right – you are far too independent for your own good. I should have known that you would never be a lady, but there is hope yet for your sister. I will not allow you to ruin her as you are ruined."

Lydia pleaded, "Father, can you not hear your own voice, your baseless accusations? These are not your words; they are the words of a woman who seeks to control you, to keep you to herself. Do you know so little of me that you would believe these things without proof?"

His answer chilled her. "I have the word of Miss Perry; there can be no doubting it as she will be the next mistress of this house. Are you questioning the honor of the next Lady Wharncliffe? I will not stand for it!" he bellowed. "You may leave Boscombe Hall at any time."

"You wish me to be gone? Are you disowning me?" Lydia asked.

"I will not disown you, but while you are here I expect that you shall remain confined to your room. There will be no more trips to London and you will not have any influence upon your sister."

"You would keep me as a prisoner if I remain here?" Lydia asked.

"Not as a prisoner, but you must not be allowed to cause any more mischief. You may choose to leave," he said coldly.

Lydia found strength deep inside her heart. She recalled the words of Colonel Harford, assuring her that she would be his wife no matter what her father's reaction was. "Then I choose to leave. You may believe Miss Perry now, Father dear, but one day when you are alone in this cold house and her smiles no longer warm you, I want you to think upon what you have destroyed."

"What have I destroyed? What is lost to me? A daughter who is willfully disobedient and deceitful?" asked her father.

"No, Father," Charlotte replied as she stepped even closer to Lydia. "You have lost both your daughters."

"Charlotte, there is no need for rash behavior," he said.

Hand in hand, the sisters left the study as their father continued to urge Charlotte to stop. Mr. Finnegan looked shocked by what he'd witnessed, and Lydia was certain he must have overhead every word of the conversation. Without a word, she rushed to her bedroom with Charlotte at her side. There wasn't much time. She did not intend to spend one more night under the roof of a man who would believe her tutor rather than his own daughters, and a secretary who had done nothing to warn her.

Sending Charlotte to pack quickly, Lydia filled only a small bag. She would send for her trunks when she (and to her sorrow, her sister) were settled. There were two places in the world that would welcome them. Of those two addresses, Lydia knew where she was likely to find peace; she was bound for Dartmoore.

Weeping as she crammed her jewelry into her purse, Lydia

vowed that this would not be the end of their family. Her father was acting like a man possessed of an evil spell. She did not believe in witchcraft, but she did believe in feminine wiles. When she was away from Boscombe Hall and could think of what was to be done, she would save her father from the heartless and treacherous Miss Perry.

———

Lydia and Charlotte arrived at Dartmoore exhausted and mournful. They had traveled through the night in a coach, one of several they were forced to hire as they made their way across Cornwall to Plymouth. Sending a message by swift rider to Dartmoore, Lydia prayed that Colonel Hartford had not yet left his residence to journey to Boscombe Hall. She also prayed that his intentions towards her were not hollow words spoken in a London drawing room. She did not wish to think of her future if she showed up at his door without his welcome, but she couldn't help but worry.

Resigning herself to being a governess once more if she was denied entry at Dartmoore, she had decided during the hours of the journey that she would gladly return to work if that meant never having to ask her father for a pound ever again. She was still angry at him and the treacherous Miss Perry, but she knew the tears would come when her anger had subsided. Her father had chosen to believe a near stranger rather than his own daughter. The heartbreak of her dilemma was too horrible to bear – but bear it she must.

How she had begged Charlotte to remain at Boscombe Hall, but her sister would hear none of it. Charlotte had grown determined in the past year, and now had an independent streak of her own, to Lydia's surprise. Charlotte would not be left behind at Boscombe Hall to endure Miss Perry becoming mistress, nor could she bear to be introduced to eligible gentlemen when her own heart and hand were promised to Hugh. Fortunately, Hugh's name had never been mentioned during that terrible conversation in the study. Lydia could only hope that he was safe from any retribution.

Mrs. Tumbridge greeted Lydia and her sister as warmly as Mrs. Peyton ever had. She fussed about how tired they must be from their journey, and led them inside to the dining room where tea and a light meal awaited them. Their bags were brought inside, and carried by footmen upstairs to their rooms, which had been prepared the moment Colonel Hartford had heard they were coming.

Colonel Hartford greeted them both in the dining room, his handsome brow furrowed with concern as Lydia and Charlotte recounted the details of the confrontation which drove them from their home. Colonel Hartford listened quietly, his chin in his hand, ignoring the steaming cup of tea in front of him.

"How venomous this Miss Perry must be. Your reputations were beyond reproach in London; there was never a word of impropriety uttered about either of you, and yet this woman has convinced your father that the worst has happened during your short season. Far worse than that, I am astonished that your father believed that I would be put off by rumors and baseless allegations. Of what need do I have of the opinion of your tutor, or your dowry? The opinions that matter to me are my own, my daughters', and those of my faithful staff," Colonel Hartford said with a frown.

"That is exactly what happened. I cannot imagine how any regard developed between them; I never noticed that they behaved towards each other in any way other than as a lord to his staff," Lydia explained, trying to make sense of her circumstances.

"Colonel, thank you for taking us in as though we were waifs upon the road. Your generosity is well appreciated," said Charlotte.

Colonel Hartford smiled warmly. "My dear Lady Charlotte, you are the sister of my future wife. You will always find welcome at Dartmoore, although I did hope you would join us here under better circumstances."

"Then you still wish to marry me, even though I shall be without dowry or character?" Lydia asked, her voice quavering.

"Do I still want to marry you? I would marry you in this dining room if our own dear Mrs. Tumbridge would do the honors. Nothing that has happened can change my feelings for you. I loved you as a governess. I loved you as a lady. I will love you no matter what you may be called, and I will call you my wife," he said as he reached for her hand, grazing it with his lips.

Lydia could feel a flood of tears threatening to fall down her cheeks. She was exhausted from the journey, despondent from the loss of her father to a vile woman, and happy that she had found refuge in the house and heart of the man she loved.

"I don't deserve you; you are so wonderful to me," Lydia whispered as she gazed at the colonel with tears in her eyes.

"You are safe now, you and your sister. Eat as much as you like, and rest. Later, when you are restored, you may wish to visit Beth and Sarah. I told them you were coming and they were overcome with excitement."

"Beth and Sarah? How I have longed to meet them; shall I see them?" Charlotte asked brightly.

"Of course you may! I daresay you will be as cherished by my daughters as your sister is," Colonel Hartford replied.

"I adored my time teaching at Mrs. Peyton's. How I miss the smiles and laughter of children. It will do me more good than all the food and rest to meet your daughters," Charlotte answered. "It will surely help me forget my own troubles."

"Oh dear, in our haste to leave Boscombe Hall, I have quite overlooked what is to be done about Hugh Burton!" exclaimed Lydia.

"Hugh? Is he the young man you spoke of, the gentleman from Falmouth?" Colonel Hartford asked Lydia.

"Yes, he is. So much has happened since our last meeting in London! Hugh is desperate to become an officer in the Royal Navy, and he has asked for Charlotte's hand in marriage. But without references or the money for his commission, I daresay the path to his success – and Charlotte's happiness – is a steep one indeed," admitted Lydia.

Colonel Hartford looked at Charlotte. Her bright smile at the prospect of meeting his daughters had darkened, and her eyes were welling with tears. "Lydia is right, Colonel. I am engaged to a man who – although below me in rank – is not below me in honor or honesty."

"I do not intend to offend you or insult the man as I do not know him, but I must ask, do you not fear that he desires only your dowry and your connections?" Colonel Hartford asked gently.

Charlotte explained, "He loved me when I was no more than a teacher at a school for girls. He never expected that my father would settle my dowry on a marriage to a fisherman. That is why he waited to propose; he would have liked to acquire a commission first."

"A fisherman, you say? You have chosen a fisherman for your husband. He must be remarkable indeed to capture your heart and your loyalty," Colonel Hartford said with a smile.

"He is remarkable. If only he had been born to a family with connections, he would have his choice of a commission or a vicarage, of that I am certain," Lydia added.

"Has he earned so high an opinion from you, my dear?" asked Colonel Hartford.

Without hesitation, Lydia answered, "Hugh has earned my respect and my regard. I was reluctant to give both at first, as I suspected him of a great many evils, but I was proven wrong. He is a masterful sailor; he saved our lives at great peril to his own upon the sea. I should be happy to be a reference for him, if only my own name was not tarnished by Miss Perry's cruel machinations."

Charlotte beamed at her sister for her recommendation of Hugh, but Colonel Hartford was not quite satisfied. "Your name is not sullied – nor shall it be, by anyone. I shall see to it. As to this Mr. Burton, how I know the rankle of men restrained by their class. I was privileged to have the power to grant battlefield promotions to men who were deserving by their deeds and valor, so perhaps there is something that I may do. I shall give the matter my attention."

"Thank you," Lydia replied, gazing at the man she loved with adoration and gratitude.

Dartmoore was more than a refuge. It was home.

CHAPTER EIGHTEEN

Two weeks after her arrival at Dartmoore, Lydia still felt the anguish caused by her father's words. Why did he choose to believe a woman he barely knew over his own daughter? What could be the cause of his behavior? Finding her way to her favorite place at Dartmoore Park, outside in the garden, she sat in the sunlight. Beth and Sarah played in the grass not far away, in Lydia's care while their governess enjoyed an afternoon off with Captain Poole.

From the sound of a piano being played, Lydia knew that Charlotte was finding solace in the music room. The music she played was mournful at times and exuberant at others, as though Charlotte was teetering between elation and despair, as her own wedding plans were far from certain. Colonel Hartford strode across the lawn and his daughters leapt to greet him. In his hand he carried a letter. Lydia smiled to see him, and he soon joined her on her favorite bench.

"You have no choice but to marry me; this must be your favorite place in all of England. This bench is where I find you when I cannot account for you inside my house. Alas, you have my daughters here with you, they shall be as you are – attached to this low bench as though it were sacred. When I search for them in the future I shall be forced to come outside to this very garden," he said as he embraced his daughters.

Lydia glanced at the garden. "You're quite right. There can be no better place in all of Cornwall than here. How I love the garden, to see it in all its glory is a pleasure. It reminds me that away from the troubles of Boscombe Hall, there is happiness."

Kissing the top of his daughters' heads, he sent them along to play. "Beth and Sarah, go play with your dolls while I speak to Lydia."

They smiled at their father before rushing back to the sunniest place on the garden's lawn, their dolls picked up from the verdant grass by eager hands.

"This has arrived from Boscombe Hall. I have not opened it, as it has your name on it."

"Boscombe Hall? Who would be writing to me from there? My father cares little for me, Miss Perry has treated me terribly, and no one else in that house is dear to me."

"It arrived with your trunks, not through the post. I doubt anyone would have suspected it, but I was in the hall when the coach was unloaded. The coachman may not have read the name on the envelope."

"How very strange," she said as she opened the letter.

Her eyes glided over the paper. The missive was not very long, but what it said was a revelation indeed. Gasping as she read the letter, she became aware that Colonel Hartford was observing her reaction. Handing the letter to him, she said, "I am not certain what to think of this letter. It is the only correspondence I have ever received from my father's secretary, Mr. Finnegan."

"Does he write on behalf of your father?"

"No, he does not; in fact, he writes on his own behalf. You may read it if you like, but his words may not be entirely clear. Much occurred at Boscombe before our departure."

"There is no need for me to read it, if you shall tell me the story in your own words," he said as he watched his daughters playing in the distance.

"Very well, but I fear it may only cast more doubt on Miss Perry's motives. It seems that Mr. Finnegan is in love with her, and he believes even now that she is in love with him. There existed an understanding between them that they would marry when her position was concluded, and myself and my sister were wed."

"Poor devil. If he is your father's secretary, I wonder if that was how she discovered your father's weaknesses. It was a masterful strategy to employ; knowing the enemy wins the day."

"He learned of the affection that had arisen between them from my father. Although he was not explicit in his language, Mr. Finnegan is his secretary, and therefore privy to his correspondence – although he claims not to have read the private missives."

"Why did this Finnegan write to you? Of what use can this information be to you? As you have said, your father does not care to listen to any defense of your actions. I hardly think he would care for any report you may give him about his bride or his secretary. How very odd that this man would confide in you with a damaging confession that – were it to be believed – would cost him his position."

"I think perhaps he writes out of a sense of duty. Mr. Finnegan is a man who behaves with such cold nature and reserve that I hardly knew he possessed the ability to love. He was my grandfather's secretary before he, like the estate itself, went to my father. Mr. Finnegan is a proud man, well educated, and he seems very loyal. I wonder if Miss Perry was able to glean any information from him at all, although she must have made the attempt."

"It sounds as though you are describing a man who is not impulsive, yet this letter, this confidence is of an impulsive nature. Can you account for Finnegan's actions? They seem contrary to what we might expect from the man as you have described him." Colonel Hartford's gaze was thoughtful.

"Yes, I'm very surprised. Although he was pleasant to me on occasion, he showed no indication that he was loyal to me in any sense other than that of a servant to a master. When Miss Perry arrived at Boscombe Hall, I did not notice any affection exchanged between them. She seemed of no more consequence to him than a house maid or a footman. How dreadfully wrong I was," Lydia answered.

"Yet here you are with a letter in your hand that would be the ruin of any secretary. If rumors that he was romantically involved with his former mistress were to ever leave Boscombe Hall, he would find employment barred to him at every reputable house in the country."

Lydia thought back to Mr. Finnegan's odd behavior, and how strangely he had acted before Miss Perry arrived from London. "I wonder if his reason for sending me this letter was more than just a man unburdening himself of a sorrow. I wonder if his loyalty to my father and to the house of Wharncliffe is greater than his concern for his own prospects. If I should manage to remove Miss Perry from my father's affections, I may restore him to his position or provide a reference for him from Boscombe Hall. Mr. Finnegan is an intelligent man; this letter ends with his declaration to resign from his post."

"He's resigning? That sounds impulsive, nearly as impulsive as this letter. A man of such reserve and loyalty driven to resign must be consumed with grief. What shall you write to him? Will you provide a reference?"

"I have no reason not to. He has been loyal, although I do wish he had confided in me about the nature of Miss Perry's relationship with my father. I would have been on my guard. Perhaps I should have been suspicious. Her circumstances were reduced upon her acceptance of the position, and yet she was so content and settled at Boscombe. I did not see what she was capable of."

"What shall you do with this information? Finnegan has trusted you with news that would surely change your father's opinion of his bride."

"If what Mr. Finnegan writes is true, and I have no reason not to believe it, she is trifling with him and my father. That is the worst sort of behavior from a woman who would claim that my own behavior was ruinous. It pains me to think that she shall betray my father, but what can be done? My father may have wronged me, but I am his daughter."

"Your loyalty to him speaks well of your character, my dear. When I look at my own daughters I could not conceive of believing anyone who presented me with such stories. How your father succumbed to her wiles is baffling to me, except to think he may have found the residence at Boscombe to be too large a place for one man. Loneliness can drive a man to despair."

"Do you suppose it was loneliness that caused him to accept the word of a woman he barely knew?" The words caught in her throat as she thought of her father choosing Miss Perry over her.

"Yes, loneliness and fear. He was nearly lost at sea; he may have faced fears you can scarcely imagine."

"I have not thought of his actions as being driven by anything but the basest of emotions. How can you account for his refusal to take my word?" whispered Lydia.

"He was not speaking as a reasonable man. She has influenced him. If he is as I imagine him to be, an old captain of the line, then he has seen many battles, and faced his own death more times than you may know. He returned to England, broken in his spirit and his body. A man like him may have hoped to die at sea with his men; he may never have suspected that he would become entombed in the walls of his own grand house. I cannot say that what I have said is the truth, but these are the thoughts many of us who have come home from war share. He was in a state which he kept well hidden from you and your sister, and she offered a comfort that he had not known since his marriage to your mother."

Troubled, Lydia held out her hand to Colonel Hartford. "You speak as though you know him; is this how you yourself feel? Do you feel entombed in Dartmoore? Do you long for the battlefield, and wish you had died upon the fields in France?"

He hesitated, and looked away at his daughters for a moment. "I will not deceive you. I have had these feelings, but I found solace in the laughter of my dear daughters – and you, Lydia. You have brought me to life. I once told you that I felt more at home in battle than I ever did in the drawing rooms of Dartmoore or London. Your father may be of the same mind. It is impossible to know him or his sorrow, but why else would Miss Perry have sought to rid Boscombe Hall of you? You were his comfort and his strength; you were the daughter he relied on as he struggled to assume a title he never wanted. She removed the only person who could put an end to her plans."

Lydia groaned. "How could I have been so selfish as to abandon him to Miss Perry? I should return to Boscombe Hall at once!"

"No, you should not. If you return now he shall not listen to you any more than he did the last day you were there. He does not yet see the danger he is in, and he has not had enough time to miss you and your sister. Time is the way to heal this terrible wound, time and the proper strategy. If you charge into the fray without a proper plan of attack, you shall lose. Write to Mr. Finnegan and assure him that your reference is gladly given, and that you will keep his confidence." He shook his head. "How it grieves me to know that a woman whom you all trusted has betrayed each of you in her own way. If she were a man, her behavior could be called out, but as she is a woman and may not be met in the field of honor, we shall have to seek other methods."

"Other methods? You sound like a commanding officer at war," Lydia remarked as she saw the sparkle in Colonel Hartford's eyes.

"This is war, my dear. Miss Perry may have won the day, but she has not won the battle."

CHAPTER NINETEEN

Late Summer
Plymouth, Cornwall

THE FLURRY of letters that arrived at Dartmoore was indeed momentous. Mrs. Tumbridge remarked nearly every day as the summer came to an end that she had not seen the like in all her time at Dartmoore. Every morning, letters appeared at the breakfast table. There were sweet romantic letters from Hugh Burton to his Charlotte, a letter from Mrs. Peyton expressing her desire to see Charlotte married at Falmouth, and letters from acquaintances in London. Lady Hilda Breakridge and her entourage of aristocratic matrons were as prolific in their correspondence as they were about all manner of gossip.

Lydia had not written to Lady Hilda about the terrible situation at Boscombe Hall, but somehow the prodigious lady had learned of many of the details – although not all the personal ones. Lady Hilda was livid, and squarely championing her girls. She wrote that Lydia and Charlotte had been under her tutelage, and therefore their reputations were entirely her responsibility. Lydia had once chafed at being called *Lady Hilda's girls* but now she was glad of it.

Miss Perry, according to Lady Hilda, was not without blemish. She had been in the husband hunting business for quite some time before snaring the Earl of Wharncliffe – a feat which Lady Hilda confided was only successful because the earl did not frequent London society. Lady Hilda, in her youth, had been dear friends with the previous mistress of Wharncliffe, Lydia's grandmother, and had been mentored by the great lady herself, much as she had tried to do for Lydia and Charlotte. She swore that she would not allow the title to fall to an unsavory fortune hunter such as Miss Perry. The letter, like the letters from the other ladies, gave Lydia a few lighthearted moments despite the bleakness of the outlook. Her father was still to be married at Christmas. Miss Perry was still entrenched at Boscombe Hall, and not likely to relinquish her position.

Colonel Hartford assured Lydia that all would be well, but Lydia's hope was beginning to fade, as was her hope for Hugh Burton ever obtaining a commission. He had not the slightest good fortune obtaining references, aside from a few merchants and the vicar in Falmouth. It seemed his prospects were truly bleak despite the letters he wrote to Charlotte, letters which she lived on as surely as though they were sustenance.

It was at breakfast one morning in late summer when the letters arrived on a silver tray brought in by a footman, as they always did. Colonel Hartford finished his tea as he read his correspondence. Captain Poole stopped in the breakfast room on his way to the study to begin work for the day. Beth and Sarah were in the school room with the governess.

Lydia was finishing a letter from Mrs. Peyton as Charlotte pouted. "There is nothing for me today. Lydia, where is my letter from Hugh? He promised to write to me as often as he could. It has been days since I received the last one."

Lydia turned her attention from the letter in her hand to look at her sister. "Charlotte, you received a letter from Hugh three days ago. He's probably busy fishing. Unlike you, he does not have the luxury of abundant free time to write letters."

"I suppose you are right, but I wish I could hear something from him. He said he may have news about a commission. I am anxious to hear that he was successful, so that we may be married. It has been two years since I met him – two long, intolerable years. How I wish for the end of this wait."

"Be patient. He will surely not disappoint you," Colonel Harford said as he buttered his toast.

Charlotte sighed, and sipped her water. "You're right. I have been patient this long, what is a little while longer?"

"That's the spirit to have, my dear," Lydia replied as she looked at the letter in her hand, her thoughts suddenly troubled. She was not married yet, either. How long had she languished at Dartmoore as a guest? Reading the letter, she tried to concentrate on Mrs. Peyton's anecdotes but found her mind was too distracted.

Charlotte was the first to leave the dining room as Colonel Hartford finished his breakfast. When Lydia was certain that the footmen were not listening, she leaned close to him and whispered, "I have been patient. Not as patient as Charlotte, but I have waited without complaint. Do you still wish to be married?"

Colonel Hartford looked at her, guileless. "Married? No, we shall remain as we are. You shall share my house and live in the garden, and I shall run the estate and my businesses. Your sister shall play music every day until she is wed. I can think of no reason why we should alter our present circumstances, can you?"

At first, she did not realize that he was teasing her. "You may amuse yourself, but that is not the answer I wish to hear. Is it the matter of my dowry, that I have none? Is that why you have delayed marrying me?"

"Lydia, what has troubled you? Are you not content with Dartmoore? Are you unhappy here? I do not care for your dowry; I have no need of it. I'm sorry, I thought you understood my reasons for delaying. I did not want to hasten into a wedding while you are forced to endure this terrible trial with your father. I have every hope that it will be resolved. Would you not prefer to wait until we discover whether what is broken between you and your father can be repaired?"

Lydia sighed. "I feel awful, perfectly awful, to speak to you about my dowry when you have opened your house, welcomed us warmly, and provided food and shelter to us without asking for anything in return. I was being foolish, and I apologize. Like my sister, I long to be married to the man I love."

"How it gladdens my heart to hear you say that. I am more impatient to be wed to you than I have said. I have endured the wait with strength, but I feel my strength is failing. If I did not believe that your father shall be reunited with you and your sister I should not wait another minute."

"Then we are in agreement. We shall not wait. We shall create a scandal by running away to Gretna Green to be married," Lydia said with a smirk of her own.

"Lady Lydia Wells, are you suggesting that we elope? Lady Hilda would never forgive us if she could not be involved with our wedding, since she introduced us."

Lydia laughed. "No, she never would, nor would Mrs. Peyton, or Mrs. Tumbridge, for that matter. Then we shall wait, although I do tire of waiting for something I believe in my heart to be as impossible as poor Hugh receiving a commission."

"I do not think you will discover that is as impossible as you might think. Learn from your sister. Be patient. I promise your patience shall be rewarded," he said with a wink as he left her alone at the breakfast table.

———

LYDIA WAS SHOCKED – ASTOUNDED beyond measure. Standing in

the drawing room of the Dartmoore Park was a man she knew well, and whom she loved and respected. Her father, the Earl of Wharncliffe, was standing beside Colonel Hartford. Lydia quickly searched his features, and found his face was stone, his mouth set in a frown.

Charlotte was pale. She seemed faint as she drifted into a chair beside the fireplace. Lydia wanted to join her but chose to remain upright, standing up to face the man who had sought to have her banished rather than listen to her. Her heart fluttered in her chest. How she wished to remain angry at her father, but she fell into her old girlish ways, seeing him as the infallible captain of the seas, and wishing for his love.

What reason could he have for being at Dartmoore? Was he not content to chastise her from Boscombe Hall? Had he journeyed across Cornwall to question why she was a guest at Colonel Hartford's estate, and why her sister was here? Bracing herself for the worst, Lydia glanced at Colonel Hartford, hoping to read to his expression, but he was as implacable as her father.

"Lord Wharncliffe, it is an honor to entertain you in my home, is there anything you require after your journey? Refreshments, tea?" Colonel Harford spoke to his guest as though the man was not responsible for Lydia and Charlotte's sorrow.

"Thank you, Colonel Hartford, but that will not be necessary. I will not stay long."

"What brings you, sir?" Colonel Hartford asked as he invited the earl to sit.

The earl looked uncomfortable, but he sat down on a chair by the fireside despite the warmth of the day. His gaze did not leave Lydia's face except to glance at Charlotte, who had recovered sufficiently to sit upright, grasping the arms of her chair.

"Father, you look unwell. Let us call for tea," said Lydia.

"No daughter, that will not be necessary. I shall not be long. The reason I came to Dartmoore was to speak with you and your sister. A letter would not be sufficient after the accusations I leveled at you, accusations I am embarrassed to say I ever considered. I have come here to apologize, and to ask for your forgiveness," he said.

Lydia was choked with emotion. "Father, I don't understand. When I left Boscombe Hall, you were convinced that I had led Charlotte astray, that I had behaved abominably. You accused me of terrible indiscretions. I was innocent of all charges, but you would not allow me to plead my case before you."

The earl replied, "I did not want to hear a word against my bride-to-be, the woman you knew as Miss Perry. How could I bear to hear any word that contradicted the woman I thought I loved?"

"Do you not love her still?" Lydia asked as she held her breath, her eyes searching his face.

"It pains me to say that yes, I still love her despite her cunning ways, but I have seen the mistakes my heart led me to. I have been reprimanded forcibly at every turn. My secretary resigned, his reason not hard to surmise after my footman witnessed a private moment shared between him and Miss Perry in the arbor. Yet I would not hear any word against her, not until the letters from London began arriving, one after another, and several from women who knew my mother. It was not until Lady Hilda came to Boscombe Hall unannounced that I knew I had been persuaded to choose between my daughter and a woman who sought me for my fortune. I have sent Miss Perry away never to return, at Lady Hilda's insistence."

Turning to Colonel Hartford, the earl spoke plainly. "Sir, I thank you for what you have done for me and my daughters, if they shall ever be called that again. Lady Hilda told me of your campaign and your patronage. I must seem a doddering old fool to you, sir."

"No, sir. I am a military officer. I know something of what makes men like us vulnerable. You see, my campaign was not mounted with the hopes of sparing your fortune or your reputation; it was waged with the intent of securing your daughters' happiness. I have no care for a dowry, but I do care for Lydia and Charlotte's joy. I have daughters of my own. When I think of their heartbreak if I should ever choose love before them, it moved me. I could not bear to see the same sorrow in your daughters' eyes, sir. Please forgive me if I have spoken too plainly."

"On the contrary, sir. I was a captain of the line before I was a lord. I prefer the plain-spoken man to the aristocrat. Is it true that you wish to marry my Lydia, to make her your wife?"

"Yes, your Lordship, it is still my intention, as it has been for many months," answered Colonel Hartford.

"Then you shall both have my blessing if you still wish it. You may not wish for her dowry, but it would please me if you would accept it," the earl remarked.

"Then it is done, but what of your other daughter? She is engaged as well," said Colonel Hartford.

"What of this young man of Charlotte's, what of him?"

"He has accepted a commission in the Royal Navy. I have seen to it personally, providing his references and securing the amount he needed, for he is a man of honor. If your daughter wishes, she may be married from this house with my blessing," said Colonel Harford.

"Charlotte, is this true? You wish to marry a man who is going to sea, as I once did, when you could have a lord?" the earl asked his youngest daughter.

"It is true, every word of it. I wish to marry no one else," she replied. Her hands trembled at the news, and her color was high.

"I suppose you know what sorrow awaits you, the months without news, the worries, and the fears. If you must marry beneath your rank, I am pleased you chose an officer. You shall have my blessing, if that is what you wish."

"Oh, Father!" Charlotte cried as she leapt from her chair, embracing him.

"Lydia, my daughter, do you forgive your father for being a besotted old fool? I cannot undo what I have said, but I can ask for forgiveness. Please, I am begging you, accept my apology before Lady Hilda is forced to visit me again. I felt as small as a child when she was done with me. She would have made a fine admiral!"

Lydia was laughing despite the tears that slid down her face. Her father had returned. He was free of Miss Perry, and asking for her forgiveness. How could she deny him that, when she knew what it was to love with all her heart? As she smiled at Colonel Hartford, she mouthed the words *thank you* before embracing her father, just like she did when she was a little girl.

CHAPTER TWENTY

Late Summer
Falmouth, Cornwall

THE CHURCH in Falmouth had never seen such an event as the one that filled every pew that summer morning. It was a wedding, but not just an ordinary wedding. All the boxes reserved for the town's elite citizens were crammed with all manner of relation, from distant cousins to in-laws of every description. The pews were crowded, except for the front ones, reserved for the prominent guests of the bride and groom. Citizens of Falmouth crowded the walls of the church, and even spilled out into the road. Everyone was craning their necks to see the coaches and carriages that formed a wedding procession of such importance and wealth that many in the crowd were quite convinced that royalty would be in attendance.

On this auspicious occasion, the gray stone church – which was hardly more than a chapel – had been decorated lovingly by the women from the church and the girls from Mrs. Peyton's. The girls were so enthusiastic in their decorating that not a single ribbon was left in any store in Falmouth that day. Fresh flowers festooned the pews, ribbons were tied into countless bows and arranged around the entrance of the church in such a way that the vicar was not terribly sure that the display was not pagan.

The weather was idyllic. The sun shone though small white clouds in the sky. A sea breeze was blowing in from the quay, carrying all the scents of the sea with it, with hints of salt, sunshine, and the mysteries of the ocean. The crowd gathered outside the church cheered with each carriage that drove up, each depositing well-dressed members of the wedding party.

If anyone was keeping a tally, and Moira from Mrs. Peyton's was charged with that duty, there were no fewer than eight titled ladies, six titled lords, several officers of the army and the navy, a knight, and a baronet. Every merchant closed his shop that morning, and so did a good number of tavern keepers as well. Ship owners rubbed elbows with fishermen from the quay and nearby villages and more than one lady was greeted by a fishwife, according to Moira, who gave the full report to Cook and Mrs. Peyton over tea later that afternoon.

To the discerning eyes of the more fashionable among the crowd, the clothes of the guests were as rich in satin and silk as any of the wedding party, a small but blissful group of four people. If the elegant coaches with their coachmen and drivers and teams of horses were not the talk of Falmouth for many years to come, the wedding party itself was sure to cause many a girl to have fairytale dreams of her own. Among the party were two young women whom the citizens of Falmouth knew well. They might now have vaunted titles, but they were daughters of Falmouth just the same.

At the arrival of the members of the party, Falmouth roared to life in a manner that was not only extraordinary for a wedding, but unprecedented in the little port town. As an anxious but joyous bridegroom waited inside the chapel for his bride, his patron standing at his side, the carriage arrived with the bride herself and her singular attendant.

Lydia Hartford, formerly Lady Lydia Wells, stepped out of the carriage to a sea of applause and good wishes from onlookers. She smiled and waved as she waited for her sister. Charlotte was standing in the carriage. As the bride, she was the queen of the day in Falmouth.

From Lydia's perspective her sister had never looked lovelier. Her golden hair shone in the sunlight, barely hidden by a light summer bonnet and lace veil. Her dress was simply tailored, but the light champagne of the satin shimmered against the blue sky. In her gloved hand she held a bouquet of sweet-smelling herbs and blossoms picked from Mrs. Peyton's garden, a present from her former pupils.

Lydia led the way into the church, her eyes tearing with happiness. How long they had waited for this day! She was newly married herself, her own wedding being held at Boscombe Hall the week before, but she felt her own heart race at the thrill of seeing her sister finally married to the man she loved.

At the altar stood two handsome gentlemen. One dark haired man Lydia knew better than any other person in the room – her husband, standing at the side of the newly commissioned Lieutenant Hugh Burton dressed splendidly in his uniform. Hugh beamed with pride as he gazed at his bride being led by her father, the Earl of Wharncliffe.

A hush fell over the crowd as the couple were joined in matrimony. More than one woman cried at the wedding, and more than one man felt pride in his heart that one of their own, a fisherman, was not only married to the daughter of an earl, but was newly commissioned into the navy. Falmouth was witnessing an event that was more than a wedding; it was a story that would be told time and time again until it became part of the town's lore.

On that morning, as the sun shone down through the stained glass, the light landed on Charlotte's upturned face as Hugh slid back her veil. Lydia looked at Colonel Harford and smiled. He was the reason that she and her sister had this moment, that Hugh was commissioned, and that her father was in attendance. She was overcome with joy and love. From her life as the daughter of a sea captain, to a governess, to a lady, to the wife of a colonel, she'd had an adventure that was more than she could ever have dreamed of when she was a girl living in the garret at Mrs. Peyton's school. And as he smiled back at her, she could feel in her heart that her adventure was far from over.

AFTERWORD

Thank you so much for reading my book. I hope you enjoyed this Regency romance story.

If you have time and would like to leave a reader's review, please do so where you purchased the book. I always love getting feedback on my books and appreciate tremendously your effort.

If you would like to be the first to know about my new releases, promotions and giveaways, please sign up for my mailing list on my my Facebook page, Victoria Hart author. For comments or questions about my books, please contact me at victoria@maplewoodpublishing.com.

ALSO BY VICTORIA HART

VICTORIA HART

A ROYAL

Renewal

THE ROYALS OF HELEDIA

VICTORIA HART

DILEMMA
The Royals of Heledia

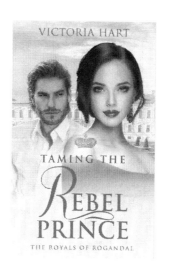

VICTORIA HART

TAMING THE

REBEL
PRINCE

THE ROYALS OF ROGANDAL

Printed in Great Britain
by Amazon